What Others Are Saying abo[u]t *[...]*
by L.B. Graham . . .

"There is a completeness to L.B. Graham's literary imagination that I don't see very often. He's a world-maker. Barra-Dohn, with its strange technologies and ruthless tyrants and wandering priests, feels like a whole world—a world you can immerse yourself in and not come out of for a long time."
—Jonathan Rogers, author of The Wilderking Trilogy
and *The Charlatan's Boy*

"The heart of Lewis and the world-building of Tolkien dwell richly in the works of L.B. Graham. Prepare yourself for high fantasy charged with suspense and intrigue . . . if you dare take the first step down the Darker Road."
—Wayne Thomas Batson, Bestselling author of The Door
Within trilogy and The Dark Sea Annals series

"Intricate world, intriguing characters, and incredible pacing equal fascinating reading. L.B. Graham has created fantasy in The Darker Road that draws the reader in and won't let go. Fun reading, but be ready for those heart-thumping pages. There is danger between these pages and the heroes needed to fight a scourge of corruption."
—Donita K. Paul, author of The Dragon Keeper Chronicles
and Chronicles of Chiril.

THE
DARKER ROAD

The WANDERING: BOOK 1

LIVING
INK
BOOKS
Writing Worth Reading

L.B. GRAHAM

The Darker Road

The Wandering: Book 1

Copyright © 2013 by L. B. Graham

Published by Living Ink Books, an imprint of
AMG Publishers, Inc.
6815 Shallowford Rd.
Chattanooga, Tennessee 37421

Print Edition: ISBN 13: 978-0-89957-772-2
EPUB Edition   ISBN 13: 978-1-61715-337-2
Mobi Edition   ISBN 13: 978-1-61715-338-9
PDF Edition   ISBN 13: 978-1-61715-339-6

First Printing—July 2013

THE DARKER ROAD is a trademark of AMG Publishers.

Cover designed by Daryle Beam at Bright Boy Design, Chattanooga, TN.

Interior design and typesetting by Kristin Goble of PerfecType, Nashville, TN.

Interior illustrations by Abe Goolsby, Nashville, TN.

Edited and proofread by Agnes Elkins, Sharon Neal, and Rick Steele.

Printed in Canada
18 17 16 15 14 13 –MAR– 6 5 4 3 2 1

"For Tom, my Deslo, who's grown up into quite a fine young man—with pride in all you've accomplished and hope that the best is yet to come."

CONTENTS

Prologue

THE PRICE MUST BE PAID

alsura stopped fastening the straps of his ceremonial vestments over his clothes. Raised voices and scurrying footsteps in the Temple proper echoed above. His fingers trembled, and as he ran for the stairs, his long silk stole fell to the ground. He hesitated but did not go back.

It had to be his father. He had pressed Armond twice in the last few days on the matter of the parade, but his father remained evasive about any intention of protesting or opposing Kartain's plans, saying only that he'd already made clear how he felt about both Kartain and his vision for increasing the power and prestige of the Kalonian priesthood. If the sympathies and desires of the majority of the priests lay with Kartain, he'd said, he had no choice but to accede to their will. When pressed further, Armond had only taken Calsura's hand firmly in his and said quietly, "I lost the election to succeed Dorrell as Amhura to Kartain, but I must answer to Kalos, as must we all."

Calsura wasn't reassured. Neither was his mother. Del had begged and pleaded with him to make sure Armond didn't do anything foolish, but what was Calsura to do? Armond was his father, and Kartain intended sacrilege. He would parade the Golden Cord around the streets of Zeru-Shalim today, fully aware that the people who all but worshiped it already would fawn over it even more, reinforcing the widespread belief that it was a talisman, a sacred relic of power controlled by the Kalonian priesthood in general and the Amhura in particular. Kartain intended to elevate himself above the king, and the parade would take him closer in that direction. The masses bowing to the Golden Cord were only a half step removed from bowing to the man that they believed controlled it.

Calsura leapt up the stairs, taking them two at a time, pushing past a gangly initiate as he emerged upstairs. Confusion reigned in the Temple, but Calsura easily spotted the commotion's epicenter. Several priests were gathered near the entrance to the Room of Life. He stood, rooted to the spot, a sudden and inexplicable fear seizing him. If they hadn't removed the Golden Cord yet to prepare for the start of the parade, it remained in the Room of Life, where only the two high priests and the Amhura could come and go freely. So what was going on there? What had Armond done?

Another temple initiate, looking nervous and afraid, ran up to him. "Come quickly, Brother Calsura. Maybe you can get him to listen to reason."

"Get who to listen? Father Armond?"

The initiate's eyes widened. "You don't know?"

"Know what, boy? Out with it." Calsura's voice was impatient and harsh, and for that he'd apologize later.

"He's chained himself to the iron brackets just inside the doorway. He won't let anyone past."

"Chained himself?"

"Yes," the initiate said, looking back toward the gathered crowd. "He says that no one is parading the Golden Cord around Zeru-Shalim today."

Calsura glanced around, inhaling slowly, trying to take in the vast expanse of the Temple of Kalos with one quick sweep. "Is Kartain here yet?"

"Not yet."

Calsura jogged quickly toward the gathered priests. As he approached, several noticed him and stepped aside. He walked through their ranks until he stood but a few feet from the entrance to the Room of Life.

There was Armond, his father and the high priest of Kalos. His legs were set in a firm stance across the base of the doorway, and his arms were held out wide across the door's threshold with heavy chains extending from both wrists until they disappeared beyond the door frame. Armond's usually gentle gray eyes burned today with a strange and desperate fire.

"What's going on, Father?" Calsura said calmly. He'd never addressed Armond with the familiar "Father" in the Temple, where the full address for a high priest would have required at least "Father Armond," even from him, but he was hoping that the deliberate omission would get his father's attention.

"I'm barring the door to the Room of Life." Armond's eyes surveyed the gathered crowd, and though his voice was calm, it was laced with anger and contempt, startling Calsura. "You see me. You see the chains. Why do you ask?"

"Father . . ."

"Has he sent you, Calsura?" Armond said, now staring at him. "Are you here to talk me down? To calm me? To maneuver me?"

"Father!" Calsura said. "The Amhura didn't send me."

"Well? What then?"

"I heard a commotion upstairs while I was dressing. I came to see what was going on. That's all."

"So now you've seen. Well?"

"Well what?"

"What are you going to do? Are you with me or against me?"

"You know me better than that," Calsura answered quietly. The question hurt, like being struck in the face without warning. "You know I'm with you."

"Do I? Have you brought chains I cannot see so you can help me bar the door?"

"Do I need chains?"

"You'll make a poor impediment without them. Too easily moved. Not me, though." As Armond spoke, he jerked his hands forward. The little slack in the chain quickly played out, snapping taut with a metallic ping and arresting Armond's arms in sudden and dramatic fashion. "No one enters today. The Golden Cord isn't going anywhere."

As though on cue, Calsura caught a glimpse of the Golden Cord over Armond's shoulder inside the Room of Life. It hung in midair, undulating rhythmically in a pattern both simple and mysterious, as though dancing to some silent inner song.

"Will you worship it too?" Armond asked quietly, a note of sadness replacing the anger in his voice.

Calsura pulled his eyes from the Golden Cord's entrancing movements and indescribable beauty and looked back at Armond, whose eyes had never left him. "You know I don't."

"Then what? Are you with me or against me? With Kalos or against Him?"

Calsura refused to look away. "I am with you and Kalos, but can't I be with Kalos and still question the wisdom of this?"

"Of course, but you can't be with Kalos and support Kartain."

"Can't he now?" a mellifluous voice said firmly from somewhere behind.

Calsura bowed his head and stepped automatically to the side as the fear seized him again. Kartain had come. Armond was lost.

Kartain walked past in the ornate attire of the formal robes of the Amhura. He didn't so much as glance aside to take note of Calsura but walked on until he stood only a few feet from Armond. "If I have understood you correctly, you have just suggested, here at the doorway to the Room of Life, something so startling as to be unbelievable."

Kartain turned from Armond and gestured with a grand sweep to take in the entire crowd, gathered and silent. "Before these priests, who serve in the Temple, do you suggest that obedience to the Amhura, who holds his position by divine right from Kalos, is in fact a betrayal of Kalos?"

"You hold nothing by divine right," Armond said, spitting on the smooth stone floor between them. As Kartain faced him again, Armond met his gaze without flinching, saying, "You hold your office because you promised a corrupt priesthood a corrupt vision of affluence and power to be gained and kept at the expense of true worship of the God they supposedly serve. That they elected you betrays their corrupt hearts."

"My, my," Kartain said, turning away from Armond again as he surveyed the gathered priests with eyebrows raised in feigned shock and surprise. "Someone is a little bitter that he wasn't elected Amhura, isn't he?"

Armond kept his mouth shut as Kartain turned back around.

Calsura could see the practiced look of patronizing tolerance on the Amhura's face and his father's clenched jaws as he held his silence.

Kartain addressed his father once more. "I will offer you one chance to end this day still a member of the Kalonian priesthood."

"How generous."

"Of course," Kartain continued, "you will have to forfeit your position as one of my high priests. The seriousness of your offense demands that a price must be paid."

"I am Kalos's high priest," Armond growled. "Not yours."

"Always the quibbler," Kartain replied, looking to the crowd as he rolled his eyes as a long-suffering adult might roll his eyes over a querulous child.

"And don't you dare talk to me of offenses or of paying the price," Armond added, the fire in his eyes and voice burning even brighter. "You are the one who must turn back, or we will all pay the price."

"Enough of this foolishness," Kartain said. "The parade is set to begin. Unlock these chains immediately and walk away."

"Zeal for Kalos is never foolish," Armond said, meeting Kartain's gaze firmly. "I'm not going anywhere."

"Unlock them," Kartain said.

"No," Armond pulled himself up to his full height and stretched his arms wide across the doorway.

Kartain turned and waved to two men in priestly garb at the back of the now sizable gathering.

As the two young priests walked toward Kartain, Calsura saw that one held a hatchet in his hands. Instinctively, he moved as though to intercept them, but several pairs of strong hands suddenly seized him from behind and held him still. "Let me go!"

Kartain turned to him. "Silence, priest, or I'll have your tongue cut out."

When the young priests came up alongside Kartain, Armond looked at the hatchet and laughed. "It'll take hours to sever these chains with that, and by then, it'll be too late for this sham of a parade. Word will spread of what has happened here."

"It would take hours to sever the chains," Kartain said matter-of-factly. "Your wrists, however, are another matter altogether."

"Kartain! This is blasphemy!" Calsura said, struggling against those who held him. "You can't shed the blood of a high priest of Kalos in the Temple, let alone at the doorway to the Room of Life."

"Can't?" Kartain said as he rounded on Calsura, his eyes flashing with sudden anger. "I am the Amhura. I do as I please."

Turning back to Armond, Kartain stepped in even closer until he was almost whispering in Armond's ear. "In just a few minutes, the parade will proceed as planned, and if any hear of this tomorrow or the next day, they won't care."

With a nod to the two priests, Kartain stepped aside.

Armond writhed but could not evade them, his motion restricted by the chains that bound him. "You dare spill my blood in the Temple? You dare stain the Room of Life?"

Kartain stood, arms crossed, watching silently.

"You think Kalos won't hold you accountable?"

As Armond struggled, the young priest with both hands free gained a firm grip and pulled Armond to one side so that his left arm was held taut in midair.

The other priest raised the hatchet, and Calsura looked away as the blow fell.

Armond screamed.

Calsura heard the hatchet fall again, the initial blow having failed to do its full work. When Calsura opened his eyes, blood covered the floor, and a weakened Armond was sagging down, now on his knees, his head lolling against his chest as his right arm still hung enchained above his head.

The two priests, the one so bloody he looked more like a butcher from the Zeru-Shalim marketplace than a priest, turned back toward Kartain.

"Why are you stopping?" Kartain said, pointing them back to Armond. "He's still in the way."

"You can kill me," Armond gasped as he was lifted and pulled to expose the other arm, "but for your sin . . ."

A sickening crunch interrupted him, and Armond fell with a thud onto the floor. For a moment, all was quiet save for Armond, who lay groaning on the stone, wallowing in his own blood. Above and behind him, now clearly visible for all to see, the Golden Cord danced its endless dance in the Room of Life.

"For your sin," Armond repeated, "the price must be paid."

The slow, rhythmic motion of the Cord stopped as it formed a circle in midair. The Kalonian priests gasped. The Golden Cord had danced its rhythmic dance for generations, for centuries. Now it rippled and vibrated like a gong that had been struck, as something like a shimmering wave of power pulsated out from it, rushing toward and through them.

Instantly, Kartain, his two henchmen, and most of the other priests gathered there fell lifeless to the floor of the Temple.

The wave that erupted from the Golden Cord and rippled through the priests, killing most and stunning the rest, also passed through the walls of the Temple. It shook the walls visibly but did not collapse them, and then it moved on out through the streets of Zeru-Shalim. As the startled silence of divine judgment settled upon the few priests that remained alive inside the Temple, the sound of hundreds and thousands of mourners wailing for the lost broke through the silence of a city in shock.

The hands that had held Calsura held him no longer. They lay lifeless beside their owner on the floor of the Temple. In a daze, he went and knelt by his father. Armond was dead, and Calsura wept.

At some point, how much later Calsura could not have said, the wailing of widespread grief pulling him from his father's body, he walked to the front of the Temple and stepped out through its great door. As far as his eyes could see, throughout the vast assembly of people who had gathered for the parade, men and women of all ages were bent over the bodies of the dead that littered the streets of Zeru-Shalim like so many grains of sand after a sandstorm.

"Kalos," Calsura whispered as he stumbled to his knees on the stairs of the Temple, "What have we done?"

Mordain looked tired and defeated. Trying to bury almost half the population of Zeru-Shalim before the heat of summer created a mess and stench beyond all imagining had been a monumental task, taking almost two days to complete.

Calsura could understand the king's reluctance to see him tonight, even given the nature of his message. Still, Mordain had agreed, and now Calsura and his five younger brothers stood in a semicircle before the king's throne.

"Kalos has spoken to you?" Mordain said at last.

"Yes."

"The Golden Cord is to be divided into six pieces?" Mordain looked from Calsura and his brothers out through the large window to his right toward the Temple, visible some distance away where it towered over the buildings around it.

"Yes," Calsura said, resisting the impulse to add that it had already been divided, that he'd found it that way when he returned that morning to the Room of Life, as Kalos directed.

Mordain turned back to him. "The Cord was a gift to Zeru-Shalim, and through it we have been blessed."

"Yes, but too many now worship the gift and forget the Giver."

"Its power has prospered and protected us."

"The Cord is powerful, another reason why this is to be done," Calsura said. "But prosperity and protection come from Kalos."

Mordain looked back to the window. "You say the Temple is to be closed?"

"It has been defiled and the Kalonian priesthood disbanded."

"Who will lead the people in worship?"

"You will," Calsura said.

Mordain looked back, a frown creasing his face. "I'm not a priest. I'm a king."

"Remember, it was in answer to the prayer of a faithful king that Kalos gave the Golden Cord to Zeru-Shalim in the first place."

"So," Mordain said, starting to lean forward, "if I am faithful, the Cord might be returned?"

"I meant that as king, you can model fidelity to Kalos for Zeru-Shalim," Calsura said. "The fate of the Golden Cord is not mine to predict."

"What will you do with it?" Mordain said, leaning back in his throne, allowing his eyes to close.

Calsura answered, "We must leave Zeru-Shalim, and we must separate."

"Separate?" Mordain said, his eyes opening again. "From each other?"

"Yes."

"You will each leave the city, and then you will leave each other? For how long?"

"As far as I know, forever," Calsura answered. "The Golden Cord is not to be reunited. Kalos has forbidden it."

"Why you, Calsura?" Mordain looked more intently at him, and then in turn at each of his brothers.

"We are the sons of the last faithful Amhura."

The frown creased Mordain's face again. "Kartain was the Amhura."

"No," Calsura said. "Kartain won the election. Armond was the last Amhura."

For several minutes, nothing further was spoken until eventually Calsura turned to lead his brothers out.

Then Mordain spoke again. "Is there nothing else?"

"Nothing else, Your Majesty?" Calsura stopped and turned back toward the throne.

Mordain leaned forward. "For me, from Kalos."

"No, Your Majesty," Calsura said, but he hesitated. He thought of the woman and her children he had passed on the way in and of the rumors he had heard about her. "There is one thing I'd like to say about Kartain's family."

"Kartain's family?" Mordain answered, leaning back.

"Punishing the innocent for the deeds of the wicked isn't just."

"Is this also a word from Kalos, Calsura?" Mordain's voice was suddenly no longer weary and sad but cold.

Calsura's skin prickled at the shift in tone. He lowered his gaze. "No, Your Majesty."

"Then you are dismissed."

Calsura led his brothers from the throne room. Their packs lined the wall of the hallway. Calsura helped Emin, the youngest at just seventeen, put his on. He hoped they would be given a little time to travel together, that they wouldn't all six be separated right away. Kalos had not said they must all part immediately upon leaving Zeru-Shalim, but what the future held for them or anyone, he could not say.

Part 1

THE TRUER WORD

1

THE RHINO-SCORPION

K aden wasn't sure he wanted to be king. However, since he was going to be one eventually, whether he wanted to be or not, he thought maybe he should have been in Barra-Dohn today. Eirmon was always going on and on about preparing him for the throne, but here it was, the day before the anniversary celebration, and Kaden was in the middle of nowhere.

He banked his slider to the left as he curved around the rock formation, then eased back up as he flew above the endless sea of desert sand.

Captain Greyer followed close behind, but he took a wider arc around the rocks and had to accelerate after they straightened out to catch up.

Kaden admitted to himself that as much as he hadn't wanted to come out this morning, he wasn't eager to return home, either. Regardless, his reluctance provided no compelling reason to linger. The terrain would only grow flatter and less interesting the farther they went from the quarry and the closer they got to

Barra-Dohn. There was little to look at and almost no sage on this side of the city to sweeten the air.

And, of course, Eirmon had to be faced eventually.

Kaden looked off to the right, a cluster of columns that marked a large colony of ants catching his eye. He had only glanced over briefly and was already turned back around, when what he had just seen registered. He banked hard to the right and decelerated quickly, coming to a full stop twenty or thirty yards from the columns.

Greyer pulled up next to him. He raised his goggles, resting them on his forehead, and looked at Kaden, waiting for an explanation.

Kaden hung his goggles on one of the slider's handles, then dropped off onto the ground. He waited as Greyer dismounted and came to stand beside him. Pointing toward the columns in the distance, he said. "See it?"

Greyer looked at the columns for a moment, then turned back to Kaden. "Sir?"

Kaden nodded and pointed again, a little impatiently. "Do you see it?"

"It's just an ant . . ."

"Look," Kaden said, stepping closer to Greyer. "The column that stands a little off to the side, there. See it? It's a little shorter than the others."

"Yes," Greyer said after a moment. "What about it?"

"Doesn't it also look a little smoother than the others? A little too smooth?" Kaden asked. "And do you see how the top of the column bends ever so slightly away from the other columns?"

Kaden looked at the column in question as he described it. "That's what I noticed first, the bend. That's what gave it away."

Greyer looked back at the columns, and this time he studied the cluster for a while. "I don't know how you saw that from the slider, but I think you're right."

Kaden smiled a big, delighted smile. "It's a rhino-scorpion, Greyer, lying in wait for something to approach the ant colony."

"Have you ever seen one, sir?" Greyer asked. "I mean, when it isn't buried like that?"

"I saw a whole herd of rhino-scorpions once," Kaden said, thinking back to that day. He remembered the herd marching in a straight line, single file, stretched out along the horizon. It seemed very long ago now. "I was just a kid, maybe not even as old as Deslo."

"I've seen one but not a whole herd," Greyer said. "Where'd you see that?"

"I was with Gamalian on a sandship," Kaden said, trying to remember where exactly they'd been. "One of his famous field trips into the desert."

"You probably learned all you ever wanted to and more about them then," Greyer said. "At least, it must have been interesting to see a herd up close."

Kaden laughed, and Greyer looked over, his eyebrows rising slightly. "I learned plenty, but from a distance, Gamalian was scared to death of them."

"Well," Greyer said, shrugging it off. "You can't blame him, really. They're nasty creatures."

"They're not so bad," Kaden answered. "Real scorpions scare me more than rhino-scorpions. Little, elusive, they can be any-where. With a rhino-scorp, if you know what you're looking for, you can spot it a mile away."

"You can, apparently." Greyer laughed. "I might not be so fortunate."

"Maybe not, but you wouldn't be snooping around an ant colony. This trap isn't for you."

"Still," Greyer said. "You can see why Gamalian would keep his distance. Those great big front claws . . ."

"Which are mainly for digging."

"True," Greyer acknowledged, "but not just for digging. And two more *pairs* of claws . . ."

"Which are mainly for walking."

"And that long, lithe tail with the sharp, curved, scythe-like blade on the end. What about that?"

"Yes, well," Kaden said, grinning, "that part of a rhino-scorp is pretty scary, but the poor things have to defend themselves somehow."

They laughed, watching the ant columns and the horn of the rhino-scorpion, whose flat body, six legs, and tail would all be buried just barely below the surface of the desert sand. The rhino-scorpion was waiting for smaller prey than them, but that didn't mean he wouldn't lash out if they got too close. Many an unaware desert traveler had passed too close to one and regretted it.

"So where were you?"

"Where was I when?" Kaden looked over at Greyer.

"When you saw the herd with Gamalian?"

"I don't know," Kaden said. "Near the coast, I think, because I did get a lesson in rhino-scorpion migratory patterns."

"How I envy your fancy education," Greyer said, rolling his eyes.

"It was interesting, actually," Kaden said. "We didn't just talk science. We talked history. That was the day Gamalian told me the Old Story about Kalos creating Zerura."

"The Old Stories," Greyer scoffed. "They're not history. Why would Gamalian fill your head with that rubbish?"

"Because it is part of a good education," Kaden said, almost reflexively. He smiled to think of how much he sounded like Gamalian when he said it. "Besides, they're fascinating."

"I'm a soldier, sir," Greyer said. "I don't have much use for children's stories about invisible superbeings and the like."

"You're hopeless," Kaden said. "It's not like Gamalian believes the Old Stories any more than you or I do, but at least he appreciates them. He taught me to appreciate them too."

"Appreciate them for what?"

"Their creativity, for one thing," Kaden said. "I mean, the whole idea that in the beginning there was no Zerura, so there was no Arua field, so there was no balance in the ecology of the living world . . ." Kaden lost the thread of what he was saying. He stared at the desert that surrounded him, stretching as far as he could see in any direction. No Arua field? Who first imagined that? Might as well conceive of a world without water or air.

"With no Arua, things could grow frighteningly large and strong," he continued when he realized his mind had wandered, "which is why we needed Zerura to give boundaries to the living world."

"Zerura," Greyer said with a frown. "Living matter. For all I know, it's as imaginary as Kalos."

Kaden shook his head, thinking of the great dig under the Academy that his father thought he'd kept a secret. "No, Zerura's real, Greyer. Where do you think the Arua field comes from?"

"Again, I'm a soldier," Greyer said, pulling his goggles all the way off his head and dangling them from his fingers. "I don't even think about such things. Besides, what does any of this have to do with rhino-scorpions?"

"I think," Kaden said, trying hard to remember. "I think Gamalian said the rhino-scorpions made him think of the Jin Dara."

"The what?"

"The Jin Dara," Kaden repeated. "It means 'dark things.' The Old Stories said that before the Arua field restrained their growth, dark things, or Jin Dara, walked the earth."

"Dark things," Greyer muttered. He turned his back on the ant columns in the distance. "Come on. Your father is expecting us."

Greyer started back to his slider, but Kaden reached out and grabbed him. "Hey, we can't pass this up."

"What do you mean?"

"The rhino-scorpion, of course," Kaden said, indicating back toward the columns. "What do you think I meant?"

"Of course, we're passing it up," Greyer said. "It's over there, we're over here, and that's just fine with me."

"Greyer?" Kaden said, "Come on, we can't walk away from this. How many chances do you get to hunt a rhino-scorpion?"

"I don't want to hunt a rhino-scorpion," Greyer said. "Why would I?"

"Well, I do," Kaden said. He let go of Greyer and turned back to his slider. He handled the bundle of spears tied to the slider's side, and bypassing the meridium ones, selected one with a plain, wooden handle. It was a long spear, maybe five feet, with a long, wicked blade—razor sharp on both sides and at the point.

Kaden turned back to Greyer, who hadn't moved. "Well? Are you going to come and help, or are you just going to watch?"

Greyer frowned and ignored the question. "Prince Kaden, this is insane. You were so angry this morning about having to come out here at all, about missing the preparations for the anniversary, and the feast tonight, and . . ."

"I wasn't angry about . . ."

"You certainly seemed angry," Greyer said. "I had to hear all about it on our way out. Now you're going out of your way to pick a fight with a rhino-scorpion. Why? Let's just go back."

"I wasn't angry," Kaden muttered, struggling to find just the right words to explain what bothered him about Eirmon sending him to the quarry. He couldn't, so he stopped trying. "I'm sorry, Greyer, but I don't have to explain myself to you. Are you coming or not?"

Greyer held his ground but only for a moment. He walked over to his slider to retrieve a spear too. When he returned, he asked, "What's the plan?"

"I'll approach from the front by the horn," Kaden said, pointing with his spear toward the cluster of ant columns. "Stay a step behind and a few steps wide of me. When I provoke it, he'll lash out with the tail. Cut the barb off, and then I'll go for the kill."

"Just like that?" Greyer said. "Cut the barb off the swinging tail?"

"Just like that." Kaden smiled.

"If I miss?"

"Don't."

Kaden started toward the columns. He approached slowly, spear held out in front. He'd never been very close to a rhino-scorpion, and he wasn't sure where they were most vulnerable. Their exoskeletons were very hard, he knew that, but perhaps if he could find an eye or a joint between the body and one of the legs, he could drive his spear through.

He'd have to make sure Greyer got the tail, of course, before he committed to his own attack. The barb was no laughing matter. It probably couldn't slice through bone, but it would tear through clothing and flesh with little difficulty. That his bones might stop it from passing clean through him was little comfort.

He was getting closer to the columns. If he stretched out the spear, he could touch the nearest of them, though the rhino horn lay a little farther out. He knew the rhino-scorpion could sense the vibrations made by their feet in the sand. It knew they were coming, probably also knew they were big, and maybe hoped they'd pass by without getting too close.

Kaden crept closer. His grip on the spear tightened. He thought he could see the faintest outline of the rhino-scorpion's body. The legs would be folded underneath. He couldn't see exactly where the tail was coiled, but that didn't matter. It was plenty long enough to lash out at anything that approached the horn with room to spare.

He glanced over at Captain Greyer. He looked tense. Even though Kaden was in his thirties, married, and a father, Greyer, who was a little older, acted at times like he was responsible for Kaden. And who knows, maybe Eirmon had given Greyer instructions to protect the prince. Kaden wouldn't have put it past his father to do that, no matter how insulting such a directive might be to him.

Of course, he thought of Greyer as a friend, as much as a captain in the army under his command could be a friend to the king's son. So maybe Greyer wasn't worried about what he'd tell Eirmon if something went wrong. Maybe he was just worried.

Greyer looked up and caught Kaden's eye. If Greyer was worried, it didn't show. He just looked ready. He nodded, and Kaden nodded back.

Moving forward, Kaden approached the rhino-scorpion's horn. He stopped a few feet away and extended his spear until it was just an inch away. He poked the horn.

Immediately, the body of the rhino-scorpion rose from the ground as sand cascaded off from every side. The tail rose whip-like into the air and flashed toward him.

Greyer swung his spear to intercept it, but he swung too high, and the blade missed. The tail, hitting the wooden shaft of the spear, swung awkwardly around and around, wrapping itself tightly around it while Greyer struggled to hold onto the spear and avoid the circling barb.

Kaden moved decisively to intervene. He swung his own spear, striking the taut section of tail between the rhino-scorpion and Greyer's spear, slicing clean through. The severed stump of a tail floundered around, and the rhino-scorpion screamed with a high-pitched squeal.

When Kaden was sure Greyer was all right, he spun to face the rhino-scorpion, but the creature was surprisingly fast and had already started away, all six legs churning the sand furiously. Kaden struck out at what appeared to be an exposed joint between one of the rear legs and the body, but he hit the leg, and his blow was deflected into the air.

He thought about giving pursuit but thought better of it. Had Greyer gotten the tail cleanly, maybe he'd have had a chance to aim a blow at the head of the rhino-scorpion as it emerged from the ground. He'd missed that chance now. Chasing it down and killing it would likely be tedious work, and he'd wanted excitement and a thrill, not tedium.

"Not going after it, sir?" Greyer asked.

"No, Greyer," Kaden said. "We'll let it go."

Greyer reached up and started unwrapping the severed tail of the rhino-scorpion from his spear. When he was finished, he stood, holding a four- or five-foot length of tail, with the long, cruel barb dangling at the end. "At least, you got this. It's a nice trophy."

Kaden took it from Greyer's outstretched hand. The tail was already getting stiff since being cut from its owner. He didn't know what he'd do with it, but he'd hold onto it all the same.

"I'm sorry I missed," Greyer said. "I just had to be sure I at least made contact."

Kaden nodded. "I know. I'd have aimed high too. Better that than missing all together."

They walked back to the sliders and put the spears away. Kaden laid the tail along the top of his bundle and tied it in. He looked over at Greyer, who still hadn't mounted, then turned to look for the rhino-scorpion. He couldn't see it anymore, but a long thin cloud of sand hovered in the air, marking out its path.

"He may not last long without his tail," Kaden said, feeling genuine regret. He didn't like the idea of leaving anything alive but bereft of its ability to hunt, feed, and defend itself.

"He may not," Greyer agreed. "Who knows? Maybe rhino-scorps are resourceful and resilient creatures. Anything that lives out here has to be, right?"

Kaden looked at the bright sun and glanced around at the barren landscape. "Pretty much."

Kaden climbed up on his slider, preparing to go, but Greyer still stood on the sand. "Something on your mind, Captain?"

Greyer stepped closer to Kaden's slider. "Life is too precious to throw away."

"What are you talking about?" Kaden watched Greyer, who was watching him. "I'm not trying to throw my life away."

Greyer didn't take his eyes off Kaden, and the intensity in them didn't fade. "I don't know all of what's between you and Eirmon, and it's none of my business. But he won't be the one you punish if something happens to you. It'll be Ellenara and Deslo."

Kaden thought of Nara and Deslo, of the gulf between him and them, of just how wrong Greyer was. If he died, they might feel relief but little else. Still, there was no point correcting the man, so he just repeated himself. "I'm not trying to throw my life away."

Greyer shrugged. "If you say so, but if I may speak further?"

"Go on."

"Driving your slider recklessly and attacking a rhino-scorpion for no apparent reason is one thing, but if war should come, and we go out together, I won't have men under me endangered because their commander doesn't value his own life."

Kaden thought about this for a moment, then nodded. "Fair enough, Captain. Can we go now?"

"We can go," Greyer said, but still he hesitated to mount his slider.

"What is it, Captain?" Kaden asked, a little irritated that they were still having this conversation.

"I'm sorry," Greyer said, seeming to sense Kaden's loss of patience. "I just wanted to say that it's hard to see you risk yourself, because when you risk yourself, you risk Barra-Dohn."

"How's that?" Kaden said, frowning at Greyer.

"Because," Greyer said, "whether you like it or not, you will one day be king. And if I may say so, sir, I think with a little work, you'll make a good one."

"Thank you, Greyer," Kaden said, as the captain mounted his slider.

They accelerated, turning back toward home. Greyer wouldn't have said what he did if he didn't mean it. The captain was a man of few words, sparing in his praise. And, it was nice to hear that specific affirmation from someone.

Eirmon had certainly never said it.

He thought of his father, of the throne of Barra-Dohn and found himself still not entirely sure he wanted to be king, whether he'd make a good one or not.

2

IN MEMORIAM

K aden dismounted his slider in the palace courtyard, letting the eager steward take it away.

Captain Greyer dismounted too and stood, waiting for Kaden's direction.

Kaden looked at the palace, wondering if Eirmon was inside, knowing he needed to find out but not wanting to.

"Do you have any idea what Eirmon's up to?"

"Sir?"

"Don't 'sir' me, Greyer," Kaden said, resisting the urge to laugh as he glanced at the look of innocent confusion on Greyer's face. "You've seen the same things I've seen. Even if you don't know what's going on, you must be asking the same questions."

Kaden ran his hand through his hair and scratched his head. "The quarry, the weapons and inspections, the drilling and the gathering of supplies—all of it. I know Eirmon thinks he can do these things, and no one will notice because of the preparations for the anniversary. But we both know there's more than getting ready to celebrate the discovery of meridium going on."

Greyer nodded. "I've noticed, but I don't know anything about it that you don't. I thought maybe you knew but couldn't tell me yet."

"You thought I knew?" Kaden did laugh now. "You know Eirmon doesn't tell me anything he doesn't have to. I guess this is one of those things he doesn't have to."

"Well, he hasn't told me, either," Greyer said. "None of the captains know anything, but he's gathering supplies and mustering men. It certainly seems like he's preparing for . . ."

"Something big," Kaden said. "The increased exercises and drilling, all in the name of being ready to defend Barra-Dohn in case someone uses the anniversary as an excuse to attack. Well, it seems a bit . . ."

"Flimsy, sir?" Greyer suggested. "I mean, who'd attack Barra-Dohn?"

"Yes," Kaden mused. "It does seem far-fetched. So what's it all about? Eirmon is paranoid, of course, but have you heard of any actual trouble with the Five Cities?"

Greyer shrugged. "I haven't, but like I always tell you, I'm just a soldier. The politics of the empire don't mean much to me."

"Me, neither," Kaden said.

"Well," Greyer said, adding a smile to his shrug, "that's going to have to change, isn't it? Otherwise, my prediction that you'll make a good king certainly won't come true."

"I don't know that I want to be king," Kaden said softly.

"Why not?"

"I don't ever look at my father and think, 'I want to be like him.'"

"Taking over for him doesn't mean you have to become like him," Greyer said, matter-of-factly.

"I know," Kaden said, "but I like to think Eirmon wasn't always like he is now. Maybe it was becoming king that made him this way." Kaden shivered, feeling a chill pass over him momentarily despite the hot day. "Sometimes, I think that maybe if he'd been older when he succeeded to the throne, then maybe it would have been different. Maybe that much power, so young—closer to Deslo's age than mine—maybe it made him like he is."

"All the more reason to think you can be different," Greyer said. "You've had time to prepare. Besides, it might be a long time before you even have to worry about it. The king is relatively young and in good health."

"True," Kaden said. "I suppose I should try to remember that whenever I find myself wishing something awful would happen to him. As long as it doesn't, I don't have to become king."

"You don't mean that, sir," Greyer said, though Kaden could tell Greyer wasn't entirely sure what to make of Kaden's comment.

"Who knows what I mean?" Kaden said, smiling and gesturing as though to wipe his own words away. "You know I talk all the time without saying anything sensible."

"I don't know any such thing," Greyer said. They stood in silence for a moment, and then Greyer added, "Do you need me for anything else?"

"No, I don't suppose I do," Kaden said. "I have to report to Eirmon and then get ready for the banquet. If you could do any of that in my stead, I'd happily let you, but alas, none of these are duties I can shirk."

"I'm afraid not, sir."

"Then go on," Kaden said. "Go home to your family. Are your boys looking forward to the anniversary?"

"Oh, yes," Greyer said, smiling. "Very much. We've talked of little else this last month. They'll probably be unable to sleep all night and will pester Maril and I relentlessly . . ."

Greyer must have seen something in Kaden's face, for he trailed off and never finished his sentence. They stood in awkward silence for a moment, and Kaden was about to take his leave when Greyer suddenly said. "It's not too late, you know."

"Too late for what?" Kaden said coldly.

"I'm sorry, sir, it's not my place," Greyer said, starting to turn away. "I'll just be going. "

"Greyer, wait," Kaden said, relenting. Greyer turned back, but Kaden saw wariness in his expression and posture. He sighed. "I'm always telling you to speak to me like a friend and a peer, not to treat me like a prince, and here I am barking at you when you do. Please, say what you were going to say. It's not too late for what?"

"Well, among other things, to forge a relationship with Deslo," Greyer said, taking a deep breath as though bracing for Kaden's reaction.

"A relationship? Like the one Eirmon had with me?" Kaden said.

"Whatever it was like having Eirmon as a father, and I can't really imagine what it was like."

"No, you can't."

"I'm sure I can't," Greyer said. "But whatever it was like, you don't have to be like that."

"No?" Kaden said. "What else would I be? That's all I've ever known. That's why I leave Deslo to his mother, Greyer. Better to be uninvolved than to be like Eirmon."

"Are those your only choices?" Greyer asked. "What about Deslo? What does he want?"

They stood together in silence once more. After a moment, Kaden reached out and took Greyer's hand. "I need to go. Thanks for speaking your mind."

"Very good, sir," Greyer said. He bowed slightly before turning away.

Kaden watched him pass through the courtyard to the gate that would take him out into the busy side yard where the butchers would already be at work, slaughtering the animals for tonight's banquet. Greyer didn't like leaving through the palace, and Kaden didn't blame him. Few but the kitchen stewards used the congested side yard, and there wasn't any chance of running into

Eirmon there amid the bloody work of preparing the fresh meat to be carried into the palace kitchens.

For his part, Kaden stood, thinking about Greyer's comments. He knew he should go to Eirmon and report, but he didn't want to. He turned and walked in the opposite direction. He would go to see his father, but before he did, he wanted to visit his mother.

Kaden hesitated before the wrought-iron gate. He hadn't been here in a while, and from the extensive network of spider webs, he could see no one else had been either. He broke a scraggly branch from a nearby shrub and used it to clear as many of the webs from the gate as he could. Tossing the branch away, he opened the gate and passed inside.

At the small table inside the gate, Kaden picked up the pitcher and poured the sweet sage oil into the lamp beside it. The pitcher had been nearly empty, not enough to fill the lamp. There was enough for a brief visit, though, and as the lamp began to glow brightly, he made a mental note to speak to Myron about making sure the stewards did a better job here. After all she'd been through in her short life, keeping the pitcher full and the gate free from webs seemed like the least his mother deserved in death.

Kaden lifted the lamp and walked down the short hallway to the stairs that headed downward into the darkness. The shiny marble floor and walls glimmered in the light of the lamp, and his footsteps echoed in the silence. He could feel the temperature grow cooler the farther he went below ground, and the air grew musty. At last, he reached the bottom. There he stood before the ornately carved, black mahogany double doors.

He reached up and ran his fingers along the cool, smooth, intricate carvings. In Barra-Dohn, where wood was rare and hard wood an extravagance, doors like this had never been seen before the king had these installed. Rumor of their opulence and the fortune Eirmon paid to buy the wood had spread far and wide, and matrons throughout Barra-Dohn and beyond had wept at this lavish symbol of the king's undying love for his queen. Even as a boy, Kaden had known better and hated his father's hypocrisy.

He pushed the heavy door open and left it ajar as he walked into the spacious vault. Two large lampstands stood on either side of the door, and at the base of one sat a large pitcher. Like the smaller one upstairs, it wasn't full, but there was enough. Kaden picked it up and filled the lamps on the stands. Light blazed out, filling the mausoleum.

His mother's sarcophagus sat directly ahead in the center of the room, turned to the side so the carved figurine lying on its top could be viewed in full by any and all visitors who came and stood between the lamps where Kaden was. For years after her death, visitors had come almost daily in a steady stream to pay their respects. Over the years, the stream had slowed to a trickle, and now, she lay alone—the forgotten queen, hidden out of sight in this forgotten place.

Kaden walked forward until he stood beside her. He reached out and touched the cold, marble cheek of the lifeless representation of the mother he'd lost so long ago, and memory stirred within. He thought of a day they'd had a picnic lunch on the royal barge in the middle of the harbor under a bright blue sky and a smiling sun. They were out on their own with just the crew of the barge and a handful of stewards from the palace. The table had been laid with a cornucopia of fruits, bread, and cheese, and his mother had entertained Kaden as though he were a royal dignitary from a far-off land.

Eirmon always scorned such playacting, sometimes even openly mocking them both when they adopted roles like these and acted them out, but that day he'd been somewhere else. Where exactly, Kaden didn't know and didn't care. That afternoon—all afternoon—they'd been free to eat and play and be every bit as silly as they wanted to be. When Kaden had grown tired, he'd curled up in his mother's lap and fallen asleep while she sang softly and stroked his hair.

Kaden stood still, his hand still on his mother's marble face. Along with the tenderness and sadness the memory provoked, he felt the corollary anger that always came too. Why were such memories so rare? His father had been king with the affairs of an empire to oversee. Why did it seem as if he'd hardly ever had time alone with her? Why did so many memories of his mother also involve his father, seemingly taking a perverse delight in ruining the joy they found in each other.

He'd never done that to Deslo and Nara. He wasn't a perfect husband or father, he knew that. Far from it. Still, he never sabotaged the relationship between his wife and son. Never. In fact, he didn't interfere in Deslo's upbringing at all. Nara didn't understand just how much of a gift this was, but Kaden knew. It was a priceless gift. One he'd have paid any price for.

But was Nara grateful? Of course not. Even when she didn't say so directly, she was always dropping little hints that he should be more involved. Maybe gratitude was too much to expect from her. Maybe she held too many things from their own strained relationship against him. Another mess with Eirmon at its heart.

A surge of anger swept through him. The anger brought the tears that his sadness had failed to bring. The hand that had moved to the marble shoulder of the figure in repose before him clasped tighter and tighter on the stone, and the fingers of his free hand trembled as they clenched into a fist.

Eirmon. He'd said and done all the right things in public, but behind closed doors, he'd treated his wife as if she was worthless. He hadn't bothered to hide his other women from either of them, and it became an open secret among the palace stewards that the king's appetite spilled over with regularity outside the royal bed.

Of course, after his mother's death, the king had continued his womanizing, moving from one lover to the next with no compunction and little hesitation. At first, Kaden had worked hard to keep up with the king's indiscretions, just so he could hate whoever was next in line. In time, he realized what wasted effort it all was.

Now, he no longer cared who the king's current paramour was. What Kaden knew without needing to know anything else was that whoever she was, and Kaden had his suspicions, she undoubtedly harbored hopes of becoming queen. She no doubt believed she was different from the others who had aspired to that crown before, which of course she wasn't. Eirmon would never crown another woman queen. He didn't have to.

If Kaden was honest, though, it wasn't the other women who made him angry. Not anymore. It was Eirmon's total indifference to his wife's memory and to this day. More than twenty years ago today, she had died in childbirth, along with the baby sister that Kaden had never even seen.

It wasn't that the king didn't remember what today was, because generally he did. Most years, he'd mention the event to Kaden in some patronizing way. Words like, "I know how hard this day is for you" would flow out of his mouth, like some grand, magnanimous gesture of comfort. He never seemed to understand that those words did little more than remind Kaden that the day wasn't hard for Eirmon at all. If the king did understand, he kept doing it anyway.

"I remember," Kaden said aloud, his quiet words echoing softly in the flickering lamplight of the crypt. The sage oil was running low. He walked to the foot of the stairs before looking back. "I remember, and I'll never forget."

Kaden blinked in the sunlight as he crossed the courtyard back toward the palace. His anger had cooled, the tears were gone, both replaced by the cold, hard determination to stand his ground that he usually carried to meetings with the king. He didn't want to cower before his father, nor did he want to react in such a way as to compromise his integrity just to annoy or defy him. He wanted merely to be himself—no more and no less.

He passed under the shadow of the palace and found his eyes once more adjusting to the dark. The door ahead was propped open, just slightly, and as he stopped and reached down to open it, it swung outward suddenly, hitting him hard in the hand. He stepped back, his hand throbbing; the anger he'd stifled and pushed down in the mausoleum boiled over. He shouted at the person he could not yet see, "Fool! Watch what you're doing."

His wife, Nara, appeared in the doorway, her arms full to overflowing with some bolts of cloth and her sewing things in a basket. She looked mortified, and it only deepened when she saw Kaden.

He groaned inwardly. Of all people to come through that door.

"I'm so sorry," Ellenara said, bobbling the bolts of cloth and struggling to keep from dropping them all over the ground. "I had my hands full. "

"I see that. It's all right."

"I pushed the door open with my foot. It was stupid and thoughtless. I'm sorry."

"No, I am," Kaden said.

For a moment, they stood facing each other. How wide the gulf between them, Kaden thought. A chasm, really. Even so, Kaden regretted his choice of words. He hadn't meant it personally, but she'd take it that way. "Nara, I shouldn't have called you a fool. I'd have done the same thing."

Tears slipped from Nara's eyes and rolled down her cheeks. She adjusted the bundle of things in her arms so she could reach up and wipe them away.

They felt to Kaden like accusations, directed not just against his angry words but against all the long, sad history between them. He tensed, hardening himself. He was on his way to see Eirmon. He didn't need this and couldn't get bogged down here, mired once more in a mess that had no solution. Nara didn't try to talk to him about their marriage very often any more. They seemed to have both conceded the uselessness of such conversations, but looking at her now, Kaden worried that she was working up to it.

"I need to report to Eirmon," Kaden said, more brusquely than he meant, but that didn't stop him. He started past her.

As he did, she reached out and seized his arm with the same hand she'd just freed to wipe away her tears.

He stopped, startled. He couldn't remember the last time they'd touched each other.

"I know how much you miss your mother. I know how much today hurts. I just wanted you to know I'm sorry, and I wish . . ." She hesitated as though considering whether or not to finish. "I wish I'd had a chance to know her too." She released his arm and strode off into the courtyard, head down, clutching her things tightly to her chest.

Kaden stood, watching her go, then slowly turned and headed inside the palace.

3

EIRMON

Despite the gleaming white exterior of the palace of Barra-Dohn, sweeping halls of red and black marble dominated much of the inside. Large windows supplied plenty of light to the exterior rooms, but the internal spaces and corridors often felt quite dark to Kaden when he stepped into them after being so long in the unrelenting brightness of the Aralyn sun.

The main level of the palace fluttered with activity. Stewards moved to and fro, working on final preparations in the kitchen and the great hall, in the smaller private dining rooms and the parlors that would be used to entertain not only the representatives from the Five Cities but the other honored guests who were coming for the anniversary.

Despite the heightened activity, Kaden made his way through the palace without difficulty. Underneath what appeared to be chaos and confusion, lay discipline and order, as the chief steward ran the palace with an abundance of both of these latter qualities.

Kaden found Eirmon's study empty, and returning to the main floor, he stopped one of the stewards in the bustling mass and told her that he'd like to see the chief steward.

Within moments, the man himself appeared. Short with thinning blond hair, he had an appearance of frailty that belied the heartiness underneath. He approached Kaden, moving with obvious purpose, though he never appeared hurried, his jacket and pants impeccably neat, as always.

"I'm sorry, Myron," Kaden said, "I didn't want to bother you. I know how busy you are today."

"No need to apologize, Prince Kaden," Myron said with a slight bow, acknowledging Kaden's apology even as he deflected it. "What may I do for you?"

"I was looking for Eirmon," Kaden started then paused.

Myron interjected. "A runner has just informed me that the king is on his way back from the Academy as we speak. I was just on my way to await his return. Should I send word to your room when he has arrived?"

"Thank you, Myron," Kaden said. "That won't be necessary. I'll just come with you, if you don't mind."

"You would be most welcome, Prince Kaden," Myron said, "but there is no need for you to wait at the door. I can . . ."

"Your staff has plenty to do already," Kaden said. "Besides, I don't really want to go back upstairs when he'll be here any moment. No point to it."

"Very good, sir," Myron said, bowing again.

Kaden followed the chief steward to the main entrance to the palace. The large double doors were open, providing a bright glimpse of the large square in front of the palace where the festivities for the anniversary would begin the next day.

Myron stepped out onto the top step and stood waiting, and Kaden stopped too, leaning against the sturdy door that was propped open.

"How has the prince's day been so far?" Myron watched the entrance into the square by which Eirmon's platform would enter, so Kaden couldn't see the expression on his face. He had no idea how privy Myron was to the king's plans, though Kaden suspected that the chief steward knew a great deal just by keeping his eyes and ears open. The man didn't seem to miss anything. Still, Kaden didn't know how much Myron might know about the specific task Eirmon had given him that morning, so he thought it best to be vague. "My day has been fine, Myron. And yours? Busy, I'm sure."

"Yes, sir," Myron said. "Very busy. I'm afraid that—ah, here they are."

Some of the Davrii had just appeared, jogging on their meridium-soled shoes several feet above the ground as they spilled into the square and fanned out to make room for the king's platform coming behind. Their plain gray pants and tunics decorated sparsely with the red trim that signaled their membership in Eirmon's private guard was perhaps the most instantly recognizable uniform in a city that preferred muted tones and wore simple garments.

Not far behind the front ranks of the Davrii came the king's platform. Eirmon Omiir rested beneath the silver canopy, enjoying its ample shade as the platform glided into the square from the main street that connected the palace on the northern edge of Barra-Dohn with the Academy at the very heart of the city. More members of the Davrii jogged beside the platform above the ground while some ahead and behind walked the actual street. Eirmon's entourage took up almost the entire width of the road, which was, Kaden thought, just the way the king liked it. Wherever they encountered traffic of any kind—pedestrians, couriers, and sliders alike—all had to wait for Eirmon to go past before resuming their journeys.

Kaden looked at Eirmon reclining in his ornate chair. The king discouraged references to it as a throne, though it evoked that terminology from the people of Barra-Dohn. Most of them would

never see the real throne inside the palace, so Kaden thought they
could be forgiven for attaching that significance to it when they
saw their sovereign passing by them on the streets of their city.
Even so, Eirmon didn't like members of his household or those in
his service referring to it that way. They were supposed to know
better.

Watching Eirmon's platform, which was some ten feet wide,
glide into the square, Kaden wondered how the people of the
city would react to the statue Eirmon had commissioned to com-
memorate the anniversary when it came gliding in from the same
street the following day. He'd had the opportunity to see the
statue at various points while it was being made. Most had not.
It was a towering and impressive piece, and Kaden suspected it
would make quite a spectacle.

As Eirmon's platform drew closer to the palace, several Davrii
moved into place around it. When it approached the stairs,
the pilot behind Eirmon shifted the rudders, and the platform
stopped just inches away.

Myron descended to meet him and bowed, waiting as Eirmon
stepped across the small gap onto the stairs beside him.

Next to Myron's thinness and apparent frailty, Kaden was
struck afresh by Eirmon's sturdiness. Short and stocky, he wasn't
overweight, simply solid. Kaden's son, Deslo, had inherited that
same frame. When they all three stood together, Kaden felt quite
out of place. Possessing the taller and more slender build of his
mother, the only resemblance Kaden could see between himself
and the other two was the trademark fair hair of the Omiir's. He
knew the reasons for the distance he experienced from his father
were many and disconnected from mere appearances, but it certainly felt ironic that the grandson Eirmon seemed to treasure
so much more than he'd treasured his own son bore a far clearer
physical resemblance to him.

There was no formal exchange of greetings between the king
and the chief steward nor between the king and Kaden. No sooner
had Eirmon's foot touched the stair on the same level as the king's

platform, than Eirmon was climbing the rest of them toward the open palace doors with Myron trailing close behind.

The chief steward was always very careful to make sure he walked a half step behind.

Kaden fell quietly in on the other side, knowing that Eirmon would want to address whatever the chief steward had come to discuss first before hearing Kaden's report.

"Is it done?" Eirmon asked as they passed back inside the palace.

"Yes, Your Majesty," Myron answered simply.

"Excellent," Eirmon said, and Kaden thought he detected a rare note of excitement in the king's voice. "I want to see it."

"Of course, Your Majesty," Myron replied.

Kaden followed as they made their way through the palace, not sure where they were going until they got there. The most formal of the private dining rooms in the palace also doubled as the council room when the king hosted a meeting with the representatives of the Five Cities. Kaden knew that the day after the anniversary, Eirmon would be hosting just such a meeting.

When they reached the entrance to the council room, a few stewards were working inside, but they did not linger once they saw the king at the door. Soon they were gone, and the three of them were left alone.

Still, Eirmon did not immediately go in. He stood, gazing at the beautiful new furniture.

Sitting in the middle of the room was a large table and a dozen chairs made from an incredibly rare redwood. Kaden had been there when the merchant who sold the wood to the king had claimed that he crossed the Madri to get it. Such a claim was dubious, of course, almost certainly made to drive the price higher. It was not impossible that he'd crossed the Madri, for he was not the cowering sort. Even so, though the merchant appeared to be the kind of person who might brave the crossing, it didn't mean he had. The northlands were not the only place where redwood could be obtained.

Still, the man had shown the king respect but not fear, and that always impressed Eirmon. Later, the king had admitted his own doubts about the veracity of the merchant's claim but added that even if the wood had been grown south of the Madri, it was very rare and of exceptional quality. It would have had to come from at least as far away as southern Golina and perhaps farther in the frigid, distant reaches of the southlands. No, Eirmon had said, he did not begrudge the merchant the price of the wood. A man of that caliber and daring deserved the price he asked, and Eirmon had given it to him.

Eirmon walked forward into the room at last. His fingertips traced lightly the back of one of the ornate chairs and then ran along the smooth surface of the table itself.

Kaden followed Eirmon inside, but he stayed back from the table and did not touch it. It would probably have been all right to do so, but without express permission from the king, Kaden thought it better not to.

The chief steward waited at the doorway.

"Can you imagine what will go through the minds of the emissaries of the Five Cities when they see it?" Eirmon said, though he didn't look at either of the others when he did, nor Kaden imagined, did he expect a reply. Both Kaden and Myron remained silent.

"They will know, if nothing else, that it cost a fortune," Eirmon added a moment later. He walked beside the table, still running his fingers along the smooth wood.

The table was beautiful, Kaden admitted. The craftsman Eirmon had hired to make the table and chairs with the wood had done well with it. Still, he didn't understand why the king was making such a fuss about it. Normally, Eirmon didn't pay any attention to the furnishings of the palace.

At the far end, Eirmon pulled out his chair, which was larger and more ornate than the others. He sat with both palms pressed flat against the smooth surface. He looked up at Kaden. "Come, Kaden." The king motioned to the chair beside his.

Kaden walked over and sat.

"It is time for a lesson in politics. Here's a question. Will showing off my new, rare, and expensive table stamp out the seeds of rebellion that are sending their deep roots down in the soil of the Five Cities?"

"Father, you don't know that. "

"Answer the question!" Eirmon shouted as he thumped the table with the flat of his hand. The king added through gritted teeth, "I'm not interested in what you think I know."

"No, a table won't do that," Kaden said this time. He stared at the table, not looking at Eirmon.

"That's correct," Eirmon said, no trace of his momentary flash of anger remaining in his voice. "It can't. Nor can it make the process of actually doing so any easier. So what then, can it do?"

Kaden shrugged. He knew that not answering verbally would annoy and possibly anger Eirmon, but he didn't care.

"Pathetic," Eirmon muttered and sighed. "I will teach you despite your stubborn insistence on remaining in ignorance. This table is a symbol of my power and my wealth. It will remind the emissaries in no uncertain terms of the supremacy of Barra-Dohn, without my having to say a word. Whatever their intentions when they arrive, in the end they will accept the yoke as their fathers and grandfathers and great-grandfathers did."

Kaden stole a glance at the king, who seemed no longer to be talking to him.

Eirmon was rising up out of his chair, which he pushed gently back in.

Kaden stayed where he was.

"Oh, yes," Eirmon continued, "they will accept it now or later." The king strode around the far side of the table, heading back toward the door. "Can you not see them, straining to conceal their admiration for my beautiful table? Putting on their usual show of insincere devotion to me and to Barra-Dohn? The wheels of insurrection turning in their minds? Full of smug self-satisfaction, even as they eat my food at my table? Preparing to lie

and deceive, as though I were a dotard, unaware of their treason-
ous hopes and plans?" Eirmon's angry face suddenly grew calm.
He stood now behind the chair opposite his own. "They will
come. They will sit. They will wait expectantly, smirking, for the
council to proceed in the usual manner, but it won't. No, it won't.
Then I will wipe the smirks from their faces." Eirmon abruptly
turned and left the room.

Myron and Kaden moved quickly to follow. Kaden considered the display he had just witnessed. Perhaps the king's growing paranoia about the Five Cities and the rebellion he feared
really did explain what neither he nor Greyer could. Maybe Eirmon thought the council would be the prelude to an assault on
Barra-Dohn.

"Is the pre-banquet reception room ready?" Eirmon asked as
they walked back through the palace.

"No, Your Majesty," Myron said.

The simple, straightforward answer would have surprised
Kaden if it were anyone but the chief steward. Most would have
squirmed to use the word *no* with Eirmon. Myron didn't.

"The representatives from the Five Cities will arrive anytime
now," Eirmon said, well aware that this was not information the
chief steward needed.

"Yes, my Lord," Myron said, "It will be ready. They will neither see nor hear anything to suggest the least corner of your palace is unprepared for their arrival and this historic celebration."

"Good," Eirmon replied, stopping to face Myron. "I want
them to find my house, like my empire, in order."

Myron bowed in reply, acknowledging the king's clear warning. Eirmon didn't like to threaten overtly, but his threats were
no less effective for their subtlety. Kaden knew that very well.
Disappointing the king was not a habit the chief steward had ever
cultivated, nor did he wish, Kaden imagined, to start now.

Eirmon, seeing that his message had been received in the
spirit intended, said, "Send word when it is done."

"Yes, my Lord," Myron said at once, but Eirmon had already turned his attention to Kaden, and the chief steward melted away into the frenzied activity still swirling around them in the palace.

"We'll talk in my study," Eirmon said, and Kaden followed as they passed upward and into the king's private residence. The noise of preparations faded below, leaving only the yawning silence between them.

Kaden was surprised to see Rika waiting outside the door to the king's study. He didn't know how she managed it, but Rika had a knack, almost as much as Myron, for knowing what was going on and quietly getting ahead of it. How she'd known the king was on his way to his study and how she'd gotten there ahead of them, Kaden couldn't imagine. She didn't have the network of subordinates that Myron did at her disposal.

Though Rika was one of Deslo's tutors, Kaden had few dealings with her, as he steadily directed such matters to Nara. What's more, Kaden knew Deslo was out hunting with Gamalian, his other tutor, which Rika almost certainly knew as well, so she wouldn't be here looking for him. It must be Eirmon, but what would bring her here to find the king? Rika had significant responsibilities at the Academy in addition to her role in the royal family, and Kaden wouldn't have thought on such a busy day that she could afford to hang out at the palace waiting for Eirmon.

"Waiting for me, I take it?" Eirmon said as they approached the door to his study.

"Yes, Your Majesty," Rika said. She wore the solid blue garb of an Academy researcher. Her clothes were modest and tailored carefully to present her as professional and workmanlike, but also, Kaden suspected, to accentuate the womanly curves underneath. Rika had always struck Kaden as a woman who knew very well that she was attractive and picked her clothes to enhance her attractiveness with subtlety rather than crassly exposing it, the way a less secure woman in her position might.

That thought stirred something in Kaden, and he appraised Rika more carefully. She was pretty, but Kaden would have said her dominant characteristic was ambition. Both were qualities the king found alluring, but both were also qualities the king mistrusted.

Kaden dismissed the matter from his mind. Neither Rika nor the way the king saw her were of any consequence to him.

"I have something to show you," Rika said.

"Now?" the king said, opening the door to his study. "It's a rather busy day."

"Yes, Your Majesty," Rika said. "The Academy wished to give you something as a surprise in honor of the anniversary. It was meant to be ready earlier, but it was only ready for installation today."

"A surprise? Installation?" Eirmon said. "Sounds intriguing."

The king started as though to enter his study, but before he could, Rika said, "May I?"

"Of course," Eirmon nodded, acquiescing. "After you."

Rika stepped through the door, reached up to touch something on the wall that Kaden could not see, and suddenly a glow of soft white light with a hint of blue flickered in the dark room.

Eirmon looked at Rika, puzzled.

She stepped farther in, smiling, and motioned for them both to come in too.

Kaden followed Eirmon through the doorway and looked at the source of the light—a small, glowing, half-globe, mounted to the wall.

The king shook his head as he stared at it, his reaction expressing well Kaden's own feeling of disbelief. He'd never seen anything like it.

"You just touched it?" Eirmon asked, looking from the light to Rika. "The sage oil is already inside?"

"It doesn't require sage oil," she said, evidently enjoying the king's wonder. "And yes, I just touched it. You can activate it the same way when you enter. The light won't last a long time, and as you can see, it's not terribly bright, but it should prove helpful to illuminate the room while you add oil to your—"

"It's my skin then? Cells from my skin activate it?"

Kaden could hear in Eirmon's voice a little eagerness to recover from what he probably saw as loss of face. Eirmon hated to appear ignorant, even if there could be no reasonable expectation that he would know something that he didn't like the specialized knowledge that the researchers who worked for the Academy possessed and had put into this light.

"No," Rika said, "the meridium core is, after all, behind a thin layer of glass. It's just the warmth of your hand that—"

"But you only touched it for a moment," Eirmon said, looking back at the light on the wall, now fading. He reached out and rubbed the glass with his hand, and the light grew stronger. His attempts to prove his own cleverness appeared lost in the increased brightness.

They stood looking at the light, and when it began to fade again, Rika looked at Kaden. "Go ahead. Touch it."

Kaden reached out and felt the smooth, warm glass. The light glowed stronger under his fingertips. "Amazing."

"Yes, it is," Rika said, walking over to Eirmon's desk, where she took up the pitcher of sage oil and poured some into his desk lamp. The light from that lamp soon overpowered the lesser light from the globe beside the door, but Eirmon and Kaden still stared at it.

Kaden felt no need to pretend he understood matters too complicated for him. He understood how the lamp on Eirmon's desk worked, as much as he understood any meridium-based technology. Like everyone else, he knew that meridium worked, even if he didn't feel anyone had ever adequately explained just how it worked.

Yes, meridium reacted to the Arua field that emanated from the earth. Yes, it needed to be mixed with biological materials from plants and animals to have those reactions. Yes, plant materials mixed in different proportions with meridium alloys created various heat and light reactions. Yes, animal materials mixed in different proportions with meridium alloys created various force reactions. Yes, the blending process of meridium in its molten state with these biological materials was a tricky, precise business. Yes, yes, yes.

He knew all this. Any child did. But *why* did it work? Kaden didn't know, and he knew Eirmon didn't either. The king liked to portray himself as a budding scholar who'd been forced to leave behind the realm of research and science when circumstances forced him to ascend to the throne. Kaden knew better. Eirmon cared little or not at all about the theoretical. Only when something showed clear indications of being practically useful to his desire to strengthen his empire did Eirmon begin to care.

Kaden gazed at the light. He wasn't Eirmon. He would like to understand; he just didn't. Perhaps questions of this nature could never be answered. Perhaps meridium's response to Arua was just a fact of nature, like the ceaseless pull of the tide or the revolving wheel of the seasons. Maybe it just was.

"It operates on the same principle as the streetlights of Barra-Dohn," Rika said from behind them. Kaden and Eirmon turned to face her. "The streetlights soak up the sun's energy all day, like a plant, storing them for energy. Then, at night . . ."

"But the globe transformed the heat from my hand into light in a matter of mere seconds?"

"Yes, it did." Rika looked proud as she said that. "The Academy is excited about this new technology. Unfortunately, it's difficult to do and expensive, so it isn't yet practical for sale and export, but we're working on that. Someday, that light, or ones like it, will make you and Barra-Dohn a fortune."

"I believe you," Eirmon said. He crossed to the glass doors that led out onto one of his private balconies, opened them, and walked out. He stood, overlooking the square below. Kaden and Rika followed him. "How appropriate, on this eve of the anniversary celebration," he said.

"That was our thinking too," Rika said. "So please forgive this intrusion on your busy schedule. Now, if you'll excuse me, Your Majesty. I'm sure you have things to do."

"By all means," the king said, without looking at her.

"Prince Kaden," Rika said, nodding ever so slightly as she turned to go. Soon, the door was closed behind her, and Kaden was alone with Eirmon.

"So?" Eirmon said as soon as the sound of the door closing signaled they were alone. The king did not turn around, did not look at him, and did not bother with any social niceties.

Kaden would have been surprised if he had. "So what?" he said. He tried to keep his voice empty of emotion, but he could hear the echo of irritation in it. He knew what Eirmon wanted, knew that if he continued to be difficult about giving it to him, the scene would get ugly. He could see all this with perfect clarity, yet it was so hard not to fall into the familiar pattern, making his stubborn protest in the same stubborn way.

"So what did you think?" Eirmon said, turning from the balcony to look at Kaden.

Kaden wondered if Eirmon felt it too, the sense that this was an old, familiar, tired dance. "You know what I think," he said. "I think I should have been here today, is what I think."

"You made that clear last night," Eirmon replied.

"Then maybe you should have listened for once."

"When did you forget that I am your king as well as your father?" Eirmon snapped.

Despite the outburst downstairs and just now, Kaden knew Eirmon didn't often yell. It simply wasn't necessary. He got what he wanted without it. Kaden provoked the king's ire like no one else. He felt some guilt about that, but he also felt his provocation of the king was not entirely without it's own provocation—a lifetime of it.

"My reasons are my own," Eirmon said after a moment, trying visibly to calm his voice, "and since I haven't shared them with you, you can't possibly presume to judge the worth of my commands."

"Then share them," Kaden said. He succeeded in keeping the impatience he felt out of his tone, but there was a risk that he might come across as pleading, something Eirmon despised almost as much as disrespect.

Eirmon grimaced, and Kaden braced himself. "I will share them when I'm ready. Now stop making a fool of yourself, always whining about things you know nothing about."

Kaden clamped his mouth shut. He swallowed what he'd been going to say, knowing it would only escalate the conflict.

"You've made your point," Eirmon said. "I've heard your protest. Can we actually talk about your trip to the quarry now?"

Kaden didn't speak right away. His lips were pursed, his hands clenched. He needed to speak, but he was determined not to do so until he was ready to keep his words simple and his voice clear of anger.

Eirmon, obviously thinking Kaden's silence was continued resistance, added one more, final, expectant word. "Report."

Kaden exhaled, then spoke. "They worked great, just like they have every other time I've been there."

"And the men? The squads who work them?"

"Fast, efficient, accurate—everything we want," Kaden said.

"In your estimation, they're ready for use?"

Eirmon studied Kaden's face, and Kaden thought he saw an unusual eagerness there. Why, Kaden wondered? Eirmon, perhaps noting Kaden's reaction, quickly added, "Should such use be necessary, of course."

Eirmon turned back to look over the square, perhaps to avoid Kaden's searching eyes. Eirmon's caveat hadn't fooled him. The king expected that the new weapons would soon see action. This had been no ordinary inspection. "They're ready."

"And the spheres with the new cores?"

Kaden shook his head. What could he say of them? "They're everything you said they were. What they did to the quarry wall . . ." His voice trailed off, but he knew the king would understand. He'd seen them himself. Words were inadequate to explain the sight. They stood in silence, looking out over the city.

"What aren't you telling me?" Kaden asked. "I have a right to know."

"Always so eager to claim your rights," Eirmon sneered. "Try earning them instead."

Despite his efforts to keep calm, Kaden felt the familiar flush of anger rise within. With difficulty, he kept it from spilling out of his mouth.

Eirmon continued, sounding a bit more conciliatory, as though even he knew he'd gone too far, pushed Kaden's buttons a little too hard. "After the Grand Council, I will tell you what's going on. Until then, you need to be patient and trust that what I have done and asked you to do, I have done for a reason."

"I'm sure you have," Kaden said, and he couldn't resist adding, "but that's not much comfort. I don't often like your reasons."

"That's too bad," Eirmon said, the sneer back. "Sadly, you have to live with them."

"You don't have to tell me," Kaden laughed, bitterly. "No one knows that better than I do. I do live with them. Every day." He added the last, pointedly, knowing Eirmon would understand the implication.

"So predictable," Eirmon said. "Don't bring her into this."

Kaden shrugged and turned away. "Are we finished then?"

"Almost," Eirmon said. "I need you to get ready to greet the emissaries from the Five Cities. They'll be here at any time."

"What?"

"Dinner is at eight, and they won't risk being late."

"But . . ."

"They won't want to get here too early either," Eirmon continued, ignoring Kaden's interruption. "Even though I know perfectly well that they've all been in the city since at least early this morning, still they— "

"Why do I have to do it?" Kaden interrupted the king. He tried never to do that, but he didn't care anymore.

"Because I want you to."

"I hate playing the royal receptionist."

"You might as well get used to it."

"Why?"

"I would have thought that was obvious, even for you."

"Why obvious? Because I'll one day be king?" Kaden said, stepping toward Eirmon and pointing at him. "You're the king, aren't you? You must be since you never let anyone forget it."

"Watch your mouth!"

"I don't see you receiving anyone," Kaden continued, a little less vehemently. "Seems to me that the best thing about becoming king will be that I won't have to do all these things you keep telling me kings have to do."

"Well then, little boy," Eirmon said, not backing down. He stepped right up to his taller son and looked up into Kaden's face with fire in his spiteful eyes. "Run along, and pay your dues. When you're king, you can pass these duties on to Deslo. Maybe, if you're lucky, he'll be more respectful about it than you are."

Kaden thought for a moment about giving Eirmon another piece of his mind, but it was no use. They had this argument at least once a week, and they'd been having it most of Kaden's adult life. There was no resolving it, so there was no point prolonging it. Kaden stalked off the balcony and out of the study, glad to shut the door behind him.

Kaden walked, preoccupied, paying almost no attention to where he was going. Greyer had the audacity to suggest that he was a bad father? Nara did more than suggest it, using words like neglect, begging him not to ignore Deslo. He'd love to be ignored and neglected.

Deslo might not understand now. That was fair; he was only a little boy, but one day he would. It was a hard lesson, no doubt, but it was not neglect; it was a gift.

It felt like all of Kaden's life, Eirmon had been trying to crush him. When Kaden had first held Deslo in his arms, he'd been seized with a terrible thought: What if he turned out to be a father like Eirmon had been?

Kaden had vowed never to let that happen. He would never crush Deslo.

4

THE HOOKWORM

Deslo squatted, and his feet dipped in the air just slightly but not so much that he lost his balance. A deft movement of his meridium soles, and he regained his footing on the Arua, as though his feet rested on solid ground.

He laid his meridium spear down gently beside him, and it dangled in the air beside his feet. On a windy day, he might worry about it becoming unbalanced and falling or at least spinning. His spear was fine craftsmanship and unlikely to fall unless he tipped it up and upset its balance. But no breeze stirred, though he would have welcomed the relief.

The merciless sun beat down, and the desert sands stretched endlessly ahead, making him feel small and lost, even though he wasn't. Had he not known that Barra-Dohn lay beyond his sight but within easy reach by sandship, it would have been easy to panic. Deslo had hunted a hookworm in the desert on his own before twice, but he still struggled a bit with being overwhelmed by the desert's raw barrenness. He reminded himself that most boys his age had never hunted hookworms alone and that he wasn't hopelessly childish to be disconcerted by the relentless heat and blinding glare reflecting off the desert sands below his feet.

Of course, he wasn't really alone. Gamalian was waiting with the sandship, hovering somewhere in the distance behind him. Even if he'd wanted to be alone, the king's grandson never went anywhere unsupervised. If he needed help, he could call out, wave his arms madly, or whatever, and Gamalian would come. Deslo was determined, though, to get a hookworm on his own this time and show his father that he could.

Truthfully, he wished his father would hunt with him, but he was running some errand for his grandfather, or perhaps he was already back in Barra-Dohn. Wherever he was, he was definitely too busy with the plans for the anniversary celebration to come along. Deslo told himself it was the anniversary, but if it hadn't been that, it would have been something else. His father was always busy.

Now that he'd put the spear down, he wiped the sweat from his right hand on his shirt, and taking the Romaia lizard he'd been carrying in his other hand firmly behind the head with it, likewise dried the left. The lizard, which had been still before the switch, must have sensed a chance to escape, for it began to squirm and twitch, its stubby tail rapidly moving back and forth in a clear display of desperation to be free. Deslo held on tightly, both because he didn't want his bait to get away and also because he didn't want to be bitten.

He returned the Romaia to his left hand, picked up his spear again, and looked around for anything that might direct him in his pursuit. At first he saw nothing, save lots and lots of sand and the occasional sandy rock jutting up out of the desert floor, but then he saw what he was looking for. About thirty paces away, what appeared to be a small basin of sand opened in the ground and began to deepen. The sand started shifting, moving slowly in a swirling fashion, like a sand whirlpool gradually seeping deeper into the earth.

Deslo launched himself forward, running above the ground with renewed strength and determination. The hookworm was diving, and if he didn't get within range soon, the worm would be too deep.

The whirlpool of sand appeared to have reached its nadir when Deslo drew near, for the sand tumbling into it was now filling in the very bottom of the newly created bowl. It might be too late. It depended on how sensitive this hookworm was to movements on the surface and how hungry it might be.

Deslo lowered his knee carefully, knowing that tilting his feet too far in the wrong direction might mean a slip and his foot dropping onto the sand, which would warn the hookworm of his presence and scare the creature off. He reached down and dropped the Romaia lizard gently onto the sand.

The startled creature wasted no time in availing himself of the opportunity to escape his captor and began scurrying across the blistering sand without delay. At first, he headed toward the sand whirlpool that had almost slowed to a stop, but then, as though detecting the anomaly in the landscape and knowing the danger that it posed, the Romaia cut hard to the right and ran, if anything, faster. Holding its little head high and erect, the four legs of the frightened lizard churned through the sand, kicking up a tiny sandstorm as it ran for its life.

Deslo jogged in the Romaia lizard's wake, watching to see if the hookworm would take the bait. The lizard showed no signs of slowing down, and Deslo knew that he'd have his answer soon. It wouldn't take long for it to be beyond the hookworm's ability to detect motion at the surface, if the hookworm hadn't already been too deep when Deslo dropped it in the first place. Deslo jogged along behind and waited. Nothing. Deslo started to close the gap in order to capture it again. The Romaia would live to be bait another day.

Just then, a long bulge in the sand appeared almost directly below him, and Deslo's pulse quickened. The hookworm had risen after all and was in pursuit. Some of the sand displaced by the worm's rise sprayed his legs as he ran. He moved instinctively to the side so as not to be right above the bulge as it plowed along behind the Romaia lizard. He was no expert, but he knew enough to know the hookworm rippling along beside him was big—very big.

Deslo began to move in an arc so that he could see the hookworm on his left and the Romaia lizard up ahead. The last time he'd tried to spear a hookworm when it surfaced for the Romaia he'd brought, he'd been directly behind the hookworm's head. When it opened its wide, gaping mouth to grab and swallow the lizard, he'd had a poor angle to drive in the spear where the creature was vulnerable. His spear thrust struck the hardened exterior of the hookworm's head instead, and it had rapidly retreated safely out of sight.

He wouldn't make that mistake again. He'd approach the hookworm's killing move from the side, and when the hard-shelled mouth opened to gulp down the Romaia, he'd put his spear in through the opening and drive its sharp point through the less dense scales below the head from the inside, just like he'd been taught.

Deslo timed his approach carefully. The hookworm was blind and negotiated its terrain based on feel alone. Even when it surfaced, it wouldn't be able to see him hovering above. Still, the Romaia was not blind, and Deslo didn't want to confuse it. Despite its current preoccupation with the danger rushing at it from below, Deslo could easily spook the lizard by running toward it from above, and if the Romaia changed course, Deslo might lose his favorable angle when the hookworm rose for the kill.

The hookworm was closing rapidly, and the Romaia knew it. Its proud head, once erect, now bobbed slightly as its legs flew faster. Sand flung up into the air by the hookworm, now almost at the surface, sprayed in all directions. The Romaia tried changing directions one more time, but safety did not lie anywhere within its reach, and Deslo adjusted his course as well. For one, brief moment, the sand grew almost still, and the sand cloud over the lizard dissipated, but Deslo knew this was certain proof that the hookworm's killing strike was coming. It had dived down from the surface in order to propel itself upward beneath his prey.

Sand erupted in all directions as the hookworm's head burst through the surface, pushing the lizard up into the air. The Romaia's legs flailed, looking for the ground that had disappeared from beneath its feet in that sudden, terrifying surge. The hookworm's mouth opened, forming a deadly trap for the now falling lizard. The rear legs of the Romaia hit the hookworm, and the mouth snapped shut, snaring one of them. Deslo moved in.

The hookworm opened and closed his mouth twice more in rapid succession, and now all but the front legs and head of the Romaia had disappeared from view. Deslo readied himself right above the thick, ugly head, and when the mouth opened again, he thrust his spear down with all the force his ten-year-old body could muster, careful to get inside the hardened rim of the worm's mouth without wasting the principle strength of his blow on the lizard still being swallowed there.

The strike was accurate and true, and he felt the spear pierce the inside of the hookworm's mouth, several inches below the hardened rim. He pushed the spear straight through on an angle and felt it burst through the outer scales into soft sand. The hookworm pulled down hard, willing to let the spear rip out through its hardened mouth rim in order to be free, but the spear was too far below the rim to pull through.

The hookworm was hooked.

Deslo was so excited that he forgot to kick off his meridium soles and step down onto the sand. Instead, he stood on the invisible Arua field, his feet several feet above the hookworm, readjusting his grip on the end of his spear so he could use it like a lever to pry the hookworm up out of the ground. Meanwhile, the injured but still powerful worm resisted, knowing that it had to submerge soon or die.

Most of its short, sharp, external hooks that it used to propel itself beneath the sand still lay below the surface, and they were clawing backward with all the hookworm's might to pull itself down and free. It would wrench the spear right from Deslo's hands and submerge, dragging the spear down with it if Deslo wasn't careful.

After almost losing his balance in this awkward position, Deslo remembered to kick off one of the detachable soles so he could lower a foot onto the sand. The ground felt odd after standing on the Arua for so long, and even though his light, leather-treated boots were designed for desert wear, he could still feel the heat radiating up from the sand. He detached the other meridium sole by tilting it just so and catching the corner of its heel against his leg. It popped off and bobbed up into the air where it floated beside its mate.

Now, with both feet set shoulder-length apart in the sand not more than eighteen inches from the hookworm's head, he maneuvered the spear shaft so he could grab it as tightly as possible, closer to the creature's head for more leverage. Hookworms, for all their prowess, speed, and mastery beneath the sand, were remarkably vulnerable to the heat of the desert sun and could not long survive at the surface. Deslo knew the creature would already be feeling the ill effects of its longer than intended exposure, and it would do all it could to pull free of his grip. Time was on Deslo's side, if he could but hold on.

Deslo strained with all his might. He couldn't believe the resistance he was getting. He'd helped surface hookworms in the past, but he must have completely misjudged how great the total pull of one could be, because he'd felt sure he was ready to do this on his own. But now, his hands were slipping on the spear shaft, and his muscles ached as his arms felt as if they were being ripped from their sockets.

Just as he was feeling sure he had lost this battle, the resistance from below slackened. He had weathered the first and mightiest pull of the hookworm, and now he pulled back with all the strength he still possessed. The hookworm lurched up from the hole a few feet, small dark hooks spaced all around its sandy red-brown body flailing wildly now that they'd been removed from the sand. And yet, despite its great counter-pull, the hookworm was not completely out. Deslo felt a sinking fear.

The biggest hookworm he'd ever seen had been about three and a half feet, less than a foot smaller than Deslo himself, and that was supposed to be about as big as hookworms grew. This hookworm was almost that far out of the ground, and yet Deslo could feel enough resistance to indicate that a healthy portion still remained below the surface. More hooks were still embedded in the sand, struggling desperately to keep Deslo from surfacing it altogether.

The hookworm thrashed to the right, and Deslo lost his balance. His left foot was jerked sideways, and he felt himself falling down as he struggled to remain upright. His right knee hit the sand mere inches from the rugged and dangerous side of the hookworm. The sharp hooks weren't searching for him to cut him open, but they were looking for sand to grab. In the worm's overwhelming desire to retreat back underground, the hooks would rip him open if he got too close.

Deslo dug his left foot in, arresting the hookworm's movement. Then having gathered himself, Deslo thrust up and out, jerking the hookworm back in the direction he'd been pulling before. The hookworm's hold on the ground broke, and Deslo drove back, step after step, until he could see several feet of sand between the tail of the hookworm and the hole from which he had pulled it. He rolled the worm, using his spear as a handle to turn the creature, and drove the pointed end into the sand, effectively staking the creature down. Exhausted, he stepped back.

For a moment he stood, more or less doubled over, arms aching and chest heaving. Sweat slid through his eyelashes, blurring his vision, and he didn't have the energy to reach up and wipe it off. Then, having regrouped, he straightened and walked around his catch, now motionless on the sand. It was remarkable how fast the desert sun could sap all energy and strength from a surfaced hookworm.

Deslo didn't know how big the hookworm actually was. He did know he'd never seen one this large. It looked to be as big as he was, maybe bigger, and he was only a shade under four and a half feet. Now that the fear and adrenaline had subsided, Deslo started to imagine his return, and his excitement grew. The court would surely be amazed. Buzz about the colossal hookworm that little Deslo had surfaced alone would fill the palace, maybe even all of Barra-Dohn.

His father would be proud of him now.

"Simply remarkable," came the voice from behind him. Deslo turned to see Gamalian, gliding up toward the fallen hookworm on the sandship. In his face, Deslo saw not only pride but wonder, confirming what the boy suspected. The hookworm was indeed very big, and his accomplishment in spearing and surfacing it alone, by extension, was all the more significant.

"Have you ever seen one this big?"

"Never." Gamalian propped up the rudder, and the sandship slowed. He dropped the sandbag anchor overboard as he stepped carefully out. Though Deslo knew Gamalian was spry for a man his age—he was even older than his grandfather—it was a big step to cross over the side of the sandship and down onto the desert floor. Deslo usually just placed his hands on the side and vaulted over, but Gamalian was tall enough that he could step over, all the way down to the desert floor. Still, the maneuver warranted caution for a man of Gamalian's years.

Gamalian approached the hookworm, and like Deslo before him, circled it, gazing intently down. He stroked his short, neatly trimmed beard thoughtfully, a distinctive habit of his, because no one else in the palace wore a beard.

Occasionally, Deslo came across the odd craftsman or servant in the city who did, but even that was rare. The only thing Deslo could figure, though his mother had laughed at the idea when he'd mentioned it to her, was that Gamalian was attached to the beard because he was attached to the gesture. Gamalian was always stroking it with his fingers while in deep contemplation as they discussed the marvels of history or geography, of economics or political theory.

"Remarkable," Gamalian said again.

"I think it's bigger than I am," Deslo added.

"Oh, absolutely. The thing is a good five feet," Gamalian said, squatting now beside it and holding his arms out as though to measure. "I've never seen anything like it. It must have been very hard to surface."

"Yes," Deslo conceded. Whether he'd admit that later when he told and retold his story for the royal court was one thing, but he wouldn't lie to Gamalian. There was no need. Physical strength was no more impressive to his tutor than any other accident of birth. Most people, Gamalian often said, acted as though brain and brawn were meritorious accomplishments by those who happened to have them, whereas there was always more accident than accomplishment involved in having either.

Deslo added, wringing out his aching hands, "I almost couldn't hold on."

"I believe it," Gamalian said, looking from the worm to the boy. "A grown man would have struggled to surface this hookworm."

Deslo glanced from the hookworm to his sun-browned skin and muscular arms. Like his grandfather, he had a stocky frame. "Built for strength, not speed," was how his grandfather put it. The marvel of meridium and Arua helped him compensate for his lack of speed, but strength was power, and power was everything, or so his grandfather always said. "Be strong of body. Strong of mind. Strong of purpose. In all things, Deslo, as far as it lies with you, be strong." The hookworm before him was testimony, undeniable testimony, that he was becoming strong.

"Do you think it will fit on the sled?"

Gamalian looked over his shoulder at the meridium sled hovering behind the sandship, attached to it by two short chains. "Maybe not, but even if the tail dangles on the way back, we'll be all right. I'll move the sled closer. This thing will be heavy."

Gamalian climbed back in and pulled up the anchor. Taking hold of the rudder, he began the careful work of maneuvering the sandship and sled. Deslo retrieved his detachable boot soles

from where they'd drifted off to and watched. He was anxious to
learn how to pilot a sandship, even if he knew it would be hard.
Learning to understand the nuances of the relationship between
meridium and Arua took time, and for Deslo, his first foray into
that world had been learning to master the subtle art of running
on meridium soles.

He'd heard that the complexities of navigating a sandship
grew exponentially with the size of the craft and the number of
rudders, but he could see that even in the simple, smaller craft,
the task was difficult. The one he and Gamalian had taken out
this morning was only a two-person sandship, so only one rudder
was necessary, but the massive ships that transported cargo and
troops and the like, both to and from Barra-Dohn, sometimes
involved fifteen to twenty giant rudders, requiring often a pair of
pilots to successfully steer the biggest of them.

Gamalian dropped anchor again. He'd succeeded in getting
the sled almost immediately above and beside the hookworm, but
it wasn't too close. Gamalian disembarked and joined Deslo in the
sand. "Do you want to get the front? I'll get the tail."

"Sure," Deslo said. He knew that Gamalian was offering him
the easy job, because the spear would make a nice handle for lifting the hookworm's head and upper half. He might have protested
had it been anyone else, but he was too tired to be proud.

He walked around to the head of the hookworm and pulled
the spearhead out of the sand. Attempts to slide the spear a bit farther through the hookworm on the blade side didn't go very well.
Perhaps now that the adrenaline of battle had passed or perhaps
because the sun had already begun to dry out the worm, he found
it hard going to pull the spear farther through. In the end, he gave
up after only jerking it through a few more inches and simply got
the best grip on the spear he could manage.

"All right," Gamalian said, squatting down to slide his hands
under the hookworm about a third of the way up from the tail,
careful to avoid the sharp hooks protruding at varied angles.
"Let's go on three."

Deslo didn't need to reply, for Gamalian had already started the count. When he reached three, Deslo gave a mighty heave. The head and tail rose readily into the air, but the middle of the hookworm sagged almost a foot below the sled.

"Just hold it where you are," Gamalian said with a puff. He draped the tail across the side of the sled so part of it hung down, but most of it was supported, and he worked his way up the side of the hookworm, lifting and rolling it on. Deslo had to twist the spear in his hands to keep up with the twisting of the hookworm. But in the end, it was firmly up on the sled with just the very end of its head and tail hanging over the side. Gamalian had positioned it well but at a cost.

Deslo watched Gamalian raise his bleeding hand to his mouth, and just like a kid might, he sucked his hand where the sharp hook had cut it. "Is it deep?"

"It's not too bad," Gamalian replied when he'd examined the cut. "I'll live, but we should get back so I can wash it properly."

Deslo folded his detachable soles at the hinges so he could pull them down toward the ground where he deftly maneuvered them onto his feet. In a flash he was hovering beside the sled. Putting one foot on the worm for leverage, he took a firm hold on his spear. It took a few moments, several violent wrenches, and most of his remaining strength to remove it, but in the end he had his spear back in hand as he settled into the sandship beside Gamalian.

"Ready?" Gamalian asked.

"Ready," Deslo said.

Gamalian pulled up the anchor and lowered the rudder, and the sandship started slowly forward.

Exhausted, Deslo watched the desert slip past as they accelerated. He was exhausted but happy.

5

STRANGE TRAVELERS

Deslo enjoyed the wind brushing his face and flicking his dark hair about in matted clumps. For the most part, the sweat had stopped pouring down him now that the hunt was over. Not completely, though. The sun was still hot, and he had no shade. He lifted the jug beside him and drank, grateful even for lukewarm water.

Deslo glanced at Gamalian, who was gazing ahead, his hands working the meridium rudder. Deslo knew the older man wouldn't say much if he tried to start a conversation because Gamalian never talked much when steering a sandship. Ordinarily, Deslo wouldn't have minded the quiet. Gamalian was quite a talker. He liked his tutor, but sometimes the sheer constancy of the words annoyed him. Not a lot, of course, because Gamalian had interesting things to say. He seemed to know about everything, even when he said he didn't. Now, though, with the excitement from the hunt swirling inside him, the boy wanted to talk, but Gamalian was silent. Deslo sighed, leaned back, and closed his eyes.

The smell of sweet sage wafted up but only for a moment, and Deslo knew the sandship must have just passed a fairly large clump of it for the scent to have been so strong. He knew most of the sage oil used in Barra-Dohn was harvested from vast fields that lay south of the city, but he was still a little surprised that here wild sage had been allowed to grow to maturity without being harvested by someone.

The silent desert slipped past, and at last, Barra-Dohn loomed on the horizon, though still a fair distance away, when the sandship approached an old, wild-looking man in a full-body, flowing black garment, walking barefoot through the desert sand. Deslo stared as they drew alongside. The man's grizzled face was covered with white whiskers, and his head was bald save for a few scant wisps of white hair on the side and back. A slender staff of gnarled wood was in his hand, and it rose and fell with each stride the man took.

Gamalian showed no signs of slowing down as they passed the odd character, who didn't turn to look at or acknowledge them, so Deslo leaned over and tugged Gamalian's sleeve to get his tutor's attention. "Shouldn't we offer him a ride?"

Gamalian shook his head, leaning over to answer. "He's a Kalosene, Deslo. He wouldn't take the ride, even if we offered it."

"But he didn't have any shoes!" Deslo said. He looked back over his shoulder at the man's bare feet as he continued on his way through the desert, as though the mere mention of such a bizarre occurrence made the boy wonder if he'd really seen what he thought he had.

"The Devoted never wear them," Gamalian said.

"But how do they do it?"

"I don't exactly know," Gamalian said. "My guess is that his feet must be too callused to feel the heat."

Deslo didn't turn back around. He kept his eyes on the man trudging along through the sand, and he wondered what it must feel like to walk mile after mile through the desert in bare feet. He knew what a callus was. He'd had one on his hands before when he first learned to use a spear, but he wasn't sure how they could protect bare feet from the heat. He tried to imagine walking through the desert in bare feet. He'd stepped in the hot sand barefoot before, and he'd danced and moved his feet as quickly as possible to spare his feet the pain until he could put his shoes back on. He couldn't imagine walking at normal speed like that for miles and miles.

All the while, he sat watching the man. The old fellow never looked up. Gradually, the man slipped out of view, and Deslo turned back around.

The sun in the sky signaled afternoon when the sandship approached the queue of ships waiting for entry at the main eastern gate to Barra-Dohn. Of course, Gamalian could have skirted the city walls around the northeastern corner and entered through the private gate about twenty minutes from here that was reserved for traffic headed to the palace, but Gamalian never used the private gate. When Deslo had asked him why not, Gamalian had said that one of the things he could teach Deslo—that no one else would—was how it felt to be an ordinary citizen.

Gamalian had seemed very earnest about that. To rule "ordinary" people, the tutor reasoned, Deslo needed to understand them, and how could he do that if he was never treated like one? So it was Gamalian's custom when leaving and reentering Barra-Dohn with Deslo, to come by the public gate and wait in line like everyone else.

Deslo had accepted this rationale when Gamalian first gave it, as he did everything else Gamalian said. However, as Deslo had gotten older, he'd begun to suspect that Gamalian's motives might not be so simple. His tutor liked, or so Deslo thought, the reaction of the guards at the city gates when they recognized Gamalian and his passenger.

Whatever the reason for it, Deslo found himself once more in the line, which today was longer than usual. Sliders and sand-ships of various sizes waited to be waved through on the left. On the right, a few were waiting to come out. In the middle, a large crowd of people on foot was also queued up to enter the city, some having stored sliders they didn't want to take inside the walls and others perhaps having walked to the city from outlying towns. Gamalian had warned him that the line might be long when they returned, as dignitaries from near and far and other curious spectators flowed into the city to be a part of the anniversary celebration that was to take place the following day.

Deslo had been around the preparations for the celebration for a while, but sitting in the queue and watching the crowd, it somehow felt more real. He felt excited. At last, all the talk and activity were becoming something tangible.

Gamalian eased the sandship forward, but several ships were still between them and the checkpoint at the gate.

Deslo leaned his weary head on his hand, feeling the toll of his exhausting day. His eyes searched the mass of people waiting to gain entrance to the city and wondered where they'd come from and how far they'd walked if on foot. He also scanned the feet of those nearby. All had shoes on. He knew towns lay sprinkled around Barra-Dohn and that many from them would be attending the celebration, for his grandfather had invited them to take part, but he wondered where all these people were going to sleep tonight or tomorrow night.

They talked with each other to pass the time as they waited, old men and young, mothers and fathers, even children of all ages.

The sandship slipped forward again, farther this time than before, and when it came to a halt, Deslo examined the new cluster of people now standing beside them. Almost immediately, his eyes were drawn to a pair of striking figures. Both were men, tall and distinct. The one nearest to the sandship was a little taller than the other. He wore thick sandals and billowing white pants that the hot desert wind, which had picked up the closer they drew to Barra-Dohn, flapped about. An open white vest likewise rippled in the breeze, revealing a muscular, dark brown chest. Indeed, though many in Barra-Dohn had dark skin, this man was very dark, like one of the island people, except he lacked the wavy shock of hair characteristic of islanders.

As a matter of fact, his head was bald or mostly bald. At the rear of his smooth brown skull near the nape of his neck, a thick, long, plume of golden hair flowed down from a knot, held firmly by a golden clasp. The strange sheen of his golden hair fit right in with the wide assortment of jewelry the man wore—all of it gold. He had several rings on his fingers and earrings in his ears. He also had bracelets on his wrists, a few necklaces draped around his neck, and a bright gold band encircling his left bicep—a vivid contrast to the dark skin beneath it.

The other man looked much the same in his attire, jewelry, and features, save only that he was a little shorter, and the plume of hair extending from his head was sprinkled with gray as well as gold. Had they not been on foot, Deslo would have been sure they were important people, some kind of traveling dignitaries.

No sooner had that thought passed through his mind, when Deslo had an idea. It was too unlikely, too improbable for him to take seriously, but as he looked more closely, he wondered if maybe, just maybe, it might not in fact be so. And then, as though in answer to the question he longed to ask but couldn't, the taller man looked in Deslo's direction.

Sunlight reflected brilliantly off of the man's eyes. Deslo had never seen anything like them. Eyes that looked like pools of solid gold—though Deslo thought perhaps there might be the smallest dark dot in the middle, suggesting a pupil after all—gazed back at him. On the man's chin was a small tuft of hair, every bit as golden as the plume on the back of his head. He saw Deslo watching him and smiled, a broad smile betraying a mouth full of large white teeth, and then he turned back to his companion.

Deslo reached over to grab the sleeve of Gamalian's tunic as he had when they passed the Kalosene, only this time he shook it more urgently as he whispered, "Gamalian. Look, look."

"Look at what?" Gamalian said, turning to look at Deslo instead of at the men or the crowd they were in.

"Amhuru," Deslo said, hardly able to contain himself or to keep his hand from pointing, but he didn't want to be obvious. "In the crowd. Look and see."

The mention of Amhuru had gotten Gamalian's attention, and he lowered the rudder so they wouldn't slide forward while he wasn't looking. Disregarding the line in front of them for the moment, he searched the crowd, and it did not take long for Gamalian to find the same striking figures.

"Well?" Deslo asked. "Are they?"

"They are, indeed," Gamalian answered, never taking his eyes off them.

"I knew it!"

"Well spotted, Deslo," Gamalian said. "You've never seen Amhuru before, have you?"

"No, I haven't."

"No, I guess not. We haven't had any here in a long time."

Deslo turned from Gamalian back to the men, who were moving forward with the crowd now, though not especially quickly. They also seemed to be deep in conversation, which they hadn't been before.

"Why now, I wonder?" Gamalian added, talking quietly to himself. "Today of all days . . ."

Deslo pondered the question, and he didn't have to think very hard before he had a possible answer. "Maybe they heard about the celebration."

"Perhaps," Gamalian said, still focused on the two men, "though I'm not sure the Amhuru really care about such things. At least, I doubt they'd care enough to come for that alone. But could it really be a coincidence?"

"I thought the Amhuru were nomadic," Deslo said.

"They are," Gamalian said, finally taking his eyes off the men. He glanced back at the line in front of the sandship before turning his attention to Deslo, as he said again, "They are."

"So they go here and there whenever they like, right?"

"Basically," Gamalian said, "though they probably have a bit more rhyme and reason to their wandering than that."

The sandship in front of them moved, and Gamalian eased theirs forward also. They were now a bit ahead of the two men, and the tutor sat quietly watching them, mumbling under his breath, only bits and pieces of which did Deslo hear or understand. "There's nothing for it, I suppose. Some conventions and obligations can't be avoided."

"What are you talking about?" Deslo asked as Gamalian's voice trailed off.

"Oh," Gamalian said, aware that he'd been mumbling out loud. "I'll need to get word to the king about the Amhuru as soon as possible. Your grandfather dislikes complications and surprises, but there's nothing to be done about this one."

Deslo stared again at the Amhuru, noticing now the axes hanging from both waists. From the little he'd heard, he knew the Amhuru were respected for their physical prowess as well as their wisdom, and he wondered what their coming might mean. The sandship slid forward again, and when it stopped, he leaned over to Gamalian. "Do you think they'll stay awhile?"

"There's no telling," Gamalian answered, shrugging. "It wouldn't be uncommon if they did. Amhuru sometimes stay in one place a couple of years, but then again, they usually travel alone. What two together means, I couldn't say."

A couple years, Deslo thought. How exciting! He looked at the intervening space between the sandship and the gate, which was no longer very large. He felt surprisingly eager to pass through and get to the palace. The hookworm, a Kalosene, and now the Amhuru. What a day it had already been!

And to think that the anniversary celebration hadn't even started yet.

6

ARUA

The adulation from the palace stewards and staff was all
Deslo had imagined it would be. Even the king came
outside to view his hookworm, after which he ordered the
chief steward to make sure hookworm bisque was added to the
menu for the feast being held that evening for the ambassadors
from the Five Cities. He also asked that the hookworm's shell be
preserved and displayed in the palace.

Deslo's father, though, was not among the onlookers.

As the crowd dissipated, returning to their work, his grandfather approached. Gamalian stepped in, however, and the two
of them moved a few steps away to speak privately. As Gamalian
whispered in the king's ear, Deslo watched his grandfather's face,
noting the precise moment when the smile disappeared. For a
brief moment, something like surprise showed there, but that too
disappeared and a more practiced look of impassive concentration
replaced it.

"You're sure?" Deslo heard him say.

"I'm sure."

Eirmon walked over to Deslo. "You have done well, and I want to hear all about it. Unfortunately, it is a busy day, and I must attend to some things before the banquet tonight and the anniversary tomorrow. But later, I want to hear all about it."

His grandfather started back toward the palace, and Gamalian followed.

Deslo blurted out. "Is Father back yet?"

The king turned back, this time leaning over and taking Deslo firmly by the shoulders, the easy smile returning to his face. "I've given him a job to do, Deslo. If he doesn't see the hookworm before it's cooked, he'll see the shell after. He'll see, and he'll be proud of you—just as I am."

Eirmon must have seen Deslo's disappointment because he lingered for a moment longer. "You know," he said confidentially. "Just between us, your father wasn't much of a hunter. Certainly, he wasn't nearly the hunter you are."

The king smiled, but Deslo didn't smile back. When he was little, he'd liked the favorable comparisons to his father, but now they just made him uncomfortable. He worried that was why his father didn't like him.

Eirmon added, almost as an afterthought. "Rika was looking for you. You should find her while Gamalian and I take care of a few things."

"I will not be hard to find," a feminine voice spoke from the shadows of the palace. All three of them looked over to see Rika emerging into the brighter light of the early evening in the courtyard. Her long dark hair was pulled back and fastened in her typical fashion, an uncomplicated bundle on the back of her head, the front of her hair left smooth and taut.

"You will stay with Deslo until it is time to get ready for the banquet?" Eirmon asked.

"Of course, Your Majesty," Rika responded with a graceful nod, and then the king and Gamalian were gone. The handoff was complete. Deslo liked both of his tutors, but he was ten now and wished it was a little less obvious that at times they were little more than babysitters.

With the king and Gamalian gone, Deslo looked once more at Rika, and only then did he notice as she stood closer to him in the light that she was dressed differently than usual. Normally, she wore the dark blue that signaled her affiliation with the Academy. Now, though, she was wearing light gray clothes that looked like they were made for traveling, but where would Rika be going at this hour?

As though in answer to his question, Rika said, "If we're to be back in time for you to get into some decent clothes, we have to go now and go quickly."

"Where are we going?"

"You'll see."

With that Rika led him swiftly from the courtyard to a place just beyond it where she had a slider parked and waiting. It would have been uncomfortable for two adults, but it was just big enough for Deslo to get on behind Rika. When he was smaller, he'd sat in front, nestled snugly between her legs as she worked the pedals and steered the slider, but he was too big for that now and so sat behind her and held on. Even that arrangement couldn't last much longer and not only because he was getting too big. Not all that long ago, the difference between snuggling up against his mother and snuggling up against Rika had barely been noticeable. It was noticeable now, and he felt a flash of embarrassment as he slid his arms around her.

Rika didn't notice, or if she did, she didn't let on. She leaned over the slider, poured in the concentrated sage oil to activate the meridium core, and in a moment they were gliding down toward the docks.

The smooth metallic feel of the slider was a sharp contrast to the wood of the sandship, as was the quicker, more responsive motion. Whereas a sandship glided almost magisterially along with the ground slipping away beneath as it turned in its wide arcs when turning was necessary, a slider zipped along more rapidly and could cut sharply either right or left depending on the skill of the rider when combining the act of steering with the timing of the all-important lean to maintain balance. As Deslo had ridden with Rika many times, he no longer needed directing. He responded to her motion and their surroundings intuitively, leaning when required and holding on fast.

Soon they were zooming along with the docks on their right. Beyond them lay the harbor, which though always full of ships, seemed more packed than usual. Consequently, the docks were alive with people, and Deslo watched them moving about as Rika navigated in the lane marked off for sliders.

Before long they'd moved away from the docks, beyond them, and Deslo began to wonder again where they were going. They weren't headed toward any part of the city he knew but were traveling parallel to it. As they left the crowds at the docks behind, Rika was able to navigate more freely, and she slowed as she worked her way down the gently sloping ground toward the water's edge. Here, the seawater came rolling in at a depth that made bringing in a ship of any size impossible.

Rika stopped the slider and stepped off, then waited for Deslo to do the same.

At least, Deslo thought, even if he were still treated as a child in need of babysitting, Rika still didn't think he needed help to get on and off the slider. Up until recently, she would have dismounted and reached over to help him. She must have picked up on his disdain and let it go.

"Still wondering what we're doing?"

Deslo looked at Rika's playful smile and knew he was supposed to say yes. He wasn't supposed to have any idea why they were there, and since he didn't, he obliged her. "Yes."

"We were talking about the anniversary of meridium's discovery last week, and you mentioned that even though you understood some of the basics about how meridium interacted with

Arua, that you really didn't understand what the Arua field was, remember?"

Deslo nodded. "I remember that you said it was complicated and you didn't have time to explain it just then but that you'd get to it before the anniversary."

"I knew you'd remember that part," Rika said, rolling her eyes in mock exasperation at Deslo's remark. It was a joke between them that he might not remember much she taught him, but he did remember everything she promised him. "Well, it is still technically before the anniversary."

"But if it's so complicated, how can we do it now?"

"I think I've figured out a good way to explain this so it will make more sense and answer your basic questions in less time. We can get more detailed and more technical later, if necessary."

Deslo must have looked skeptical, because Rika added, "Trust me."

"All right," Deslo said, looking around at the shore and the sea. "But why are we here?"

"Ah, great question," Rika said, becoming more animated. "But first, what prompted your question about Arua?"

"Our discussion about the discovery of meridium."

"Yes but more specifically?"

Deslo frowned and after a moment shrugged his shoulders. "I don't know."

"Deslo," Rika groaned, the exasperation this time only partly feigned.

"Sorry, I don't remember."

"All right," Rika continued. "We were talking about the discovery of meridium, and you asked me how we could *know* if the story was true. Remember?"

"Oh, yeah," Deslo said, a little sheepishly. "I remember that."

"You were wondering why some stories from long ago, like that one, we treat as fact, and why others, like the Old Stories, we don't."

"Yeah, how do we know what stories are history and what stories are myths?" Deslo asked.

"Exactly," Rika said, starting to pace a bit, which she did whenever she started to get on a roll. "I tried to explain how historical stories, like the one about the discovery of meridium, have facts as their foundation, and how others, like the Old Stories, are based on superstition and lies."

"But," Deslo interrupted, "Gamalian says there is truth in the Old Stories, that they communicate lessons about how our ancestors used to . . ."

"I'm not really interested in what Gamalian says," Rika said sharply. That she was not overly fond of his other tutor, Deslo knew, but the obvious disdain in her voice was strong, even for her. Rika usually stopped short of direct subversion. "I'm sorry, but I don't really have time to correct all his mistakes tonight."

She seemed to consider saying more but instead moved on. "Basically, the story of the discovery of meridium is history because it is based on facts, on a real event, an event that was documented and can be trusted. Right?"

Deslo nodded.

"And we trust it also, at least in part, because of the actual, useful knowledge that came from it."

Deslo noted the clear emphasis on the words *documented* and *actual, useful knowledge* and wondered what Gamalian would say if he were here. He wasn't though, and Rika didn't pause long enough for him to consider it further.

"Anyway, we were talking about how the craftsman cut himself on the slender, sharp piece of meridium, which at the time was a fairly common and unremarkable metal."

"You said craftsmen liked to use it because of its durability," Deslo added, wanting to show he remembered something of the story.

"That's right," Rika said, acknowledging his contribution. "Of course, as you and everyone else knows, his blood ran along the edge of the meridium, and when he dropped it in his pain, it didn't fall to the floor as he or anyone else would have expected. It fell just a short distance and then stopped, several feet above the floor. There it hung, apparently suspended in midair before falling the rest of the way a few seconds later."

Deslo, having seen great ships suspended above the ground, found the image unremarkable. But he knew what happened when you dropped ordinary things. He could imagine that if you expected everything to behave that way, then something not falling to the ground when you thought it should might be surprising.

"You know how it goes from there," Rika went on. "How he wondered afterward if it had even really happened, how he tried to re-create the event, how he eventually succeeded in doing it again but only with blood spread along the blade of a meridium knife in just the right proportion."

Deslo did know. Every child knew this story.

"What I told you last time," Rika said, "was that as research into the properties of meridium got seriously under way, the dominant theory that emerged in those early years was that there was some sort of invisible, bio-magnetic field that the bloody meridium had reacted to. Remember?"

"Yes," Deslo said. "You said that the way meridium could hover above the ground when mixed with blood suggested the existence of a magnetic force that was also, somehow, biological."

"That's right," Rika said. "And this was the prevailing theory for a long time, even as researchers experimented with mixing different types of animal materials with meridium in its molten form. They also discovered the reactions meridium mixed with plant materials could have.

"Of course," Rika went on, "this theory was mistaken. Arua is not a magnetic field at all. And yet, it's understandable why the early scientists who explored it might think this way. Magnetic reactions were the closest analogy to what they were seeing— invisible forces pushing metallic objects away. It certainly *looked* like something magnetic was going on."

"So what is Arua, if it isn't bio-magnetic? That idea at least makes sense."

"I know it does," Rika said. "The surface parallels of the theory are easier to see than the problems, which is why so many clever researchers were fooled for as long as they were. But we discussed one other thing last time before I told you we'd come back to this, something I told you to think about."

"You told me to think about the similarities and the differences between a big sandship's response to Arua and a single-seat slider's."

"That's right. Well done, Deslo!" Rika exclaimed, smiling. "See, you can remember what we discuss if you concentrate. And did you?"

"Yes," Deslo said, his mind racing back over the matter to see if he could find anything in that moment that he'd missed before. "But, I don't know what I was supposed to figure out."

"Let me help," Rika said, as though expecting this answer. She reached into her cloak and withdrew a flat, black disc about the size of the palm of her hand.

"What's that?"

"Come and see," Rika said, walking over to a flat rock not far away and setting the disc down. "Now, sit down next to the rock and watch."

Deslo sat down, and Rika took a small metallic pin and held it out just above the black disc. "All right, in this experiment, the pin represents the slider."

Rika let go, and the pin popped up higher in the air. It hovered there uncertainly for a moment and then fell to the side of what Deslo now understood was a powerful magnet. "Now," Rika said, leaving it there, "this will serve to represent a sandship in our experiment." She reached her hand out over the magnet at about the same height with a substantially larger bar of metal and let it go. It immediately dropped toward the magnet, hesitated for a moment just above it, then rolled to the side where the pin was and fell on top of it.

"All right," Rika said, looking at Deslo carefully. "What did you see?"

"Neither one really hovered very well or for very long."

"True," Rika agreed, nodding. "The stability of motion that Arua makes possible is one thing that suggests it isn't simply magnetism at work. But just for the sake of argument, let's imagine you could solve the stability problem. What else did you see that would suggest the Arua field isn't magnetic?"

Deslo thought back over what he'd watched for a moment. He frowned in concentration, then shook his head. "I don't know, Rika. I don't understand."

"That's all right," Rika said, reassuring him with a smile. "Remember, compare what you saw with the magnets with what you've experienced and seen yourself with wearing meridium soles or riding in small sandships as opposed to watching and riding on great big ones. What happened right after I let go of the metallic objects that suggests a difference?"

Deslo pondered this, picturing each of these things. Rika watched him, expectantly. Then he saw it. "The little one went up, and the big one went down!"

"That's right!" Rika said, pleased at Deslo's evident excitement. "So?"

"So, if the Arua was a bio-magnetic field, then lighter objects would be pushed way up high, and big heavy ones, like large sandships, would sink down low, right?"

"Yes! If Arua were a magnetic field of any kind, pushing up out of the ground with uniform strength, then something strong enough to hold a vast sandship a few feet off the ground should be able to push a boy like you, when you're wearing meridium soles, way, way up into the sky."

"But it doesn't."

"That's right, it doesn't," Rika agreed. "It doesn't because Arua isn't a bio-magnetic field."

"Then what is it?"

"Ahh, that is the question."

Deslo looked around them again. "That's why you brought me here. You could have shown me the magnet trick at the palace. You brought me here to see something else."

"My bright, bright little Deslo," Rika smiled. "You are exactly right. I did bring you out here to see something else, but what?"

Deslo frowned, looking from the grassy shore to the water to the sun hanging low above it. He shrugged. "I don't know."

"Well, I wouldn't ordinarily let you get away with that half-hearted attempt at answering my question or non-attempt as the case may be, but we are pressed for time. So, unfortunately, I'll have to cut to the chase. Let me first say that the best analogy for helping someone understand Arua is actually snow, but as it never snows anywhere in Aralyn, let alone in Barra-Dohn, I figured that fact might not help much."

"I know what snow is," Deslo said, a little indignant at the suggestion that he didn't understand the idea of snow.

"I didn't say you don't know what snow is, but you've never seen it in person, and it would take me a month on one of your grandfather's fastest ships to get you to southern Golina where we could find some. But I'd need a lot of snow to make my point."

"Why?"

"Because the idea is something like this. Imagine three feet of snow is on the ground all around us."

Deslo blinked and looked around. "Does it really snow that much in Golina?"

"I don't know, but it snows that much in some places, which is how this analogy was developed by scientists far from here and eventually worked its way back to Barra-Dohn."

Deslo must have betrayed that his thoughts were now far away trying to picture vast snowfields, because Rika snapped her fingers in front of his face. "Deslo! Are you with me?"

"Yes, sorry."

"Now, imagine snow all around us at about the level of your chest. Walking through that would be tough and tiring. You'd always be pushing snow out of the way. That's why people who live in places that get so much snow wear things called snowshoes. Snowshoes actually allow the person wearing them to walk on top of the snow."

"Like meridium shoes allow us to walk on Arua!"

"Yes, just like that."

But the excitement passed quickly through Deslo. "But snow is real. You can touch it. Arua isn't like that."

"That's the point," Rika said. "Arua *is* like that. It's real, even though you can't see it or hold it. That's what took so long for scientists to figure out. Come."

Deslo rose and followed Rika down toward the water's edge. To his surprise, she didn't stop but continued into the water itself, wading in until she was standing waist deep. "Come on. Don't be shy. I don't have snow available, so I have to make due with what I have."

Deslo waded out until he was standing beside Rika. The water was up to his chest but under his shoulders. He understood now why she wasn't wearing her normal clothes.

"All right," Rika said. "The water is the Arua field. Let's run in it, or perhaps more properly, through it. Follow me!"

With that she turned and started running through the water. Her pumping arm motions seemed exaggerated until he also tried to run.

It was hard, and he had to work to make sluggish progress behind her. Even though it felt as if he were taking giant strides every time he pushed off the seafloor, he never seemed to be able to build up momentum or speed.

At last, Rika stopped and turned around. "So, imagine we've just been running through the Arua. Now it's time for my next point. Stay here." She waded back to the shore until she was standing on dry land, dripping wet from the waist down. "Let's run back the direction we came from. I'll run here on the shore to demonstrate the difference between running on Arua and running in Arua. Go!" And she was off, running along the shore.

Deslo didn't even have time to protest, and the frustration he felt as he moved through the water back in the direction from which they'd come was magnified as he watched Rika move effortlessly along the dry ground. When she had gone a fair distance, she turned, spotted him struggling in the water far behind her, and came running back along the shore toward him again. "I thought I told you to run?" she said, smirking.

"It wasn't fair," Deslo objected. "I can't run in here like you can out there."

"Precisely!" Rika smiled triumphantly.

"I don't understand," Deslo said. "Water isn't like Arua."

"I'm telling you that it is. Like snow is."

"But you said yourself you can't see Arua or feel it," Deslo protested, growing irritated. "You can see and feel water! Besides, when you ran just now, you were in Arua, and you ran just fine."

"You're missing the point."

Deslo crossed his ams and turned away, shaking his head.

"Deslo," Rika said, gently. "Come out, and I'll explain."

Deslo turned back and walked out of the water onto dry land.

Rika waded back in. "Okay, let's review. The water represents Arua, right?"

"So you keep saying."

"You're the king's grandson," Rika said firmly but not angrily. "I am your tutor and a member of the Academy. I expect you to treat me with respect, even if you're frustrated."

"Sorry," Deslo said, mostly meaning it.

"If the water is like Arua, as I am saying that it is, then Arua does act on us like water does. But since we are born in Arua, as it were, and we learn to crawl and walk and run in it from birth, we don't know how it acts on us, that is, until we move on top of it and feel the difference. The sluggishness you feel in water is unnatural because it is stronger than the effect Arua has on you, not because it is fundamentally different in nature. But what happens when you put on your meridium shoes? Now, you're on top of Arua. Are you slower, faster, or the same?"

"Faster," Deslo said, beginning to see the point. "Because Arua isn't slowing me down. I move more freely."

"Yes, more or less," Rika said, nodding as she waded out of the water again. "When you move on top of Arua, you are quicker than when you move through it, and we believe this is because Arua is a real thing, like water or snow, not just a force like a magnetic field, even though we can't see or touch it. Do you see now?"

"I do, but why did you say only more or less just now?"

"Because, and this is where the discussion gets too complicated for us to finish tonight," Rika paused. She took hold of the bottom of her wet gray coat and squeezed water from it. "You said Arua isn't slowing you down when you are on it, as though it was only under you. That's probably not the case. While it may be that Arua is concentrated in the distance between the ground and the surface on which you walk or ride, we now believe that there are concentric circles of Arua, circles that rise well above this first, initial layer—what we've come to refer to as Arua, as though it was all there was."

"We believe that?"

"We do."

"But why?"

"Because if Arua somehow explains what meridium does when mixed with biological material, why do lights created by meridium and plant material still work when put on walls or the tops of poles well above the surface of what we call Arua?"

"I hadn't thought of that? Why do they?"

"I don't know exactly," Rika said. "We're trying to figure that out. We assume, as I said, that there may be concentric circles of Arua. That might explain it."

"Will you tell me when you figure it out?"

"Of course." Rika laughed. "But right now we need to get back. I think we've covered enough for today. Besides, I'll be in trouble if you're late."

7

TWO AMHURU

Eirmon looked over his city, thinking of tomorrow. The weather would be hot, so the parade and speech were the only things planned for the afternoon. The rest could wait until the night fell, taking the edge off the heat.

Once the celebration got under way though, people would eat and drink, sing and dance and generally carry on in the streets, savoring the free food and music provided by Eirmon for their enjoyment. Most would linger late into the night and some until morning. When they awoke, if indeed they slept at all, they'd shrug off their weariness, their hangovers, and their headaches and put in a meager day's work, but no one would fault them for it. By the following day, their lives would return to normal.

At least, their lives would appear to return to normal, but soon word of the war would slip out and make its way through the streets. Perhaps it would already be making its way as they rose on the morning of the second day. Soft the whispers would be, for soft they always began, but they would spread throughout the city nonetheless. Rumors of war always did.

It was inevitable that the rumors would begin before the war itself. The sudden departure of a significant portion of the army couldn't very well be hidden. Word would spread, and in certain quarters the whispers would become rumblings. The usual objections would arise from the usual places, but they would have to be carefully worded, carefully handled, for the people of Barra-Dohn would be basking in the fresh afterglow of a grand holiday—a holiday provided by the king, no less. All too clear would be the memories of lingering through the night, drinking the king's wine, and eating the king's food.

That's why it would take more time than usual for any significant objections to the king's plans to form, to spread, and to gain traction among enough people to cause concern. And by then, what would it matter? The war might well be over, for what city and what army could resist the power Eirmon planned to unleash?

The king laughed. Celebrate the discovery of meridium? Sure. Why not? It was a cause worth celebrating. Was meridium not the key to Barra-Dohn's rise to power? Was it not the very foundation of the city's greatness? What better occasion than to serve as a distraction, a mere diversion, so Eirmon could preserve that power and extend that greatness? He would give the people a party, and they would enjoy it, though none as much as he. He would celebrate but not with them. He would celebrate but not the past. His best days lay before him.

And when the war was over? When the soldiers who departed in secret returned in glory? What would be left of the whispers and objections then? What's more, the most vocal of his detractors would be in the most precarious positions, for he would give another party then, one the city would greet even more eagerly. Nothing excites joy and celebration more than soldiers coming home amid the jubilee of victory. Nothing. Perhaps, if things went well, he would be able to use the army's return and its successes as occasions to clean house at home as well. If so, then the war would prove almost as useful internally as externally.

Eirmon was under no illusions that even if the war turned out to be every bit the masterstroke he hoped it would be that he would then be able to rest. A king could never rest. No throne was ever completely secure. Constant vigilance would always be required. It was the price of power, and it could never be paid in full.

But of course, though complete security was a fantasy, relative security was achievable, and he would give that relative security both to Barra-Dohn and to his son and grandson. Kaden, and after him Deslo, would inherit as secure a throne as he could give.

Eirmon turned and looked at Gamalian, waiting inside his study for his return. The king knew his plan was a good one. He'd prepared as well as he knew how to deal with the enemy he knew, so it was more than a little disconcerting to hear this news.

Two Amhuru had come unforeseen and unaccounted for in his plans. The timing of their arrival was unfortunate. Today of all days, not that Eirmon wanted them in Barra-Dohn on any day. The Amhuru injected uncertainty that had been wholly lacking before. At least, if they'd come a month from now, it would have been too late to interfere with what he planned to set in motion tomorrow. Of course, Amhuru were famous for not interfering in the places where they sojourned, but could he count on that?

No, Eirmon had a different reason to be concerned about the arrival of the Amhuru, a reason only he understood. A reason that involved a different kind of secret than the military plans Eirmon had been orchestrating. He would have to be careful with Gamalian. His old friend and sometime counselor didn't know about either one.

"You think they will come here tonight?" Eirmon asked, re-entering the study.

"I would expect them to find their way here shortly," Gamalian replied. "Coming to the palace directly makes the most sense."

The king sighed. "As if there wasn't enough to juggle with the emissaries from the Five Cities here, not to mention the anniversary."

"I suppose," Gamalian said, "though there's another way to look at it."

Eirmon turned to Gamalian, waiting. Most would wait for an invitation from the king to proceed.

But Gamalian did not. "Generally the arrival of an Amhuru creates an uproar."

"That's my point," Eirmon said. "We're a bit busy to organize a special reception."

"But we're already organized," Gamalian said, smiling. "Why can't they join the banquet? With no extra effort, they will feast like honored guests, and your other guests will feel even more honored to be feasting with them."

Eirmon nodded, catching the thread of Gamalian's point. "And tomorrow they will wake to a day of celebration, a citywide revel that will be grander and more extensive than any that could have been arranged at the last moment."

"Precisely," Gamalian said. "It will be a spectacular, gala event, all following hard on their arrival, with none of it requiring any special arrangements."

The king turned away from the window and paced for a moment. "Assuming they follow the usual protocol, will they both offer service? I'm unclear about what to expect from two of them."

"As am I," Gamalian agreed. "I'm not aware of Amhuru ever traveling together."

"Ever?" The king frowned. "You mean this never happens?"

"I don't know about never, but it is certainly unusual. I don't know of more than one ever visiting Barra-Dohn at the same time."

Eirmon walked over to his desk and leaned against it. "Well, since we're left with only speculation, what do you think? Surely, you've got a few ideas already."

"A few. The Amhuru are essentially nomadic, yes?" The king did not verbally assent, so Gamalian hastened on. "As far as I know, they drift alone from place to place with no particular plan behind their movements."

"You don't need to qualify everything," Eirmon said impatiently. "Your ignorance of Amhuru ways is duly noted. Proceed."

"Well, my point is, they must sometimes cross paths with other Amhuru, right? They might have just bumped into one another on their way here and agreed to travel together."

"An accident?" Eirmon said, his brow furrowed. "That's your theory? They just bumped into each other and said, 'Hey, what a coincidence. Looks as if we're both going to Barra-Dohn.'"

Gamalian weathered the king's sarcasm, unfazed. "I didn't say I think that's what happened. You asked me to recount the scenarios that have occurred to me, and it seemed logical to start with this one."

"Why logical if you don't think it's what happened?"

"Because," Gamalian said, "the inference in your question about why they would choose to travel together was that it was intentional, and I thought we should establish that it might not actually be so."

If anything annoyed Eirmon about Gamalian, it was his tendency to sometimes adopt his tutorial tone with him. He'd stopped having to regularly endure that about forty years ago, but he chose to overlook it, lest the conversation be completely derailed.

"After all," Gamalian continued. "Even a cursory reflection on the events of daily life reveals that one of the most common errors we make is drawing causal inferences from unrelated events, reading purpose and intentionality into things that lack them."

Eirmon raised his hand, conceding defeat. He had stepped on Gamalian's intellectual pride and was now paying the price. "I surrender. It might not have been intentional. What else?"

"Well, it is the day before the anniversary. They might be here to honor Barra-Dohn."

"I suppose the timing means we have to consider that, but it doesn't seem like the Amhuru to travel here for something so ceremonial and brief," Eirmon said, pacing again. "Though, I suppose if the anniversary is the reason, they'll only be here a short while."

"It's possible," Gamalian said. "Traveling in a pair is already unusual, so other anomalies may follow."

"You think they intend to stay longer?"

Gamalian shrugged. "They usually do. Even if the anniversary is the occasion that brings them, we have no reason to assume they won't stay beyond it."

"True."

"Though maybe," Gamalian added, "maybe one of them will move on afterward and maybe only one will stay, as is the custom."

Eirmon found some comfort in that thought but not a lot. "Any other ideas?"

A knock at the door prevented Gamalian from replying. The chief steward entered and informed Eirmon that the two Amhuru had just arrived at the palace.

"We'll be right down, Myron," Eirmon replied. "Summon Kaden, so he may join us with the Amhuru."

"Yes, Your Majesty," Myron said. He always agreed first and then added later any information he thought Eirmon might want to consider about the directive being given. "Two of the emissaries from the Five Cities have arrived. Kaden is with them now."

"Tell the emissaries about the Amhuru once Kaden has left to come to us. The significance will be clear to them."

"As you wish," Myron said.

"Well," Eirmon said to Gamalian, "We're out of time. Anything else I should consider before we go down?"

"Not really. All we have is conjecture and questions, to which they will presumably provide answers. Let's go find out."

Eirmon nodded and motioned to Gamalian to lead the way.

Nothing Gamalian had said confirmed his own budding fear about why two Amhuru had traveled together to his city, which was somewhat comforting, though only somewhat.

As far as Eirmon knew, there was no precedent for the facts and events that constituted the king's most deeply held secret, so what precedent could there be for how the Amhuru might react? But as Gamalian had said, all they had was conjecture.

It was time to see if there were any answers.

When Lord Kazir arrived, Kaden thought that entertaining the emissaries before the banquet might not be so tedious a job. He liked Kazir, and he would have enjoyed discussing life in Garranmere with him. But unfortunately, Lord Fehrin arrived shortly after Kazir, and that meant the end of any hopes Kaden had for an enjoyable evening. Fehrin was a blustering fool, as loud and thoughtless as Kazir was quiet and thoughtful.

Almost an hour of Fehrin had Kaden sinking in the depths of despair. None of the other emissaries had arrived, Kazir hadn't contributed a single word to the conversation, and Kaden had been left all that time to feign interest in whatever drivel Fehrin offered. Kaden wished he'd lingered longer at the quarry or perhaps that Greyer had missed the rhino-scorpion's tail that afternoon. Even having his throat cut would have been better than this.

The arrival of Myron and his strange but wonderful news that the king required Kaden's presence immediately almost brought tears of joy to the prince's face. He excused himself and headed eagerly to the parlor where Myron had told him he would find the king and Gamalian. There he knocked and entered, unprepared for what he found.

Amhuru.

Despite the presence of half a dozen plush chairs, they stood side by side. Kaden sized them up as Gamalian made the appropriate introductions. In that brief moment, he saw in both men something that he rarely saw in guests of the palace and the king—complete ease and comfort.

Their composure wasn't the only thing unusual about them. The gleam and glimmer of gold flashed from all over their bodies, contrasting sharply with their dark skin. Jewelry, hair, and bright piercing eyes were all gold and all striking. The thought flickered through Kaden's head that one piece of gold jewelry on each of them must really be Zerura, at least, according to the traditions about Amhuru. But before he could look any closer to hazard a guess, his attention was drawn to their weapons.

Both men carried knives tucked into the front of their waist-bands and short-handled axes hung at their sides. The weapons all had elaborate but fine gold lines traced up and down them on both the handles and the blades. The axes especially drew his gaze. Their blades were both beautiful and menacing with a line of gold running along each of the razor-sharp edges. Usually, only the Davrii moved armed within the palace. Never was Eirmon alone, or essentially alone, in a room with armed men he didn't know. Kaden wondered how the king was handling it.

Gamalian had finished, and Kaden bowed toward the Amhuru, who returned his formal courtesy with bows of their own. The man that appeared older, with flecks and streaks of gray sprinkled through his golden plume, spoke for them both.

"As we offered a blessing for your father and his reign, so we offer a blessing for you, Prince Omiir."

"Thank you," Kaden said, not knowing if more was expected from him. "And welcome to Barra-Dohn. We are honored."

"I am Tchinchura," the elder Amhuru said, "and this is Zangira," he added, motioning to the slightly taller Amhuru beside him, who again bowed at the mention of his name.

When the younger Amhuru straightened, he grinned at Kaden, revealing a mouth full of white teeth and at least the hint of a wicked sense of humor.

Kaden thought Zangira didn't look a whole lot older than he was, though it was hard to fix a specific age to either of the men. He returned the man's grin with one of his own.

"Barra-Dohn," Zangira said, "of all the great cities of the world, carries for us the distant memories of home. When we entered its gates today, we who cherish the memories of our ancestors like a lover cherishes his beloved, heard those echoes of the past. We are very pleased to be here."

"Again, you honor me and you honor Barra-Dohn with your words and your presence," Eirmon said. "As I was about to say before my son arrived, it has been many years since we had even one Amhuru among us. Now, to find we are being graced with two is a joy words cannot express."

Both men bowed again, and Eirmon indicated toward the seats. "Please be seated. Rest from your journey."

The Amhuru moved toward the seats. Slipping their axes from their sides, they sat down.

Kaden saw Gamalian and the king exchange glances that almost looked like disappointment, but it passed quickly. He wondered what that was about.

"Your Majesty," said Zangira as they all settled into their seats. "We learned on the way here of the celebration tomorrow. We do not wish to interfere or inconvenience you and your household in any way."

"There is no inconvenience," Eirmon said. "We're glad you can join us in our time of celebration."

"Even so," Zangira continued, "if you would prefer to wait until later to discuss the specific manner in which you would like to receive our service, then we understand and will wait."

"There is no need," Eirmon said. "My son Kaden has a son of his own. While Deslo has been educated by the best tutors Barra-Dohn has to offer, including my own advisor and friend, Gamalian . . ."

Gamalian nodded as Eirmon indicated him, and the king paused to allow the Amhuru to acknowledge Gamalian in return. "Even so, to have an Amhuru for a teacher and a tutor, even if only for the brief duration of your sojourn, would be a rare and priceless gift. If one of you would accept a place in my son's household to tutor my grandson, the other may serve here in the palace with me, though the tedium of such a position might wear thin before long."

Kaden was trying not to stare openmouthed. His father liked everything arranged carefully in its proper place. He hated surprises, and he hated change. He must have known, or at least suspected, that this was coming to offer a place to one of the Amhuru in his own household and to handle it so calmly. For his part, Kaden was excited. He hoped the younger Amhuru would be assigned to tutor Deslo. That would give Kaden an excuse to get to know him.

"You are gracious, King Eirmon," Tchinchura said in reply, "I have served in the courts of many kings, so I will happily offer you what service I may, and Zangira would be delighted to serve in the household of your son, should your son desire it."

Kaden almost couldn't respond. Eirmon had to be furious. No one ever questioned his will. That the Amhuru would dare to even suggest it possible that Kaden would want anything other than what Eirmon pronounced had to gall his father to no end.

He accepted the Amhuru's offer as graciously as he could muster, glancing sideways at his father. Eirmon wasn't looking at him, and his face didn't give much away. Still, Kaden knew him well and could see he'd been right. Eirmon was most displeased. Kaden turned back to find the younger Amhuru watching him. He had the distinct impression that he had been watching to see how both father and son reacted to Tchinchura's comment.

Always watching, he noted. *The Amhuru are always watching.*

Now that Kaden was looking at him, though, Zangira grinned again and nodded, ever so slightly. Kaden nodded back. For a day that had started slowly, things had certainly taken an interesting turn.

8

THE BANQUET

Nara lay back and let the warm water rush in and fill the void where her face had been. She kept her eyes closed so the exotic salts that enhanced her luxurious bath would not sting her eyes. She would happily have stayed submerged all day, but the feast and her duties as royal hostess tugged at her.

She stood, starting toward the smooth marble stairs that led up from the large rectangular bath where the waves caused by her sudden movement lapped up against her legs. She stood dripping on the edge of the large dressing area of her private chambers. Several feet away, a large wall of glass separated her from the exterior world. In her lonelier moments, looking through that window felt like looking through the bars of a cage.

The fading light of day was slipping away, but it warmed her through the glass, nevertheless. She thought of the feast, of the formalities and her duties, and suddenly the long years stretched out before her interminably. She wondered how she would find strength to go on once Deslo was no longer little and consequently no longer needed her.

She dried herself and slipped into the blue silk dress she'd laid out for the evening. The dress was exquisite, sleeveless and snug without being tight. It suited her perfectly, showing well but with subtlety the feminine curves that marked her graceful form. She was proud of the way she had regained her figure after Deslo's birth, though that pride was mitigated by the fact that for all her efforts, she had failed to gain Kaden's love.

There it was again—the lurking disappointment that Kaden didn't love her. She knew this, was resigned to this, didn't care about this—or did she? She must care to feel this way. But why did she care? She'd been chosen for him just as he'd been chosen for her. They'd barely known each other when they married. She'd harbored a hope that love would grow over time, the hope of youth, but she hadn't known what she was marrying into. She hadn't known Eirmon.

Kaden had been in love with someone else, and Eirmon hadn't cared. That situation had been dealt with, once Eirmon had settled on Nara. The fact that Kaden had loved another had been difficult, but on its own it would have been a surmountable problem. Old loves like old wounds fade with time. Nara knew that personally. The real issue was that Eirmon had picked her. That was something that Kaden might never forgive. Certainly, he'd never forget.

There'd been moments, early on, when it had looked like she might break through, moments of real tenderness between them, real caring. During her pregnancy, Kaden had shown genuine interest in her, and when Deslo was first born, in them both. But something had happened in that first year, and Kaden had pulled back, leaving a distance between them even greater than it had been before. She'd tried to understand it and failed, so she had tried to make her peace with it, but that had failed too.

A persistent something lived inside her, unquenched—a deep, native longing to be desired, hungered for, yearned after.

Not by anyone, by Kaden. To be desired by Kaden. She could not deny that the urge came to her in moments like these, unbidden and unwelcome, a thought she did not want but could not suppress.

Her mother had always said the human heart was mysterious. Nara believed her, but she'd had no idea just how mysterious it could be.

Nara turned from the windows and the outside world and moved to her dressing table. She took a deep breath and pushed away distracting thoughts about things she wasn't sure she understood but knew she couldn't change. She busied herself about her hair, burying her attention so effectively that she did not at first hear the knocking at the door. Only when it grew more persistent and she heard the voice of her attendant, Wynn, calling "Mistress, Mistress," did she answer it.

She opened it and there was Wynn, standing with Deslo, freshly bathed and dressed for the evening in a sharp, red tunic and pants of a cool, white fabric. It was possible she'd hear from Eirmon later that Deslo had not been formally enough attired, but she didn't especially care. Her son's comfort was more important to her than the king's satisfaction, and so long as she didn't openly flaunt her disregard for some of his preferences, she got away with ignoring them at times. It wasn't as if the representatives from the Five Cities would care what Deslo was wearing.

Wynn, noticing that Nara was not quite ready, said, "He can stay with me a little longer if you'd like."

"That's all right," Nara said. "Leave him with me."

Wynn bowed and left, leaving Deslo to come into Nara's chambers. "Tell me about the hunt with Gamalian," she said as she returned to her dressing table. "I hear you caught a little something."

"A little something?"

Nara turned to Deslo with a knowing smile.

Deslo rolled his eyes, probably annoyed that he'd not caught the joke. She turned back to her mirror, at least glad that she could still sometimes get her son, even if he was getting to an age when he didn't always appreciate being gotten.

"I saw the hookworm just as they were cutting it open to make the bisque," Nara continued without turning around to look at Deslo. Her focus was on her hair as the final fold was tricky. "I came down when I heard about it. I looked for you, but someone said you'd gone out on a slider with Rika. I must have just missed you."

Deslo didn't say anything. Once upon a time, just the simple fact that she'd spoken would have prompted a reply, but it was different now. Now she needed to ask a question if she wanted an answer, probably twice. She wished she knew if it was just normal separation from her as mother that would continue as Deslo matured, or if there was more at work. "Where'd you two go?"

"Down to the water, past the quay."

"Oh?" No response. She added. "What was down there?"

"She just wanted to finish a lesson."

"Strange time for that, I guess, but I suppose everything's a little crazy these days."

Deslo didn't say anything, and Nara figured that she'd tried. She would finish getting ready, and then she would take Deslo and go down to the feast. Now was not the time to wonder about how Deslo was doing. If something was bothering him, she probably couldn't fix it even if she knew. He'd talk when he was ready. If he didn't want to, then all the questions in the world wouldn't make him.

She finished her hair, took one last look at herself in the full mirror, slipped on some comfortable sandals and turned to join Deslo. She stopped when she saw him. He looked like he was trying hard not to cry.

"What is it, sweetie?"

"He didn't come."

"Who didn't come?"

"To see it. The hookworm. It was like a record or something. Everybody was saying so, and everybody else was there.

Grandfather and Gamalian and stewards and servants and every-body." Deslo paused as he vigorously wiped a tear from his eye. "Rika came to see it. You went to see it, but he didn't. I know he was back. If he'd been somewhere else, Grandfather would have said to make me feel better, but he didn't. That means he was here. He just didn't come."

Nara walked over to where Deslo was sitting on an oversize chair by the window. He made as though to turn away from her, but when she sat down with him in the chair and gathered him up in her arms, he didn't resist. She held him, and the tears could be restrained no longer.

Deslo sobbed quietly, struggling not to and frequently wiping the tears away with both hands. "I thought," he started, "I thought if he saw it, if he saw what I'd done, that maybe . . ."

"I know, sweetie," Nara said when Deslo left the thought unfinished. Perhaps it was too unbearable for Deslo to say the rest out loud. Nara hugged him and held him close.

"It's complicated," she said, finding herself in familiar ter-ritory, trying once more to explain what she herself did not understand. She was growing weary of the hollow statements and empty explanations, and she thought Deslo was too. It might have been her imagination, but she thought that she could feel Deslo physically bracing for the onslaught of her various excuses for the inexcusable.

Not tonight, she thought. Not tonight. I won't say all that should be said, but I will speak truth tonight.

"All I can say, Deslo, because really, it is all I know, is that it isn't you. There's something going on in your father, in our family, something I don't really understand. I will try to, though, and I will try to help you understand it too. I promise. I don't know if I can make it better, but I'll try."

The crying slowed and stopped. For the first time, really, Nara had not excused or explained; she had simply acknowledged. As Deslo regained his composure and dried his tears, Nara real-ized that just the fact of that acknowledgment had real power for him. At the moment, it appeared to be power to comfort, to confirm that he did indeed know what he thought he knew, but Nara wondered what other power that acknowledgment might have.

She wondered, but there was no time now to contemplate it. The time for leaving had come and gone, and though she might try the king's patience with Deslo's clothing, she preferred not to try it unduly. "Come," she said, standing. "Let's go down."

Deslo rose and allowed Nara to take his hand as they walked toward the door. She opened it, and Deslo stepped out into the hall. Nara paused as she reached back to pull the door closed behind her. She looked over her sitting room, the stairs down to the lovely marble bath, and the door on the other side leading to her bedroom. It was true that when she looked through her windows, she often felt that she was peering out of a cage. At the same time, it was genuinely difficult sometimes to leave this place behind. After all these years in this city and in this palace, these rooms were the one place that didn't feel alien. They were a cage, but they were her cage, and the distinction between a cage and a sanctuary was not one she could make anymore.

For perhaps the first time in his life, Deslo found a formal banquet fascinating. Excruciatingly boring was the norm. Part of the interest was the presence of the emissaries from the Five Cities and their elegant wives. Lord Jona from Amattai, his fierce blue eyes staring out from under the bushy shag of red hair that fell about his head in a disheveled disarray sat quietly, eating, drinking, and most of all, watching. Close by him, Lord Fehrin, his thin wisps of dark hair combed neatly, sat discoursing loudly on the cyclical nature of fishing in and among the cluster of smaller islands offshore from Perone. The two couldn't have been more different.

Lord Kazir of Garranmere, farthest inland of all the great cities of Aralyn, sat talking more quietly with Lord Venn of Jerdan, his nearest neighbor. Though Jerdan was also inland, it sat

nestled at the foot of the Dibos Mountains near the headwaters
of the Olin River, the only real river in Aralyn. Unlike the Behrn,
which only flowed with water for about six weeks a year, the Olin
actually had water in it most of the time. Thus Jerdan had a fairly
constant supply of water, unlike Garranmere, which was dependent on the madly rushing waters during the rainy season from
the Behrn to fill their great underground cisterns for another year.
This had been a dry year for most of Aralyn, though Barra-Dohn
had been fine, and Deslo knew Garranmere had been hard hit by
the drought.

The fifth emissary, Lord Saris of Dar-Holdin, the city farthest
from Barra-Dohn and the most isolated of all the Five Cities, as
far southeast in Aralyn as Barra-Dohn was northwest, sat occasionally talking with the others. Deslo noticed, though, that he
tended only to speak when spoken to first. He was watchful, like
Lord Jona, but at the same time not quite like Jona. Lord Jona
watched everyone and everything, it seemed, as though he were a
hungry animal and the people around him were prey that might
get away. Saris was different, watchful but without conveying
the same sense of a being about to pounce. He watched, Deslo
thought, like his mother sometimes watched him when she didn't
think he noticed, sober and sad and at a distance more than
physical.

All the emissaries and their wives were draped with finery
appropriate for a banquet with their king.

Deslo knew enough to know that they represented cities subject to his grandfather and Barra-Dohn, but he had only the vagu-
est notion that being in such a position might bring with it certain
resentments and jealousies. If any of those things were evident in
the conversation, he didn't notice.

Of course, the presence of the emissaries was only part of
Deslo's excitement at this particular banquet, and it was by no
means the greater part. Far more interesting was the presence
of the two Amhuru. Deslo had only just discovered that the one
called Zangira, who was sitting at a difficult angle for Deslo to

be able to observe him during the meal, was to be his tutor. This news made it hard for Deslo to pay attention to much of what was going on. He wanted to hear and see Zangira better, but his grandfather didn't like anything that looked like "fidgeting" at the table, so he had to be patient, at least for now.

Before the banquet, a trio of performers, dressed in colorful robes and bright body paints, came out to entertain them. They were contortionists who had used paint mixed with a meridium alloy, so they could work the power of Arua into their act. They tied themselves up in knots, all suspended several feet above the ground, working them into increasingly impossible positions. When at last they had untangled themselves, applause erupted from everyone at the banquet as they took their bows and exited the room.

The highlight of the meal was the moment the hookworm shell—his hookworm shell—was brought in and displayed when the bisque was served. The king told the story of Deslo's hunt with evident pride, and the emissaries and the Amhuru clapped for him. It was a little overwhelming, and he could feel himself blushing at the attention. The elder Amhuru, Tchinchura, smiled and nodded at him, his golden eyes glimmering in the firelight of the hall.

The banquet seemed to go on and on, with course after course, and each dish rarer and more delicious than the one before. Deslo's favorite was the Baiya fruit, imported from the Maril Islands. With little thought to how late it was getting, Deslo ate and watched and laughed, enjoying it all, much to his own surprise. For the first time, he thought that perhaps the world of adults was not merely an intolerable bore, that it might in fact possess certain delights.

It came as a rude shock and disappointment then when his mother motioned to Wynn, who had entered the room unnoticed by Deslo, to take him off to bed. It was not unusual and normally not unwelcome, but Deslo wanted very much to protest. Was his mother not always saying that he would soon need to stay at the table and participate in the adult conversation? Here he was eager to do just that, or to listen to it anyway, and she was sending him away. He turned to her with a look of disappointment, but she ignored it. She simply kissed him on the forehead and whispered, "Go with Wynn."

His grandfather was watching; otherwise he might have appealed. He knew instinctively that to do so would probably make his grandfather angry, not at him, but at his mother, and he didn't want to do that to her. Still, as he left the room, he felt cheated. The gathering would go late into the night, and he would not be there.

Eirmon stood in the open doorway that looked out over his private garden. The nighttime sky was cloudless. The stars shone bright above. Eirmon was beginning to despair that he wouldn't get any sleep. He'd had his share of sleepless nights as king, of course, but all things considered, he would just as soon begin the day of the anniversary celebration with a little sleep as not.

He walked across the room to the door that separated his sleeping chamber from the large front room of his private apartment and slipped into it. The room was only dimly lit by faint rays of light slipping in from outside through the great wide windows, but he could negotiate it even in total darkness with complete ease. He walked out onto the front balcony, overlooking the great square and Barra-Dohn beyond.

The brilliance of the city at night was one of the things he deeply loved about Barra-Dohn. Ever since he'd been a boy, he'd been mesmerized by how lovely and alive the city appeared, even in darkness. When the sun ran her course through the heavens around the other side of the world and when the dark of night crept over the land, it served only as a foil to the greater beauty of Barra-Dohn when captured by the city lights that rested atop the slender silver poles throughout the city, soaking in the sun's rays by day only to recast them as blue-white light at night.

The restlessness he felt was beginning to irritate him. Nothing he had seen that night from any of the emissaries of the Five Cities had given him cause to worry that his imminent move against them was anticipated, and all along that had been his sole concern. Not that all the anticipation in the world on the part of any or all of the Five Cities would be able to stop him, but it could complicate matters, and he disliked complications.

Still, the presence of the Amhuru had interrupted the quiet pleasure of his impending triumph. He had looked forward to the banquet and the joy of hosting as guests the very men who had arrived in relative security and self-satisfaction, their confidence growing that at some point, perhaps even soon, they would loosen if not shed entirely the shackles that held them in partial servitude to him, the king of Barra-Dohn.

The whispers of rebellion had always come and gone, but they had grown of late and reached the king's own ears. Whispers that Barra-Dohn's hegemony over Aralyn would soon be over, that the age of empire for any one city was coming to an end, and a new age of power and equality was coming to pass, made possible by the widespread availability of meridium, of all its benefits and wonders. The technology gap between places like Barra-Dohn that had pioneered the use of meridium and those cities that had been made subservient to them because of that power had decreased until it was now negligible, or so it was widely believed, even by many in Barra-Dohn itself.

Soon, the Five Cities and all Aralyn would find out just how wrong that belief was. This was a fact, a fact that should have provided the king with immense satisfaction throughout the evening, but the quiet smiles and piercing gazes of the two Amhuru punctured his silent smugness at every turn until he was so annoyed that at one point, after being grinned at one too many times, he almost rose and left the room to avoid them all together. He didn't, but the fact that he had been so out of sorts when he should have been in full gloat bothered him. He had only suspicions about the reason for their unexpected arrival, but he couldn't shake the feeling that if right, all his plans and even his very throne might be in terrible jeopardy.

"Trouble sleeping?"

Eirmon turned to see Rika standing in the doorway leading back to his bedchamber, her lustrous hair set free and hanging down about her shoulders.

"Yes," he said, turning back to look out again over the city. She walked slowly across the room and put her arms around him, pulling him back against her tightly. Since she was soft and warm, he was almost distracted from the thoughts that had driven him from her side in the first place.

"Come back to bed."

"In a moment," Eirmon said.

She did not let go immediately, but she did not ask again either. When she had first become his mistress, she had not always taken no for an answer, and while he admired her courage and insistence, he liked to be obeyed. She had, in time, made progress, and a moment later she released him and returned to the bedroom to wait.

He didn't know for sure why the Amhuru were there, but so long as they did not interfere with his business, he would worry about that later and direct Kaden and the army of Barra-Dohn to pursue his purposes precisely as he had planned. And then, when the small matter of preemptively re-subduing the Five Cities had been taken care of, he would take care of the Amhuru as well.

Tchinchura and Zangira squatted in the darkness. Several large and comfortable chairs sat unused nearby. While Amhuru did at times spend months and even years in the service of the wealthy and powerful from nations all over the world with luxury that boggled the mind at their disposal, they were raised to be hard and to be strong. As a matter of course, they declined the comforts that made most men soft and weak. When they separated later, each to his own room, they would leave their beautiful beds untouched and sleep on the less inviting floors beside them.

"Something is wrong here," Zangira said, his golden eyes gleaming slightly in the relative dark of Tchinchura's sitting room.

"Only one thing?" Tchinchura replied, a hint of amusement in his voice.

"Maybe more than one, but at least one. The fault lines ran deep in that room tonight."

"Tell me," Tchinchura said, the humor gone. "What did you see?"

"These men, the emissaries from the vassal cities of Barra-Dohn paid almost no attention to their king."

"Very little," Tchinchura agreed.

"In what royal court do the courtiers ignore their sovereign?" Zangira continued. "Perhaps in a place where fear and terror held sway, where fear of coming to a tyrant's attention might be fatal."

"Perhaps there," Tchinchura agreed.

"But these men did not seem afraid. They talked and ate and laughed, and all the while barely acknowledged that their king was in their midst."

"I agree. They did not seem afraid." Tchinchura nodded. "And the king? Do you think he saw what we saw?"

"He must have," Zangira said. "But that was even stranger. He seemed content to keep to himself, neither angry nor nervous. But if the king feels secure in his power, why is he not angry? If he's insecure, why is he not nervous?"

"Perhaps he was not surprised by it."

"Yes, I wondered." Zangira nodded. "So, if the vassals feel secure enough to ignore their king?"

"Then there is some agreement between them. Perhaps only a shared vision or a common goal. Perhaps more. Perhaps they feel their liberation is at hand."

"And if the king is not disconcerted by their confidence?" Zangira asked.

"He may be aware of what they intend, and either he is resigned to it, or—"

"He has plans of his own," Zangira finished Tchinchura's thought. His companion nodded, and for a moment, they both squatted in the dark, thinking, until Zangira added, "He did not strike me as the kind of man to be resigned to losing his throne."

"No," Tchinchura agreed. "He did not."

"Either way," Zangira continued, "something is wrong here. We may have walked into a storm."

"We may have," Tchinchura said. "Did you see anything else?"

After a moment, Zangira said, "Tell me, what did you see?"

"There were cracks in the king's aloof demeanor. He may not have been surprised by the behavior of his guests, but I think he was unsettled by us."

"Perhaps, if a storm is indeed brewing, he may not want us here to witness it."

"Perhaps," Tchinchura said. "Or perhaps our search is nearing its completion."

Zangira did not reply, and Tchinchura did not let the silence hang between them in the darkness for long. "I could be wrong, of course. I've been hopeful before. Even so, be careful. If I'm right, it won't be safe here. Whoever has what we seek has killed Amhuru before."

"One other thing," Zangira added. "There's something between Eirmon and his son. The relationship is strained. If the king has what we seek, Kaden's help might be crucial to recovering it."

"Maybe," Tchinchura said, "but many sons protest against their fathers, even as they become them. Whether he has what we're looking for or not, this king is a strong man. Try to make a connection, but tread carefully."

9

FORTY DAYS

On the morning of the anniversary, Kaden had an unexpected chance to talk at some length with Zangira. Charged with introducing the Amhuru to Deslo, Kaden made the most of the opportunity to discuss Zangira's recent travels. He was amazed and envious of how far the Amhuru had roamed.

"I wish I were free to travel like that," Kaden said, wistfully, as they walked out in the courtyard.

"Why not?" Zangira asked. "Surely Barra-Dohn has commerce with many places. Would it not be worthwhile to see the larger world?"

"I'm sure it would," Kaden agreed, "but my father thinks that kings who spend too much time away from their thrones lose them."

"But you are not yet king," Zangira said. "Surely your travel wouldn't jeopardize his throne."

"Of course not," Kaden said, a little embarrassed and not wanting to sound as impotent as he felt. "I think he feels that my time is better spent here, learning how to rule."

"I see," Zangira said, and Kaden was relieved when he didn't press the matter further. "For my part," the Amhuru added, smiling slightly, "I can grow weary of travel and sometimes wish for the stability of a less nomadic life. Perhaps it is inevitable that we would each wish for what we don't have."

"Maybe." Kaden nodded, returning the slight smile. "How about I trade with you? You stay here and do my job for a year, and I'll travel and do yours."

"Ah," Zangira said eagerly. "Our problems solved. We'll just have Eirmon and Tchinchura work out the details."

They laughed, and Kaden wondered if the Amhuru had already, in such a short time, figured out just how much control Eirmon exerted over not just Kaden but all things in Barra-Dohn.

Up ahead were Gamalian and Deslo, so Kaden summoned his son to meet Zangira. The boy came eagerly, Gamalian trailing just behind.

"Deslo," Kaden said, stopping a few feet away. "Come and meet Zangira. As you heard last night, he will be assisting Gamalian and Rika as your tutor for a while."

Deslo walked slowly forward, and the younger Amhuru stepped out to meet him. A broad smile of shiny white teeth flashing in his dark brown face, and his bright, golden eyes glinted in the noonday sun. Zangira reached out and gripped Deslo's hand firmly in his own.

"It's a pleasure to meet you, Deslo," Zangira said warmly. "I'm sure we will be friends."

"How long are you going to be here?" Deslo asked.

"Deslo," Kaden said sharply, embarrassed by his son's lack of decorum. He knew better. "That is up to the king and the Amhuru. It isn't something you need to worry yourself about."

Deslo's hand, released at last by Zangira, fell to his side, and he looked down, staring at the stones of the courtyard before his feet.

The silence hung heavily around them, and Kaden regretted his sharp tone. The boy did know better, but he was just a boy and just as curious as Kaden was.

Zangira leaned over, and Deslo looked up as the Amhuru said, "Here is something we have in common already. I was always saying things I shouldn't when I was your age." His eyes sparked now with laughter as much as light, and he added quietly, whispering in Deslo's ear, "Sometimes I still do. Like now, probably."

Deslo smiled back, and Kaden felt both relieved and chastened. The sting from Greyer's challenge the previous day returned, *What about Deslo? What does he want?*

"Deslo," Kaden said, almost impulsively, and Deslo looked from Zangira to him, warily. He winced at his son's apprehension. "I saw the hookworm, and I wanted to tell you how impressed I was. I could never have handled one that size when I was your age."

If Deslo had smiled when Zangira joked with him, he positively beamed now.

Kaden was glad, but he felt a little embarrassed too. Zangira had watched the exchange, and once more Kaden couldn't help but suspect the Amhuru saw more than most would have seen. He wondered how much Zangira saw and hoped that the Amhuru didn't think less of him for it.

Together they walked inside, and Kaden led the small entourage to Nara's door. The door was open, and Wynn was waiting. She took Deslo off his hands, though the boy looked rather mournful at being whisked away. Kaden empathized. He was growing older, and he remembered being at that age when everyone still treated him as a child when inwardly, he had started thinking of himself as a man.

He pushed thoughts of Deslo away. They would see him again soon enough. It was time to get ready for the start of the anniversary. A busy day lay ahead.

The whirl and blur of the morning finally culminated in Deslo's rejoining his tutors and father in a room where not only they but Tchinchura and Rika were waiting. No sooner had they arrived when Kaden took a breath, glanced around the room, and said, "Ready?"

He didn't wait for a response but opened the door that led onto the large balcony that overlooked the public square outside the royal palace. Kaden walked outside, and everyone else followed him.

It was there on that balcony where he had stood before many times that Deslo was suddenly conscious that the eyes of a multitude were upon him. He inched closer to his mother.

Except for the openings right below them and in the center of the square, along with the entrance from the main thoroughfare of the city, every last inch of space was filled with people standing, jostling, and trying to hold their ground against the vast press of humanity that surrounded them. Though a mass of people that large could never truly be quiet, Deslo could sense the hush running through the crowd as faces male and female, large and small, near and far, were raised to look at the royal family and their guests. Deslo looked at the Amhuru, their long ponytails knotted tightly at the base of their skulls and their simple white attire, strikingly contrasting with the brownness of their skin and the goldenness of their hair and eyes. He knew that the hush wasn't just for his family.

Then, accompanied by the blare of horns from below, the tall glass doors from the smaller balcony beside them, a private balcony belonging to the king, swung open and Eirmon walked out. Strutted, really, more than walked, but Deslo was just beginning to be old enough to tell the difference, so he merely observed it without further analysis. It occurred to him then, though he supposed he'd already known it, that his grandfather liked to make an entrance.

Eirmon wore a tightly fitting jacket of black silk embroidered with red designs that embellished his cuffs and lapel and danced down the center where the crimson buttons were. Above his left breast, a simple golden circle sat, which was easily lost at first glance in the busier activity of the red embroidery.

Deslo did notice it, though, and he wondered what it was there for. It was no emblem he'd ever seen his grandfather wear before.

From below his jacket, the king's loose, slightly off-white pants clung here and there to his muscular legs. The king, having come to a stop, stood erect and proud at the balcony. "Meridium has given us our great power and wealth," the king said, his voice echoing in the crowded but quiet square. "So it is meridium we celebrate today. Behold the statue that I commissioned for this celebration, which shall stand always in Barra-Dohn, an enduring reminder of where our power comes from."

With those words and a flourish of the king's arm, the horns blared again, and all eyes turned to the entrance to the square. The sight that greeted them was marvelous to behold. A huge platform inlaid with simple yet beautiful gold and black patterns, carefully designed to be as wide as the road would allow and yet navigable so that it could move between the palace and the Academy, was gliding from the street into the square.

Rising up from the great, moving pedestal was the statue of a man, kneeling on a single knee and holding with his outstretched arm an enormous knife that was nevertheless proportional to the man's huge body. His face was upturned slightly to view the blade, and his piercing eyes were focused intently upon it. Though dark gray like the statue, the knife glinted crimson where the rivulets of blood that had stained the craftsman's knife were brilliantly portrayed.

Deslo understood enough about art to guess that the muted color of the rest of the statue, for there were some bits of color in the eyes of the craftsman and elsewhere, had probably been deliberately designed to show off all the more vividly the bright red streams on the knife.

The statue, riding smoothly on its platform, flowed majestically into the square as a handful of men dressed in the simple blue of the Academy worked the rudders at the rear of the pedestal. The statue of the ancient craftsman and his knife towered above the assembled crowd, even as it confronted at last in the palace, a building sufficiently tall and grand for it to rest before. Then, having steered the statue to its predetermined place, carefully chosen to make it central but also to obscure the king as little as possible before the gathered assembly, the platform slowed to a halt.

It was not lost on Deslo, nor did he imagine that it was on many of the people gathered there, that the very means by which so great a statue could be suspended above the ground and transported in a seemingly effortless way through the streets of Barra-Dohn bore witness to the power and importance of the discovery of meridium they had come to celebrate.

"At the cost of a few drops of blood," Eirmon said, seizing once more the attention of the crowd, "the secret of meridium was unlocked. Power like none other was placed in our hands. With that power, we built an empire. And while more blood was required to build that empire, far more was spared because of the power meridium gave us. Now, meridium lights our streets, cooks our food, and unites Aralyn through commerce in ways that wouldn't have been possible without it. Meridium has been the foundation of a thousand years of power and prosperity for Barra-Dohn, and today we celebrate that glory.

"People of Barra-Dohn, as your king, I invite you today to leave your cares behind. There will be time tomorrow to deal with your worries and your fears, your struggles and your sorrows. Not today. Today I call you to the great feast, but let it not be a celebration of yesterday alone. Yes, we have enjoyed a thousand years of glory, built upon the solid foundation of meridium, but let us also celebrate a thousand years of even greater splendor. For who can doubt that the future of Barra-Dohn will be even brighter than her past? Who can doubt that standing upon the power of meridium we will yet do even greater things?" The king paused as he spoke and motioned to the crowd that filled the square and spilled into the streets beyond. "What can we not do, you and I, with so great a people, so great a city, so great a power?"

The excitement of the day, which had been accumulated over so long a period of anticipation and pent up inside the quiet crowd, finally found release. The people roared in response to the king's theatrical wave of his hand and to the stirring emotion of his voice. Cheers, shouts, and clapping hands mixed together in thunderous approval, and the king stood quietly with his own hands now clasped behind him, soaking in their evident adoration.

But as the gathered spectators gave enthusiastic expression to their embrace of Eirmon's words and as the king most willingly received it, Deslo noticed down below, a man moving out from among the crowd. It was the same Kalosene he had seen the day before walking in the desert. He was bald, dressed in black, and walked barefoot toward the front of the great pedestal upon which the statue rested, though without the walking stick he'd been using yesterday. The Kalosene moved out of Deslo's line of vision, and so Deslo dropped lightly down onto all fours, knowing that few would take note of him with everything else that was going on. He scooted forward to the edge of the balcony where he could look down through the slats with an unobstructed view.

Hardly had he done so, when the roar of the crowd began to subside. Whether the king had indicated that he had more to say or whether they had noticed the figure moving toward the statue or whether the crowd's response had simply run its natural course, Deslo couldn't have said. All he knew was that quiet descended again upon the square, and that it was the Kalosene and not the king who seized it.

"Do not believe that a thousand years of prosperity lie before you, men and women of Barra-Dohn," the Kalosene said, his voice ringing through the square loud and clear. "This is no more true than is the absurd notion that your past glories rest upon a foundation of meridium."

"You dare contradict me?" the king exclaimed, anger evident in his face and echoing in his words as he pointed accusingly at the Kalosene, who seemed very small, standing alone beside the vast statue. "Guards, deal with that man!"

Several members of the Davrii, stationed around the edge of the crowd, moved out into the square, spears in hand.

As they did, though, Tchinchura leapt up onto the balcony rail not far from Deslo, and the boy looked up in surprise and wonder at the Amhuru, who stood there, half crouching, like an animal preparing to strike. His balance was remarkable, for he drew his great axe from his belt and ran the blade along the golden ring on his left bicep in one fluid motion. Then, raising it, he hurled it down into the square in a flash and without any apparent worry of losing his footing and falling.

Deslo's head jerked to follow the trajectory of the axe as it flew downward, rotating rapidly, toward the place where the Kalosene stood. Deslo's first thought was that the Amhuru had thrown it at the man, but the axe actually struck the stone of the square between the Kalosene and the Davrii who had advanced the closest, and sparks burst from the paving stone where the axe blade hit it, so that the Davrii stopped their advance in surprise.

What happened then seemed unreal, like an image recalled from a dream. The axe, which had stopped as though lodged in the stone of the square, started rotating backward up through the air just as quickly as it had descended until it was retrieved into Tchinchura's hand. It looked to Deslo like the axe had been attached to a rope or chain and then been jerked back up along the same line it had descended. Only there had been no rope or chain, and Deslo couldn't fathom how it could move backward from the square into the Amhuru's hand. With another flash, it was once more flying downward, this time striking the ground between the Kalosene and the next closest Davrii. In a shower of sparks, the axe arrested the motions of more soldiers nearby, then returned through the air into the Amhuru's outstretched hand.

At this point, all attention in the square was focused squarely on the Amhuru, who retained his aggressive stance upon the balcony, the axe held threateningly where he'd caught it. He did not throw it again, though, but instead spoke for the first time, looking down at the men below as he did so. "Whatever price the Devoted may have to pay later for his words, he will first be heard. Has Kalos sent you, Devoted One? Have you said all that you came to say? Or is there more?"

"Kalos?" the barefooted man below laughed, looking up at the striking figure of the Amhuru balanced on the balcony rail. "You use a name foreign to this place, traveler. I fear that those who hear you will not know who you mean. Even so, I have been sent by Him," he continued in the silence that now filled the city, a silence even more complete and profound than any Deslo had yet noted that morning. "For I bear a message for all Barra-Dohn, though it is to the king that I must deliver it."

He took a step closer to the statue and raised his hand, tracing the golden inlay on the side of the pedestal. Abruptly, he pulled it back, and turning back around, directed his gaze to Eirmon, standing proud and defiant on the balcony above.

"Forty days, oh, king, is all the time you have left. Forty days. Even now, your doom comes, and before the sunset of the fortieth day, Barra-Dohn will be destroyed, and her empire shall fall. For elevating a created thing above the Creator, for forgetting where you came from and what matters most, for pride and for arrogance, the price must be paid."

The silence was broken on all sides now as whispering and murmuring raced through the crowd.

The king turned angrily to Tchinchura, who remained perched on the balcony. "You have encouraged this, Amhuru! This man foments rebellion in my kingdom while you protect him and threaten my soldiers! Stand down. Put your axe away, or I will have my guards deal with you after they have dealt with him."

Tchinchura lowered his arm slowly and slid his axe back into his belt.

The king, not waiting for Tchinchura to complete the action, was already motioning to the Davrii below. They moved in quickly and took captive the Kalosene who did not resist.

Tchinchura dropped down from the railing and stood once more beside Zangira.

As Deslo stood to his feet again, he looked up at the inscrutable face of the elder Amhuru. Across the way, on the king's private balcony, the king was motioning to the crowd to be quiet once more, but before anything more could be said, Deslo was pulled back inside the palace by his mother's strong and insistent hand.

10

THE KALOSENE

Eirmon wanted to slam the door to the balcony behind him, but he didn't want the people in the square to have anything else to talk about. Rage boiled in him, and while he managed to close the door firmly and not slam it, he could not contain himself once it was shut. He stepped over to the desk nearby and swept the papers off the surface so that they went swirling across the room. Still unsatisfied, he picked up the lamp on his desk and threw it across the room so it shattered against the wall. Shards from the lamp scattered across the floor, breaking into even smaller pieces as they fell on the hard stone floor. And still Eirmon's anger swelled. He wanted more than a broken lamp and displaced paper. He wanted blood.

The door to the small study swung open a little way, and Gamalian's head popped in uncertainly. Seeing the clay shards and papers strewn across the floor, he looked over at Eirmon. His mouth opened as though to speak, but perhaps catching a glimpse of the depth of the king's rage, he thought better of it and said nothing.

"Get in or get out," Eirmon snarled.

Gamalian stepped all the way into the room, closing the door quickly behind him.

Eirmon paced, small bits of the shattered lamp crunching under his feet. "Who else is outside?"

"Kaden and Myron," Gamalian replied, and then glancing at the door as though to deflect the king's attention away from him added, "and the Amhuru."

Eirmon practically growled at the mention of the Amhuru. "They should be staked out in the desert beyond our gates. Food for the buzzards."

"It is unfortunate . . ." Gamalian began, but he swallowed whatever he was going to say next as Eirmon shot him a look of warning. After dry-washing his hands a bit, he went on with what might have been an amended version of what he'd started to say or perhaps something else all together. "There are, umm, protocols . . . Well, that's maybe too strong a word. Traditions, rather, when dealing with a Kalosene, my king." He didn't get any further.

Eirmon's pacing stopped as he rounded on Gamalian. Striding over to where the older man stood, the king screamed in his face, his own face red with fury. "Traditions! You speak of traditions?" Eirmon could feel himself shaking almost uncontrollably, but he didn't care. He wanted to reach out and grab Gamalian by the throat. The Kalosene had stolen his moment, and the Amhuru had undermined his authority. All in plain view, so that not only his people but the emissaries from the Five Cities had witnessed the spectacle.

This was not only personally embarrassing, but the Kalosene's so-called prophecy—the ludicrous warning that Barra-Dohn would fall within forty days—could only embolden the whispers and rumors he'd been hearing of rebellion brewing in the distant reaches of Aralyn. Surely, stories would go back with the ambassadors, stories that would feed the hopes of those cities that they might be free if some unspecified doom was coming to Barra-Dohn.

"Don't speak to me of tradition," the king continued, calmer but still angry. "The Kalosene will be dealt with. And if the Amhuru interferes again, I will deal with them too."

"But Your Majesty . . ."

"Don't!" Eirmon said, wagging his finger right in Gamalian's face. He held it there until he was sure Gamalian understood he was not to make so much as one more sound. "I am going to the Great Hall. Tell Myron he is to have the Davrii bring the Kalosene to me there but not until I am on the throne to receive him."

Gamalian nodded. "Yes, Your Majesty."

Eirmon walked to the door but paused, studying Gamalian who had made no move to follow him. "If you are half as wise as you pretend to be, old man, you will watch the proceedings there without comment—whatever happens."

Gamalian did not reply.

After a moment, Eirmon swung the door open and stalked out into the hallway.

Kaden stood nervously, watching his father fuming as he sat upon his great throne. He knew Eirmon was working hard to contain his anger, but the king couldn't hide it entirely. It was visible to any but the least observant, and Kaden hoped all those assembled would see his fury and beware. Especially the Amhuru. After Tchinchura's daring move on the balcony, Kaden knew they were on dangerous ground. No matter who you were, it could be very costly to oppose the king.

The Amhuru, for their part, stood completely still alongside Gamalian and himself. Kaden had always thought Eirmon's self-control was remarkable, but his skill at managing his emotions was nothing compared to theirs. They stood together, registering no clear emotion, as though they had passed indifferently from one formal ceremony to another.

"Your Majesty," Myron said as he entered the room, "the Davrii have the Kalosene outside the hall."

"Have him brought before me," Eirmon said.

Myron turned back toward the door.

The king glanced at Kaden and Gamalian, standing immediately on his right and beyond them to the Amhuru. Kaden knew that strictly speaking, having been accepted into the service of Kaden's household specifically to tutor Deslo, Zangira didn't have cause to be there. Still, though the king could have removed him at least and possibly both of them, Eirmon allowed their presence. Perhaps he wanted them to see what was coming, and if so, that didn't bode well for the Kalosene.

"Myron," Eirmon called as he stood. The chief steward slowed and turned. The king raised his hand and motioned to him to stop. "Wait a moment."

Myron stopped. He stood, facing Eirmon, hands clasped behind him. Eirmon walked down the steps that led up to his throne, past Kaden and Gamalian until he stood before Tchinchura. The Amhuru was quite a bit taller, but the king drew himself up to his full height and stared into the other's inscrutable, golden eyes.

For his part, Tchinchura never moved. He stood, arms folded across his chest, watching Eirmon as he came all the way from his seat on the throne until he stood before him. The king stared, and the Amhuru matched him stare for stare.

Kaden felt the discomfort of the silence, almost unable to watch.

At last, the Amhuru spoke. "Your Majesty is angry that I interfered," Tchinchura said, as though he were noting nothing of any more importance than the time of day or the color of the sky.

"Angry?" Eirmon repeated. "I am angry, and I have cause to be angry. You didn't just interfere. You helped a traitor spread his treachery."

"Treachery, Your Majesty?" Tchinchura replied. Whether he was really confused by the king's statement or only feigned it, Kaden couldn't tell.

"Yes," Eirmon said, growing louder and stepping closer. "Calling for the fall of Barra-Dohn would qualify as treachery."

"If Kalos has granted the Devoted a vision of the future, then warning us about the calamity to come is hardly treacherous," the Amhuru said, his deep voice magnifying the incredulity in his words.

"Amhuru," Eirmon said, scoffing. "I don't even know where to begin. There are no visions of the future from Kalos or anyone else."

The king turned away as though to walk back to his throne, shaking his head, but then he turned back and went on. "And there is no need to give warnings of what cannot happen. No army in the world could conquer Barra-Dohn."

"If it is impossible, why be upset?"

"Because some in Aralyn would like to see Barra-Dohn fall," Eirmon replied, shouting now, his practiced calm disrupted. "And I don't want to defend my walls against attack, even if that attack is futile and misguided."

"The Devoted keep to themselves," Tchinchura replied. "It is unlikely his words were part of any larger plot against your kingdom."

"So?" Eirmon said. "What do I care why he did it? The result is the same. If he has encouraged those who wish me and my city harm, he is guilty."

Tchinchura said nothing further. He remained still, watching the king, who had grown more and more animated during their exchange.

The king, though, wasn't finished. "Let me be perfectly clear," Eirmon said, speaking much more softly. "If you try in here what you did out there, you may find that you join the prisoner and share his fate." Eirmon turned to go.

Tchinchura spoke, and if Eirmon's words had been intended to intimidate him, there was no evidence in the Amhuru's tone that they'd had the desired effect. "Let me also be clear, Your Majesty. This is your realm. I accept that. I am here only to advise, but I am an Amhuru, and your threats of violence do not frighten me."

Tchinchura paused, and for another long moment the two men matched stares, until the Amhuru continued. "I will speak and act as I see fit, and so long as my words and actions do not violate your laws or threaten your person, you have every right to disagree but no right to threaten. If necessary, I will defend myself. You would be wise to make sure that is never necessary."

Kaden watched Eirmon's eyes grow wider with every word until his eyes bulged like they were about to pop out of his skull. The king clenched his hands into fists that grew tighter and tighter until at last he had to forcibly unclench them. "You dare threaten me? In my palace? In my throne room? You dare?"

Silence. Tchinchura had never so much as moved toward the axe that hung at his side.

Eirmon's eyes now flitted between the weapon and the Amhuru's face. He looked to Kaden, increasingly uncertain even as he grew increasingly outraged.

The king backed away from the Amhuru. "Have a care, Nomad. I don't care what the traditions and protocols say; you are a guest under my roof. I will not be spoken to like this. I will deal with the old man, and you will be silent. You will be silent, or you will be sorry."

Eirmon called to Myron as he stalked back to the throne. "Bring the prisoner before me!" Eirmon resumed his place on the throne, clasping the curved end of the armrests tightly as he leaned forward, expectantly. He turned toward the doors.

Kaden could no longer see his eyes. Quietly, Kaden exhaled.

The doors opened wide, and into the Great Hall poured a hundred of the Davrii, who took up positions on either side of the hall, two rows to a side, the two sides facing each other with a large open space between. Another ten came in next, walking close together with the Kalosene in their midst, his hands bound and his legs chained so that he took short, shuffling steps.

From their midst stepped a large man, wearing the simple dark gray of the Davrii but with two red bars on the left side of his breast, revealing his rank. With his hand, he guided the Kalosene forward until he stood at the foot of the throne. Neither the captive nor his captor said a word.

The Kalosene stood barefooted, his feet almost leathery. His black robe hung loosely on his scrawny frame, and dark, penetrating eyes stared out of the grisled, gaunt face. He looked intently at the king upon his throne with no outward sign that he was afraid of Eirmon. He seemed, not calm exactly, but still, like a wary animal when it knows it is being hunted.

"You have been summoned before me to give an account for your actions today," Eirmon said. He waited, but the man did not speak. "Well, old man? You had a lot to say earlier. Have you nothing to say now?"

"Did you not hear me the first time?" the Kalosene asked, his voice surprisingly free of insolence, given his question.

"Your life is in my hands," Eirmon growled. "Think carefully how you address your king."

"My life slips away like sand before the wind," the Kalosene said. "I knew when Kalos sent me that there was little chance I would be coming back."

"Kalos?" Eirmon muttered, his disdain evident. "Why do you hide behind myths and shadows? Why have you really come? Why do you foment rebellion in my empire?"

"I can only speak what I am given to say, oh, king," the Kalosene answered, and as he spoke, Kaden thought he could see sadness in the old man's eyes. "The problem is not that I spoke. The problem is that you did not listen."

If Eirmon was at all inclined to be merciful, which Kaden doubted, the Kalosene's words would squelch that mercy if he continued on like this. Kaden found himself desperately wishing for the impossible—for the man's life to be spared.

The king, meanwhile, motioned to the captain beside the prisoner to come forward. The man walked up beside the throne, and Eirmon whispered silently in his ear. The captain turned and promptly walked out of the room.

"So," Eirmon said. "My problem is that I did not listen?"

"That is one of your problems."

Eirmon's face grew darker. All traces of amusement disappeared from his voice. "I should listen? To you? To your absurd claims that Barra-Dohn will fall?"

"The city will fall," the Kalosene replied, "and not only will it fall, but it will remain empty and in ruins for seventy years while a small and harried remnant wanders in exile. This is the price Kalos has decreed."

Eirmon stood on the pedestal before his throne, towering over the Kalosene. "Empty and in ruins? You fool! No power in the world can threaten me or this city. In forty days, this city will remain as it ever was, proud and indomitable, while you lie moldering in the ground. In seventy years, Barra-Dohn will remain, and no one will remember that you were ever alive."

"No, Your Majesty," the Kalosene replied, shaking his head. "In forty days, Barra-Dohn will fall, and you will join me in the grave."

"You hear that?" Eirmon cried, turning to look at Tchinchura and Kaden and all the men on his right hand, before surveying the Davrii around the room, still standing at attention. "From your own mouth is your fate sealed. You speak of the death of your king and the fall of this empire without shame. Your life is forfeited. Even now your executioner comes."

"Which means my fate had already been decided," the Kalosene said, looking steadily at Eirmon.

As though on cue, the door opened, and the captain returned with two more soldiers, who carried a rug rolled up between them. They marched up until they stood right behind the Kalosene, who did not turn to look.

"For treason against my person and my throne, I sentence you to death, the sentence to be carried out immediately."

"Your Majesty," came the words from the deep voice of the Amhuru beside him. Kaden's heart sank.

Eirmon whirled angrily, still upon the pedestal, still towering over the others in the room. "You were told to keep silent! Do as I say!"

"I do not speak to challenge your ruling but to request a word
with the prisoner before his execution. A final word cannot hurt.
Just a moment, please, while your men prepare."

The soldiers holding the ornamental palace rug were already
unrolling it behind the prisoner, the pretty colors an odd foil to
the scene playing out before it.

The king stared at Tchinchura, who looked not at him but at
the Kalosene, who waited patiently for his fate to unfold.

"A moment, but leave your axe with your friend," Eirmon
said, and then added with a dismissive gesture. "Make it quick. I
have a celebration to attend."

Tchinchura handed his axe to Zangira and walked over to
the Kalosene, who only turned to look at the Amhuru at the last
moment. The Amhuru put his hands gently on the Kalosene's
shoulders and leaned over to whisper in his ear. Kaden could hear
a soft murmur to which the Kalosene replied just as softly. Then
the Amhuru spoke again as both men stood, heads bowed low.
Then the Amhuru walked back to where he had been, and the
captain led the Kalosene onto the rug.

Positioning him in its center facing the king, the captain made
the Kalosene kneel. Pushing his head down until his neck was
exposed above the top of the black robe, the captain let go and
drew his sword. The Kalosene never moved and never flinched.
The blow was swift and sure, and both head and body toppled
onto the rug as the Kalosene's blood seeped out, adding a new,
darker red to its more festive hues.

"Drop him in a hole somewhere, and cover him in sand," Eirmon said as he descended from his throne. Sneering, he looked at
the Amhuru. "I don't want to be accused of failing to give one of
the 'Devoted' a proper burial."

Turning back to the Davrii, he added. "Burn the rug."

11

THE WIND-RAY

A strong breeze blew off the harbor as Deslo ran along the quay. The soldiers at the entrance didn't stir as he turned in past them and ran onto the king's dock. The waves were larger than usual from all the activity out in the harbor, and as they broke against the pylons beside the dock, water sprayed up into the air. Deslo impulsively shot out his hand and caught the tail end of the spray. The water felt warm as it ran down his palm onto his arm.

"Deslo!" Nara called from back along the quay. "Be careful!"

Deslo didn't answer. Instead, he turned back toward the royal barge that lay at the end of the dock, walking now rather than running. The barge was the only vessel docked there, and though it was quite large, the substantial berth all the other boats in the harbor gave the king's dock failed to provide an adequate foil to display its true grandeur. The white curtains of the grand pavilion that dominated the barge billowed in the strong wind, and servants loading roasted meats, fruit, and wine were hard at work getting the final provisions onboard and in place, no doubt well aware that the king was almost there.

Deslo took the gangway in several big strides. For some reason, though the expanse of water to either side of the dock had never frightened him, he'd always had a fear of falling into the gap between the dock and whatever ship was moored there, so he routinely made quick work of getting onto and off of any ship. Perhaps it was the darker hue of the water down there or the fear of somehow being crushed between a ship and a pylon, but whatever it was, he scampered up onto the barge and felt relief when he stepped onto the broad, open deck.

Knowing that he'd be in the way of the servants working to prepare the barge at the top of the gangway, Deslo darted across to the port side past the open entrance to the pavilion, where most of the onboard activity was going on. Reaching the far rail, Deslo leaned against it to survey the vessels both large and small out on the harbor.

As Barra-Dohn had grown over the years, space within the walls had grown tightly. For the wealthier citizens, expansion had taken the form of vessels like this one, where they'd spend warm evenings hosting parties of friends on the water, often not even moving from their exclusive docks out into the harbor. Even many of those in Barra-Dohn who couldn't afford a luxurious barge like this kept smaller vessels for fishing and recreation in one of the many public docks. Sometimes traffic in the harbor was so busy that it felt as though you could walk from one side to the other just by stepping from ship to ship.

Of course, that kind of crowding never bothered the king's barge. No other docks lay within a hundred yards in either direction. Vessels both large and small would sit becalmed and unmoving, waiting in long lines for their chance to get where they wanted to go rather than move too close to the king's barge on those rare occasions the king had it moved from the dock out into the harbor. Smaller vessels were always nearby filled with the king's soldiers. No one wanted to risk being boarded, having his vessel commandeered and moved, and facing the displeasure of the king, even if the worst anyone had suffered to date was a substantial fine for impeding the king's barge.

Today was one of those rare days when the king would have the barge moved out into the harbor, and Deslo was excited. He liked being on the water, even when the ship stayed at the dock, but it was always more fun when it actually moved. Deslo had known for a long time that he'd be spending the day on the barge, as it had been clear early in the planning for the anniversary celebration that the king had no intention of staying in the city for the noise and crowding that the whole affair would bring. Plenty of lesser officials and soldiers were on hand to deal with whatever might happen there, and of course, word would be sent to the king if necessary.

Eirmon, however, intended to steer well clear of the many headaches a public holiday like this would bring, and the barge was the best way to do it.

"Tell me, Deslo, what do you see?"

Deslo turned to see Zangira walking up behind him. He hadn't thought anyone from the royal party would be on the barge so soon, and he was surprised to see the Amhuru there, his golden eyes gazing out over the harbor as he stood up to the rail beside him.

"What do I see?" Deslo asked.

"I'm sorry," Zangira said, turning from the water to the boy, a broad smile splitting his dark face. "Force of habit. It is a common question among Amhuru."

Deslo nodded, wondering what kind of people asked one another what they saw while looking at the same thing.

Perhaps Zangira saw the lingering confusion in his eyes, because he went on to explain. "It is often said that the wise listen before they speak," Zangira began. "We believe looking is like listening. It is a skill we teach our children to develop. Early in life, we learn to ask our friends what they hear and see, since two are less likely to miss something than one, and ten are less likely to miss something than two. Do you see?"

"I think so," Deslo said. "Gamalian tells me sometimes when we're talking about history that unless I've read three different accounts of something, I don't know anything about it. Is that what you mean?"

"Something very like," Zangira said. "Gamalian is a wise man. So tell me, Deslo, what do you see?"

Deslo looked out at the harbor. He felt like he was being tested, and the only thing he could think about was how he didn't want to fail. He peered at the rippling water, the sun shining in the clear blue sky, at the ships in the distance, at the people on those ships standing in clusters, enjoying their wine. He thought he must be missing something, but he told the Amhuru what he saw.

"That is also what I see," Zangira said, when Deslo was finished describing what he saw. "Thank you. I feel better, knowing it is what you see. As a stranger in this place, I was afraid that I was missing something."

Deslo stole a glance at the Amhuru beside him, who stood staring out over the water. The golden hair knotted at the base of his neck fell halfway down his back, and his big hand rested on the axe hanging by his side. At that moment, Deslo decided he liked Zangira.

"Will you teach me the trick Tchinchura used with his axe today?" he asked, hopeful.

"Trick?"

"You know," Deslo said, getting excited as he recalled it. "He threw it, and then, it came back to him."

"Ah," Zangira said, nodding. "You could call that a trick, I suppose, but it is not something I can teach you."

"Why not?" Deslo asked. "Am I too young?"

"No, you are not too young."

"Is it an Amhuru secret?"

"You could say it is a secret, but mainly, it is skill that is hard to learn and that requires the right equipment. Perhaps another time, I can explain more, but your family has come, and we should probably join them."

Deslo turned and looked across the barge. The king and Deslo's parents, along with Rika, Gamalian, and Tchinchura had indeed come up the gangway. He looked up at Zangira, wondering how the Amhuru had known, since he'd not been looking that direction any more than Deslo had. If he could learn to be that observant by asking others what they saw, he would start doing it himself.

"Come," Zangira said, and Deslo fell in behind the Amhuru as they crossed over to meet the others.

The sun was low in the evening sky, and Deslo stood by the table, plucking juicy chunks of chicken off the bones left behind from their dinner earlier in the day. His mother often marveled at his appetite and sometimes discouraged him from indulging it too much on days like this. But she was paying no attention now, sitting outside the pavilion on one of the padded benches by the rail, talking to Zangira. They had been there for quite a while, gazing out over the water and talking, and Deslo wondered if his mother had decided it was all right to like the Amhuru as he had.

The soft white sides of the pavilion had been rolled up and tied, all save the very back, so that standing at the table in the heart of the pavilion, Deslo still had a panoramic view of the bow and sides of the barge, as well as the water glinting with sunlight out beyond. A soft breeze blew across the harbor, and Deslo closed his eyes for a moment as he chewed, wondering if anything was better than eating to his heart's content on the king's barge, surrounded by everything he could reasonably desire.

The pavilion was almost deserted. Nearby, his grandfather was sleeping on what he referred to as his daybed, which was plush like his real bed in the palace but nowhere near as big. The king was snoring softly, and Deslo knew that not wanting to disturb the king's rest was one reason why everyone else had vacated the pavilion. Deslo wasn't worried, though, as he peeled off another piece of chicken and put it hungrily in his mouth. He could move quietly when it suited him, and if the king awoke while he was there, it would have nothing to do with him.

Gamalian and Tchinchura were in the bow, standing together, gazing out over the water. He'd heard them laughing just a moment ago, a rare intrusion of sound on the otherwise silent barge. There'd been plenty of talking and laughter earlier before and during the meal, but the food, wine, and pleasant afternoon sun had done its work, and now several of the others were asleep like the king on various padded benches scattered around the deck. Rika had spent a little time with Deslo, talking about some of the more peculiar marine life that lived in the harbor, but eventually she'd excused herself to lie down and now lay fast asleep in the sun.

Kaden was also sleeping, having retired shortly after the meal. They hadn't exactly talked while they ate, but his father had taken a seat next to him, itself unusual, and asked Deslo what he'd thought of the statue.

Deslo had been so surprised, he didn't even remember what he'd said, except that the statue hadn't been nearly as interesting as what the Kalosene had said.

His father had agreed, and then they'd sat through the rest of the meal eating in silence but together.

Movement on the port side of the barge diverted Deslo's attention away from the food in his hand. One of the boats manned by soldiers from Barra-Dohn was moving up alongside the barge, much closer than normal, and as Deslo looked at the boat, he could see the attention of the men on it fixed on something out ahead of them. In fact, looking up from the smaller vessel, he could see that Tchinchura and Gamalian had shifted around from the bow to the port side of the barge and were looking and pointing in the same direction. Deslo swallowed what he was chewing and moved quickly out of the pavilion to join them.

"What is it?" Deslo asked as he came up alongside them.

"A dark shape, gliding above the water," Tchinchura said, pointing as he stooped down so he could get the correct angle to help Deslo see.

And then Deslo did see. Whatever it was, from this distance it was clear that it was no bird. Huge and dark, it was gliding well above the surface of the water from the direction of the mouth of the harbor. Vessels of various sizes were scrambling to get out of its way, but it was moving quickly and they seemed to be crawling by comparison.

"I think it's a wind-ray," Gamalian said after a moment, his tone betraying his own surprise.

"I believe you are right," Zangira said.

Deslo turned to see that the younger Amhuru and his mother had come up behind them. His mother said nothing, but she took Deslo's hand and held it tightly.

"There have been several reports recently of larger than normal wind-rays bothering ships out at sea," Gamalian added, recovering his more usual matter-of-fact manner.

"But surely none have ventured into the harbor," Nara said, and Deslo detected worry in her voice.

"No," Gamalian said after a moment. "I've never heard of one in the harbor."

For a moment, they watched the wind-ray, which was growing larger as it came closer. Two of the smaller boats with soldiers had moved out in front of the barge, taking up what Deslo now understood was a defensive position to protect the barge, should the creature threaten it. He knew wind-rays could glide a long way above water before needing to dive back down again, but he had no idea if the one up ahead was capable of coming this far or not.

"I think I should wake the king," Gamalian said, turning away from the rail and heading back toward the pavilion.

"What about Father?" Deslo said, peering up at his mother. She looked back over her shoulder at Kaden, still fast asleep.

"I'll tell him, Deslo. Stay here with Zangira."

She walked away, and Zangira slid closer, putting his big hand firmly on Deslo's shoulder. The Amhuru looked down at him, a serious look in his golden eyes. "Wind-rays are very dangerous creatures, Deslo," he said, and then a slight grin crept over his face as he bent down and added with a whisper in his ear. "But don't worry; so are we."

Deslo wondered if maybe this was something Zangira had said simply to make sure he didn't worry, but he suspected that the Amhuru were not given to idle boasting. Whatever the case, he did feel reassured and relieved, and for a moment at least, it looked as if he might find out just how serious Zangira was. The wind-ray grew bigger by the second, large and dark gray with purplish hues streaking its back, the lighter pink on its under-side glinting off the water it glided above. With every moment, it became clear that on its current course it would pass close beside if not above the king's barge.

Soldiers in the smaller boats nearby no longer stood and stared. Rather, they moved with frantic energy. Their swords had been loosed and dropped behind so as not to impede their throw-ing motion as they took up the bundles of slender meridium jav-elins that lay in their boats. The javelins were very effective when used on land, as they could be thrown for hundreds of yards on a line along the surface of the Arua field and still be deadly when they struck their target. Over water, where the force of the Arua field was greatly diminished, they were less effective.

Deslo wondered how close the wind-ray would need to come before the soldiers could have any hope of striking the creature enough times to take it down.

And then, when the wind-ray was a few hundred feet away and still out of range, it tilted and banked to the right, gliding now almost on its side for several hundred yards. As it did so, the twin, deadly, undulating tails rippled in the air right in front of Deslo. They came out at sharp angles from each other, not far behind the great wings of the wind-ray. Deslo tried to stifle a shudder but couldn't, and Zangira tightened his grasp on his shoulder.

The wind-ray was heading straight for a ship that was a little bit larger than the king's barge, lying at anchor but with a deck crawling with people. Then some fifty or sixty feet from the bow of the ship, the wind-ray suddenly turned completely upside down and plunged into the water.

Shouts and screams echoed across the water in the brief moments of semi-stillness as the people on the ship waited. The wind-ray had vanished from view, but everyone knew what was coming.

"Surely, it can't take down a ship that size," Kaden said, and it was only then that Deslo saw his father, his hair unkempt and his shirt disheveled, standing a little way down along the rail.

"I'm afraid it can," Tchinchura said, "and will."

"Then that will be the last thing it does," Eirmon said defiantly, striding up past them all to the bow of the barge. He leaned over the rail and barked orders at the soldiers in the boats. "Get closer to that ship. When it latches on, put so many holes in the bloody thing that if it takes the ship down, it never comes back up."

After a brief protest from one of the captains below about leaving the king undefended, a protest that was summarily and firmly overridden, the boats were moving as quickly across the intervening distance as the oarsmen could take them. Even so, hardly had they began to pull away from the barge when the wind-ray came up underneath the ship, its two great wings wrapping up around the ship, latching onto either side with deadly force. The long powerful tails rose out of the water, and with a loud cracking that split the silent evening, the first blows from the wind-ray punctured the sides of the ship with ease.

Deslo watched in horror and amazement as one of the sharp, solid tails splintered the side of the ship that faced them. The tail sank inward for several feet, then pulled back out, whipping away from the vessel only to be redirected with equal force at a different exposed part of the hull. Over and over, again and again, both tails slammed through the sides of the ship, which was soon a fractured shambles, smashing wood and whatever else lay within.

A few hardy souls tried to discourage the wind-ray by throwing down from above whatever was at hand on deck, but all to no avail. Staves, chairs, benches, and even empty and near-empty casks bounced off the wind-ray, completely ineffectual, falling into the harbor like the shattered pieces of the ship itself. Others, less hardy, having decided the cause of the ship was lost, chose to take their chances in the water and leapt from the shaking deck into the roiling waters below.

"It's taking too long," Kaden growled under his breath. "There'll be nothing left but splinters."

"The wind-ray will never leave this harbor alive," Eirmon said, as though in answer.

"That won't be much consolation to the people who've been skewered, or swallowed whole, or crushed by its wings."

The king said nothing further, and they watched as the wind-ray finished its deadly work. Parts of the ship were caving in while others seemed to be crumbling out. The bow was noticeably lower in the water, and Deslo thought he could see the stern tilting forward, not out of the water yet, though he didn't doubt that might yet come.

Then, somewhat to Deslo's surprise, though he'd been half expecting it, a volley of meridium javelins struck the wind-ray's wing on the side nearest the king's barge. The tail closest to the soldiers whipped out in a dangerous arc, but their boats were far enough away that it couldn't touch them. Instead, they unleashed another volley, and by now some dozen or so javelins were stuck to the wing of the wind-ray.

Surely, Deslo thought, the creature would now let go and try to escape, but instead it redoubled its blows on what remained of the ship, with a renewed frenzy, as though determined to leave nothing behind whatever the cost. The soldiers threw and threw, emptying their substantial arsenal into the creature, and still it held on, and the tails ripped in and out of the fragmented hull.

Suddenly, the ship pitched forward, and the few people left on deck were tossed into the sea. The bleeding wing of the wind-ray, with dozens and dozens of javelins sticking out of it, detached itself and struck the water with surprising force. After several more strokes from its wings, the wind-ray had slipped out from under the sinking ship, which quickly slid beneath the surface of the water.

One of the boats full of soldiers boldly darted forward while the wind-ray was extricating itself from the destruction it had caused. As the creature moved here and there to open its gaping mouth and swallow a few of the thrashing people, the boat glided almost on top of it. The soldiers unleashed another strike at the more vulnerable underside of the wind-ray, which until that moment had been attached to the ship and inaccessible to them.

The backlash of the wind-ray was fierce, and a swipe of the wing struck the little boat and flipped it, scattering the soldiers into the harbor. But rather than moving to finish them, the wind-ray pulled with its wings to put distance between itself and the rest of the soldiers. After a moment, it slipped beneath the waves.

"It's going to get away," Deslo said, distraught.

"No," Zangira said, "I don't think it will."

"But they can't see it, Amhuru," Kaden said. "It's swimming away underwater, beyond the reach of our soldiers."

"It will try, but the wounds are too numerous and the hurt too grievous. It will die."

"How can you be sure?" Kaden was now looking down the rail at Zangira, but Deslo noted that the Amhuru never took his eyes away from the place where both the ship and wind-ray had disappeared from view.

"I cannot be sure. I am only telling you what I think," Zangira said.

"I don't suppose we'll ever know," Kaden said.

"We might," Gamalian said. "If it does die, and if it doesn't get beyond the mouth of the harbor before it does, it may wash up on shore."

"Either way," Eirmon said, turning from the bow and walking back toward the pavilion. "There's nothing more to be done. I'm hungry."

Deslo turned from the rail as though struck. It wasn't as though his grandfather had said anything particularly cruel or nasty, and he'd heard plenty of both from the king's lips before. Still, his nonchalant tone and apparent lack of concern for what they'd just seen was inconceivable.

The king took his seat at the table and helped himself to leftovers.

Deslo stared as though he'd never seen him before.

12

ULTIMATUM

The room was dark when Zangira slipped quietly in, but the tall glass doors to the balcony were propped open, and he could see Tchinchura standing there, leaning on the rail, gazing out at Barra-Dohn. The sound of a city in celebration echoed from the darkness beyond. Zangira crossed the room and stepped out onto the balcony to join him.

"Is the boy asleep?"

"He is," Zangira said.

"You have earned the mother's trust, at least," Tchinchura said, reaching over and patting Zangira on the back before taking a firm grip on his shoulder. "That she would ask you to stay with her while she comforted her son at bedtime is no small thing."

Zangira looked at Tchinchura. The elder Amhuru was the most observant man he had ever known. He was used to Tchinchura stating as fact things he could only have surmised by watching the world carefully. How he could know this, however, was a mystery. "How did you know?"

Tchinchura turned to Zangira with a broad smile, laughter in his eyes. "I ran into Wynn, Ellenara's servant. She told me what had happened."

Zangira shook his head as Tchinchura enjoyed his joke. "Then you also know, no doubt, that it was the boy who asked me to stay in the room, not his mother."

"I know that a mother would not let a man she did not trust remain with her as she whispered words of comfort to her son, any more than the son would ask for the man to remain if he did not also trust him."

Zangira shook his head again, but this time, not about Tchinchura's joke. "I should not have stayed. It was Kaden's place."

"I know," Tchinchura said. "But the fractures run deep here. It is good that you stayed. Perhaps that is one service you can render Kaden as you tutor his son, to model for him what caring for a son looks like. I doubt he could have learned such a lesson from Eirmon."

They stood side by side, gazing out at the bright lights of the city and listening to the night song of the city's revel. There was music and laughter aplenty, and it illuminated the night every bit as much as the glow of the meridium lights. Zangira could not help but wonder if the news of the wind-ray in the harbor had spread yet. He had seen many battles in his time and fought them, but the vivid contrast of the sudden and violent attack on a day like today, in the midst of apparent safety and celebration, had been striking. He could understand why Deslo had been uneasy and afraid of bad dreams. It had been a scene out of a nightmare.

Somewhere out there, while their neighbors toasted their collective good fortune, families were mourning the deaths of those who had been on that ship. Some had survived, of course, but many who had been eating and drinking, dancing and laughing, had hardly had time to understand what was going on before the ship was being destroyed beneath their very feet.

"I've never heard of a wind-ray coming into a harbor like that where maneuverability was so limited and eventual escape so unlikely."

"Neither have I," Tchinchura said. "It was very strange."

"A coincidence?" Zangira asked, turning to face Tchinchura so he could see him better. "Two such strange events on the same day?"

Tchinchura shrugged. "That is the question. The Devoted prophesied doom. A few hours later, a wind-ray swoops all but directly over the king's barge and crushes a ship right in front of him."

"But the king," Zangira said, shaking his head at the memory. "He acted as though nothing had happened. He sat at his opulent table stuffing his face."

"And no one else made the connection either," Tchinchura said. "At least, not out loud."

"They must have been afraid," Zangira said. "Even if it was a coincidence, surely they could not have failed to see at least the possibility of a connection."

"Perhaps," Tchinchura said. "But you have traveled much, and you know as well as I do, that people can manage to not see a great many things when they will not open their eyes."

"Do you think the wind-ray's coming was a coincidence?"

"No," Tchinchura said quietly. "I don't doubt that there is much going on here I don't understand, but I think Kalos was sending Eirmon another warning."

"Will he heed it?"

"As little as the first, I'm afraid." Tchinchura turned from the rail and started back inside. "Come, it has been a long day."

They reentered the room, closing the doors to the balcony almost all the way to drown out most of the noise from the city but not all the way in order to allow for fresh air. Back inside, Zangira asked Tchinchura the question he had waited all day to ask. "What did you ask the Devoted, and what did he say?"

"I asked him if his prophecy about this city was fixed," Tchin-chura said. "If Kalos had firmly decided to overthrow it, or if there was still time to save it."

"And?"

"And the Devoted told me that the moment Eirmon gave credit for Barra-Dohn's prosperity to meridium, the doom of the city was sure."

"Then as surely as the wind-ray destroyed that ship, Barra-Dohn will fall."

Tchinchura nodded in the dark, and for a long moment, they sat in silence. At last, Zangira added. "Is that all?"

"No," Tchinchura said. "He told me that the collapse of Barra-Dohn would be quick and complete. He said that whatever brought us here, we would do well to leave before it comes."

"Then," Zangira said, "we have forty days to find what we came for."

The reaction of the emissaries from the Five Cities to Eirmon's beautiful new table was most gratifying. Some voiced restrained compliments on the craftsmanship and elegance of the rare, red hardwood. But after Eirmon brought up the claim of the merchant who sold him the wood that it had come from above the Madri and feigned skepticism about such a claim, nothing more was said. Nevertheless, planting the idea that the wood was even rarer than the men had suspected produced the desired effect. Eirmon noted several of them examining it closely when they didn't think he was paying attention. He even caught Jona of Amattai running the thick fingers from his huge hand along the smooth edge, almost caressing it as his eyes burned with envy. Very gratifying.

As the palace stewards brought and set before them the fruits and nuts, the soups and breads, the water and the wine, the emis-saries talked among themselves primarily about the feasts they had enjoyed the previous evening. Eirmon had, of course, invited them to join him on the royal barge, knowing full well that they would decline. The men and the cities they represented had important trading interests in Barra-Dohn, and they needed to maintain strategic friendships. But none of them wanted to spend one moment more with Eirmon than the formal courtesies of their offices required. So after the official ceremony outside the palace, they had dispersed into the city. Of course, Eirmon was well aware of where they had gone and who they had visited, as several Davrii in plain garments had shadowed them, and he had already heard their reports earlier this morning.

None of them said a word about the disruption to the official ceremony by the Kalosene. Eirmon knew full well that the striking scene in the square with the Kalosene at the foot of the great statue proclaiming the imminent fall of Barra-Dohn was obviously the most interesting thing that had happened to them the previous day. Not to mention the Amhuru standing on a balcony rail, hurling his axe like a madman and then somehow retrieving it back into his hand. The king also knew that they would avoid the subject of that disruption like the plague, at least in his presence.

Even so, it irked him that they did just that. They expressed neither the sincere regrets of friends that a deranged lunatic had interrupted the ceremony, nor the obsequious palaver of fearful servants lest their angry master would take his anger out on them. They ignored it, like men who feared that the strange incident might strike too near the truth and perhaps alert the king to their own hopes of one day pulling him down, even if the time and manner of that fall were still hidden from his view.

However, the emissaries had talked about the incident with the wind-ray. Not surprisingly, more than one of these men had been on other barges in the harbor when it happened—three, in fact, according to the reports of his soldiers. They hadn't had front-row seats to the destruction of the ship as Eirmon had, but some had seen the wind-ray at a distance soaring above the water. It appeared that all of them, even if they'd been nowhere near the harbor, had heard of the ship the wind-ray had destroyed.

"Of course, you know," Lord Fehrin was saying, eating a pomegranate as he talked, "I've seen plenty of wind-rays in my time." He spat out a couple of seeds, and while most landed on the plate before him, one landed on Eirmon's new table. Fehrin made no move to pick it up, and the king watched the fool chew and talk while the seed sat untouched on the table. Eirmon didn't know if the pomegranate seed would leave a stain on his dark redwood or not, but it irritated him, and he felt his anger begin to rise.

". . . and from time to time," Fehrin continued, "a wind-ray does attack a fishing boat out at sea, but to see one enter a harbor teeming with ships and then to attack and sink such a large one, well, that was something else."

Eirmon looked at his chief steward standing by the door on the far side of the room, and the slightest motion of the king's head brought the man gliding across the room.

Myron approached and leaned down so the king could whisper his instructions into his ear.

As the chief steward departed, Eirmon returned his attention to the emissaries. Thankfully, Fehrin had either finished or been cut off. Eirmon suspected that while these men might agree on their opposition to him and Barra-Dohn, they probably agreed on little else. Either way, Lord Kazir was now talking, expressing some disappointment that he had missed the chance to see the creature, while adding as something of an afterthought that he was sorry for the destruction it had caused. Still he moved on after a quick glance in the direction of the king. Living in Garranmere made opportunities to see a wind-ray fairly rare.

A procession of stewards filed into the room. They took the bowls and platters of food from the center of the table and carried them out, and then they returned to clear away the dirty plates before each of the men.

"Ah," Jona said, as a huge platter holding several large chunks of roasted lamb was set on the table. "Time for the main course."

A few more bowls of vegetables and another loaf of bread followed, and all were set in a small arc around the king. Then

Myron returned with a clean silver plate for Eirmon and put it at his place. The stewards who had brought the main course then slid in among the five emissaries and took their goblets, most full or almost full of both water and wine and then left the room.

When the last stewards had left, the five emissaries, now with neither food nor drink before them, not even with plates or cups, sat looking at one another in stunned surprise.

Meanwhile, Eirmon pulled the platter with the roasted lamb closer and began to carve it with the utensils provided. As he cut, he leaned over toward the fresh loaf of bread and inhaled, long and deep. "That smells good," he said.

Utter silence had fallen on the room, and the confusion among the emissaries grew. Most now looked to the door, half in hope and half in fear. The moments slipped away, and Eirmon heaped more food on his plate, taking large servings from all the dishes. When he was finished, he did not wait but began to eat. Then at last as he ate heartily before them, anger replaced confusion on the faces of his guests.

Some of them leaned together and began to whisper. Their murmurs, at first soft, grew louder. Jona, for his part, glared at Eirmon, his furrowed brow growing redder and redder with rage. Even so, he did not speak. Not even when Eirmon looked up from his plate at him, meeting his gaze, stare for stare.

"Lord Jona," Eirmon said, between bites, "you seem upset about something."

"Don't play the fool, Eirmon," Jona said in a low voice that was almost a growl. "It does not become you."

"*King* Eirmon, you mean, Lord Jona," Eirmon replied. "Let us at least be civil."

Jona's eyes gaped, and he fairly spluttered as he spat out his reply. "You lecture me about civility after this deplorable failure of hospitality?"

Eirmon took a bite of lamb and chewed, watching both Jona and the others around the table. They were less bold than Jona but no less angry. The king took up his goblet and washed down his food, then lifted his napkin and wiped his mouth. He leaned forward, placed his elbows on the table, clasped his hands together and sat staring at the emissaries, who were each staring back still as stones.

"You think that you can come to my table, eat my food, enjoy the hospitality of my home while you plot and plan against me?"

For a moment, at least, the cloud of anger on Lord Jona's face passed.

Whether fear or uncertainty or something else showed through, Eirmon couldn't have said for sure. As quickly as it had come, it was gone. Whatever it had been was replaced by an animosity that ran far deeper than any social insult could create.

Surveying the other four, though, Eirmon could see that his words were having a more profound effect. Fear was visible on several faces, though to differing degrees. Lord Kazir showed very little, while Lord Fehrin looked like he might pitch over and collapse on the floor at any moment.

"What evidence do you offer, King Eirmon," Lord Saris of Dar-Holdin said, his voice admirably steady as he spoke, "that this baseless accusation is true?"

"The accusation is not baseless," Eirmon replied, taking another large bite of lamb as he replied. "And I will waste neither your time nor mine with providing proof. Let us instead consider that the various formalities of producing evidence and establishing my case have been completed, and let us instead focus on the consequences of your crime. For which, as our eccentric visitor yesterday put it so memorably—before I disposed of him, of course—'the price must be paid.'"

"You cannot treat the rule of law as a formality," Lord Venn objected, slamming his fist on Eirmon's table. "You cannot!"

"I do as I please, Lord Venn," Eirmon said, his voice cold but clear. "That's one of the privileges of being king. Or hadn't you heard? No matter how much you wish to deny it, I am your king."

There was only quiet then and tension so palpable that even Eirmon could feel it. He took another swallow of his wine, glad he had it there to calm him and keep him steady. He wondered how parched the five before him must be feeling.

"Now," Eirmon said, setting his goblet down. "Here's the situation. You want more independence from Barra-Dohn; you shall have less. Barra-Dohn will now require as tribute a fourth, not a fifth, from each of your cities."

All around the table, eyes bulged, and mouths dropped open as Eirmon, in a single sentence, increased by 5 percent a taxation rate that had held steady for centuries and which the Five Cities had been campaigning for years to *drop* by 5 percent. In fact, that very discussion was supposed to be the main agenda item for this council. Of course, as staggering as this proclamation was for them, Eirmon knew it was nowhere near as staggering as the next one was going to be.

"What's more," he continued, "I hereby disband the assemblies of each of your cities. Instead, I will install vice-regents who will report directly to me and to me alone. They will govern the day-to-day affairs of each of the Five Cities, making sure that the interests of the king are fairly and consistently upheld."

Lord Jona was on his feet. In a single motion, surprisingly fluid for a man of his bulk, he had pushed back from the table and risen into the air as though pulled up irresistibly. "You cannot! There will be rioting in the streets! In seeking to avoid an imaginary uprising, you will create a real one."

"Sit down!" Eirmon said, and as he spoke, members of the Davrii slipped quietly into the room and spread out along the wall. They stood well back from the table, but nevertheless, all eyes in the room were upon them, and Lord Jona quietly took his seat again.

"Is it not enough that you insult us? Accuse us?" Lord Saris said. "Now you threaten as well?"

"Oh, no," Eirmon said, a wicked grin appearing on his face. "I haven't threatened you. Not yet, anyway. That comes now."

Saris and the others stared back, and Eirmon let the moment stretch out before finishing what he had to say. "You will return home. Now. And I mean now. This very hour you will each depart. Your things have already been packed and await you outside this room. You will inform your cities of these changes and of the likelihood of more to come, and you will send word back to me that your city both understands and accepts my will."

"And if we don't?" Jona asked quietly, gazing not at Eirmon but at the soldiers standing silently around the room.

"Then I will crush your cities and leave them in ruins. They will become a symbol, much like Rezin, of the folly of rebelling against Barra-Dohn."

The men at the table did not reply. Each of them remained rooted to his seat, none wishing to be the first to speak or move.

"Oh," Eirmon said, as though adding an afterthought. "Since, apparently, Barra-Dohn only has forty days left, or thirty-nine, I guess, if we count yesterday, we'd better make this snappy. I think we should abide by the Kalosene's timetable. You have forty days from yesterday to send word of full compliance, or my armies march, and your cities will be destroyed."

Eirmon thought that even Jona blanched at that one, and he felt satisfied at the degree of fear and uncertainty that now registered on each of their faces. He had known that he would enjoy this day. He had, however, underestimated how much.

"You'd better be on your way," he said, reaching for the fresh loaf of bread and tearing off a large chunk. "You don't have much time."

13

THE REAL PLAN

Kaden made his way to the throne room, vaguely aware of the buzz beginning to make its way through the palace. The emissaries were leaving. Eirmon had given them an ultimatum and threatened them with war. The details were still unclear, though Kaden figured he was about to find out more.

He entered and found Eirmon, not on his throne but on the steps leading up to it. Kaden wondered why they were meeting here instead of in Eirmon's study, especially if he had been summoned simply to learn what had happened. For the first time, Kaden felt misgivings about this meeting.

The king looked tired but happy, and Kaden moved closer, eyeing Eirmon cautiously. "You sent for me?" Kaden asked, stopping a short distance from the throne.

As he did, Kaden's eyes flickered from Eirmon to the throne above him. The symbol of kingly authority was obvious and a bit heavy-handed. The king must have wanted to send him a message by meeting here, but what did he have to say that he felt made this necessary?

"The army leaves for Garranmere tomorrow," Eirmon said simply. "And you are going with it. It marches under your command."

Kaden scrutinized Eirmon, peering closely, trying to read the king's eyes and face, but Eirmon was well practiced at making them inscrutable. At last, Kaden resorted to words and asked the obvious question. "Why? Have the cities already refused to comply?"

"Ah, so you have some awareness of the situation already," Eirmon said. "Good!"

"I don't know much," Kaden answered, seeing that smug look on Eirmon's face that said, *You don't really know what's going on here.*

"We are not going to wait for their answer. It is unimportant."

Kaden's countenance darkened, a frown creasing his face. "I don't understand. I thought you'd given the Five Cities an ultimatum."

"I did," Eirmon said. "I gave them forty days to comply with my demands. It was a ruse."

Kaden stared at his father. He'd always known his father was tough and determined, even ruthless, but this was more than that. This was dishonor and treachery of the worst kind. Kaden was embarrassed for Eirmon, who apparently didn't see the need to be embarrassed for himself. "Why the pretense? If you were going to attack all along without warning or provocation, why not just do it?"

"No provocation? You consider plotting against Barra-Dohn and my throne to be something other than provocation?"

"But Father, you suspect rebellion, but do you know? Is there proof? And even if there is proof, isn't this response a bit severe?"

Eirmon rose and drew himself up to his full height as he gazed down at his son on the floor below. "You'd better believe it's severe. That's the point. I'll raze Garranmere to dust, and the 'Four Cities' that remain will never forget the price of rebellion."

"They'll never forgive you, either," Kaden said, recoiling before his father's vehemence. "They'll hate you all their days. Children born a hundred years from now will curse your name."

"It would be a waste of my time if they didn't," Eirmon replied crisply as he walked down the stairs.

Kaden watched the king come and stand in front of him, face-to-face, and it was all he could do not to back up and move farther away. He felt sick.

When Eirmon spoke again, it was almost a whisper. "When will you understand? You think you can rule an empire with respect, but you can't. People don't like to be ruled, not even by people they respect."

Turning just far enough so he could motion toward the throne, Eirmon waved his hand in its direction. "Fear is the only thing that can keep this throne secure for you and for Deslo, and the only thing people fear is power."

"So you say," Kaden said.

"Yes, I do," Eirmon replied, "And I'll keep saying it until you listen. I want my grandson to hold that throne as firmly as I do long after both of us are dead."

Kaden turned away. He couldn't look at Eirmon anymore. He stood gazing neither at the king nor at the throne behind him. He looked past both of them at the wall in the distance. "Father, I beg you . . ."

"Don't!" Eirmon spoke with renewed vehemence. "The weak beg. Paupers beg. Dogs beg. A prince never begs. Be a man."

Kaden took a breath and held his tongue. Lashing out would do no good. He knew his father, and he knew he could not alter what had been determined. He forced himself to speak. "What is the king's command?"

"You are to proceed directly to Garranmere. You are not to communicate with the city in any way before executing my command. Take the field, destroy the walls, lay waste to the city."

"And the people who live there?"

"Kill those who resist. Those that don't, let them leave. They will scatter to the other cities, spreading the fear of my mighty hand as only eyewitnesses can."

"And then?"

"You will send messengers to each of the other cities, demanding immediate capitulation to my terms. You will warn them that unless they confirm immediately their willingness to obey, you will crush them like you crushed Garranmere."

"And if one of the cities calls my bluff?"

"It is no bluff," Eirmon scoffed. "If any of the other four fails to heed my warning, if you receive anything but immediate, complete compliance, well, then you will proceed to that city and do to it what was done to Garranmere. I don't care if I rule four cities or three. They will understand that I am their Master."

"If more than one disobeys? If all four?"

"Then pick one and go. With the weapons I've placed at your disposal, you will make short work of it. If after two cities have been razed, any still resist, keep going."

"You may have nothing left to rule over but sand."

"I will do what is necessary," Eirmon replied. "Besides, the futility of resistance will be clear. Two assaults won't be necessary, I don't think. Certainly not three."

Kaden didn't want to look at Eirmon, didn't want to speak, didn't want to even be there. He could refuse, simply refuse to do it, but what good would that do? Eirmon could assign the attack to someone else, and it would be done anyway. Kaden didn't think his father would actually harm him for refusing, but how could he know what Eirmon was capable of?

"As my Lord commands," Kaden said at last, starting to turn away.

Eirmon didn't let Kaden get far. "That's not all."

Kaden stopped and turned. "Yes, my Lord?"

"I want you to take Deslo with you."

Kaden gaped at his father. "Deslo? Why?"

"Because he will one day rule after you. He must know the price of power so that he may keep his throne secure in his turn."

"He's a child," Kaden said, disgusted and growing angry. "This will be bloody work."

"If you wield the power I have given you wisely, the blood will be theirs, not yours."

"You know battles are never that neat."

"I know," Eirmon said. "I also know that Deslo is ready for more than you think he is."

"That may be," Kaden countered, "but I will be commanding an army. I won't have time to watch over a ten-year-old."

"No, but Zangira will."

Kaden paused. "You want the Amhuru to come along?"

"I wouldn't have said it if I didn't."

"Aren't you worried," Kaden said sharply, losing the battle to control his anger, "about what the Amhuru will think of your lies and deception?"

Eirmon smiled. "I told you the deadline was a ruse. Ruses don't work, unless they deceive."

"Ruses are meant to end battles already, not as pretexts to start them."

"And I will win this battle before it begins. It is more merciful that way to all concerned," Eirmon said, managing to sound as though he actually believed what he was saying.

Kaden almost choked over Eirmon's reference to mercy, but he swallowed it and when he spoke again, said nothing about it. "I suppose Gamalian knows what you are sending me to do?"

"He does not," Eirmon answered.

"He won't like it."

"It doesn't concern him," Eirmon growled. "Now, I believe we're finished here. You have things to do."

Kaden hovered there a moment, not speaking but not leaving either. There was one more move, one more chance to spare Deslo from being a witness to this barbarity. "Ellenara won't like it."

Again, Eirmon smiled. He leaned in close and murmured. "Really, Kaden, you are so predictable." He turned and ascended the stairs until he stood once more before his throne. He looked at Kaden and sat. "No, she won't like it, but since when have you cared at all about what she liked?"

Kaden recoiled as though he'd been struck. He wanted to reply, but what could he say? He'd set himself up for that. For fifteen years, he'd blamed Eirmon for forcing Nara upon him, so how could he possibly use concern for Nara's feelings as a pretext to keep Deslo home?

He turned to go, and Eirmon called after him. "Tell Nara what you're doing and where Deslo is going. At least, be man enough to take care of that before you go."

Kaden did not look back as he left, trying to ignore the sting of Eirmon's words as he went.

Kaden walked as if he were in a dream or a nightmare. His feet moved mechanically as he negotiated the palace halls by force of habit. Three times he'd avoided turns that would have actually taken him where he was ostensibly going, choosing rather to roam a little longer, but he couldn't avoid it anymore.

He sighed and turned down the hall that led to Nara's rooms.

He felt sick. His whole life he'd rationalized his father's domestic failings, thinking that at least he was a competent if sometimes an iron-fisted king. Those illusions had just been shattered. Eirmon was the same dishonorable wretch as a king that he was as a husband and a father. He hadn't successfully compartmentalized anything. He was the same man in every facet of life and not a good one at that.

Kaden stopped. Something about that thought was vaguely unsettling, but he didn't exactly know why. He knew that below his anger was disappointment, but that wasn't what was bothering him. So what was it? There was no time to figure it out now. Nara's door lay just ahead, and he had to figure out how he was to tell his wife that her little boy was going to war. He knocked lightly on the door.

A moment later, soft footsteps approached, and the door opened to reveal Nara in a silk robe. She looked up at Kaden in total surprise and drew her robe tighter around her reflexively.

Kaden colored with embarrassment as she murmured awkwardly, "Kaden, I thought you were Wynn."

"I'm sorry to disturb you, Nara," he said, fumbling with his hands, not quite sure what to do with them. "But this couldn't wait."

"No, it's all right," Nara said, regrouping. She reached down with her free hand and pulled her hair back behind her shoulders. "I was just surprised."

They stood for a moment, and Kaden looked up and down the hall. "Would it be all right if I came in?"

"Of course," Nara said, opening the door farther and stepping back to let him pass inside. "Should I summon a steward for anything?"

"No, I'm fine," Kaden said. "May I sit for a moment?"

"Of course," Nara said, and she remained standing as Kaden sat on one of her plush chairs. She looked as though she were trying to decide whether she would also sit, and then she motioned with her hand toward the door to her inner room and said, "There's a bit of a draft in here. Would you mind if I grabbed something a little warmer to put on?"

"Not at all," Kaden said, and Nara quickly slipped from the room. The room felt anything but drafty to Kaden, and he grabbed the front of his shirt and shook it briskly to engineer a cool breeze. He'd started to sweat and was feeling miserable.

When Nara returned, she was wearing a thicker, longer, more all-encompassing robe that covered her from neck to ankles thoroughly. She smiled as she took a seat opposite him, saying, "That's better."

He smiled weakly in return and cleared his throat. "Please, let me apologize again, Nara. I know this is . . ."

"Don't mention it," Nara interrupted. "You're the prince, and I'm your wife, and you can do what you like."

Kaden looked at Nara in surprise.

She had mastered the art of always being pleasant, even when she had no apparent reason to be. The biting tone and words were completely unexpected. Nara looked a bit surprised by it too. "I'm sorry, Kaden," she said, now looking mortified. "I didn't mean to speak to you like that. It was rude . . ." Nara's eyes were now brimming with tears.

All Kaden could think of was that she was crying, and he hadn't even gotten to the part of the conversation that was supposed to be difficult. Why must every exchange between them be so hard? Because he'd consistently made them hard came the sudden, inescapable answer. This was his fault, not hers, and it was time to finally admit that. "It's my fault, Nara, not yours," he said softly. "You'd have to say or do far worse to ever owe me an apology."

She looked like she was about to say something conciliatory like she normally did, try to smooth things over and take blame on herself.

So he hurried on and didn't let her. "Please, Nara, we both know it's true, and it's not why I'm here. Tonight we'll drop the pretense and speak candidly, all right?"

"All right," she said, wiping her eyes and looking at him with a little apprehension.

"Good."

"Are you feeling all right?" she asked. She seemed to be really looking at him, perhaps for the first time since he'd arrived.

Kaden looked at her as she looked at him. She seemed genuinely worried, and that made him feel guilty. "I'm leaving in the morning."

"Oh?" she said. Uncertainty had crept into her tone. "Where are you going?"

"You will find out soon enough, so I might as well tell you," Kaden said, but the thought of actually saying out loud what his father was doing galled him. "Eirmon is sending me to war to crush Garranmere."

Puzzlement replaced worry and uncertainty. Nara looked confused. "Why?"

Kaden shook his head knowing he had no good answer to that question. He stood and paced, unable to sit still. "Eirmon is

convinced that rebellion is brewing in the Five Cities. He wants
to crush it before it has a chance even to begin."

"He may well cause it," Nara said.

Kaden stopped pacing and shook his head. "No, he won't.
You have no idea how strong Barra-Dohn really is, Nara. The
new weapons the Academy has developed. They're . . ." His voice
faltered as he sought for words. "They're unstoppable."

"Well, if they are," Nara said softly, "at least you should be safe."

There it was again. First the worry and then relief. "You care
about me, Nara. Why?" he asked, looking sorrowfully at her.

If his question surprised her, she recovered well. "Because
you're my husband."

Kaden inhaled. This wasn't the time for this. What was he
doing? "I'm sorry, Nara. I shouldn't have interjected that. Now's
not the time for such things. Maybe when I get back."

"I'd like that," Nara said, almost eagerly before he'd even finished. "To talk to you, genuinely, honestly. It's been a long time,
Kaden."

"I know," he said, nodding. He hadn't meant to bring their
history into this, but now that he had, he felt that he'd earned the
right to proceed.

"Eirmon wants me to take Deslo," he said, simply, sinking
back into his chair.

"What? That's ridiculous! He's just a child," Nara gushed,
beginning to pick up steam. "He can't go to war! That's absurd."

"It's decided," Kaden said quietly. "Eirmon's determined."

"You have to go back to him, Kaden. You have to explain."

"It's decided."

An awful silence hung between them. Kaden knew that Nara
understood as well as he that the king's will in matters like this
was irresistible. It wasn't a fight that either of them could win. So
he sat watching Nara, wondering if her recent tears would return.
He wouldn't blame her if they did.

But they didn't. Nara rose, smoothed her robe calmly, and
walked slowly toward Kaden. He tensed with every step, bracing

for anything. When she reached him, though, she slowly slipped to her knees before him and reached carefully up to take one of his hands in her own. He was so shocked at her gentleness and affection that he did not resist or pull back. Nara knelt, looking up at him, and then she smiled a sad, weary smile, but it was a smile.

"If Eirmon is determined, Kaden, then we can't stop it," she said. She'd faltered a bit on the word *we*, but Kaden appreciated her effort to avoid communicating blame. "If Deslo must go, then I beg you . . ."

She squeezed his hand and lifted up off her knees slightly as she repeated herself. "I beg you, Kaden. Reach out to him. Take this chance to be his father in fact and not just in name. If there must be war, and if you both must go, do some good along the way. He loves you, and he's so desperate to be loved by you."

Kaden had heard enough. He'd been harangued by Eirmon only now to be lectured by Nara. He started to pull his hand back.

Nara seemed to realize she'd run out of time, but she clasped his hand tightly and would not let go. She had one more thing to say. "I know Eirmon will always stand between us. It hurts, but I understand. Don't let him stand between you and Deslo. You're a good man, Kaden. At least, I know you want to be, and I believe you can be. You're not like him. You'll never be like him. Just be you, and let Deslo in." She bent over and kissed his hand gently with her warm lips. She rose to her feet, still holding his hand.

Kaden looked up at her, stunned. He didn't know what to say. "Zangira is coming," he said, apropos of nothing. "We'll take care of Deslo."

"I know you will," she said with a smile, squeezing his hand as she let go.

Kaden walked to the door and paused before he opened it. "I'll bring him back safely."

"And come back safely yourself," Nara added.

"I plan to," Kaden said, acknowledging her good wishes. He knew he should go, but he hesitated, looking at Nara. How long had it been since he'd really looked at her? She watched him, no doubt wondering why he didn't leave. He smiled at her as he opened the door. "The silk robe suited you better."

And he left, treasuring the look on Nara's face that had been equal parts shock, embarrassment, and pleasure.

Tchinchura watched the massive sandships, laden with soldiers and supplies, gliding along before him. A somewhat smaller, faster vessel was anchored nearby, and Zangira waited upon it. Once they had said their farewells, Kaden and Deslo would join Zangira on it, and they would sail away with the others.

He'd learned of this late last night when Zangira had brought word of their departure at dawn to his room. Where precisely they were going, Zangira had not known. What he had known was that Eirmon and the army of Barra-Dohn was going to war and that Zangira was to accompany the king's grandson.

They had talked late into the night, but neither knew enough of what was going on in Aralyn to feel they fully understood. Some of the dynamics they'd observed between the king and the emissaries from the Five Cities made more sense in light of it, however. Unless Tchinchura was greatly mistaken, this attack had been planned long before the anniversary. He also assumed that the target of the attack was going to be one of those cities. Anything smaller didn't make sense, given the size of the army being dispatched.

Whichever city it was, it was going to be greatly surprised. None of the men they'd observed on the night they'd arrived in Barra-Dohn had seemed as if they were wary of imminent threat. Perhaps they were aware now, which might account for their sudden departure the day before. But with the army following hard on their heels, Tchinchura doubted there was much that could be done unless provision for their defense had been made some time ago.

When at last it had been time for bed, he had warned Zangira to be careful. Eirmon clearly did not like the Amhuru being in Barra-Dohn. His son Kaden might feel differently. He seemed less calloused and more conflicted in general about this venture than his father, but there was no guarantee. Splitting up the two of them might have been Eirmon's main reason for sending Zangira with the boy rather than one of his other more familiar tutors.

Of course, Zangira had pointed out that if Eirmon had ill intent toward them, then it might well be Tchinchura who needed to be careful. He would be right under Eirmon's nose and just as alone as Zangira.

Tchinchura had not needed the warning. Something was very wrong in Barra-Dohn, and wherever it ended, it certainly started with the king.

At last, Deslo's mother stopped hugging the boy, and Kaden led the child up the gangway onto the sandship. Zangira stood on the deck waiting for them, and he greeted Deslo with a big smile when he boarded. The gangway was hauled up, and the men in the stern began to work the large, meridium rudders. As the ship gathered speed and began moving away across the hot sand, Zangira looked at Tchinchura and nodded.

Tchinchura returned the nod, then turned back to the small party that had come out from the city, which of course included the king. In turning, he caught the king staring. Eirmon had been watching him, and his look had been dark and brooding.

The king turned quickly away, and Tchinchura trailed a short distance behind the others to the small sandship they'd come out in. The look didn't confirm anything Tchinchura didn't already know. He was living in the home of an enemy, of that much he was sure.

Whether the king possessed what was missing, well, that was a different question all together.

14

THE JIN DARA

The man with reddish hair, flecked here and there with spots of gold, whose eyes flashed brilliant blue in the bright morning sun, stood in the bow of the ship as it bobbed up and down in the gently heaving water. The launches he'd sent to the city in the morning were visible in the distance. He would soon have an answer.

To some extent, the answer didn't matter. He'd come a long way and gone to great lengths to make this day possible. What he desired lay within reach, and he would have it one way or another. Of course, some roads forward would be easier than others, so he certainly hoped his proposal was met with favor.

He felt uncharacteristically impatient. He had learned patience the hard way, as indeed his whole family had. They'd been forced to. And over the long years, the old hatred had not lessened, had not spent its fury, and had not diminished, not for all the delay or any of the setbacks. Instead, they'd all learned to focus on the hope of this very moment of their return and the wrath that they or some of their descendants would bring. And now he was here, and that wrath was about to be unleashed.

To stifle the impatience, he allowed himself to be distracted by the memory of Alaxundra, and the day he had realized this moment was finally within his grasp.

The pungent smell of incense that always hung like a cloud over the part of Alaxundra known as Old Town was thick and strong. Perhaps the decreased circulation of people affected the circulation of air or maybe it was just the narrower streets and cramped spaces. A slider zipped by, emerging out of the darkness of the side road, hovering a few feet above the ground as the rider worked the meridium pedals for the turn onto the busier street. From his new vantage point beneath the shade of the midsize building beside him, he looked back at the sunny street. His companions had separated, melting into the crowds and shadows as he made his way through the city. They would wait for his return.

A courier running above the narrow lane marked out on the paving stones beneath him, the lane designed for the rapid transport of essential messages and information that was vital for a large city like Alaxundra, ran past the opening to the side street and disappeared again on the other side. The man turned his back to the road from which he'd come, smiling to himself. Either that courier had a hopelessly ill-designed pair of meridium shoes, or his employer wasn't getting the lad's best effort. He felt sure he could have outrun the boy on solid ground without the benefit of the specially designed soles, and the courier was a young man in the prime of life while he was not, though his appearance belied his years.

The entrance to the building that sheltered him even now from the blazing Alaxundran sun appeared ahead on his right. A small flight of broad stairs proceeded up to a grand-looking entrance where a large door stood recessed behind several great pillars that spanned the entire height of the building. Though it would not have been all that impressive in the commercial center of modern Alaxundra, for Old Town, it was obvious that this had once been a valued and important place.

The cracks in the pillars and the scratches on the great wooden doors betrayed a different fact. Whatever the building had meant to Alaxundra in centuries long past, it no longer meant that anymore. The man climbed the stairs and paused on the spacious front portico. No doubt, in the days before meridium had become both the foundation and the currency of power, the great library of the Alaxundran Hall of Records and the information it contained had been valued far more than it was now. He valued information still, regardless of who else did or did not, for words were power as was knowledge, though they were a more subtle power than the power of meridium.

The ability to harness and use the perhaps limitless strength and benefits of the Arua was a power like no other. No one knew that better than he did. But to think that it was the only power worth having was a mistake of colossal proportions. Had his father and his father's father before him not bothered to learn the wisdom of the ancients from the Old Stories that were now all but lost to the world, except in places like this, he would not be on the verge of avenging a millennia-old grievance, and avenge it he would.

There was but one thing he still needed to know, and perhaps this was the place where he would find the missing piece. Then nothing would stand in his way. He stroked the smooth, golden necklace lying warm against his bare skin. Unlike a chain, it encircled his neck like a single, solid ring. He let it go and opened the great wooden door.

As he pushed the door closed behind him, the musty smell of the room made him wish the pervasive odor of incense from outside was more successful in penetrating the grand stone walls of the hall. Even coming from the shady side street, it took a moment for the man's eyes to adjust to the dimly lit interior. A single bulbous lamp sat upon the extensive counter that faced him, beyond which row after row of great shelving stood with scrolls and portfolios piled high throughout. The lone occupant of the room, aside from himself, sat reading by the light of the lamp, an ancient clerk with but a few wisps of hair upon his aged head.

"Welcome to the Alaxundran Hall of Records," the clerk said in a deep and surprisingly sonorous voice as he looked up, the dim light throwing his grisled face into sharp relief. It sounded too strong and sure to match the failing vessel from which it flowed. "What can we do for you?"

The visitor crossed the smooth floor to the counter, ignoring the apparent incongruity between the solitary figure before him and his use of the plural. He greeted the clerk with a practiced grin that was all warmth and charm. "Your library is every bit as magnificent as I have been led to believe. Most impressive."

The clerk nodded, a look of gratification for the compliment showing in his face.

The visitor's piercing blue eyes caught every detail of the clerk's reaction. Flattery was the supreme social lubricant. Wherever one went or whatever one wanted, there could be no better method to ensure help and compliance along the way. Where flattery failed, there was always force, but force should only be the last resort.

"Have you come for something in particular or simply to see the hall, sir?" the clerk asked. "If so, I would be happy to show you around."

"Something particular has brought me. Still, I'd love to be shown around. The grandeur of the hall is unparalleled in the great cities of the world or so I've heard. That is, if you have the time, and I'm not interrupting important work."

"Our time is usually our own. Visitors are rare enough these days. What I am doing can always wait until tomorrow or the next day. Let's begin downstairs." The clerk smiled, rising from his seat and leaning toward the man across the counter. "That's where the real treasures lie."

The tour was tedious, almost beyond endurance, for the aged clerk proved quite long-winded about the history of the hall and at times, the whole city of Alaxundra and even the extensive realms of Faalimun. At one point, he became moved while relating the tale of a minor fire that had either damaged or destroyed certain records that contained critical demographic information drawn from detailed and extensive census work. Until the clerk mentioned that the fire had taken place more than two hundred years ago, he was quite sure the clerk had witnessed it personally and put it out with his own copious tears.

At last, though, they found themselves back at the counter where they had started the tour. The clerk renewed his offer to help as he lifted a small pottery pitcher and poured what must have been some local variety of plant seed oil into the lamp. The oil mixed with the lamp's meridium core, and the light brightened considerably, illuminating the room far better than it had been upon the man's initial arrival.

"Yes," he said as the clerk looked at him patiently, waiting to hear what had brought him to see the hall, for by now it must have been perfectly clear that he was a visitor to Alaxundra, not just to the hall itself. "I was hoping you could help me locate a city."

The clerk's eyebrows lifted slightly. "Well, we do have many fine maps, but I must say that cartography is not our strongest area. Even so, I will help as I can."

"The city that I seek is not so much lost in space as it is lost in time," he continued. "That is, I am sure it would be easy enough for me to locate on a map, if I could but connect it to its more modern name. The name I have for it, I believe, has not been used in many, many years."

"Ah," the clerk replied, a look of positive delight crossing his face. "Very intriguing. What is the name?"

"Zeru-Shalim." The man said the name softly but with a certain, quiet hardness. "I believe it is of the southlands, like Alaxundra. None of the stories I know of it suggest it is north of the Madri. It is very old, or so I have been told, and once it was great.

It may still be great, for all I know. That there is now no city called Zeru-Shalim, however, I am fairly certain. I've looked."

"Hmm," the clerk replied, his brow furrowed in thought. He stroked the sagging skin on his wrinkled chin. "Nothing comes immediately to mind, and yet . . ." His voice trailed off into silence.

The man did not speak, leaving the clerk to his reverie, knowing it was important to let him first search through the extensive records of his own mind.

"And yet," he began again. "Zeru-Shalim. Something, yes, there's something. I don't know what. I've heard that name, though, or seen it somewhere before."

And that was all. A change came over the clerk. He was suddenly all business and competence, moving with purpose and determination. Mumbling half to his visitor and half to himself, he moved between the stacks and the counter, depositing and arranging dozens of single-sheet documents, bound portfolios, and ancient scrolls. And then, when great mounds of information lay scattered in semi-organized fashion across the counter, he began to pour over them, moving the lamp as he worked through the materials from one side of the counter to the other. For an hour or two, he poured meticulously over the contents he had gathered together.

The man with the reddish hair and bright blue eyes settled into the less than comfortable stone bench by the great door through which he had entered. He left the clerk to his work until the clerk systematically returned to the shelves all the documents he had first removed. He rose and went to the counter again. "You've found something?"

The clerk, without looking at him, replied while continuing his work of returning the documents to their rightful places. "Nothing yet," he said, reaching up to set a handful of loose sheets under a smooth stone. "But don't fear. I've narrowed it down, I think. A great city of the south, once called Zeru-Shalim, but so long ago that the name has passed from collective memory, reduces the options tremendously. I've ruled out all the other major cities of

Faalimun, as well as Nercissa, so this go around, I'll focus west of here and look to Aralyn and Golina."

With that the clerk began to assemble another mound of documents, and the stranger went back to the stone bench. This time, rather than sitting, he stretched out along it, lying on his back. For a while he lay staring upward, watching the shadow cast by the clerk from the solitary lamp as it played on the distant ceiling, but after a while he closed his eyes and lay in the darkness of his own thoughts.

"Aha!" the clerk exclaimed.

The stranger sat up. "Aha! Aha!" the man repeated, and he rose, moving quickly over to the counter.

"Look at this," the clerk said without looking up as he approached. He held up an ancient-looking portfolio so coated with dust that a steady stream fell from it and swirled like fog around the lamp. Then he set it back down before the visitor could even focus his eyes upon it. "Come, I'll read it to you, for the script of this era is particularly difficult to read for moderns who aren't specialists.

"It says, *The deal is done. Negotiators from the palace have reached an agreement with the emissaries from the city formerly known as Zeru-Shalim. The first shiploads of the new metal should be arriving within the year, along with scientists and technicians to demonstrate the special properties within. All the possibilities this opens up commercially, technologically, militarily, and more, are hard to conceive, for the chief emissary assures us that they have entered into like agreement with no other city from Faalimun but Alaxundra alone. Our return to supremacy among our sister cities seems assured.*

"It goes on from there, but even without reading further, we can safely assume that the new metal referenced therein is none other than meridium, for this document is more than eight hundred years old. It can't be anything else, can it?"

The man fixed his bright blue eyes firmly upon the clerk, who had looked up and was watching the visitor expectantly. Without reference to the question he had been asked, which had no doubt been offered rhetorically anyway, he returned to the matter that had brought him to Alaxundra in the first place. "And the city once known as Zeru-Shalim is mentioned there?"

"I'm sure it is," the clerk said, "but we need hardly look for the name, surely."

"Why?"

"Because everyone knows who first supplied meridium to Alaxundra. That commercial partnership was fundamental to our return to glory, wasn't it? Absolutely fundamental." The clerk's excitement bubbled out from him as he spoke. He fairly glowed with it. The heavy years written on his face seemed to fall away as a boy's countenance was reflected in the yellowish light of the lamp, and a child's wonder gleamed in his eyes.

"Would you mind checking for me anyway, just to be sure?" the man asked, his calm tone a stark contrast to the clerk's eagerness. "I've come a long way for this information."

The clerk answered by leaning in closely. For a moment he scanned the page, and of all the hours over all the years that the man had been searching for the answer to his question, this moment felt the longest. Ages came and went in the brief span of time it took the clerk to say, "Ah, here it is. Exactly as I thought."

"Yes?"

"Barra-Dohn," the clerk said, looking up with a knowing smile. "Of course, it is. It's Barra-Dohn."

"Barra-Dohn." The name slid from the man's mouth in echo of the clerk. He formed the word again with his lips and tongue but did not say it out loud. He said it only for himself, for his own ears, for his own heart and mind. Barra-Dohn. He had heard that name before. Barra-Dohn. It was indeed a great city, though he had never been there. It had to be great to be so widely known, like Alaxundra itself. Barra-Dohn. Until this moment, he had never known that every time he'd heard the name of Barra-Dohn, he was hearing about Zeru-Shalim. Now he knew, and now his course was set.

"You have done me a great service, friend," the man said. "May I offer you something for your services?"

"No, no," the clerk said emphatically. "Alaxundra may not put as much public funding aside for the maintenance of the hall of records as it should, but we are of course paid for our work here. There is no need. No need at all."

"Are you sure?"

"Yes, yes. It was a wonderful distraction from my more mundane duties. I'm delighted to have been of help. No reward is needed. To have found the answer to your question, to have been of service, that is all the reward I need." The clerk leaned over the counter, closer to the man. "To tell you the truth, it was the first question I've had in years that required even a moment's reflection. Usually the questions that come my way these days are so basic that I don't even need to think about the answers."

Riffling his hand through his reddish hair, the man smiled and nodded. "Then let me at least thank you verbally most profusely for all your help. I am in your debt."

"It is nothing," the clerk said. "In its heyday, people came from all over the world to seek information from this place. It's why we're here. It's what we do."

"Truly, the reports of the greatness of the archives of Alaxundra are not exaggerated. In fact, they do not do it justice. In my travels, I heard only of the greatness of the place, but surely the resourcefulness and wisdom of its keepers should also be boasted of. After all, of what value would all the knowledge and wisdom in the stacks behind you be if you and your colaborers did not know where to look for it?"

At that, the clerk behind the counter seemed absolutely too happy to speak. He was as bashful as an adolescent boy who has been told by a beautiful girl that he is handsome. Having gotten what he came for, he smiled and nodded, turning back toward the door. "I will be on my way and take no more of your time, my friend."

"But good sir," the clerk said suddenly, as though snapping out of a daze when the man turned to go. "I have not yet gotten your name."

"My name?" he replied, a slight frown passing over his face as he turned back around to look at the clerk behind the desk.

"Yes," the clerk said, lifting a large portfolio from a shelf below the countertop. He opened it, placing it upon the other materials that lay spread around him. "It is required that I log every visitor to the hall and that I provide a brief summary of the information they sought here."

"I see," he said, rubbing his hands gently together as he looked down at the floor. After a moment, he walked back over to the counter and looked carefully down at the book that the clerk had set upon it. Line upon line of entries—dates, names, and more—were visible. There were no doubt thousands of names from across the years recorded in that book and of no great consequence to him. He stood for a moment, thinking, and then looked up into the eyes of the clerk who waited expectantly. "My name, my real name, is of little consequence. It could hardly matter to you or anyone else. Still, I will give you a name for your book so that you may fulfill your obligation to your masters. You may write, if you wish it, that this request was made to you by one who called himself *the Jin Dara*."

When he said *the Jin Dara*, his voice became a clear, soft whisper. At the same time, a smile appeared like daybreak across his face as a twinkle gleamed in his strikingly blue eyes. Then saying no more, he turned and walked swiftly from the room, cherishing with every step how the innocuous grin of the ancient clerk had slipped away when he had spoken those words and was replaced with a sudden, wide-eyed look of horror.

Outside, evening had come to Alaxundra. The last light of day was fading though the thick smell of incense remained. He stretched, feeling no weariness, then jogged down the steps, feeling energized and happy. Barra-Dohn. He knew now. He finally knew.

The sound of footsteps on the deck chased the memory away. He turned to see Devaar standing before him, a rare smile on his hardened face.

"They've agreed," the Jin Dara said.

"Oh, yes," Devaar replied. "They hate Barra-Dohn almost as much as you do."

"Good," he said, nodding. "When will they meet with me?"

"They said you could come ashore anytime, and I told them you would come at first light."

"Very well then," the Jin Dara said, turning back to gaze across the water at the outline of the city. Evening was advancing, and pinpoints of bright meridium lights were beginning to sparkle throughout.

Devaar walked up and stood beside him. For a long while, they stood quietly, gazing at the city. At last, Devaar broke the silence. "They said that Barra-Dohn lies just over a week away by sandship, but it will take them a little while to gather their forces."

"That's fine," the Jin Dara said. "I'll need some time myself. Even I can't bring nightmares to life with the snap of my fingers."

"No, sir," Devaar said, chuckling. "I guess not." After a moment, he added. "It's strange, isn't it?"

"What's strange?"

"To have looked so long and to be here at last."

"Yes. It's strange," he answered, turning his piercing gaze on Devaar. "Strange and wonderful."

"Indeed," Devaar answered. "Somewhere out there, the mighty city lies. But the people have no idea what's coming."

"No, they don't."

"They wouldn't believe it possible, even if someone told them, would they?" Devaar looked at him, then turned back to the city in the distance. "Without seeing it, without experiencing it, how could they? But it's already over. Their fate was decided the moment we learned the name. Their city is dust, and they don't even know it."

"Devaar," the Jin Dara said, "you've never said a truer word."

Part 2

THE STRONGER HAND

15

FRIENDS AND ENEMIES

The morning sun glinted off the slender rod in Nara's hand. On one end, the rod flared out into a somewhat broader base, while the other end simply ended in a solid, smooth surface. The first rod was short, so placing the disc on top of it once she'd balanced it on the Arua field would be relatively simple. She stood it up, the end with the flared base at the bottom, and held it firmly but gently between her fingers until she could not feel it leaning in any particular direction. Removing her fingers as gently as she'd placed them on the rod, she stepped back and examined the collection of colorful discs behind her on the ground.

It wasn't any harder to play Rainbow Sevens with pottery discs. They just shattered when they fell off a rod unlike the meridium ones. Nara was quite good at the game, though, having had lots of time to herself in which to practice, so she didn't mind the challenge. She took up the bright, large, flat yellow disc, and with relative ease, placed it atop the slender rod.

She moved on to the next rod, which was slightly longer, placing it on its end not far from the first. Picking up the orange disc next, she carefully placed that one too. The red and green discs also went onto their respective rods fairly quickly, but the next play almost ended the game. The fifth rod was tall enough that the top was just above head level for her, and reaching up to set the blue disc in place required more careful attention. Letting go too soon, the disc tilted and fell, but her hands were nimble and not far from the top of the rod when it fell off, and she caught it on the way down.

Nara looked around a little guiltily, but no one was watching. The smaller courtyard on this side of the palace was not on the way somewhere else, so people didn't just pass through. She was rarely disturbed while she was there, a major reason why Nara gravitated to it in her abundant free time.

She had no need for guilt, Nara realized. Yes, strictly speaking, you weren't supposed to touch a disc again once you'd taken your hand off it. But Nara wasn't playing against anyone, so it wasn't as if she'd cheated. She leaned forward up on her tippy toes, though it wasn't necessary yet, and placed the blue disc again, this time more carefully.

She wasn't surprised that she'd faltered with the blue disc, for she had a lot on her mind. Deslo was on his way to war, which would have been enough all by itself to disconcert her, but there was also the fact that Kaden had flirted with her. The words themselves could have been taken more than one way, but the tone in his voice and the look in his eye were a giveaway.

But now he was gone too, leaving her to wait and wonder what, if anything, might come next. She tried to occupy herself with things like this, but since Deslo filled so much of her time ordinarily, it was difficult to stay busy. She forced her thoughts back to her game.

Having left the pink and purple discs to last, she decided to play pink first. It was tricky maintaining her own balance as she tried to balance the disc on the sixth rod. But she managed after a few moments and turned to pick up the seventh rod, only to see Tchinchura watching now from the entrance to the small courtyard.

When she didn't turn back to the game, he smiled and spoke. "Please, I didn't mean to interrupt. Continue."

Nara hesitated, not sure she wanted to make the final play while being watched, especially not by the Amhuru. His golden eyes were penetrating at the most innocuous of times. But now as she turned her back on him and moved to set up the final rod, she felt as though they were burrowing right through her. She didn't need to move in order to shield the main length of the longest rod from the man, but she knew that the top part, the part he'd want to watch anyway, was clearly visible over a foot above her own head.

She took up the purple disc and strained upward, standing as tall as her toes allowed. She approached her placement a bit clumsily, and the rod wavered a little but didn't fall over. It wasn't a game-ending error, but it was bad form. She adjusted her stance and tried again, this time coming in almost perfectly so the disc was very nearly centered upon first touching the rod. Her fingertips gently manipulated the disc until she was almost certain she had scored the win. The only reason she didn't step back and admire her work right away was that it felt too quick. She was genuinely surprised to have the disc in place already.

She didn't linger, though, since she didn't trust her fingers not to tremble and ruin the precision of the placement if she left them on it much longer. So she removed them and stepped back, holding her breath even though she knew the disc was exactly where it needed to be. The big purple disc didn't so much as move at all atop the rod, and from behind her, Tchinchura clapped his hands and laughed.

He walked up beside her. "I like it," he said. "It is a far more delicate sculpture than the one the king commissioned for the anniversary."

"Sculpture?" Nara said, looking up at him, momentarily distracted by what sounded like criticism of the king or at least his taste. That wasn't the kind of thing you heard anywhere in the palace, even in out-of-the-way gardens. "Oh, no," she said finally. "This isn't art. It's a game."

"Art, game. There's no reason it can't be both," Tchinchura said. "Games all over the world have artistic elements."

"All over the world," Nara echoed him a little wistfully. "You've really been all over the world?"

"Not all over, I suppose," Tchinchura said with a smile. "But I have seen many places."

"But you didn't recognize the game. You haven't seen it before?"

"I haven't," Tchinchura said, "but I have seen ones like it that combine the Arua field and fine dexterity. Is the game over?"

"Since I'm not playing anyone, I guess so," Nara said.

"I see," Tchinchura said. "The game is for more than one player?"

"Yes."

"If you fail to place your disc, you lose?"

"That's right."

"And if both of you place all seven," the Amhuru asked, turning from the discs, still sitting atop the meridium rods, "what then?"

"You go again, in reverse order, from tallest to shortest," Nara said. "On and on, until the pressure gets to someone, and they misplay."

Tchinchura walked forward into the middle of her placement of the rods. "Does the order of the colors matter?"

"Not really," Nara said.

Tchinchura surveyed the rods one more time and then turned back to her. "Would you like help taking them down? Or will you leave them like this?"

"Sure," Nara said. "Help would be great."

"I'll grab the taller ones," he said, reaching over and taking the purple disc down. In a moment, all seven discs were piled back on the ground, and the seven rods lay beside her on the Arua, floating, the wide bases now on top, the shafts of the rods pointed down at the ground.

"We can leave them here," Nara said.

"Maybe I can play with you sometime," Tchinchura said. "I'd like to try my hand at it."

"I'll see if there's a set around the palace for someone your height," Nara said. "If not, we can pick one up in the city somewhere."

"Ah, yes," Tchinchura nodded. "It would be a little unfair if mine weren't any taller."

"A little," Nara said, looking up at him. "You wouldn't have to stretch at all if you played with my set. It would be unfair."

Tchinchura made a faint bow. "Then we will find a suitable set, and if you can be patient with a beginner, we will play sometime."

Nara frowned, remembering the Amhuru's balance when he leapt onto the stone rail of the balcony, remembering as he hurled his axe and retrieved it out of the air. Novice or not, self-deprecation or not, she very much doubted if Tchinchura would play like a beginner.

She realized he was watching her carefully, and not wanting him to think she was frowning at the thought of playing with him, she smiled and said, "I will be happy to play with you, though I doubt you will require much patience. I suspect you'll be just fine."

He grinned but said nothing further about the game. Instead, he changed the topic to something else altogether. "I was going to walk out in the city. Would you like to walk with me?"

Nara was a bit taken aback. From what she had observed, the Amhuru had kept his own company in the week since the army had set sail for Garranmere. She imagined that he'd been trying to remain near Eirmon, since ostensibly he'd offered his service to and been accepted by the king. But Eirmon seemed to be carrying on as usual as though there wasn't an Amhuru lurking around his court, and he hadn't just launched a surprise attack that would start a war.

"All right," she said, not even sure why she'd hesitated at the request. Any initial reluctance she'd felt about the Amhuru had passed quickly. She believed they were good and honorable men, which might not serve them well with Eirmon, but she didn't mind having them around her and Deslo.

Then it struck her. Her hesitance wasn't really about him. It was about her. Other than Wynn and some of the other female stewards in the palace with whom she'd formed a strange sort of friendship, no one visited her, no one attended her, no one paid her any attention. The thought of walking in the city with any man, let alone someone as striking as Tchinchura, was simply odd.

"That would be nice," she added after a moment.

"Good," Tchinchura smiled. "I haven't been out in the city much yet. With you, at least, I know I won't get lost."

She laughed. "Somehow, the thought of you lost is almost as hard for me to imagine as the thought of you having difficulty playing Rainbow Sevens."

Tchinchura laughed with her. "You might be surprised."

"I might," Nara said, eyeing him again. "But I doubt it."

The market district of Barra-Dohn was busy as usual, smelling of fresh bread and sage oil, but it seemed to Nara to be somewhat subdued, nonetheless. The hawkers selling their wares seemed less eager, while the people going to and fro running their errands seemed more preoccupied. Across the way from the market, more couriers than usual raced through the space set aside for them and their business. It was clear to Nara that even those who didn't have any family members or friends in the army were showing the nervous effects of a nation waiting for war.

The ebullience that had characterized the city for weeks if not months leading up to the anniversary had disappeared. Gone, just like that. Nara couldn't work it out. Eirmon was too savvy to squander in a single senseless stroke all the goodwill he'd bought with the anniversary celebration. Then again, Eirmon might have found a perverse pleasure in doing just that.

Up ahead, a mother leading her young son by the hand crossed the street. Nara's eyes lingered on the boy. He looked a few years younger than Deslo, but he was stocky and walked a bit like him. She caught her breath for a moment, thinking of Deslo in the midst of all those soldiers, but he was far away and worry could not help him.

"All will be well," Tchinchura said as they walked on. "You'll see."

"Pardon?" Nara said, looking over at him.

"Your son," Tchinchura said. "All will be well."

Nara looked back at the boy walking with his mother. They were just turning into a bakery. "How can you be sure?"

"Beyond even the army he's with, he's with Zangira, and Zangira will not let anything happen to him."

Nara peered at Tchinchura's inscrutable face. His golden eyes watched her, betraying nothing. "They're going to war, Tchinchura. Wars are dangerous and unpredictable."

"I know," Tchinchura said. "But Zangira has seen war before. He will keep the boy safe. He would give his life before he would let harm come to Deslo."

"I hope you're right," Nara said, then corrected herself. "Not that I hope Zangira will have to make that sacrifice."

"I know what you meant," Tchinchura assured her, squeezing her arm gently. "And besides, whatever the fractures in the family, Kaden will do all he can to make sure Deslo is safe."

Nara felt herself blushing and looked away. "It's that obvious is it? The trouble between us?"

"Yes," Tchinchura said, not dancing around the subject. "Understand, Nara, I will not lie to you, even if it would be easier. I will not offer false consolation for your heartache over Kaden's detachment, nor would I reassure you about Deslo's safety unless I really was sure of Zangira."

Nara nodded, wondering how the Amhuru had seen so much in so short a time.

"However," Tchinchura said when she didn't reply, "though I will not offer false consolation, I will offer real consolation when I can. I don't think Kaden is as detached from you and the boy as he first appears. It seems his real struggle lies elsewhere, does it not?"

So perceptive, Nara thought, and she smiled gratefully at Tchinchura as they walked on. Perhaps the hope she'd felt beginning to blossom since Kaden and Deslo had left that maybe, just maybe, they could one day be a family, was not entirely unwarranted.

"Eirmon," Tchinchura started and then stopped. The Amhuru looked momentarily uncertain, and it caught Nara by surprise. She hadn't seen anything even resembling hesitation in the man before. He did continue, though, after a moment. "He isn't a very open man, is he?"

"Kings bear the weight of nations," Nara said, noting the emphasis Tchinchura put on the word *open*, and wondering what exactly he was getting at. "That's what Kaden used to say, anyway, when I'd make observations about his father."

"It's true," Tchinchura said. "I have known a few and served them. But it's more than his responsibility, isn't it? Fault lines are here, all through the family and even the city itself. Secrets are here too, and they trace their way back to Eirmon, don't they? Even a stranger like me can see that."

Nara was beginning to feel uneasy. Even if Kaden might not be as lost to her as she'd feared, she'd always felt like the unwanted wife of the king's son, of little use to either Eirmon or Kaden other than to dress up for decoration on state occasions and to nurture the king's grandson. Talking about the fractures and problems in the royal family was not something she did with anyone. She had no real friends since the king had employed all the servants and stewards in the palace. To be suddenly asked a serious question about Eirmon by someone other than Deslo was something she was wholly unprepared for. She stopped, feeling disinclined either to answer or to evade the matter, and the Amhuru stopped too. She sighed and said, "What do you want from me?"

"A fair question," Tchinchura said. "And it deserves a fair answer. Amhuru offer their services as a matter of course when they visit a place like Barra-Dohn, and we are glad to serve."

Nara nodded. She had known a little about the Amhuru before Tchinchura and Zangira came, and she had learned a little more since.

"However," Tchinchura continued, "I have rarely felt the misgivings I feel now in any court. The events that followed upon our arrival, what I've observed in Eirmon's household, and his wariness around me—these things cause me great concern."

Nara found herself again taken aback by his candor. She lived a life of routine wrapped in artifice and disingenuousness, but Tchinchura seemed incapable or unwilling to dissemble. "I'm still not sure what you want from me."

"Only a friend," Tchinchura said, smiling. "Anything you can tell me that will help me understand better what kind of place I've landed in and what kind of man I am serving would be a great help."

They had started walking again, and as Nara kept pace with Tchinchura's longer strides, her mind raced. She was well aware of the conflict over the Kalosene that had, as she saw it, gotten Eirmon and Tchinchura off to such a rocky start. And she was well aware that Eirmon had been keeping the Amhuru at arm's length ever since. To be seen too much in his company, to become too close a companion, could be unwise for someone whose own position was by no means secure.

But she wanted to help him. She liked him, and his reassurances that Zangira would protect Deslo with his life did comfort her. After only a little more than a week, she found it easier to believe the Amhuru would be both good to and for Deslo than to believe the lies of the king. Besides, she had certainly wished for a friend to help her understand what she'd landed in when she'd

first come to Barra-Dohn. Now, at least, she could be that friend
to him.

"All right," Nara said. "I will do what I can to help you understand Eirmon. But, the first thing you should probably know is
that I don't think anyone really knows Eirmon, because he doesn't
let himself be known."

"Perhaps not," Tchinchura said, "but no one can really hide
himself from the world around him. A man's character won't be
concealed. It finds ways of coming out, for better or worse."

Eirmon reclined on a plush white chair on his barge. He was
drinking wine but carefully. The water was choppy, and even
though the barge was still moored at the dock, Eirmon could feel
it surge and swell beneath him. Although the carcass of the wind-
ray had washed ashore near the mouth of the harbor, as Gamalian
had suggested it might, he'd been uneasy about heading out into
deeper waters. Still, he chafed to be away from the dock, already
castigating himself for not going out but not enough that he actually gave the command.

"Your Majesty?"

He turned to see Rika standing there, her hair pulled back
snugly and her well-tailored blue Academy attire hugging her
curves closely and flatteringly. Eirmon doubted many of the stewards were in the dark about what was going on between them,
but he never flouted these things. Removing even the pretense of
secrecy was always a bad idea, as it encouraged a freedom in others to see his business as their own. So in public he performed the
charade required of him and expected her to do the same.

"Since your charge in the royal family is far from here, I
assume that you bring news from the Academy?"

"Astute as always," Rika replied. If there was a hint of gentle
sarcasm in her voice, it was the barest of hints, so well hidden that
he wasn't even sure himself that he'd heard it. She sometimes protested the necessary rituals in surprisingly silly and pointless ways.

"Well?" he asked, not caring if she thought him grumpy. It was the prerogative of kings not to care if their moods annoyed or displeased those around them.

"I come with confirmation that my earlier request was indeed correct," Rika said, showing no signs that the king's shortness had bothered her in the slightest. "Barreck says that more is indeed needed. Much more, in fact, if the experiments are to proceed at their current pace."

The king set his wine down and fidgeted with his tunic. The rate at which the Academy was using or consuming the supplies he was giving them had definitely accelerated, however Rika might subtly infer that she wasn't convinced. He'd begun keeping private records of his own, something he should have done ages ago, and they definitely showed a marked acceleration in how often these requests were made.

On the one hand, it didn't really matter. It's not like he couldn't supply the research of the Academy indefinitely, but he had always felt a certain misgiving about it. So much power was at stake. So much, that to willingly, voluntarily, give away even the faintest echo of that power, gnawed at him. It gnawed at him even though he knew the experiments in question had already produced the means by which he meant to secure his throne for generations to come.

Still, if someone with access to the work had decided to lay aside a stash for himself, it could prove troublesome. Rika thought him paranoid but why not? Why couldn't one of his enemies have someone from the Academy in their employ? And if so, why couldn't they be gathering more than just information for their employer?

"Is Your Majesty of the same opinion as before?"

"Yes," Eirmon said. "I want you to proceed as directed."

"I think that's wise," Rika said, and the simplicity of her agreement surprised him. She'd been dismissive of the idea a few days ago.

"You do?" Eirmon said, peering at her cautiously. "You've changed your mind?"

"Yes," Rika said matter-of-factly. "I've thought about it since, and I suspect you might be right."

"Really?"

"It's not that unprecedented."

"What isn't?"

"Your being right," she said with a smile.

He frowned, even though he knew that none of the stewards were close enough to hear. "I meant my changing my mind, of course," she added.

"Yes, of course," he said. "Well, we'll figure out who is to help later."

"In the meantime?"

"I'll go down with you tomorrow."

"Good," Rika said. "I'll take word to Barreck myself."

"He isn't to know about the other."

"I know," Rika said, seriousness displacing the playfulness that had been twinkling in her eye. "Whatever passes between us, I always do as you command."

"If thievery is going on at the Academy," Eirmon said, "I want it stopped, and I want anyone who so much as considered being a part of it apprehended. This isn't just stealing from the Academy. This is stealing from me."

"If there is theft going on," Rika answered him, placing noticeable emphasis on the *if*, "then it will be discovered, along with the guilty party or parties."

"I'm counting on it."

"I will do my best," Rika said.

"See that you do," Eirmon replied, then changed the subject. "And don't forget that I asked you to report back to me about how our experiments are affecting the ecology of Barra-Dohn. Do you have anything more for me on that yet?"

"I'm afraid I have nothing concrete, Your Majesty," Rika said, shrugging her shoulders. "The anecdotal evidence that there are effects on all aspects of our ecology seems pretty strong. Beyond the unusually productive crop yields of recent years and stories of oversize rats and vermin, people are beginning to notice an upward trend in birth weights. I even heard several reports about the increased height of many children under ten and most children under five."

"Deslo's not any taller than I'd expect a boy in my family to be," Eirmon said.

"No, but he's ten already, isn't he?" Rika said. "And since we're not sure how exactly our work is doing this, we wouldn't want to extrapolate too much from one counterexample."

"So are we doing harm to our children?" Eirmon asked, examining Rika carefully. "What good will all my work be to secure Barra-Dohn's power if we poison it along the way?"

"I understand the concern, but we don't have any reason to think that," Rika replied. "Think about it. The increased crop yields are good changes. The larger, stronger rats, though bad for us, are good for the rats. Even if our kids are being affected, which we don't know for sure yet, why wouldn't we assume that being bigger and possibly stronger isn't a good thing? Perhaps we'll even be able to deliberately manipulate this effect going forward to ensure larger, stronger, faster, and even healthier children."

"Well, I want you to make sure that some of those researchers I'm funding down there are working on this," Eirmon said. "I want them gathering more than anecdotes."

"Yes, Your Majesty." Rika nodded and began to withdraw, but Eirmon didn't let her get far.

"I had an interesting report today," he said.

"Oh?" Rika said as she stopped.

"Yes," Eirmon went on. "It appears that my daughter-in-law spent quite a bit of time in the market yesterday."

Rika looked confused. "What's interesting about that, Your Majesty?"

"She was accompanied by the Amhuru, Tchinchura."

Eirmon saw Rika processing what he'd told her, but if it struck any particular chords, she gave nothing away. "Is this association a problem?"

Eirmon shrugged. "It's probably nothing, but as I've told you already, I don't want him to know anything about what we're doing."

"I agree," Rika said, "but Nara can't tell him what she doesn't know."

"I understand," Eirmon said, "but does she know more than I think she does? Or even more than she thinks she does? Can the Amhuru glean from her those things I desire to keep hidden?"

Rika frowned. "If you'll allow me, Your Majesty. That seems . . . unlikely."

"Perhaps," Eirmon replied. "But even if you think I'm being paranoid, you will tell me if you observe them together."

"As you wish."

"You may go," Eirmon said after a moment, and Rika left him without comment.

Eirmon picked up his wine and turned back to the waves. He didn't think his son's wife could tell the Amhuru anything important that he didn't want the man to know, but his anxiety over even this remote possibility underscored the untenable nature of the situation. Even if he managed to keep Tchinchura in the dark, it was all but assured that Zangira would discover his secret. That was a price he'd been willing to pay to separate the Amhuru, but he was kidding himself if he thought he could keep the secret and avoid more drastic action.

The hope he'd harbored that they might just go away had disappeared. It was unrealistic. He would have to take care of them, but how? And what would happen then? Would more come? How many Amhuru were there? Even with all of his power, how many could he handle?

He was getting ahead of himself. At the moment, two were here, and he hadn't even handled them yet. He would need to rectify that and fairly soon. Tchinchura needed to die, and it needed to happen before Zangira returned.

16

SANDSTORM

The sand on the wind was growing thick. At first, only a few grains had been detected in the mouth or nostrils, irritants in the eyes. The wind had since picked up, and, whirling clouds of sand were growing ominously to the north. As awareness of the coming storm had spread, men on each ship had passed out goggles and scarves. That they'd not needed them before on the trip had been fortunate, for the crossing from Barra-Dohn to Garranmere could be perilous.

Kaden adjusted his thick, clear goggles and smiled as Zangira fumbled a bit with his own pair.

The Amhuru had waited to don both the goggles and the scarf, but as the storm had intensified, he had decided to put them on. He wound the scarf around his head, cinching it tightly after getting it just right across his mouth and nose, doing all this without turning his eyes away from the approaching clouds.

Kaden looked back at the storm too. He didn't think the whirling heart of the sandstorm would pass over them, but it would be a near miss, and the going might be rough for a while.

"Have you been in a sandstorm before?" Deslo asked, looking up at the Amhuru, his voice faint above the wind.

"Yes," Zangira answered.

"Was your sandship capsized?"

"I wasn't on a sandship."

Kaden and Deslo exchanged looks of surprise as Zangira added, "I was on foot."

"Walking?" Deslo said, voicing Kaden's own thoughts. "You were caught in a sandstorm while walking?"

"Yes," Zangira said. "More than once."

Deslo shook his head. "I'm glad I've never been out walking in a sandstorm before."

"Me too," Kaden said, shaking his head.

"Are you afraid?" Zangira asked, stooping beside Deslo and placing his hand on the boy's shoulder.

"A little."

"Good. You're right to be," Zangira said.

"Why? You two aren't," Deslo said, looking from Zangira to Kaden and back.

"No, but fear can be good. It can teach us wisdom," Zangira answered. "If you forget that a storm in the desert, on the sea, in life can kill you, you may already be dead."

"You're supposed to be helping him not be afraid," Kaden said, leaning over toward the Amhuru, a touch of scolding in his voice.

"Am I?"

"Yes," Deslo said. "And you're not helping."

Zangira bent over so that his well-wrapped face was just a few inches in front of Deslo's. "This storm won't capsize these ships, and you are safe from both the wind and the sand. Does that help?"

"A little."

"Good, but don't turn that comfort into folly by forgetting that wind and sand can kill."

"I won't," Deslo said, looking as if he didn't understand completely why Zangira was picking now of all times to remind him that sandstorms can kill.

Zangira seemed to be considering saying more, but something distracted him, not on the ship but on the distant horizon. He walked to the rail and searched the desert behind them, through the sandy maelstrom that was building in intensity.

Kaden couldn't see anything, but he followed the Amhuru to the rail. "What is it?"

"A handful of sliders," Zangira said. "They're some distance away, and their riders are standing beside them watching the fleet. A man just arrived on another slider and dismounted. That's how I saw them. I can't see how many men."

Kaden peered through the swirling sands. He'd suspected before that the Amhuru had remarkable vision, but if what Zangira was saying were true, then he hadn't guessed at nearly how amazing it was. "I don't see anything."

"You can send for a looking glass," Zangira said, "and maybe you will be able to see them with that, or you can trust me that they're there."

Kaden looked at Zangira wondering, not for the first time, about those piercing golden eyes. Did they have anything to do with this? Anything to do with the legends that said Amhuru wore Zerura and that Zerura changed the Amhuru over time until they could see and hear things ordinary men couldn't? Could do things ordinary men couldn't?

Kaden had seen Tchinchura balance on the stone rail at the palace and had seen the thrown axe fly backward up into his hand. He was inclined to trust Zangira. "How many do you see, and how far away would you say they are?"

"I couldn't have said with certainty before and with less so now, but there appear to be four or five sliders. The clump of men is harder to make out."

"How far?"

"Across this terrain in these conditions?" Zangira said, shaking his head. "I don't know. Probably not as far as I think."

"I doubt they're scouts," Kaden said, thinking out loud. "Garranmere would have no reason to be looking for us."

"Unless they have no intention of abiding by your father's ultimatum and know this might be coming. They may already be looking to the defense of the city."

"They might not intend to obey," Kaden said, "but I still think it unlikely they'd already be watching for us. My father's unwillingness to wait forty days surprised even me."

"Despite yourself," Zangira said, turning his piercing gaze upon Kaden. "Perhaps you want to believe the best about your father, and you are disappointed when that desire is disappointed. Garranmere might not share your hope and so might actually prepare for the worst."

"Possibly," Kaden said, wondering if it were true. Had he been surprised at Eirmon's move because deep down he wanted to believe better of his father?

"I guess," he continued, "in the end it doesn't matter much if they're soldiers, hunters, merchants, or just passersby in the wrong place at the wrong time. It doesn't even matter if they're looking for us or not. They've seen us, and I don't want word to reach Garranmere ahead of us if I can help it, even though we should be within sight of the city by tomorrow night, and the secret will be out."

"Perhaps they already know," Zangira said. "Maybe they've already been warned and these are scouts sent to track our movements."

"All the more reason to stop them."

"Would it not be wise to take them alive so we can find out why they're here and what they know?"

"Yes, I'd prefer capturing to killing," Kaden said, "but I also prefer killing to escaping." He turned from the rail and for a moment hesitated before Zangira. "Thanks for the warning."

"I am in your service," Zangira said with a slight bow. "And as your son's safety is the chief service I can render you now, your success is as important to me as it is to you."

Kaden nodded and moved quickly back down the sandship toward the bow. It wasn't long before some twenty or thirty sliders, gathered from their own ship and the others nearby, were racing through the howling wind and swirling sands in the direction of the group Zangira had seen.

Kaden knew that sending sliders out into a sandstorm was a risky move. Bright beacons were lit and lifted onto poles so that they hung high above each of the nearby ships, glowing in the storm, to guide the sliders home once they were free to return. Still, depending on how things went out there and how far the chase might lead the men who had gone, finding their way back might be tricky no matter what they did.

Kaden also hoped that the men who had been watching the fleet would be taken alive, especially since he didn't know if they were soldiers. His task at Garranmere hadn't become any more palatable since leaving Barra-Dohn, and he didn't want any more blood than necessary on his hands. So he stood and waited.

As he stood at the rail, several sliders emerged out of the sand-fog, moving quickly toward the ships. When the sliders in front saw the beacons ahead, however, they veered away, so Kaden realized these were not from his ships and wanted to avoid them.

As they turned more parallel to the fleet, though, more sliders emerging out of the sandstorm behind cut them off. He watched as soldiers riding behind the drivers of those sliders unleashed a volley of bolts that shot across the intervening distance, almost impervious to the wind and storm that raged around them. Several bolts struck both the slider out in front and its driver, who was pierced multiple times and knocked out of his seat. The slider rolled to the side as the driver was thrown off, and the slider fell from the Arua field, slamming into the sand below. The body of the unfortunate driver fell equally hard, landing headfirst with an inaudible thud where he lay, half-buried and still, a pair of meridium shafts protruding from his body.

The second slider was not hit, but the driver was struck in his right leg and his foot slipped from the pedal. The slider slowed and veered off to the side, back in the direction of his pursuers. The sliders behind him swarmed in, and he was quickly surrounded. The wounded man reached down with his hands to lift his damaged leg back onto the pedal, but he seemed unable to make his foot work properly and never did get the slider going again. He was hauled off the back of the slider unceremoniously by a handful of soldiers and fell into the sand. He was soon bound and thrown over the back of another slider and was soon on his way to the sandship.

When the wounded man was brought on deck, Kaden spoke briefly with the soldiers who had captured him, directing that the frightened man, who certainly didn't look like a soldier, be taken below. Zangira stood with Deslo at a distance, watching. The soldiers got back on their sliders and disappeared out into the storm.

Kaden walked back to Zangira and Deslo. He noticed that his son was staring at the overturned slider embedded in the sand near the sandship. Actually, he was looking in that direction, but Kaden couldn't tell if the boy was looking at the slider or its dead driver, which the wind was already burying with ruthless efficiency.

He reached out and put his hand on Deslo's shoulder. "Even though we talked about the ugly side of war, it's a different thing to see it, isn't it?"

Deslo nodded. His hands firmly gripped the rail of the sandship, and he did not turn from the scene beside them. "More men are going to die, aren't they?"

"Yes."

"A lot more?"

"Yes," Kaden said again, wishing he had a different answer to offer.

"Why?" Deslo asked, and when he turned to look at his father, Kaden saw that the look on his face wasn't sadness but anger.

Kaden couldn't think of a satisfactory answer to this question, and he looked at Zangira, but he knew the Amhuru couldn't help. In the end, silence was the only answer Deslo received.

"The king shouldn't be doing this," Deslo murmured, so quietly that Kaden almost didn't catch the words above the wind.

"It is important to be careful when we judge," Zangira said.

Kaden was glad for the Amhuru's prudent interjection. Kaden had been tempted to agree.

"Often, there are things we don't know, factors we haven't considered," Zangira said. "They can make all the difference."

"But isn't it also important to treat people fairly?" Deslo asked, turning toward Zangira, the anger still clear in his tone. Deslo pointed. "That man is dead, and I don't understand why."

"You're right," Zangira said. "Justice is important. Lives are not to be taken lightly. But what I'm saying is that not knowing the reason why this is happening isn't the same thing as saying there is no reason. There might be an explanation."

"I think we would have heard it by now if there was," Deslo said, turning back to Kaden, who felt the implication.

Deslo had heard and understood his silence.

The sea was a little choppy beneath *The Sorry Rogue,* but Captain Elil D'Sarza held the looking glass steady. She'd given up trying to count the ships in the Amattai harbor, but it was still difficult to stop looking at them. All the ships she surveyed bore the same light green sails with the same bizarre insignia—a golden fist clenched tightly. She'd never seen a ship with that particular sail before here or anywhere else, and today that was all she could see.

She lowered the looking glass at last. Geffen watched her closely, waiting for her to react, but she didn't know how to react. What was she to think?

"You see, Captain?" he said finally, breaking the silence.

"I see," she said. She slid the looking glass closed and slipped it into the small leather case that hung by her side. "What are the chances Amattai suddenly and without warning built a vast navy, merchant, or otherwise?"

"Slightly less than none," Geffen replied, his bewilderment at what they had found showing again. "I doubt Barra-Dohn has a fraction of this many ships at their disposal. You don't think King Omiir would stand for Amattai to have so many, do you?"

"I've never met the man," D'Sarza said, "but from what I've heard, no. No, I don't."

"So they've come from somewhere else, right?"

"That would appear to be the only other choice, Geffen," D'Sarza said, glaring at her first mate. He knew that stating the obvious was one of her pet peeves, so he at least had the decency to look sheepish under her scrutiny.

"But I've never seen that insignia before," Geffen said, as though trying to recover a bit of lost ground with the observation. "Not at sea, not at port, not on shore, and I've served beneath the mast for more than thirty years, Captain."

"I've never seen it either," D'Sarza murmured. "It's very strange."

"Strange doesn't even begin to describe it," Geffen said, then hastily added before D'Sarza could fix him with her glare again, "though what would begin to describe it, Captain, I'm sure I have no idea."

D'Sarza reluctantly agreed with him. "Neither do I."

"So what do you want to do?"

"Sail on," D'Sarza said, then turned from Geffen to survey the distant harbor again. "Now, before we're spotted."

"What will we do with the cargo?"

"Sell it somewhere else."

"But Carmeran . . ."

"Carmeran can get his supplies elsewhere."

Geffen nodded.

She knew he was aware of how reluctant D'Sarza was to lose business. She'd sail just about anywhere and do just about anything to make or keep a customer. Just about. Sailing into that harbor with those ships, though, was something she wasn't going to do, and she knew that despite his halfhearted protest, Geffen didn't want her to. He liked profit more than adventure, as did she, though both were willing to put up with a fair amount of the latter if an even larger share of the former was on the line. Still, D'Sarza was a profiteer, not a gambler, and too many variables—all green and gold—did not make sailing into that harbor worthwhile.

"So, where to?"

"We'll head down the coast for a couple of days and take shelter in a cove I know. From there, we'll take samples inland to Garranmere and see if we can't drum up some interest. Maybe someone there will be as willing to pay for quality as Carmeran."

"Garranmere?" Geffen said. "You never do business there. Shouldn't we just head on to Barra-Dohn?"

"It may come to that," D'Sarza said, "but let's try Garranmere first. Dealing with kings is risky."

"Risky but lucrative."

"Sometimes, but dealing with envious neighbors who want desperately to have what even their king does not can be even more lucrative."

"But Captain, you can't be sure about what King Omiir does or doesn't have."

"Very true," D'Sarza agreed, "but very possibly, neither can they. Carmeran wasn't."

Geffen smiled. "Oh, Captain, you are a rogue."

"I am indeed, Geffen," Elil agreed, sighing as she turned her back on the Amattai harbor. "And a sorry one at that."

17

THE MISSING PIECE

E irmon didn't like doing anything that felt even vaguely like sneaking. Sneaking felt like hiding, hiding felt like fear, and Eirmon wasn't afraid of anything. He liked the effect fear had on others, but for the most part, he was immune to it. Even his suspicion that the two Amhuru had come to Barra-Dohn because they suspected what he had and what he had done to get it or even worse that they didn't just suspect but knew—even that, didn't elicit fear. There were only two of them, and they could be killed if necessary. Would be killed, just like the Amhuru he had taken it from in the first place, because he didn't think it wise to wait to find out what they did or didn't know.

Besides, he did have one of the six original fragments of the Golden Cord at his disposal. That kind of power lying curled around your calf, nestled against your skin, touching you all the time went a long way toward dispelling the things that caused fear in ordinary men.

Still, entering the Academy through a small back entrance with only a handful of Davrii who accompanied him in near concealment through the streets felt like sneaking. He knew it was necessary, that his increasingly frequent trips to the Academy would occasion comment and attention that had been wisely avoided hitherto. The issue wasn't so much the people of the city but the rank-and-file scientists and researchers who worked in the Academy but didn't know about the ongoing research sustained and made possible by his periodic donations. Even so, he didn't like sneaking.

Rika met him inside and silently guided him swiftly to the small, secure room where the work was to be done. He stepped in behind her and waited while she closed and locked the door behind them. He insisted on the door being locked, even though the Davrii would patiently wait in the hall, standing guard against no one in particular. This area of the Academy was off limits to all but the few who knew what the king was there to do. As they knew Eirmon didn't want to be disturbed while he was doing it, they would not come until Rika took them word that he was finished.

With the door locked, Eirmon bent over and slid his pant leg up over his right calf, exposing the fragment of Zerura. He tapped it lightly three times, and it began slowly to uncoil from around his calf until it lay wriggling almost rhythmically in that odd almost semisolid state it assumed whenever he took it off. The sheen of the Zerura always appeared to him a little brighter when he took it off, perhaps especially here because the room was dim.

Eirmon took it over to the plain wooden table with the small hatchet lying upon it. "Bring the box."

Rika took up the large box from beside the door and carried it over, setting it on the side of the table beside the place where the king had set the Zerura fragment, still quivering where it lay. With a swift blow, the king cut about a third of the fragment off. For a moment, both pieces lay wriggling near each other.

Then they began to shake and vibrate much faster than the Zerura fragment had been moving previously, and suddenly both pieces seemed to stretch and expand. The one that had grown from the shorter piece grew still and lay motionless on the table. Eirmon handed it to Rika, who put it in the box. The one that had grown from the longer piece did not stop moving. It merely slowed down, resuming its more rhythmic and methodical motion upon the table as though nothing had happened.

"It doesn't matter how many times I see you do that," Rika said. "I still marvel at it."

Eirmon cut again, and while he waited for the smaller piece to expand and come to rest so he could give it to Rika to put in the box, he nodded. "I know. I've cut this thing thousands of times, and if I had all the pieces back, it would fill a room larger than this. Still I cut over and over. Still it yields more, never exhausted, never consumed."

Rika set the second piece in the box while the king waited for the larger piece to expand so he could cut it again. "I know you don't like the idea of leaving the orginal here, but if we could study it, perhaps we could figure out how the replication . . ."

The hatchet struck the table hard, and the king looked up at Rika. "We've settled this. You know I won't leave it."

"I would supervise it myself."

"No," Eirmon said, as he took up the next piece and handed it over. "You have all the other pieces to examine and use in your experiments."

"And we're grateful," Rika said, "but you know they can't replicate endlessly like the original. These pieces don't replicate at all."

"What I know is that . . ." Eirmon started and then paused as he cut again. "Each piece I give you is cut from the original. Each piece I give you is Zerura, even as the original is Zerura. How could they be different?"

"I don't know," Rika said. "That's what we want to find out."

"I also know that every Amhuru bears a piece of Zerura somewhere on his body, derived from one of these originals." Eirmon handed the next piece to Rika and struck the Zerura on the table in front of him again. "Somehow those replicas not only retain the power of Zerura, like the replicas we produce, but they also can be put on and taken off like mine can. They're sensitive to the touch of their bearers, as I've told you before."

"I know you have," Rika said. "I don't doubt it. Still, we can't figure out how to 'activate' the pieces you give us so that they can be worn like yours. They don't respond to any of us, no matter what we do."

"Which means," Eirmon said, cutting again, "that we still don't know lots of things about how the Zerura works. Perhaps with more study, you'll figure that out. Maybe how the replication works too."

"Perhaps."

Eirmon handed her the next piece, and she carefully placed it in the box along with the others. "You sound uncertain."

Rika shrugged. "We've figured out how to do all kinds of things with Zerura, but we're no closer to understanding how Zerura does these things than when we first began to study it."

"You haven't given up, have you?" Eirmon asked, looking up after his next blow. He rested the hatchet on the table as he looked at Rika, a smile that was almost cruel curling on his lips while he wiped beads of sweat from his brow. "After all, you were the one who insisted that mystical explanations that required imaginary deities were nothing but foolish fancies. You insisted there was a physical explanation for Zerura and everything it could do, that time and patience and careful research would unlock those mysteries."

"And it will," Rika said, a look of cold determination appearing on her face. Eirmon nodded, acknowledging her answer, and then cut again. "Good," he said.

"I'd hate to think my confidence in you and in the Academy, which I so generously fund, has been misplaced."

He handed her the next piece, and she said nothing further. He continued to cut and she to collect, and conversation interrupted the process no further.

Rika accompanied Eirmon as he exited the Academy. He bid her a terse farewell and soon was gone, disappearing with his escort around the nearby corner. She watched him go, being careful to keep her anger concealed, even after he was gone. She hadn't gotten where she was in the world by being careless or by wearing her emotions on her sleeve. Schooling herself to reveal nothing, even when she didn't think anyone was looking, helped to ensure that she never did give anything away in those times when she might be observed unawares.

She went back inside, trying not to think of the request to attend the king in his chambers that would undoubtedly come that evening. His obvious enjoyment of the verbal jabs he took at her, both in public and in private, didn't seem to diminish his physical appetite for her. In fact, if anything, those jabs seemed to increase it, a fact she'd struggled with at first. She knew she'd put herself in the way of this situation and worked steadily to engineer it, and she also knew that if things went as planned, it wouldn't last indefinitely. Neither of those things consoled her at the moment.

She made her way through the halls until she reached the room where Barreck would be waiting. Reaching up, she pulled her ponytail tightly and tugged the bottom of her neatly tailored jacket, straightening it out again. Then she stepped into the room.

Barreck looked up from the box of Zerura on the desk before him and smiled. His light gray eyes revealed the hint of a smile, and he swept his fingers lightly through the tuft of blond hair that hung down over his forehead.

Rika pulled the door closed, peeking out into the hall quickly to see if anyone was coming first and then crossed the room to Barreck.

He pulled her tightly and kissed her hungrily. She didn't want to let him go, but she knew it was foolish to linger. Still, it was difficult to step back, and she could feel him hesitate too.

No sooner had they separated, though, when the door opened a short way and another of the Academy scientists poked his head inside. "I'm supposed to take the box downstairs?"

"Sure," Barreck said, pushing the box further out in front of him as a silent invitation for him to come and take it.

The man at the door stepped quickly into the room. Without need of further encouragement, he took up the box, mumbled his thanks, and disappeared quickly.

Rika stared thoughtfully at the door as it closed. "You don't think people know, do you?"

"About us?"

"Yes."

"Why?"

"He didn't look at me," Rika said. "I mean at all. The whole time he was here."

Barreck smirked. "The whole time? The whole twenty seconds he was here?"

"Don't do that," Rika said, frowning. "I just had to put up with him, thinking he's clever as he mocks me."

"Sorry," Barreck said, instantly repentant. "You know I'd never mock you, not seriously."

"I know," Rika said. "You really don't think his behavior was odd?"

Barreck shrugged. "Not necessarily. He's important enough to be working on the Zerura project but not enough that you know his name, so he's a bit nervous around us."

"Do you know his name?" Rika asked.

"Of course, I do. It's Jastin."

"Jastin?"

"Or something like that," Barreck said, smiling. "Hey, I'm here all the time. I don't spend most of my days in the palace with the king's grandson, do I?"

"Well, it's paid off, hasn't it?" Rika asked, hoping she didn't sound as defensive to Barreck as she thought she did.

"It will, I hope," he replied, "though technically it hasn't paid off yet."

"No, not yet," she agreed. "But soon. It will pay off soon."

She glanced back at the door for a second, then turned back to Barreck. "Speaking of paying off, you did lay some aside before Jastin took the box, right?"

"Of course, I did," Barreck said, motioning to an old, tattered cloth lying in a dingy corner of the room. "Ten pieces are wrapped in there. I'll lock the room when we leave and take them out later."

"Good." Rika nodded. "We're going to need to squeeze out as much as we can each time if we're going to be ready to go in a couple months."

"About that," Barreck began, a bit hesitantly. "I've been thinking . . ."

Rika groaned. "Oh, no."

"Hey," Barreck said, feigning a hurt look. "I thought we weren't going to mock."

"I'm just giving some of your own back."

"Fair enough," Barreck said, but he hesitated before going on. When he appeared convinced that Rika was ready to be serious, he continued. "I don't see why we don't just go now. We have plenty, and with so much of the army and the king's attention diverted by the war, the timing seems right."

"Then Eirmon will know we're the thieves," Rika said. "Even just now before he left, he reminded me to be diligent in investigating the missing Zerura. If you and I just disappear in the night, he'll figure it out, Barreck."

"So what? Whether we leave tomorrow or next week or next year, he'll figure it out when we go, won't he?"

"Not necessarily. Not if we stick to the plan. If we use enough of our stash to set up the fall guys like we talked about, he might not connect our disappearance with the Zerura at all."

"Not even when we disappear a month or two later?"

"Maybe," Rika shrugged. "Maybe not. He might just think I fell in love with you. That we ran away because we knew he'd never allow it."

"And when some of the weapons we've made for him and some of the technologies we've researched start showing up in Amattai or wherever we sell the Zerura and the secrets we've discovered about it, won't he know then?"

"He might," Rika said. "But what do we care? We'll be so far gone by then, he can be as angry as he likes. He'll never find us."

"I still think it would be safer if we go now," Barreck said, frowning as he gazed down at her. "He won't just let you go, even if he doesn't connect us to the Zerura theft. You know that. That makes his current preoccupation the most important variable in this equation."

"Listen," Rika said, reaching out and taking Barreck's hand firmly. "Remember what Eirmon told me. He intends to destroy Garranmere utterly. He wants refugees to flee throughout Aralyn, taking tales of the city's destruction with them so all will know the power he possesses. Remember?"

"I remember."

"Then remember why we don't want to move too soon," Rika said. "When we show up weeks or months after the arrival of these refugees, after the people of Amattai or Perone or Dar-Holdin or wherever have heard both the king's threats and the stories of his power. Then, Barreck, then the offer we bring of the very power Eirmon wields and the information they need to wield it too will be at maximum value. They will give us anything. Pay any price. We will leave with more wealth than you could ever imagine."

Barreck had listened patiently to every word, and when she finished, he took her hand gently in his own. "Will you tell them Eirmon has a limitless supply of the Zerura?"

"Probably not," Rika said. "If they ask where Eirmon got it, I'll probably say I don't know."

"They'll think they can fight him," Barreck continued. "They won't understand that as powerful as the Zerura is, he can overwhelm them with the sheer quantity of the things he can produce."

"I know," she said.

"They'll be slaughtered if they rebel against him."

"They might be," Rika said. "But they might be planning to rebel anyway. I would be. At least, we'll provide them with a fighting chance. They sure don't have one now. Besides, we have enough to worry about if we're going to pull this off without losing sleep over decisions that aren't ours to make."

"No," Barreck said, "I guess not."

Rika fixed Barreck with a level stare and said, "I need to know that you can do this, all of this. Setting up Academy scientists and accusing them falsely will hit a lot closer to home than wondering as we sail off into the sunset about what will happen once we're gone to people we don't even know."

"I know," Barreck said. "I'm prepared for that."

"Good," Rika said, reaching up and giving him a tender kiss. "We've come too far and paid too dear a price to turn back now."

"I know," Barreck said. "I wasn't thinking about turning back, just wondering how best to proceed is all."

Rika nodded and turned back toward the door. "Well, we should go down to the dig if we're still going to do that today. Eirmon will be expecting me back at the palace before too long."

"Sure," Barreck said, kissing her again. "Unfortunately, we're finished here anyway."

"Hold on," Rika said, remembering the king's admonition on the barge the previous day. "I almost forgot. Eirmon brought up the issue of Zerura's ecological effects again."

"Oh," Barreck said. "That's too bad. I guess we need to set up a team to look into that after all."

"Yeah," Rika begrudgingly agreed. "I think we do. I know we wanted as many people on the Zerura team working in development as possible, but we'll have to set some aside for this."

"That along with those we're going to set up to take the fall for the missing Zerura will slow down the work."

"I know," Rika said. "But it can't be avoided. I have to comply with his wishes or risk drawing unwanted attention. Besides, there's no guarantee we'd leave with substantially more insight into Zerura even if we didn't."

"No, we have no guarantees," Barreck said with a sigh. "There's no use bemoaning it. I'll let you know when I've set it up so you can report back to Eirmon."

"Thanks," Rika said, and they slipped out of the room.

It was cool, as always, in the tunnels near the bottom of the dig. Rika looked at the light glowing dimly overhead and wondered to herself for the hundredth time why the meridium reacted so differently down here. This many lights would have been almost too bright to bear in a space this small aboveground. Down here, though, they provided barely enough light to make out the rough contours of the passageway. It was counterintuitive. If veins of Zerura in the ground created the Arua field, and if the effects of the Arua field diminished the farther aboveground you went, why wouldn't those same effects intensify and increase the deeper you delved?

With Eirmon's taunts about not understanding Zerura still lingering, this mystery rankled rather than delighted her. It was another sign that he'd struck a nerve. Not knowing something, like why the Arua field did what it did or how it worked, wasn't usually frustrating. It was invigorating, a spur to explore and investigate the wonders of the world. It was her nature to find pleasure in puzzles, not frustration. She realized afresh just how much she needed to be free of Eirmon. His attention and affections were suffocating her. Even so, she would endure him as long as she had to, and when she left, it would be on her terms and with her fortune made at his expense.

Up ahead, Barreck stopped and turned to wait for her. "Can you hear the work now?"

She stopped and listened. The distant ringing of tools against rock echoed in the half light of the dimly lit tunnels. "Yes, I hear them now."

Not too far ahead, the tunnel opened up into a wider space, a staging platform for the work going on below. Ropes, boxes, and tools of all shapes and sizes lay stacked on either side of them. Rika stood with Barreck at the edge of the mine shaft, a large gaping hole that opened up before them. A narrow rim went in both directions around the shaft, wide enough for two men to walk side by side but not comfortably. Rika looked down at the men hard at work, almost seventy-five feet below them. A handful of others were operating a pulley system on the other side of the hole on another broad platform, unloading rock from large buckets before sending the empty ones back down.

It had taken eight years to get down this far, some three hundred feet beneath the Academy. It would have been easier and quicker if they hadn't had to keep moving the central shaft, but the plan drawn up by the engineers when the dig began had advised it. In truth, they had advised Eirmon not to dig beneath the Academy at all, but when he would not be dissuaded, they had at least insisted that he not dig straight down.

Rika, though not a specialist in the finer points of structures and engineering, could see their concerns. The Academy, which had long ago been a temple or something, was a mammoth building, and the prospect of digging out a large portion of the ground that supported it had been concerning to the engineers given the task of making this dig possible. Even so, Eirmon, despite his generally dismissive attitude toward the Old Stories, was determined to mine for Zerura here, so here the work went forward.

And to the engineers' credit, their strategy of boring down only so far in one place, then carving out a small horizontal tunnel parallel to the surface, then boring down the next distance in a different spot, thereby distributing the growing structural weakness below the Academy, certainly seemed to have worked so far. All fears of settling in the Academy's foundation and of possible foundational cracks had proved unfounded as the ongoing work was having no obvious effect on the building above at all.

Rika looked at the workers across the way and down below, though she doubted they could hear her even if they'd been paying any attention to her, which they weren't. She leaned in close to Barreck's ear. "Wouldn't it be something if they found a vein? Think of what we could take away with us then."

Barreck nodded, also surveying the scene around them before he turned to whisper back. "They'd have to find it fast."

Rika nodded. She knew that the plans were to take the shaft down just a little more, then burrow through the rock a few hundred feet in whatever direction the engineers figured was safest, before starting another shaft down once more. This would be the fifth vertical shaft, intended no doubt to go down another seventy-five feet, unless they struck a vein of Zerura first.

Unless. It was the big gamble of this project. Rika and her peers discounted the mystical language of the Old Stories as the product of a time steeped in superstition before the glories of science had liberated their forefathers from ignorance. They knew Zerura was real. They'd held it in their hands. They knew it could do wondrous things. They'd seen those wonders with their own eyes.

It was as easy to believe that veins of Zerura lay far beneath the world's surface and generated the Arua field as it was to believe any other hypothesis about the field and its effect on meridium. Easier, in fact. So Rika felt that this whole dig was a waste of time dependent entirely on a legend that seemed as unbelievable as all the other Old Stories. Yet, she wondered how great a change the discovery of a vein of Zerura here might bring.

If Zerura were found and if the Zerura mined here could be replicated like Eirmon's piece over and over without any apparent limit, then everything would change. That much she knew. Whether the changes would be for good or ill, that was another matter.

18

GARRANMERE

Kaden yawned and stretched as he walked across the deck of the sandship. After being so long in transit, it was odd not to feel the ship in motion, though admittedly, across the smoother stretches of desert there hadn't been much to feel. For now at least, the ship was still, like the sands beneath its hull.

His sleep had been broken, his dreams unpleasant, and no doubt like many others both on the sandships and in Garranmere, he now waited uneasily for the uncertain dawn. The light of the summer moons, as they slipped slowly toward the horizon in opposite directions, shone wanly on the quiet desert. The last hour of night was one of Kaden's favorite times of the day. Soon the light of morning would break, and the new day would be upon them. A new day full of blood and death, fire and smoke. Many of those who would rise to greet it would not live to see its end nor would they walk the cool sands again beneath the gentle moons.

When the sandships had at last anchored for the night a few hours after sunset for most of the soldiers, the walls of Garramere must have appeared as indefinite grayness, glinting slightly in the pale moonlight. Zangira, though, saw more than that. He could see distant figures moving back and forth on top of them, or so he said to Kaden, and he could see where the solid wall ended and the enormous gate began.

By now, Kaden no longer questioned the Amhuru's remarkable ability to see what he could not. He simply accepted Zangira's testimony as fact.

Garranmere sat beside the Behrn River, which this time of year was only a sandy channel that hadn't seen water in months and wouldn't see water again for almost as long. In fact, a portion of the currently waterless Behrn ran beneath the vast city walls for several hundred feet. From that section of the river, several long sluices and aqueducts ran down beneath the city to feed a network of enormous cisterns. The quantity of water that could be stored there was staggering, and yet the rushing waters of the river during the rainy season were generally adequate to fill them. They were in turn generally adequate to keep the city well supplied during the long arid months of the dry season.

Even so, a small army of water managers took daily measurements of the water levels and kept meticulous records of Garranmere's water usage. They released frequently updated projections for how many more weeks the cisterns could keep the city supplied at current rates of use. An outlander might find that they and their reports bordered on the paranoid. But most outlanders had never known the fear of parceling out tepid, sandy water by the cup from the cistern dregs while neither cloud nor rain were anywhere visible on the horizon and when each morning's sunrise brought only the promise of heat and misery without hope of relief.

The Behrn ran almost north to south here, though it tailed off a bit to the southwest and ended not far away in an inglorious stretch of ground that was little more than a mudhole. But during the rainy season, the water not siphoned off for use by

Garranmere formed a small lake that appeared and disappeared within the space of a month. Small thick doors dotted the city walls on that western side of the city, so people from within could have direct access to the river during the rainy season. But the main gate faced southwest so that large sandships both entered and left, moving essentially parallel to the river.

It was that massive gate that Kaden watched in the waning moments of the peaceful dark. He had circled below the city in the night, and now the entire fleet sat anchored in a wide arc facing that southern wall and gate. The left flank of the fleet extended right up to the Behrn riverbank, which wasn't much of a natural defense without water, but it was a natural demarcation line, nonetheless. The right flank extended far to the east of the gate, with Kaden's sandship fairly close to the middle of the line, placing it just a little east of the gate.

Garranmere was built to withstand siege. The walls were thick and tall, the solitary gate strong, and the sections where the riverbed entered and exited beneath the walls were protected with massive gates that would allow for the entrance of water and little else. Controlling the only large stores of water for hundreds of miles in any direction in the middle of a vast desert, the city always had a clear advantage over any would-be invaders, who had to haul water with them. Bringing some water was, of course, not only possible but necessary, but how could an army big enough to actually smash through the walls or the gate and pose a threat to the city also bring enough water to endure until they did? Especially in the heat of summer, when no rain would bring relief by providing a natural supply?

Kaden wondered if those inside the walls felt reassured by these facts as they gazed out on the vast fleet now arrayed against them. Perhaps they did. Perhaps they didn't. Garranmere's strengths were well known throughout Aralyn, so if an army had come in midsummer, they must have brought a certain confidence with them that a protracted siege would not be necessary. Even if Garranmere's defenders trusted the thickness of their walls, they must have some questions about what gave this army hope. What had they brought? What devices and what strategy had induced them to brave the desert crossing with so many men and ships? What were they planning that they believed would either get them inside or draw the defenders out?

Kaden ran his hand through his thick hair. What were the defenders of the city thinking and feeling as they stood their posts this morning? Were they confident in themselves and their strength? Were there chinks in their courage? Did unspoken fears slip in and plant seeds of doubt? Did those seeds find ready soil in fear, and did they grow unchecked in many hearts at the thought of strength and wonders they could not imagine? Did the simple fact that they could not conceive of what an army might have brought that would threaten them make them even more afraid, unable to see the danger for which they could not prepare?

The man captured in the sandstorm had confirmed that Garranmere wasn't expecting an attack, at least, not imminently. Since he was no soldier, he denied any official purpose for being out on his slider. He was only a hunter who had been out with some friends for a few days. The first signs of the coming sandstorm had induced them to head back, only to find that the fleet from Barra-Dohn had cut them off from their most direct way back to Garranmere. He was just an unfortunate man who happened to be in the wrong place at the wrong time.

None of the others from his party had been brought back alive, but from what Kaden could gather from the sometimes confusing reports of the soldiers sent out to hunt them, one or two men might have evaded capture in the storm. So word of their approach had perhaps preceded them, but by how many hours and to what effect it was hard to tell. When the sandships had coasted within sight of the city just after sunset, the big gate had already been shut, and no one had stirred from Garranmere during the long night.

Kaden did not doubt that many people had endured sleepless nights inside Garranmere. The city's defense must be looked to.

Eirmon's ultimatum had preceded them, and now a giant fleet had come. It had come too early to fit with the timetable given by the king, but it had come. There could be few plausible reasons why such a fleet would come with peaceful intent, so it would now be clear to all that the intent was not peaceful. Perhaps the only questions for the people of Garranmere about the intention of the fleet were these: how long before the city was attacked? Were any conditions going to be offered by which such an attack could be avoided?

Aside from those, they had another deeper and more fundamental question, but it was not a question of intent. It was a question of power. And as fundamental as it was, it was a question the defenders of Garranmere would not voice, for the real answer to it they could not fathom. If hostilities could not be avoided, would the gate and walls be strong enough? Did the ships from Barra-Dohn hold some secret terror they could neither imagine nor resist?

Kaden knew the answers to these questions, and he knew the new day would bring an end to hope for those who asked them.

Deslo was still sound asleep when Zangira went up on deck, and the Amhuru was glad to let him sleep. Whatever the day held, the boy could use the rest. The Amhuru heard voices and turned to see a pair of soldiers leading the prisoner taken in the sandstorm between them. Kaden followed a few steps behind, and the party stopped beside a slider resting by the gangway.

As soon as they stopped, the soldiers moved quickly to open the gate and lower the gangway. Kaden stood by the man, whose hands were tied securely with rope. Zangira could see the man was trembling, even from a distance and through the pale moonlight. Kaden looked uncomfortable too and stood staring at Garranmere while this went on, so both captor and captive stood side by side, paying no visible attention to one another.

When the two soldiers had walked the slider down the gangway so that it now hovered waiting on the Arua field, they walked back up and stood before Kaden. For the first time since coming out onto the deck, Kaden glanced at Zangira. The look said little, perhaps nothing more than "I know you're there." Zangira nodded to the prince, who nodded wearily in response.

Then Kaden turned to the prisoner. "You will take a message back to the city."

Zangira could see the prisoner relax as Kaden spoke. Perhaps he'd thought he was being brought on deck to be executed, but the prince's words spoke not of death but of freedom. As he had to know by now that most if not all of his hunting companions lay buried beneath the sand somewhere in the desert, the signs of palpable relief were appropriate.

"The message you are to take is both simple and important. You may not be admitted to the city right away. By your strange appearance, some may fear a ruse to get a door or even the gate itself open. Still, when the slider that drops you off heads back here to the ships, and when no one follows you to the gate, they should let you in eventually. When you're in, you must not delay. There won't be much time. Ask to see Lord Kazir or whichever high official of the city you prefer. Ask immediately. Do you understand?"

"Yes," the man said haltingly, no doubt unsure about what made Kaden's directive so urgent and perhaps afraid of what the rest of his message would be.

"When you are admitted, you will certainly be detained. Some gate captain or petty official will interrogate you to see what you can tell them about us and what explanation you offer for being dropped at the gate by one of our sliders. You can't spare time for that. Insist from the beginning, from the very first moment, that you must talk to Kazir, to someone important. You will step on the toes of whoever thinks they're in charge there. You will insult their inflated ego, and you might be mistreated for it. You're going to have to put up with it. Lives depend on it. Understand?"

"Yes," the man said again, this time more confidently.

"When they take you to Kazir, only then are you to tell them that Kaden Omiir gave you a message. Do you know that name?"

"Yes," the prisoner said, a little less confidently this time as he kept his eyes on Kaden.

"Tell him that Kaden Omiir wants him to know that the defense of the gate and walls must be abandoned immediately. Furthermore, anyone living on the southern side of the city should leave their homes and head to the northern half. Do you understand?"

"I think so."

"Not I think so. Yes. Everyone must go. Soldiers. Civilians. Everyone. Don't take anything with you. There may not be time. Just go. Clear the southern half of the city and don't delay. When the attack starts, it will be too late."

Kaden had finished talking, but he hadn't asked the man a question.

Zangira could see the prisoner's growing anxiety displayed in his jittery motions as he stood, waiting for Kaden to speak further, waiting to be given some clear command. Zangira knew the relief from realizing he wasn't going to be executed was gone now, replaced by a growing fear that something terrible was coming.

Kaden did speak again but not to the prisoner. He looked at one of the soldiers and said, "Take him as close to the gate as you feel safe going. Don't endanger yourself. He can walk whatever distance remains."

Kaden turned back to the prisoner then and added, "Though running might be a better idea."

The soldier led the prisoner down the gangway. He didn't sit him on the slider; he draped him over its seat. Then, taking the controls, he was soon on his way, speeding over the level sands between the ship and the Garranmere gate.

Zangira didn't watch their progress long because he was soon aware of Kaden's approach. When he turned to face the king's son, he noticed that the other soldier was now nowhere to be seen.

"You know they'll never abandon the wall or the gate," Zangira said.

"I know," Kaden said. A deep sadness lingered on his face and echoed in his voice.

"Would you, if the tables were reversed?" Zangira asked, watching Kaden carefully.

"No," Kaden said, and then thought for a minute. "Although, if I knew that the army threatening me had what we have, I might."

"But they don't know what you have," Zangira said.

Kaden, who had been gazing off in the direction of the city, turned and looked at Zangira.

The Amhuru knew Kaden must be wondering what Zangira had meant by that. He would be wondering if Zangira knew more than he really did know. Kaden had been surprisingly warm and friendly on the trip, certainly much more welcoming than Eirmon, but he had been tight-lipped about their mission to Garranmere and how he planned to defeat the city. Still, Zangira knew that if Eirmon had what the Amhuru thought he had, any number of terrible possibilities could explain Kaden's confidence.

"No, they don't," Kaden said at last.

"So why do it?"

"Why do what?"

"Why send the man back with a warning they won't heed?"

"Some might," Kaden said, looking out at the city again. "The soldiers won't, but word will get around, and some might. Besides," Kaden added, turning from the city to Zangira, "it's just as much for me as for them."

"For your conscience?"

"Yes," Kaden said. "Eirmon wouldn't have warned them. He'd just have destroyed them. I can't do that."

"Is your conscience that easily assuaged?" Zangira asked, ignoring Kaden's attempt to justify himself by comparing himself to his father. It was a hard question, and he knew it, but he spoke gently.

"No, but I have no choice." Kaden sounded bitter and made no effort to hide it.

"We always have choices," Zangira replied, speaking now even more gently. "We don't always like them, and we frequently misunderstand or avoid them, but we always have them."

"If I don't do this, he'll send someone else," Kaden said, the bitterness now gone, replaced with something much closer to despair. He turned to Zangira in the fading moonlight, and while the Amhuru could have been wrong, it certainly looked to him as though Kaden's face almost pleaded with him to understand. Understand and perhaps absolve. "He'll send someone else who will, and I will suffer needlessly for something I cannot change."

"Ahh," Zangira said. "You may be right, but that is a different matter. What's more, whether such suffering would be needless could be debated. Either way, the choice remains."

"The choice has been made," Kaden said, turning away from Zangira to face Garranmere once more, "and by a stronger hand than mine."

19

IRRESISTIBLE FORCE

Barely had the morning sun begun to peek over the horizon before the line of sandships began to disgorge their contents onto the desert sands. Everywhere Zangira looked, men moved along on the Arua, moving with purpose even if it was hard for the Amhuru to make out what those purposes were from where he stood as he watched their deployment. Sliders and sandships likewise shuttled among the men, usually slowly, though some darted quickly here and there as they carried out their orders.

Among the moving vehicles and milling companies of men were odd circular platforms that soon arrested Zangira's attention. Wooden and round, they hovered just as well as any slider or sandship. Nevertheless, they were obviously not vehicles of transportation, for they had neither seats nor sides, and no one rode on any of them. In fact, each one was surrounded by a small team of soldiers, walking not on the Arua field but on the sand.

These teams used wooden handles spaced periodically around the edges to push and pull the platforms in whatever direction they intended.

On top of every one of these floating circles were two strange metallic rails running parallel to each other, three or four feet apart. The metal appeared to be a meridium alloy, but the rails were not dark gray like pure meridium; instead, they glinted with a hint of gold in the morning sun. It was precisely these rails and their golden tint that drew Zangira's attention, and he quickly surmised that the metal mixed with the meridium base must be Zerura.

If he was right, if they were made of a Zerura-meridium alloy, then Eirmon must have one of the missing pieces of the Golden Cord. There were perhaps a hundred of these circular platforms being walked out before the line of sandships below, each traversed by two of these strange metallic rails. Two hundred rails! How else could Eirmon acquire so large a supply of Zerura and produce them all?

He would inspect one of these platforms when he could, of course, to be sure about it, but he felt sure, absolutely sure. It explained Kaden's confidence, among other things. If Zangira was looking at weaponry made from Zerura-enhanced meridium, he understood why the prince did not fear the walls of Garranmere.

Zangira looked from the weapons being deployed to the city with mixed feelings. He didn't want to see Garranmere destroyed, but today might be confirmation that they had finally found what they had long sought. The trail that he and Tchinchura had been following for almost ten years had led them to Barra-Dohn, and they had approached the city with as much optimism that they were as close to the answer as they had felt in years. It was true that they had been wrong before, but Zangira believed an answer was finally at hand.

Despite the promise of a hot day to come, Zangira felt a chill. It rippled through his body as he watched the men on foot continue to walk the circular platforms out in front of the rest of the soldiers and ships below. He watched the line of small sandships sail along behind them, carrying heavy loads of metallic balls and rods. If these were also weapons made with Zerura, then why would Eirmon send Zangira with Kaden, where the evidence of his theft would be on display? He must suspect they had come to Barra-Dohn to look for it. Why place one of the Amhuru where the spoils of the king's crime would be dangled in front of his face?

If Eirmon had meant to keep his theft a secret, it would be unthinkably careless of the king to send Zangira with Kaden when exposure must be the result. He was arrogant, yes, but Eirmon didn't seem the careless type. Zangira's mind was racing, thinking, searching for an explanation. Could Eirmon have thought Zangira wouldn't recognize what he was seeing? That an Amhuru, brought face-to-face with the Zerura-altered meridium and Zerura-enhanced weapons, wouldn't know it? Surely, not. So what then?

Eirmon didn't care. Sending Zangira would mean discovery, but the king didn't care. Perhaps Eirmon had realized as soon as the two Amhuru had announced their intent to stay that eventual discovery was unavoidable. And he was right. Sooner or later, had he sent Zangira or not, he and Tchinchura would have uncovered Eirmon's secret. So if he didn't care, if he wasn't hiding, then perhaps he'd sent Zangira simply to separate them to make them easier to kill. Had Kaden been given orders to kill Zangira?

Zangira glanced around. Activity was buzzing on this ship, as on all the others, but none of it was concerned with him. He thought back over his various conversations with Kaden since the beginning of the trip. Zangira couldn't see it. Despite the obvious awkwardness between Kaden and Deslo, Kaden had gone out of his way to include Zangira and the boy as much as he could in what he was doing. He seemed to be genuinely trying to reach out to both of them.

Maybe no such orders had been given. Maybe the king was not yet sure how to proceed, and dividing them with this commission had enabled him to put off making that decision. More likely,

Zangira thought, it might be that Eirmon simply intended to deal with the problem of Tchinchura first. Whether Eirmon had been involved in the taking of the fragment of the Golden Cord directly or merely acquired it later, he must know that killing an Amhuru presented challenges for men not equipped with Zerura or as intimately acquainted with its possibilities and potential as Amhuru were. It would make sense for the king to minimize the risks and difficulties of disposing of them by dividing them and doing it one at a time.

He had to warn Tchinchura. Zangira turned from the rail and walked toward the door that led into the small cabin that he shared with Deslo. The boy was near the bow of the ship, watching the deployment of men and materiel with Kaden. Zangira glanced quickly around, though he had no reason to think anyone would be watching, and then stepped into the cabin, shutting the door quietly behind him.

Zangira whispered to the Zerura ring on his left bicep as he stroked and tapped it in the prescribed sequence. The piece began to pulsate as it unwound from around his arm. A moment later, it hung in the air above his open hand, writhing rhythmically to the inner music to which all pieces of the Golden Cord danced— whether an original or a replica—even though it was inaudible even to Zangira's remarkable ears. He carefully and quickly tapped and stroked the piece further, and it formed a ring again in the air, but a different kind of ring to the hard, solid one that was usually wrapped around his arm.

This ring rippled and hovered, and the air within it shimmered, almost rippling too. Zangira leant in close to the rippling ring and whispered quietly into the space within. The words flowed out of his mouth and into the ring and there were lost, becoming just as inaudible as its own inner tune. When his message was complete, he replaced the ring around his bicep and slipped back out of the cabin.

He couldn't help feeling anxious, even though he knew Tchinchura could take care of himself. For now, he could do nothing else. He needed to focus on the battle ahead and on whatever else the day might bring. Tchinchura might not be alone, or he might be asleep, but soon enough, assuming he wasn't out of range, he would make time to be alone in order to receive the message. The rest was out of Zangira's hands.

Zangira joined Deslo and Kaden at the rail of the sandship. Much of the movement down below had ceased as a long line of circular platforms stretched out between the sandships and Garranmere for almost as far as Zangira could see. Behind the line of platforms, soldiers waited in large companies both on sliders and on foot, waiting now, Zangira assumed, for the order to begin the attack.

"The city is to be destroyed as a sign, I take it?" Zangira asked.

Kaden looked at the Amhuru and nodded. Though Zangira had guessed that this must be the intent of their coming, even if he didn't know all the reasons why, he had not spoken of the matter with Kaden before. "It isn't too late to let them evacuate the city first."

Kaden looked away. "I have already given more warning than I should have."

"Yes," Zangira said, "if your father's wishes are the only measure of what should be done."

"Are they not?" Kaden said, looking uncomfortable with the conversation as he glanced aside at Deslo. "He is the king, after all."

"He is the king," Zangira agreed, "but he isn't God."

"God?" Kaden replied, frowning as he turned back to Zangira. "Are you as crazy as the Kalosene?"

"Was the Devoted crazy?"

"You heard him," Kaden replied. "He raved like a lunatic."

"He may have raved," Zangira said, "but as to whether it was lunacy, I am unconvinced."

"Well, when his forty days have passed and Barra-Dohn still stands, I guess we'll know."

"If his forty days do pass and if Barra-Dohn still stands, all we will know for sure was that he was wrong," Zangira said. "Being mistaken doesn't necessarily make one a lunatic."

Kaden waved the matter off, turning his attention back to the army arrayed before him and the city in the distance. "Whatever he was, I have my orders, Zangira. I may not like them, but I don't question Eirmon's right to give them. I will proceed as directed."

Kaden's tone made it perfectly clear he didn't want to discuss it further, and Zangira didn't press the point. "When the attack begins, your attention will be required elsewhere," Zangira started. "Would you like me to remain here with Deslo, or should I take him down onto the sand to watch from there?"

Looking from the forces arrayed below to his son, Kaden appeared at something of a loss. "It would be safer here," he began, "and the view of the field is better."

"It might almost be too good," Zangira said, looking intently at Kaden. On the passage to Garranmere, they had both talked some with Deslo about what battle was like, what he could expect, and why his grandfather might wish him to experience it. For his part, Deslo had put on a brave face almost from the first, seeming resolved to prove his readiness to see the events of the day. All the same, while Zangira and Kaden admired his courage, both had agreed to spare him some measure of the ugliness of what must unfold. "Besides, unless your attack goes very much awry, there will be little danger to him if he is with me down below. And should things go very wrong, the ships might not be a whole lot safer."

"Yes," Kaden nodded, showing that he understood what Zangira was intimating with a look of gratitude. Knowing that he needed to convince Deslo that this wasn't for his protection, he added to the boy, "You have come too far not to experience what the king wants you to experience. For that, you had best watch from the same vantage point as the soldiers below. Go with Zangira, but stay close to him, and do exactly as he says. Now go, wait at the top of the gangway. I need a word with Zangira."

When Deslo had gone, Kaden turned back to the Amhuru. "You're right that I don't expect much trouble to threaten us out here, but as you know better than I do, war is often full of surprises."

"I do," Zangira replied. "I will keep Deslo safe, even if trouble should find us."

Kaden nodded, then added just before Zangira left to join Deslo, "I'm not like Eirmon, you know."

"I know that you don't want to be," Zangira said, "but it can be hard not to become what we don't want to be, if we do not clearly see a better way."

Zangira joined Deslo and walked down the gangway with him, waiting patiently as Deslo slipped his detachable soles on and stepped off onto the Arua.

"Aren't you going to put on meridium soles too?" Deslo asked as he stood comfortably on the Arua, looking at Zangira.

Zangira grinned. "No."

"Why not?"

"Because," Zangira said, leaning in to whisper, "and this is a secret between you and me. I don't need them."

Deslo's eyes widened as Zangira slid off his Zerura bicep ring and rubbed it along the soles of his sandals. Then stepping from the gangway, he stood beside Deslo on the Arua as he put it back on.

"That's your Zerura!" Deslo said, pointing at the bicep ring.

"It is," Zangira said, smiling.

"I knew you had to have some," Deslo continued. "You are an Amhuru. I even wondered if that ring was it."

"You wondered correctly," Zangira said. "Now let's move to a place where we can see the city a little better. Unless I'm mistaken, your father won't wait long. I think he wants to get this over with."

Deslo followed Zangira as he led him among the soldiers waiting in reserve until they'd found a place where they could observe more directly one of the circular platforms not so far ahead and yet not be in the way of any of the companies waiting to move forward should they be needed.

As Zangira expected, they didn't have long to wait before the attack began. The crew of this platform, like those of the others in line, reacting to some signal unseen by him, began to fire upon the city. Pairs of men on the ground carried between them the large, heavy meridium balls from the small sandships that waited behind each of the circular platforms. As they stood at the rear of the platform near the two rails, another man would pour a liquid into a hole in the ball. Then moving forward, they would gingerly lift the ball up above the platform between the rails. When caught in some invisible force they couldn't see, the ball would suddenly be ripped from their hands and hurled across the platform at speeds that dazzled Deslo before being launched across the intervening distance at Garranmere.

"Zangira, how are they . . ."

But Deslo had little time to wonder about how the rails on the platforms managed to grab hold of and thrust the balls forward with such force, before the effect of the projectiles had obscured their spectacular launching from his mind. Even from this distance, the sound and sight of the damage they were doing to the walls of Garranmere silenced him. The contents of those balls were blowing such large holes in the great stone walls that Zangira could see columns of smoke beginning to rise from within the city. Some were punching right through the wall before exploding, and some were penetrating through the breaches created by the first ones in the attack.

Zangira studied the platform before them and admired the genius of the simple design. The Zerura-enhanced meridium rails created between them the powerful field capable of shooting meridium objects with great force. Moreover, they could easily be rotated on the circular platform so they could hit different spots on the wall with little inconvenience or difficulty to the team manning it. What's more, the soldiers at the rear of the platform, by tilting the back downward ever so slightly could significantly raise the trajectory of the projectiles so that they hit the walls much farther up. They could even fling some of the deadly balls over the top of the walls to maximize the destruction farther inside Garranmere.

It was only a matter of moments before showers of stone and rock, of dust and ash began to spray rubble far and wide across the sands that surrounded the city. Great clouds of smoke arose, not only from the walls but also from what must be multiple, enormous fires within the city. Great gaping holes appeared everywhere along the walls, so it did not surprise Zangira that the battered and half-demolished gate began to swing outward.

When it had become apparent in the last few minutes to everyone within Garranmere as well as without that their great walls could not save them, a counterattack was being called for, no matter how unlikely it was that any such attack could possibly succeed. It was a desperate move.

As men raced out of the opening, they formed quickly into battle lines on top of the Arua. Accompanied by teams of soldiers on sliders, they prepared to advance against the army from Barra-Dohn. Zangira watched the crews at the railguns turn from the bombs to the other stash of projectiles in their waiting sandships, the piles and piles of meridium rods. He watched and his heart sank. Having fought in many battles, he was no squeamish observer, but he knew that what was coming would be a scene more like something from a slaughter yard than a battlefield. Instinctively, he put his hand on Deslo's shoulder and gripped the boy tightly. "You've seen what the weapons are capable of," he said. "You don't have to watch this."

"I'm all right," Deslo said, looking up at the Amhuru.

Zangira saw that the boy didn't understand what was coming, and he didn't want the boy to think he thought him unable to do what Eirmon had sent him to do, so he said nothing further. He kept his hand on him though and stood his ground waiting.

The first wave from Garranmere was advancing. Sliders began to outstrip the soldiers running on the Arua. Slender meridium javelins were in their hands as they fanned out to attack the teams manning the railguns that they knew were pounding their city to dust.

Long before the Garranmere soldiers were close enough to launch an effective attack, those same railguns opened fire at their new targets. Instead of placing solitary bombs into the field created by the railguns, the soldiers working each platform were now placing armloads of the bolts inside. The soldiers holding the handles around the edge moved the railguns gently from side to side. This technique sprayed bolts in a remarkably destructive arc, and they flew at speeds almost too great to be tracked by the human eye. Dark gray blurs ripped through the lines of the attack as both men and sliders tumbled from the Arua and slammed roughly into the sands below in staggering numbers. Soon great clouds of sand rose in puffs all over the battlefield, imitating on a smaller scale the large clouds of smoke rising from the city behind. From those clouds, few men and fewer sliders emerged to continue pressing forward.

The few that remained were easily taken down by more careful and more concentrated shots. Behind them, a second wave of attackers from the city, though larger, was shredded almost as easily. Some of these got closer, though, and the indistinct slaughter at a distance was painfully contrasted with some clear and particular scenes of death. One man, who'd somehow reached almost a midpoint between the city and the line of railguns, became clearly the target of several at once and was hit by so many volleys at the same time as to be fairly ripped to pieces in midair.

Deslo, who had been watching the horror before him unfold as in a ghoulish dream, was shaken most severely out of his half-reverie by this horrific scene. He turned away and buried his face into the vest hanging loosely on Zangira's chest, clasping him tightly as he did so.

"The face of war is terrible," Zangira whispered, as he stroked Deslo's hair.

"I want to go back," Deslo said quietly, the words muffled by the soft fabric of Zangira's vest.

"All right," Zangira replied.

Deslo looked up at him, tears in his eyes. "I've seen enough, haven't I?"

"More than enough."

"Father won't think me a coward?"

"No, Deslo," Zangira said, stooping so that he was face-to-face with the boy. "He won't think that."

Deslo raised his sleeve and wiped the tears from his eyes. He was careful not to turn his head back toward the battlefield, which had become a killing field. Zangira had seen many battles, but there wasn't much here that resembled those.

Zangira could see the Barra-Dohn soldiers moving forward. The great bulk of their work had been done by the powerful rail-guns, and now it was time for the men on foot and on sliders to perform the cleanup and secure the field.

"There isn't much left to see," Zangira said, raising his dark hand to Deslo's face and wiping the tear from his eye that was hanging there stubbornly, as if trying to decide if it really wanted to fall or not. "Do you want to just wait here with me for a minute before we go back?"

Deslo exhaled and nodded again, visibly relieved.

20

ONE MORE TIME

Zangira didn't fully understand the hierarchy of the Barra-Dohn military, but he had figured out at least two things on the way to Garranmere. First, most of the officers who served under Kaden were commonly referred to simply as "Captain," their real power or lack thereof somewhat obscured by this lack of variety. Second, of those many "captains" of varying import and seniority, the one who functioned as second in command under Kaden was a man named Greyer.

Zangira wasn't sure what to make of Greyer. Perhaps not quite ten years older than the king's son, Greyer paid Kaden every respect due him by right of birth and the king's appointment to lead this army. He also addressed Kaden with confidence, looked him in the eye, and voiced his own opinions respectfully but freely. All in all, Greyer seemed completely comfortable in his place at Kaden's side. That was a decided contrast, as the other men of rank that Zangira observed with Kaden were obsequious panderers to a man, and the men without rank, or at least without any to speak of, seemed too afraid of Kaden to say much of anything in his presence.

Self-possession was a trait Zangira admired, and he'd come to respect Greyer as much as anyone he'd met in the brief time he'd spent serving Eirmon as a "tutor" to his grandson. However, that level of self-possession in the face of so much power was unusual, and let there be no mistake about it, despite Kaden's private misgivings expressed on occasion with Zangira, he radiated power. Indirect power, perhaps, but real power, nonetheless. Not only did he represent Eirmon's power vicariously, but he also represented, even if in a remote way, his own latent, kingly power. Those who were wise enough to look to their future felt it when Kaden was near.

It might just be that Greyer was that rare man who was steady, competent, and sure of himself, unwilling to be anything but what he was by nature in the face of anyone or anything else. Or maybe Greyer's comfort with Kaden was rooted in an understanding that the son was not like the father. Perhaps he knew Kaden didn't feed on the fear he caused in those who served him, at least not yet, and perhaps knowing that was freeing.

Zangira hoped so, because the other possibility that sometimes tugged at him as he watched them interact was that Greyer's self-possession might be rooted in a confidence that came from knowing that he answered to Kaden's father, not Kaden. That would mean that Kaden—whatever his rights and privileges of command on this particular mission—could not touch him, and he knew it. Maybe Kaden knew it too. Neither man gave much away, so Zangira was left to speculate. Most of the time, in his speculation, he couldn't envision any reason why Eirmon would have Greyer harm Kaden, but Zangira had interpreted his commission to watch out for Deslo broadly and intended to watch out for Kaden as well, just in case.

Soon the two Amhuru and Eirmon were going to be at odds, and blood would be spilt, maybe a lot of it. It was entirely possible that Kaden would choose at that point to support his father against them. Maybe he wouldn't. Either way, Zangira wasn't going to relax while Greyer was around until he'd figured out if the man's principal allegiance was to Kaden or to the king.

So Zangira watched Greyer silently as the captain stood before Kaden on the sandship with only the Amhuru and Deslo nearby. At first, when Zangira had brought Deslo back, the boy had stayed in their room. He'd eventually come back on deck after the railguns had finished their deadly work, but he'd kept close to Zangira and avoided looking at either the still smoking city of Garranmere or the expanse of sand before it, now littered with the bodies of the fallen. Studiously avoiding those things, the boy watched Greyer as Zangira did and listened as the captain spoke.

"I still say you shouldn't go to them."

"And I still say I am," Kaden answered.

"It's needlessly risky and foolish," Greyer replied. He spoke evenly but added the "and foolish" as though "needlessly risky" was a phrase in need of further explanation. Zangira watched the interchange, and if Greyer's challenge annoyed Kaden, it didn't show.

"It's riskier than not going, true," Kaden conceded. "But it isn't risky. The fighting even inside the city subsided an hour ago."

"Which doesn't mean it's safe, especially for you."

"It's as close to safe as it's going to be before we burn it. Even if I gave you the rest of the day, you'd still tell me not to go since it's a big city and you'd never feel quite sure that every possible threat had been neutralized."

"That's right," Greyer agreed. "Which is why I'm telling you not to go—not now and not later today."

Kaden put his hands on the smooth wooden rail and leaned upon it, gazing across the distance at the devastated walls of Garranmere. The gates were completely gone. A gaping hole even larger than the other gaping holes now yawned there, where they had stood as silent sentries until a few hours ago. Smoke poured steadily out of all the various holes in the city walls, coiling up in thick plumes until it joined the now massive cloud that had grown until it dominated the afternoon sky, a perverse mockery in the expanse of blue where always before dark clouds had signalled the coming of rain and with it hope.

"Let me bring you one of the officials of the city," Greyer continued, perhaps reading Kaden's silence as openness to what he saw as reason. "You can deliver your message then and be done with it. You need never set foot in Garranmere again."

Without looking back at Greyer, Kaden shook his head. "I want to set foot in Garranmere again." He continued to stare at the city. "The first time Eirmon brought me here, I remember holding his hand so tightly. I was just a boy, and the walls loomed above, impossibly high. So high, so strong, and now, I've pounded them to dust." Kaden grew silent. He stood, staring at the city, shaking his head.

"Much of the city inside, like the walls, is in ruins," Greyer said quietly. "If you're hoping to relive some fond memories, you'll find little that reminds you of the Garranmere you remember. Stay, and keep your memories intact."

"No," Kaden said, turning now. "I'll look one more time, and besides, as I told you before, it's important that the people of Garranmere see me. They need to see Eirmon's son walking unharmed within their walls, through their streets. If there's any doubt in any of them," Kaden continued, raising his arm and pointing at the city, "that they are vanquished, and that it is Eirmon who has vanquished them, then seeing me will remove it. You know how many people need to see or experience something tangible, to have a symbol of their defeat, before they are willing to admit it."

"I know that, but there's no doubt about who has done this," Greyer said. "And if doubt remains for any that this battle is over, the fires that will smolder through the night and the cries of the fatherless wailing in the darkness should be tangible enough to remove it."

Zangira could see Kaden clench his jaw, but when he spoke it was without any sign of anger. "Captain Greyer, please ready my escort. I'll be with you directly. Then we will enter the city, and I will deliver my father's message."

"Yes, sir," Captain Greyer said, acknowledging that the conversation was over and that he was dismissed.

When he was gone, Kaden turned from the rail and looked thoughtfully at Deslo. "I'm sorry that you've never seen Garranmere before today. Would you like to come with me now and see it?"

Deslo looked up at his father, took a deep breath and said, "Yes."

Zangira thought he could see a little of the war inside the boy. He had no desire to see more of the battlefield, more bodies, and more destruction. As a measure of how much he wanted his father's approval, his willingness to go inside the city was telling.

"Greyer is right. It won't be the place I remember," Kaden said. "And if you come, you will see unpleasant things inside the city as well as out."

"I don't care," Deslo said, shrugging dismissively as though he'd seen a hundred conquered cities.

"All right," Kaden nodded, looking from Deslo to Zangira. "Come on then."

Despite his bravado, Kaden watched Deslo draw closer to Zangira as they approached and entered the city. Long before they'd reached the gate, the smell of the burning dead assaulted them. Many men had manned the walls or been massed behind the gate when the railguns had launched the first bombs. These had pounded through, demolishing and ultimately burning whatever stood in their way. The space just beyond the wall now contained a disproportionate number of the Garranmere dead, and though not visible from a distance like the plumes of thick smoke billowing out from the city, the stench of death billowed from Garranmere just as steadily.

The smell, which was somewhat dissipated beyond the confines of the wall, struck them fully as they passed through the gate, as did the sight of the charred and burning bodies. Kaden felt nauseated. He'd have called for a scarf to cover his nose, but he doubted it could have filtered out the terrible smell, and it couldn't remove the terrible images either. Kaden felt he needed to experience the full horror of what he had done to Garranmere. He had done it, even if it had been for Eirmon. He had done it.

Sight and smell weren't the only senses assaulted as they entered. The sounds of weeping and wailing rose up throughout Garranmere, mingling together to make an awful cacophony of misery. And the smoke that billowed up into the clouds outside the city hung everywhere inside. Even at ground level it lingered, making the eyes water as it penetrated through the nose and mouth and stole into the lungs where the acrid taste of death seemed to infest everyone through and through. Kaden coughed, and, for a moment, seemed almost unable to continue forward.

"Are you all right?" Zangira said, bending over to rub Deslo's back soothingly.

Kaden turned and saw Deslo nod when he saw that he was looking, quickly going on as though afraid his father would change his mind about taking him along if he didn't prove he could handle passing through the gate. Kaden smiled at the boy's stubborn determination. He'd been like that too, once.

Greyer appeared out of the smoke. A few soldiers followed him, and they were escorting a soldier of Garranmere, who was dirty and bleeding. Kaden thought he looked weary but not altogether dispirited. They brought the soldier before him, and Greyer, without looking at the captive, addressed the king's son loudly enough for all in the vicinity to hear. "This man is, as best as I can tell, the ranking officer of the surviving soldiers within the vicinity of the gate," Greyer said, and then added an after-thought. "At least, this is the man who did not try to hide his rank from me as I searched for someone with at least some authority to concede the city upon your entry."

There was a slight pause, and when the captured soldier didn't fill it in the manner he'd obviously been expected to, Greyer turned to him and took a firm grip on his neck. In a moment, he was down on his knees with his head bowed toward Kaden.

Without raising his eyes to look at those to whom he spoke, he said in a soft voice with Greyer's hand still firmly gripping him. "Garranmere is yours, Your Majesty. Enter our gates, and do with us as you will."

"I fully intend to," Kaden said, walking as the man raised his angry eyes in defiance.

Greyer saw, and with a firm shove, he sent the man sprawling on the street. The other soldiers took over then, and lifting him none too gently, led him back through the smoke.

Where they took him, Kaden never saw. He had to play his part for those of Garranmere who were watching, but now that he was here, he wanted to be finished and away.

As they passed down the streets of the city, Kaden quickly realized that the real danger in Garranmere wasn't the survivors but the ruins. The projectiles launched all morning by the railguns had done their work with brutal efficiency. Most of the buildings they saw had been hit and damaged to some degree, and all around them broken chunks of stone and shattered clay ceiling tiles lay sprawled, often intermingled with the dead. On multiple occasions, parts of buildings tumbled into the streets they were walking along, so that they soon found themselves stealing furtive glances upward as they progressed inward, for fear that the next tumbling section of a building might come right down upon them.

It was this tendency to look upward that kept Kaden from noticing the girl until he was almost upon her. She was probably younger than Deslo but not by much. She'd been crushed from the chest down under a large piece of stone and lay whimpering on the side of the street. The soldiers with them didn't seem to notice her, but Kaden saw that Zangira did, and he watched Deslo to see if the boy would too.

He did. Looking down after scanning the sky above yet again, he saw and hesitated, unsure of what to do. Tears leaked from the girl's staring eyes as her mouth worked almost noiselessly, the faintest of sounds coming from her collapsed lungs. Kaden knew the stone upon her was too heavy for Deslo to lift, and that even if it wasn't, moving it couldn't help her. Still, Deslo moved quickly toward her, and then looked at him and Zangira. "We can move it if we all try."

"Perhaps," the Amhuru replied, stepping up beside Deslo without hesitation.

Kaden joined them with a smile for Deslo. "Let's see what we can do."

They reached down together, and with some trouble, they did manage to slide it off. The wreckage beneath was bad, as Kaden had known it would be. The girl's eyelids seemed to grow heavy, and her mouth stopped opening and closing mechanically, as though the removal of the physical weight gave her freedom to stop fighting for the breath that would never again come.

Zangira reached down with his fingers and lightly closed her eyes the rest of the way.

Kaden took Deslo's hand and led him away. "You were right to want to help," Kaden said as Zangira hustled to catch up.

"It was stupid," Deslo said bitterly. "It didn't change a thing."

"Perhaps not," Kaden said. "But it was right, nonetheless."

Deslo stopped. "Promise me that when you're king, you'll never do anything like this."

Kaden looked at Deslo and hesitated. "Deslo, sometimes wars are unavoidable, even for kings."

"I'm not talking about war," Deslo said.

Kaden knew from the look in the boy's eyes what he was asking him to say.

Kaden nodded, understanding passing between them. "I promise."

A little while later, Kaden and a reasonably large cluster of soldiers from Barra-Dohn gathered in a large open square at or near the center of Garranmere. In the middle of the square was a fountain comprised mainly of a statue of a boy playing a musical instrument. It had survived the bombing and remained intact with the water still flowing—a strange sight in the dry and smoky world of Garranmere. Kaden helped himself to a drink from it. The water was lukewarm but satisfying, and for a moment at least, the smell of death and the taste of smoke were washed away.

Greyer, who had led their little expedition into the city, had disappeared once they reached the square. He reappeared now, leading behind him a nearly bald, elderly man who shuffled behind him a bit unsteadily. Like the man from the gate, Greyer led this fellow to Kaden.

This time, though, it was Kaden who spoke first. "Lord Tannen," he said. "I was expecting Kazir."

"Lord Kazir is dead, Prince Kaden." Tannen's voice, at least, was not as shaky as his body. "It falls to me to act in his stead, and I surrender Garranmere to you, though I admit, I am confused about what we have done to incur your wrath. The forty days have not yet passed."

Kaden looked at Tannen for a moment, then glanced about him, as though surveying the buildings that surrounded the square in various stages of disrepair, many burning. "At this point, what you have done is not important, Lord Tannen."

"Not important?" Tannen echoed him incredulously. "Thousands upon thousands of civilians dead in their homes and in the streets, not to mention the soldiers blown to bits or cut down outside the wall, and you say the cause of all this is not important?"

"Don't play the fool with me," Kaden said, impatiently, feeling he had little choice but to play the role his father had assigned him. "You know full well that Garranmere happily participated in the talk of rebellion against my father that even now runs rife through the Five Cities."

"I know nothing of the sort . . ." Tannen began to reply, but he didn't get any further.

"Enough!" Kaden shouted, grabbing the front of Lord Tannen's robe roughly, all but lifting the frail old man off his feet as he did so. He let go, almost immediately, disgusted with himself for allowing his frustration with his father to show as anger against this man who had every right to be indignant. He took a deep breath and continued. "Lord Tannen, I'm not interested in your denials. Your sentence has been decreed, and I am only here to ensure that it is carried out. The 'why' no longer matters. What matters now is that you hear and obey."

Whatever courage Lord Tannen had been holding onto seemed to have slipped away, and when he spoke now, he sounded as uncertain and shaky as his body appeared. "What more is to be done beyond what you have done already?"

"The city is to be evacuated within twenty-four hours. By this time tomorrow, my men will be working their way methodically through Garranmere, burning what remains."

"Twenty-four hours!" Tannen stared, eyes wide. "But even if there weren't so many sick and wounded, it would be impossible."

"Nothing's impossible," Kaden answered him, adding urgently, "You will do it, because you must."

"But," Tannen sputtered, "surely you see the state of the city, the damage that has been done. It is already destroyed. Fire will already take much of what remains. What need is there to do more?"

"I have my orders, Lord Tannen," Kaden said darkly. "You know my father. If Eirmon wants it all to burn, then it will all burn."

Tannen looked about him uncertainly, desperately, as though hoping to find support or at least understanding in the faces of any of those gathered nearby. Finding none, he was reduced to little more than begging. "Please, Prince Kaden, even if you must burn it all to obey your father's wishes, surely giving us a little more time to get out cannot be impossible. We will go if we must, but if what matters is that we hear and obey, give us a real chance to do so."

Kaden stood, his arms crossed, staring beyond Tannen at nothing in particular. After a long moment, he shook his head once and then said quietly. "All right, Tannen, I will give you forty-eight hours, but that is the best I can do, or Eirmon will have my head as well as yours. In two days, the city burns."

"Thank you," Tannen said, reaching out as though to shake Kaden's hand, but Kaden had no heart to take it, and soon it was withdrawn. After a minute, though, Tannen did speak again. "We are to leave, you say, but where are we to go?"

"Where?" Kaden said. "Go wherever you will find shelter. After forty-eight hours, there won't be any here."

As Tannen turned to be about the business of ordering the evacuation, Kaden murmured to no one but himself. "Not then, not ever."

In the dark of the room he shared with Deslo, Zangira lay thinking about the railguns and their golden sheen. There was little need for any formal test. They had revealed their power, and he had felt echoes of it as they were used.

The room was quiet. Deslo had gone straight to bed without fuss, without questions, without requests for a story, in other words, without any of the usual bedtime formalities.

Zangira had given him the space his silence requested, but as he listened now for the rhythmic breathing that marked the boy's sleep, he didn't hear it. "Trouble sleeping, Deslo?" he asked.

"No," the boy replied. "I'm just thinking."

"You saw a lot today."

"I did," Deslo conceded. "You know, Zangira, we've talked about how awful war can be, and I know what you meant now, but is it weird to think parts of it are pretty exciting too?"

"No, Deslo," Zangira said. "That's not weird. I have fought in battle and felt the rush, the excitement it can give. It's like nothing else. It is terrible, but it isn't only terrible. There are those, in fact, who grow attached to it, who feel after a while that they cannot live without it, who need it to feel whole."

"That doesn't seem right," Deslo said. "I mean, I've been hunting, and I've felt the excitement of trying to win the battle with my quarry. I guess battle could feel like that too, only on a bigger scale, but it's people. In war you kill people, not hookworms."

"That's right, Deslo, which is why some part of us should always hate it, even when fighting a war may become necessary. When you are king one day, I hope you will remember what you saw today and how it felt."

"I think," Deslo started then hesitated.

"What do you think?"

"I think that my grandfather wants me to remember what I saw here too," Deslo said. "But I don't think he wants me to remember it like you do."

"You're a clever boy," Zangira said, figuring that truth from the boy's mouth deserved more truth in response. "I don't think so either. Even so, I hope you will remember what you saw and how it felt, because I think, despite your youth and inexperience with war, you might just see it more clearly than he does."

"Zangira?"

"Yes?"

"It's hard not to feel ashamed."

"Because of what happened here today?" Zangira asked.

"Yes."

"But you didn't do this, and you couldn't have stopped it."

"I know," Deslo replied simply. "But my grandfather ordered it, my father did it, and I watched it."

"True," Zangira said. "But you still aren't responsible. You will, though, be responsible for Barra-Dohn and its armies someday. So you must remember today. We always learn from those who go before us. Sometimes we learn what to do. Sometimes we learn what not to do. The failure, Deslo, is to learn nothing."

For a moment, they lay there in the silent dark. Zangira thought that perhaps Deslo was falling asleep, and he had almost decided to try to get some sleep himself, when Deslo spoke again.

"Zangira?"

"Yes?"

"My dad took my hand."

"Yes," Zangira said. "He did."

"And he promised me he'd never do anything like this again."

"He did."

"Do you think he meant it?" Deslo added after a moment. "Or do you think he just said that to make me feel better?"

"I think," Zangira started but then hesitated as he thought hard about what to say and how to say it, "that maybe your father is also learning on this trip some lessons that Eirmon did not intend."

For several moments, there was silence in the room, and then Deslo said, "Good night, Zangira."

"Good night, Deslo."

"I'm glad you're my tutor."

"It's my privilege," Zangira said. He lay listening, and after a while, the regular breathing that signaled Deslo slipping away into sleep came from across the room. He smiled and shook his head.

Incredible weapons. Irresistible force. Bloody battle and a battered city. And yet, the thought that lingered in the boy's mind, the thing that he couldn't set down at the end of the day was the tiny seed of hope. Hope that his father cared for him, hope that they were both agreed that what Eirmon had done to Garranmere was something neither of them would ever do.

Kaden's words and actions today had fallen like rain in the arid desert of the boy's heart, and Zangira hoped for Deslo's sake that they held the real promise of more to follow.

21

TREACHERY UNMASKED

Tchinchura sat cross-legged on the cool, stone floor in the corner of his room. He had taken the colorful rug that covered the open floor, rolled it up, and slid it under the bed to keep it out of the way. The first few days he'd been in Barra-Dohn, he'd returned to his room each evening to find the rug back where he'd found it, and each time he'd rolled it back up and tucked it away. The steward responsible for his room had eventually gotten the hint, and now the rug remained beneath the bed.

Tchinchura replayed in his mind the message he'd had from Zangira the day before. If true, the weapons used to attack Garranmere had been enhanced by Zerura, and that would mean his long hunt was drawing toward a conclusion. It would also mean that he was in great danger, but that was no surprise. Recovery of what had been stolen had always been the goal, and he'd known when he accepted this task that whoever had taken it in the first place would be reluctant to give it back.

On the floor before him lay his axe and knife. The thin veins of Zerura that ran through them gleamed even in the dim, early morning light. They'd been made with Zerura derived from the same piece that he wore as a ring on his left bicep. Thus, they could be wielded by him with remarkable speed and power, controlled in ways that defied even the ordinarily wondrous capabilities of meridium and the Arua field. And now they probably would be needed to protect him against whatever threat Eirmon posed.

Tchinchura didn't doubt that Eirmon posed a threat. It didn't really matter that Zangira hadn't yet examined one of the railguns he'd witnessed in action against Garranmere. Even if Zangira's suspicion proved wrong, though Tchinchura thought that unlikely, Eirmon had murder in his heart. Not just anger, murder. A deep hatred had burned in Eirmon's eyes when he'd rebuked Tchinchura before the execution of the Kalosene, and the Amhuru understood that the king had wanted to execute more than one man that day.

He'd not seen that same hatred in those eyes since. But the cold detachment he found in the king now, combined with the way Eirmon completely ignored him as though he'd never been accepted into service only confirmed what Tchinchura believed. Eirmon did not keep short accounts, and he bore him a grudge regardless of whether or not he possessed one of the original pieces of the Golden Cord. Tchinchura had no presumption of safety, despite the clear expectations of hospitality that applied to all, especially to the Amhuru.

And so Tchinchura wrestled this morning with the same question that had plagued him last night. Should he leave the palace? It would be safer to leave, without question, but it would also make his task more difficult. He'd lose the chance to observe Eirmon firsthand, and he had not yet given up hope of finding the missing fragment.

What's more, as long as he stayed, Eirmon couldn't help but feel somewhat secure, even if he knew why Tchinchura had come. He had been having men follow Tchinchura, and his close proximity would give the king at least the illusion of being in control. As soon as he disappeared, though, the uncertainty of his location and activities would change that. Steps would be taken to secure both the palace and the king even more than they already were. Those steps wouldn't be insurmountable, but they'd make his life more difficult and put more men in danger. While Tchinchura wouldn't hesitate to kill any soldier who tried to stop him from recovering the lost fragment, he didn't relish the unnecessary loss of life. If he had a chance to recover what he'd come for without the bloodbath an assault on the palace would require, he'd take it.

There was just too much he still didn't know, and he didn't want to strike without the certainty that he was striking in the right direction. He suspected Eirmon had the piece with him, probably on him—it would be hard for such a man to resist its allure—but Tchinchura didn't know that yet. He didn't know that the original wasn't locked away somewhere far from the palace. He didn't know for sure if Eirmon had figured out how to replicate it the right way so duplicates could also be worn and used much like the original. Perhaps he wore Zerura but not the original. An attack on Eirmon personally, then, might not only fail to recover it, but also it might set in motion a plan to keep the original safe that would make it even harder to get in the long run. It might even, Kalos forbid, lead to the fragment disappearing from Barra-Dohn altogether.

That, more than any danger to himself, had led Tchinchura to be cautious in his search and reckless with his safety. He felt close, and he couldn't bear being turned away empty-handed. Staying in the palace was dangerous, but it would likely put him in the way of information he needed. If he could just get a break. He knew, though, that breaks were less often caught than made, so it might be time for a gamble. He'd already reached out to the king's daughter-in-law, Ellenara, but he hadn't told her much. Perhaps it was time to reveal more.

To do so, he'd need to take her away from the palace or the bustling streets of Barra-Dohn, but that could be dangerous. He imagined Eirmon was at least subtle enough to eliminate him discreetly, and an assassination in the palace would be hard to pass off as an accident. He didn't know if a plot against him was already in motion, or if the king would dare while his own daughter-in-law was with him, but he would have to be careful.

He reached out and picked up his knife, wrapping his fingers around the sturdy yet light handle. He flourished it effortlessly, then flipped it in the air where it stopped in mid-rotation at a slight flicker from his finger, dangling like a plate resting on the surface of Arua. He gazed at it for a moment, both admiring it and wishing it wouldn't be necessary, then flicked his fingertips again, every so slightly, so that the knife flew back into his hand. He took up his axe, tucked both in his belt, and walked to the door.

Eirmon's platform stopped in the square beside the Academy. The king rose to his feet and walked to the edge, while two of the Davrii took the portable stairs and put them in place to enable his descent. It was quickly done, but Eirmon remained on the platform.

He gazed at the statue of the craftsman, which rested in the middle of the large open square. It loomed over even Eirmon's platform and faced forward in the direction of the street that ran past the front of the Academy. Eirmon stared, focusing on the man's face. There was something he couldn't quite put his finger on in the mood portrayed there.

He'd thought the look was awe. Certainly, the man was posed in such a way as to communicate amazement at the wonder of his discovery. The knife, despite the blood running along its blade, was held aloft like a beloved treasure or even a sacred object, harkening back to a time when people believed in such things, investing the ordinary with dreams of transcendence. He was kneeling, too, which strengthened that impression. But those eyes. Something was there that didn't seem like awe.

Maybe it was surprise, which would fit, since surely the discovery of meridium would have evoked it. But then again, Eirmon thought, surprise wasn't quite it. Was it uncertainty? Sadness? Maybe that was too strong. Sobriety seemed closer. A gravity, a seriousness was captured in the man's face that had at first eluded him.

Eirmon stared. Even though he knew the statue was a mere guess, the product of a sculptor's imagination as much as his hands, he wondered why that sobriety had lurked behind and beneath the man's wonder. Had he sensed the power of meridium right from the first? Had he foreseen the changes it would bring?

And now, Eirmon thought, turning away from the statue and descending from the platform, the world was changing again. Meridium would still be at the forefront, but it would be meridium mixed with Zerura, and he would control its production. At least, that was the basic plan. There were still two major obstacles. He hadn't figured out how he could profit from selling what he could now produce without equipping his enemy with power commensurate with his own or drawing down on himself the ire of the Amhuru. Still, he was confident that he'd find a way, and then he'd replicate both the military and the commercial successes of his forefathers.

But first, the traitors who thought they could steal from him had to be dealt with.

Eirmon walked up the wide stone stairs at the front of the Academy, accompanied by a large escort of the Davrii. People passing by stopped and stared, wondering what was going on. The king didn't doubt that the word of what was to happen today would get out in one form or another. He couldn't stop such tales from spreading, even had he come in secret, as he did when he came to add to the Academy's store of Zerura. Despite that, he'd do what was necessary to keep the details of the secret work going on inside the Academy from spreading, but he couldn't hide some of what would happen today.

Eirmon was fine with that, since he didn't want it entirely hidden. Let all of Barra-Dohn know that betrayal of the throne was a grave offense, even for members of the prestigious Academy. He needed to send a message to the rest of the Academy in case anyone else harbored plans or even hopes of self-advancement at his expense. If that message also served as a warning for others outside the Academy, so be it.

The great doors at the front of the Academy swung open, and Eirmon, followed by his retinue, swept inside. The large foyer was almost empty, but directly in front of him stood Rika, beautiful but sober in her neat, dark blue attire. Her eyes watched Eirmon all the way from the door up until the moment he stopped in front of her.

She wasn't alone, of course, as Barreck was with her. He was a capable man, which was why the king had entrusted him to head up the research being done on Zerura both to discover its properties and to apply its power. If competence at his job had been the only factor informing Eirmon's opinion of him, the king suspected he would have liked the fellow. As it was, though, he wasn't sure what he thought of the man.

Eirmon knew that Barreck desired Rika. It was obvious, even though Barreck worked hard to conceal it. The king noticed the way Barreck looked at her, though of course, the man thought he was being discreet. What Eirmon didn't know was whether or not Rika desired him in return.

She knew of Barreck's interest, of course. That much Eirmon could see. If she didn't, then sooner or later she would have caught Barreck gazing at her with that look in his eyes and been embarrassed in front of Eirmon, maybe even worried about what he would think. She never did catch him, though. In fact, she studiously avoided looking at the man almost entirely. That was how Eirmon knew.

That she might desire Barreck was a real possibility and one that didn't bother Eirmon. At least, not much. His interest in her was waning, and he'd always known her interest in him was insincere. She was ambitious, and the king had furthered her ambition as she'd hoped he would. He'd seen from the start what she wanted and had been willing to give it to her. That she might move on to someone else once he was through with her didn't bother him. It was generally better that way.

What did bother him was the fact that she clearly thought he didn't know about the game she was playing. Eirmon was an expert at carrying on a charade just far enough to give people enough reason to accept it, even if they knew it was a farce. Trying to actually fool and deceive everyone was far too taxing, but Rika seemed to think it was necessary to keep Eirmon in the dark in order to get what she wanted. More than that, she evidently thought she was being successful. Even when he provoked her, hoping to push her to show her real hand, she labored to act like it didn't offend her. She didn't even see that this betrayed her, since if she'd really loved him as much as she claimed, his injustice toward her would hurt. She might have suppressed that hurt, since he was king, but she wouldn't have been able to hide it. Instead, when he caught glimpses of her emotions at those times, he only saw her anger.

He would need to give careful consideration to what should be done about Rika when he finally finished with her. Her position in the family as tutor to Deslo would of course end, and Eirmon had thought at one point to leave it at that. But perhaps allowing her to continue in her current role at the Academy would also need to be rethought.

This couldn't be put off forever. He had recently decided who his next mistress was going to be, and the initial seduction was always the best part. He would resolve the situation with Rika, so any unpleasantness from that wouldn't mar his enjoyment of the new girl. When Kaden returned and Eirmon could rest easy about his larger plans, he would attend to the matter. Now, though, he had other business.

"Where are they?" Eirmon asked.

"They're a level down under guard, Your Majesty," Barreck answered.

"How many are there?" Eirmon asked. "The message I received this morning just mentioned that a few men were in custody."

"There are three," Rika said. "When I had that message sent to you, we were as yet unsure if we had unmasked the entire conspiracy."

"Are you sure now?"

"We believe so."

"You believe so?" Eirmon echoed her. "You'd better know, because I intend to execute these men, and when I do, any secrets will die with them."

"I should have said that the soldiers Your Majesty left behind interrogated the men in question, and it is their opinion that they have nothing further to tell us."

"I see," Eirmon said. "How'd you finally figure out who it was?"

"We were lucky," Rika said. "A spot check of some workers leaving late last night uncovered them."

"How were they taking it out of the Academy?"

"Tied to their upper arms, inside their shirts. Each of them had a piece."

"Just one?"

"Just one."

Eirmon nodded thoughtfully, envisioning the slender piece of Zerura tied carefully out of sight. "You've recovered more than those three pieces, though?"

"We have," Barreck said. "During their questioning to see if there were any others, they gave up their hiding place."

"Which was?"

"One of their houses. One of them is a widower with grown children, and the Zerura was just sitting in a box in his spare bedroom."

"Sitting in a box? How much had they taken?"

"About thirty of the duplicates."

"Only thirty," Eirmon mused, tapping his forefinger on his lips. "I'd thought there would be more."

"Thirty is quite a lot," Rika said. "Taking it out, one at a time, even if there were three of them involved every time, would have been difficult. They'd have had to get access to the storeroom without anyone else around on at least ten separate occasions, and that would have been hard. I'm a little surprised there was this much."

"Well," Eirmon said. "I suppose you'd better take me to them."

Half a dozen soldiers stood outside the storeroom where the men were being kept. Inside, with the prisoners, another two were waiting. The men in question lay curled on the floor in the corner. Their faces were bruised and bloodied. In fact, Eirmon could see that one of them had both eyes swollen shut. At the sound of the door and the footsteps entering the room, all three instinctively pressed back farther into the corner, as though doing so might spare them from what was to come.

"Bring them before me," Eirmon said, and several of the soldiers that had entered along with the king moved across the room, secured the three men, and dragged them across the floor until they were lined up before him on their knees.

At the sound of Eirmon's voice, the two who could still see looked up at the group that now stood before them. The third man raised his head too, as though lifting his head might make some difference in the proceedings. Perhaps it was simple awareness that he was in the presence of his king that drew his sightless face upward.

"Why have you conspired against me?" Eirmon asked. "And what made you think you could get away with it?"

Each of the men before him trembled, but finally the one with both eyes swollen shut spoke. "Your Majesty, we have not conspired against you. Whatever you have been told is not true."

Eirmon looked at Rika in mild surprise. Nothing she or Barreck had said had prepared him for this protestation of innocence. "Why are you here, if not for stealing Zerura from the Academy?"

"I have never stolen anything from the Academy in my life," the man replied. "And I don't think Marin or Eldis have either."

"So you deny that you were each found with Zerura last night, trying to sneak it out of the Academy?"

"I do," he said. "We were leaving to go home as usual when we were detained, then searched, then brought here, at which point we were beaten repeatedly. And here we've been all night. We are innocent of wrongdoing."

"Rika? Barreck?" Eirmon said, looking from the prisoners to the two beside him.

"This must be some new ploy," Barreck said, shrugging his shoulders, looking puzzled. "They didn't hesitate to admit their guilt during the night."

"That's a lie!" One of the other men shouted out, staring angrily at Barreck. "We didn't admit to anything because we didn't do anything."

The other man also jumped in, thinking it now safe to speak his mind. "If anything's missing, it was probably you."

He tried to raise his arm to point at Barreck, but one of the Davrii struck him across the face before he got very far, and he fell back down.

Eirmon looked at the three men, wondering what purpose it could possibly serve for them to deny this if they had been caught red-handed. Surely men who were guilty and knew they'd been caught would be pleading for mercy, since disproving their guilt would be impossible. "Who interrogated these men?"

The two soldiers who'd been leaning against the wall when Eirmon first entered stepped forward. "We did."

"Just the two of you?"

"Yes, Your Majesty," one of them said, looking at the other soldier. "It only required two. We bound them all, then untied them one by one as we asked the questions."

"And did they admit to stealing the Zerura when questioned?"

"Yes, sir."

"Liar!" Screamed the man who had shouted before but not been hit. He didn't make the mistake of making any sudden moves, but he was still struck hard by the soldier nearest to him.

Eirmon looked at the two soldiers still standing at attention, then back to Rika and Barreck who were watching the affair. "Rika, any ideas why these men would claim to be innocent instead of begging for my forgiveness, which would have seemed the more logical choice?"

"No, Your Majesty," Rika said, shaking her head. "Though, the move does fit well with the brazen nature of their crime. Since these two soldiers are the ones who discovered the Zerura on them in the first place and only they and we heard their admission of guilt, they must think that if they can cast enough doubt on the four of us, they might have a chance. It's unexpected and desperate but clever—a not unexpected attribute of men employed by the Academy."

The man who could not see, still on his knees, turned his head toward Rika as she spoke. The other two had retreated into silence, but Eirmon could see that this man was not easily cowed, which helped to explain why his earlier beatings had been more severe. "It's you, isn't it?" the man said. "You took it."

Rika looked back at the man, shaking her head in disbelief. "You can't escape your fate by accusing me, Treslan. You have broken your vows and betrayed your king."

"I have not!" the man called Treslan began, but he didn't get very far.

"Silence," Eirmon said firmly enough to cut him off and prevent anyone else from speaking too, but he did not shout. "I have heard enough."

He turned to the officer of the Davrii who had stood silently, a half step behind him throughout the whole process. "These men are to be executed for treachery against their city and their king. See that it is done."

The men before him blanched but dared not speak as he turned to exit the room. Rika and Barreck started to follow him out, but he lifted his hand to stop them. He gazed for a moment at both of them. "Stay and watch so you can teach the rest of those working on the Zerura project the price of greed and ambition."

They nodded and stopped. He left the room, walking with his personal guard back through the Academy. Before long, he had emerged out into the warm daylight, pausing on the front steps of the Academy to consider what had just happened.

Almost certainly, he had ordered the death of three innocent men. He knew that, but if he was to convince Barreck and Rika that he didn't suspect them of wrongdoing, he wasn't sure how he could have avoided it. They were small casualties in a larger war.

The world around him was whirling. Various vague notions and suspicions began to come together and crystallize into a definite conception of what had just happened and why. Unless Eirmon missed his guess, he wasn't the only one already planning the future after his dalliance with Rika was over. She appeared to have plans of her own.

Plans he intended to uncover and expose.

22

BLOOD ON THE QUAY

"He knows," Barreck said, gripping the table he was using to steady himself, his fingers blanched white.

"He doesn't know anything," Rika said, leaning in from beside him, trying to get his attention, but he wouldn't look at her. Ever since they'd come to Barreck's office after the executions, he'd avoided looking directly at her. Perhaps he was angry, though she didn't know why he would be. They'd both agreed to the plan and known its risks.

Or maybe it wasn't anger. Maybe it was shame. He should be ashamed, Rika thought, to show so much weakness in front of her.

She really didn't understand Barreck's reaction. They'd gotten away with it, hadn't they? Eirmon had executed the three men they'd accused, just as she'd known he would. Whatever momentary doubts he'd had, she'd allayed them. If any more lingered, she'd allay them too. She'd show the king in the days and weeks ahead that he'd not even begun to plumb the depths of the pleasure she could bring him. Soon he wouldn't remember having had any doubts, if indeed he did.

And if she were wrong, if the doubts did linger, it wouldn't matter. Before long, they'd be gone. If they could keep their heads just a little while longer, literally, they'd disappear from Barra-Dohn with the means to become wealthier than either of them could even imagine.

Barreck, though, from the moment they'd gotten here, had been acting as though the whole thing had failed, as though it had been their heads chopped off and thrown into a sack to be fed to the buzzards outside the city walls. He would have to get his act together. She couldn't risk having her efforts undermined by Barreck's weakness.

"He knows," Barreck repeated, shaking his head slowly. "I could tell. He didn't buy it. Not at all."

"No? Then why execute the others? Why not lock them up until he'd had a chance to investigate further?"

"I don't know," Barreck answered quietly, "but he knows."

"Well, if we're arrested after we leave here and then executed for betraying him, then I guess we'll know."

"Don't joke about it," Barreck said, turning to her at last and grabbing her arm with the same vise-like grip he'd been using on the table. "He just might."

"Let go of me," Rika said angrily, pulling her arm away. "And control your emotions, would you? If he suspects something, that's all the more reason to get it together. He might suspect, but he can't know, so don't give him reason to think he does. Leave the rest to me."

"That's hard to do when it's my life dangling in your hands too, not just yours."

"Well," Rika said, stepping closer and looking into his eyes. "You should have considered that before now. Your life has been in my hands from the moment you conspired with me to steal Zerura from Eirmon and sell it to his enemies."

Barreck turned away from her and leaned back over the table. After a moment she added, "My life is in your hands too."

"I know," he said quietly, nodding but still not looking at her. "Are you sure we can trust those guards?"

"They're the greediest soldiers I know," Rika said. "They were much easier to corrupt than you."

She said the last with a smile and a hint of playfulness, hoping to help Barreck come back to himself, but he didn't respond. He just stood, leaning over the table, staring at nothing. "And what's to stop them from selling us to Eirmon?"

"They know Eirmon, that's what," Rika said. "They know that lying to the king in order to make money from us would get them in as much trouble as we'd be in, or if not as much, still more than they want."

Barreck looked up at last and gazed at her with a semblance of calm, showing his usual self for the first time since they'd begun this conversation.

Rika continued, "They don't even know that we've really stolen Zerura from Eirmon. They completely bought my story about those three trying to sabotage my career at the Academy because I'm a favorite of the king."

"You're sure?"

"Yes, and the fact that they believe my motive was really that petty, by the way, is all the more reason they won't say anything. They had nothing personally at stake in this other than money, and yet they helped me get three innocent men killed."

After a moment, Barreck nodded. "I guess they only need to keep our secret long enough for us to get away."

"Yeah, well," Rika said, "if Eirmon does suspect us and we go missing, they'll have bigger problems to worry about. If Eirmon thinks we've swindled him out of a supply of Zerura and that they've helped, they'll be joining Treslan and the others pretty quickly."

"I'm sure you're right about that," Barreck said. "But I still think you're wrong about Eirmon."

"I'm not," Rika said, exasperated. "And I think I should know. I know him better than anyone."

"Sleeping with him doesn't mean you know him," Barreck said. Rika glared at him. "I know that. Give me some credit."

For a moment they stared, eyes locked in a silent contest of wills until Barreck relented. When he did, Rika stepped closer and placed her hand gently, soothingly on his back. "Hey, we did it. The worst is behind us. We had to do this to divert his attention from the missing Zerura. Let me divert it some more, and before you know it, it'll be time to go."

"We should go now," Barreck said, turning and taking both Rika's arms in his hands and touching her firmly but more gently this time. She didn't resist as he pulled her closer, slid his hands to her waist, and kissed her. "We have plenty of Zerura left, and taking more would be too risky now. I know we said we'd wait and see, but we can't take more. Let's just go. The sooner the better."

"Patience," Rika said. "You know why we're waiting."

"I do," Barreck said. "And we can wait for the price to go up somewhere other than here, Rika. Let's get out of Barra-Dohn."

"If we disappear now, we might as well leave Eirmon a note, taunting him that we tricked him into killing those men and then took his Zerura."

"So?"

"So? If he knows we took it, if he knows we duped him, then he'll hunt us down for sure. He won't be able not to. There needs to be real doubt about whether we did it to make him hesitate to commit time and men to the search."

"Then we wait, but weeks, not months."

"I don't know . . ."

"Just think about it," Barreck said. "Promise me you'll think about it."

"All right," Rika said. "I'll think about it."

The morning sun glistened on the harbor as Tchinchura walked with Ellenara. She'd been more than willing to walk with him, her initial reluctance to his overtures of friendship having faded with time. She readily received his suggestion that they walk past the quay and along the waterfront.

And yet, though they'd been walking for some time now, Tchinchura had found it more difficult to direct their conversation toward his own purposes than he'd thought he would. Not because Ellenara wasn't willing to talk. Quite the contrary, she talked most readily today, more so than on any previous occasion. She confided in him now easily, and today her years of heartache and confusion over her treatment by Kaden came pouring out. Tchinchura didn't have the heart to stop her. He could see and hear how much she needed to talk, so he walked beside her, listening.

Something had happened just before the fleet left for Garranmere, and now she had hope as well as heartache.

Then her talking turned to Deslo. It often did, as she was understandably anxious not just about his physical safety but also about his time with Kaden. She was hopeful that Kaden had taken her seriously about using this situation that neither had asked for or wanted as an opportunity to work on becoming more of a father, but she didn't trust that hope. It was too much of a stranger to her heart.

They walked beside the water, which murmured gently as it lapped up against the quay, and he listened to her pour out her heart. She checked herself a few times, making self-deprecating remarks about his having to listen to an anxious mother prattle on, but she didn't stop. Maybe she couldn't. Maybe now that the dam was breached, she couldn't stop the flood that flowed out, so Tchinchura listened. As he did, he thought of the report he'd had of the battle and of his knowledge that Deslo was indeed safe with Zangira and Kaden. He knew that he could offer her at least some measure of peace on that score, but that would mean telling her how he knew.

He smiled, then quickly suppressed it lest Ellenara think he was trivializing her concerns. He had the entry he was looking for, and he would use it to introduce her to the world of secrets he inhabited, though he hadn't decided how much he was prepared to tell her.

"Nara," Tchinchura said, using the abbreviated form of her name that everyone else used and that she seemed to prefer. "Deslo is all right. I'm sure he'll be coming home to you soon."

"You're always so kind to reassure me," Nara answered, "and I'm sure Zangira is looking after him like he promised he would, but . . ."

"You don't understand me," Tchinchura interrupted her, and Nara looked up at him in surprise. He never interrupted her. "I know he's all right."

She frowned. "You can't know."

"I can," Tchinchura answered, and before he said anything else, he quickly removed the Zerura from his bicep. "You know what this is, don't you?"

"I do now," Nara said, looking at the Zerura undulating in the air above his outstretched hand. "I knew you had some, of course, but not which ornament it was."

Tchinchura deftly put the Zerura back on his arm as they continued walking. "Well, that's it."

"And how does that explain what you claim to know?"

"Zangira has another piece, just like this one," the Amhuru said. "When used a certain way, they become a kind of messaging device."

Nara watched him, looking incredulous. "You can speak to him with that?"

Tchinchura nodded.

"Anywhere?"

"Not exactly anywhere," Tchinchura said. "We can pass each other messages when we're apart and the distance isn't too far, at least for a while, until we get our separate pieces back together."

Tchinchura's caveats hadn't diminished the look of wonder on Nara's face. In fact, the more he talked, the wider her eyes grew.

"What matters," he continued, "is that I know for a fact that the army of Barra-Dohn laid siege to Garranmere a few days ago and that Deslo came through the battle just fine."

Nara's eyes seemed to bulge even more, then began to fill with tears. "You're serious."

"Of course, I'm serious," Tchinchura said with a smile. "I wouldn't make something like this up to give you false comfort. Deslo is fine. And," Tchinchura added, "so is Kaden."

They walked in silence as Tchinchura let Nara think about what he had told her. Up ahead, a warehouse sat up close to the water, and a handful of men were loafing where the quay narrowed in front of it. He would let Nara consider this, and when they were past these men, he would work the conversation around to what he still wanted to tell her.

As they drew nearer to the warehouse, though, Nara spoke, sounding excited. "If you can speak to Zangira like that, then would it also be possible for me to speak to Deslo?"

"Well," Tchinchura began, but he cut himself off as he looked again at the cluster of men ahead. Something about them was wrong.

Maybe it was the clothing that didn't fit dockworkers. Maybe it was the way they seemed too unaware of a pair as conspicuous as Nara and Tchinchura. Maybe it was the furtive glance one of the men sent their way before hastily looking away. Maybe it was all of these things, but Tchinchura pushed Nara back away from him, telling her to get out of the way and get down, as he drew his axe in a fluid motion, preparing for what he now knew would inevitably come. He didn't have to wait long.

They turned, almost in unison, drawing knives and starting to fan out. One of them, right in the center of the group and a step in front of the others, raised his arm to throw the long knife with its jagged blade that he held, but before his arm was in position to let it fly, Tchinchura's axe struck him in the chest, hard, crushing his sternum.

Then, just as quickly, the axe was flying back through the air to Tchinchura, who grabbed the handle firmly, ignoring the blood that spattered off the axe onto his chest and arms as he caught it. The man who'd been hit slumped to his knees, his body lifeless and his eyes rolling back in his head, but Tchinchura didn't have time to chronicle the rest of his collapse. He ran right toward the water and the front of the warehouse, away from the direction he'd pushed Nara for fear that a blade thrown his way might somehow miss and strike her.

A knife from one of the others came whistling through the air, but the man who'd thrown it had been startled enough by the death of his friend that he'd thrown carelessly, misjudging Tchinchura's speed. The knife flew behind Tchinchura, who by this point had drawn his own long slender knife so that he was ready to strike with both hands.

A quick flick of his left wrist, and the knife was flying toward another of his assailants. He didn't have time to watch it, though, as another knife was coming his way, and this one was on target. He slowed, his axe raised, and dodging a little to the side, swung the axe so that it struck the speeding knife coming toward his chest and knocked it from the air. He spun and threw the axe at the man who'd thrown the knife. The man barely had time to look stunned, whether because his own knife had been deflected or because he'd been struck by Tchinchura's axe, it was hard to say, and he was down.

As his axe flew back to him, Tchinchura looked to see the man he'd hit with his knife, pulling the blade from his arm. Enraged, the man gripped the Amhuru's own knife by the blade and threw it at Tchinchura. This was a mistake.

Tchinchura held up his left hand, and the blade slowed to a virtual stop as he caught his returning axe with his right hand. The Amhuru took a step toward the knife, plucked it neatly from the air and hurled it back with great force. It hit right in the center of the man's neck, sunk in to the hilt, and he fell clutching awkwardly at the bleeding wound.

Tchinchura dropped low to the ground in a crouch as two more knives flew overhead, just a bit too high to hit him. He pushed forward into a roll, and as he did, he slid the soles of both feet lightly along the Zerura on his bicep. When he came out of his roll, he leapt up into the air, landing on the Arua field and running straight at the two remaining assassins.

For their part, they looked at the Amhuru speeding across the Arua field without any shoes whatsoever, let alone meridium-soled ones, and looks of sheer terror broke across their faces. One reached desperately for the small club hanging from his side as the other turned to run. Tchinchura swerved toward the man fumbling with the club, and the fellow didn't even get a chance to raise his arm before Tchinchura had dispatched him on his way after the final man.

Running on top of the Arua field meant that Tchinchura closed the gap between them quickly. When only a few steps away, he called out, "Surrender and live."

The sound of Tchinchura's voice brought the man to a stop, but it wasn't surrender he had in mind. He turned, flinging a small knife that he'd had tucked up his sleeve at Tchinchura.

A deft move with the axe, and the little knife struck the side of the axe head and fell clattering onto the smooth stones of the quay.

"I want information. I don't want to kill you," Tchinchura said, holding his position, axe raised. "But I will if I have to."

The man stood, watching Tchinchura, as though weighing his options, but then he charged the Amhuru, trying to get in close enough to knock the axe from Tchinchura's hands. He never got the chance. Tchinchura stepped aside, and with a quick, strong stroke, dropped the man with a single blow.

Tchinchura looked around. All five men were indeed down, scattered a small distance from one another, small pools of blood encircling each of them now, splotches of crimson on the other-wise dark gray stone. Tchinchura stepped down from the Arua and jogged over to the man who lay crumbled over on his side, his legs bent under his body awkwardly, the handle of the Amhuru's knife still protruding from his neck. Then, with both his axe and knife in hand, he went in search of Ellenara, his eyes scanning the quay for any further danger.

Eirmon was eating in his private dining room while Myron stood nearby, a neat stack of papers tucked under his arm. The man was certainly efficient, Eirmon thought as he took another swig of his wine. But the king could have wished that granting the chief steward's request for an audience over lunch hadn't meant quite so much of his time. He'd forestalled many of these conversations in the weeks leading up to the celebration, using the excuse that the preparation for the anniversary precluded him from giving these matters his full attention. He'd even dodged some of the less important things on Myron's list during the first few weeks after Kaden had gone, pleading that his mind was elsewhere because of the attack on Garranmere. But now, at last, he'd run out of excuses to put the man off further.

Sooner or later, even for a king, the piper had to be paid.

Myron shuffled through his papers, perhaps realizing that Eirmon's patience was wearing thin and that his time might be running out, adding pressure to move next to whatever remained that he felt was most important. As he considered what to present next, the door to the room swung open, and Tchinchura, his dark skin and white vest both stained with blood, stalked into the room.

Immediately, everything in the room changed. The handful of Davrii standing along the walls on either side of the room drew their spears and stepped to the table, surrounding Eirmon. Though the Amhuru wasn't holding a weapon, his axe and knife both hung from his belt, and the soldiers, sensing a threat to their sovereign, blocked instinctively both avenues by which Tchinchura could approach him.

Myron, in turn, disappeared almost immediately from Eirmon's side, sliding back into the shadows against the wall.

Eirmon looked up at the Amhuru, who'd stopped at the end of the table opposite him and now stood, staring with those penetrating, golden eyes at the king as he calmly set his fork down and finished chewing the bite of roast lamb in his mouth. The soldiers held their ground as the two men stared at each other, and after a moment, Eirmon leaned forward. "You look rather the worse for wear," Eirmon said, looking the Amhuru up and down.

"Indeed," Tchinchura said, "though I'm sure Your Majesty will be pleased to know that none of this blood is mine."

"I am pleased, indeed," Eirmon said. "Since you're a royal guest at my palace, it grieves me to know you were ever in danger."

Tchinchura stared back, and Eirmon wished he could read something of the man's mood. Clearly he was angry, but there were many kinds of anger, and all the king's practice and skill at reading the moods of men seemed lost on this man.

"I was set upon by five men, Your Majesty, walking out by the quay this morning."

"Indeed!" Eirmon said, trying to muster something that sounded like genuine surprise and sympathy. "Alas, as much as I try to eradicate crime in Barra-Dohn, we still have trouble with footpads and the occasional bandit."

"You have bold footpads indeed if they would attack a man who was obviously a guest of the king, since surely no one remains in Barra-Dohn who doesn't know I am your guest."

"Boldness, perhaps, or folly. Maybe both."

"Yes, boldness or folly," Tchinchura said, and then added as though an afterthought, "especially since the king's own daughter-in-law was with me."

Eirmon tensed. The fools. They'd been supposed to attack him while alone. "I trust that Nara is all right?"

"I protected her."

The subtle but clear emphasis on the "I" in that sentence grated on Eirmon. "Then I owe you a debt of gratitude."

Tchinchura nodded. "Perhaps these bandits were emboldened by the jewelry I wear. I have many valuable pieces." He motioned to include all the golden ornaments that hung from his body, but he never looked away from the king, watching to see his reaction.

Eirmon listened but didn't flinch. The Amhuru wasn't the only one who could control his emotions and conceal his reactions. "You've evidently had a very difficult morning," Eirmon said at last. "Why don't you clean up? Myron here can see to it that your clothes are washed right away. Perhaps they can still be salvaged."

Tchinchura easily slid the blood-stained vest off and flung it across the room in the direction of the chief steward, where it fell on the floor. He remained where he was, his muscles taut and body slick with blood and sweat.

The king remained still, watching, and the soldiers stood. The tension in the room was as thick as it had been the moment Tchinchura had entered.

The Amhuru spoke, breaking the awkward silence. "Nara's gone to her room. She's a bit shaken up."

"Thank you again for seeing her safely home."

Tchinchura started to go, but he stopped at the door and turned back toward the king. "Perhaps we've finally found how I may be of service to you and to Barra-Dohn."

"How's that?" Eirmon asked, curious.

"Well, if the streets are really this unsafe, I might be able to lend you a hand. I'm good at cleaning up messes. Even bandits and footpads often take orders from someone. Perhaps I will find the man responsible and purge this city of what ails it."

With that, Tchinchura slipped out the door.

The soldiers finally relaxed while Eirmon leaned back in his chair, fuming.

23

THE CITY OF LIFE AND PEACE

A re you sure this is a good idea?" Nara asked.

"No," Tchinchura answered.

They passed through a patch of relative darkness between bright streetlights as they walked down one of the larger streets of Barra-Dohn.

Tchinchura had decided against using any of the smaller streets with fewer lights, as doing so would have made it easier for anyone sent to follow them to keep to the shadows and stay close. Here on one of the somewhat brightly lit major thoroughfares of the city, they might be easily seen, but so would anyone following them too closely.

Nara pulled her shawl closer against the slight chill of evening and kept pace beside him. They'd not talked since the day Tchinchura had been attacked, but as time slipped away and he considered his options, he felt increasingly like whatever action he took, he'd be safer away from the palace, no matter how important it might be to stay close to the king.

Since their confrontation, Eirmon was never alone in the palace without at least twenty of his private guard around, so any concern Tchinchura had felt before that leaving the palace would put Eirmon on guard had been rendered pointless. Eirmon was already on guard.

Tchinchura did not waste any energy second-guessing his decision to walk in on the king upon returning to the palace. It might have been a mistake, but even if it had been, he could do nothing now. The king wanted Tchinchura dead, and letting Eirmon know that he knew the attack had come from him didn't affect that central fact. Eirmon hadn't come at him in the palace, and while Tchinchura still doubted that he would, that doubt was weakening. Eirmon must fear Tchinchura's reunion with Zangira, so if no other opportunity presented itself, he might just attack the Amhuru in his room.

He glanced around, making sure no one was near. Eirmon had seemed genuinely surprised when he'd mentioned Nara the other day. He suspected the men who'd been charged with killing him were not supposed to attack with her nearby. He hoped that walking with her tonight was not putting her into danger, but he had to trust that if danger came, he could once more keep her safe. He couldn't talk to her in the palace, as propriety would not allow either of them to be alone in the other's chambers. Wherever they went these last few days, they were constantly interrupted by stewards seeking after their comfort and well-being. Obviously, Eirmon had instructed his stewards to keep close tabs on them.

That's why Tchinchura had made Nara promise to walk with him tonight just at sundown. Going out after dark was risky, but it was also unexpected. They'd never gone out at night before. Tchinchura hoped that at least this once, he would catch the king and those appointed to keep an eye on him unprepared. Still, he had no time to waste. He'd lost his chance to have this conversation last time by delaying too long. He needed to move things along.

"Eirmon wants me dead," he said, keeping up his pace.

Nara didn't react in any way that would show surprise. Obviously, she'd considered the possibility.

"You're sure it was Eirmon?"

"Yes."

"But why?" she asked, looking his way now.

"That's what I want to explain to you," Tchinchura said. "The short answer is that he's stolen something, and I'm here to get it back. The long answer will take some explaining, but that's why I brought you out tonight."

"You don't need to, you know," Nara said.

"Don't need to what?"

"Give me the long answer," Nara said. "If you think I need convincing to help you, I don't. If you say Eirmon took something, and you're here to get it back, I believe you. I don't know what I can do, but I'll help if I can."

Tchinchura reached over through the dark and squeezed Nara's upper arm appreciatively. "I'm glad you trust me, but I want you to know anyway."

"Know what?"

"The story that should never have been forgotten. It is, after all, both your story and mine."

Nara looked confused. "I don't understand."

"I know, but listen as we walk, and you will."

Barra-Dohn was once known as Zeru-Shalim, "the city of life and peace." The Old Stories say Zeru-Shalim was the oldest city in the world, but that is more than I know. What I do know is that once, a long, long time before the discovery of meridium, a king in Zeru-Shalim grieved over the fact that many in the city did not worship Kalos. His name was Amhir, and he sought to lead the people by his example of faithful worship, but while most knew the king was devout, many ignored his wishes and did as they pleased.

Some of his counselors told Amhir to bring the force of the law to bear on those who did not serve Kalos, but the king was reluctant to do that, believing that the worship of Kalos should be freely given. Instead, he decided to fast and pray while he sought the face of Kalos, asking for wisdom to better lead the people of Zeru-Shalim.

While he was alone in his throne room, Amhir heard the voice of Kalos calling to him. Kalos instructed Amhir to go at dawn to the great square in the center of the city, carrying a pack with food and water for three days and nights. What exactly he would find there, Kalos didn't say, only that he was to go on a journey, and no matter who came with him to the square, he would have to go alone.

Amhir obeyed, and in the morning he went down to the city square. Like any king, Amhir was never alone, and a handful of his servants and advisors followed him to the square, despite Amhir's protests that their coming could serve no purpose. Kalos had called him alone. As they stood waiting for the dawn to break, the earth shook, and a great chasm opened in the center of the square as the voice of Kalos spoke again, and this time not only the king but all the men with him heard.

Kalos instructed Amhir to descend into the chasm. He told him that he would find a steep and narrow way, leading down, down, down, farther than Amhir could imagine, and that it would take him three days and nights to get to the bottom and back. When Amhir asked what he would find there, Kalos replied only that there was no time to waste, but that at the bottom Amhir would know what to do.

As the voice of Kalos faded away, Amhir made his way to the edge of the great hole, and though several of his friends and advisors expressed their concern about the king's safety and offered to come with him, all had heard the voice, and none dared suggest that he not go. Amhir insisted that he must go alone as Kalos had instructed, and he directed them to remain and pray—not for him but for Zeru-Shalim—that this journey might be the answer to his prayers for the city he loved.

During the next three days and nights, the small band of advisors waiting by the chasm grew and grew until virtually everyone in Zeru-Shalim had come and was now camped, day and night, near the hole, waiting for their king to return. Work and trade in the city ground to a halt, and the closer the end of the third day came, the more reluctant the people were to leave, even when hunger gnawed at them. The king's chief steward summoned carts stacked with barrels of water to the square when he realized that many people would not leave despite their growing thirst during that last, long, hot day.

Finally, the morning after the third night came, and as the first rays of dawn broke upon the city square, Amhir emerged from the chasm, dirty but alive. His pack had been left behind, and in his hand he carried only one thing—the Golden Cord.

The Golden Cord was a piece of Zerura, the living matter that Kalos placed in deep veins throughout the world near the beginning of time to generate the Arua field and regulate the ecological cycles of all living things. As Amhir emerged from the great hole in the square, the ground shook and groaned again, and the chasm closed behind him. All Zeru-Shalim stood silent, staring at the beauty of the Golden Cord as it danced to its own inner song in the air above Amhir's hand.

The Golden Cord became a symbol of Kalos' presence in Zeru-Shalim. That year the rains came early and stayed late. The ground yielded better harvests than anyone could remember ever receiving. Sickness became less frequent, fewer mothers and babies died in childbirth, and the elderly seemed to live longer with fewer health problems than ever before. In the face of such things, even the least devout couldn't help but acknowledge that the loving and merciful hand of Kalos had blessed Zeru-Shalim. The prayer of the king had been answered.

To house the Golden Cord, Amhir ordered a temple built in the very square where the chasm had opened. At the time, it was the largest building ever undertaken in the city, and it wasn't finished in Amhir's lifetime. The king also established the Kalonian priesthood, which was created to care for the Temple and the Golden Cord. Over time, the highest office in the Kalonian priesthood was given the name "Amhura" as a tribute to Amhir. And when at last the Temple was completed, a room in the very center was dedicated to house the Golden Cord. It became known as the Room of Life.

Tchinchura paused in his telling of the story, and Nara looked at him until he turned his golden eyes to meet her own inquisitive look. "Amhir, Amhura—Amhuru?"

Tchinchura smiled and nodded.

The sound of a door swinging open and sudden laughter broke the stillness of the quiet night, and Tchinchura instinctively pulled Nara closer as he turned to see what was happening behind them. Three men had just stumbled out of a nearby inn and stood laughing raucously. Even from across the street, the pungent smell of cheap wine wafted toward them in the warm night air.

While they were stopped, Tchinchura seized the opportunity to survey the long street behind them. A handful of people were moving here and there, all of them walking with purpose and determination. He saw a man slip into a doorway a few streets back, but even though he lingered with Nara, the man didn't show himself. He turned, urging Nara forward, and picked up his pace.

Nara watched the three men from the inn walk the opposite direction on the other side of the street for a moment, but eventually she turned back to him. They started walking again. "After the other day, I'm a little jumpy."

Tchinchura smiled. "So am I."

Nara nodded, appearing relieved that she wasn't the only one. "So I think you were going to tell me how the Amhuru are connected to the king in the story?"

"Ah, yes," Tchinchura said. "I was indeed. But you'll have to bear with me. You should know more, though some of this story you may know already, for it involves the anniversary Barra-Dohn has just celebrated."

"The story of the discovery of meridium?" Nara said, frowning a bit at Tchinchura. "Everyone knows that story."

"They know some of it, but the most important parts, the parts they really should remember, they have forgotten."

Nara frowned. "This isn't an elaborate way of dodging my question?"

"No, I promise."

"All right," Nara said. "Tell me."

At first, the Temple and the Golden Cord served as a visible symbol of Kalos for the people of Zeru-Shalim, just as Amhir had hoped it would. The city prospered and for many generations was peaceful. Over time, though, a fracture developed between the Kalonian priesthood and the kings of Zeru-Shalim. The more the people of the city attributed their success to the Cord, the more prestige the priests garnered for themselves, and the wider the gap between the kings and the priests grew.

It didn't happen overnight, and there was blame on both sides, but the distance between them expanded until it was a gaping divide. Along the way, one of these kings, locked in the ongoing struggle for control of the city, proposed that Zeru-Shalim change its name to Barra-Dohn—"the city of might and power."

Perhaps it was insignificant, this suggested change of name that didn't even happen in truth until it was proposed again, some time later, but it summarized changes going on in the heart of the city that remained the most prosperous in all of Aralyn but that no longer showed gratitude to Kalos for its prosperity. The kings and priests who should have been concerned for the well-being of their people cared only about their own power, and the people gradually lost sight of what the Golden Cord represented and began, in effect, to worship the Cord itself.

Then disaster came. To those who lived in those days, it seemed to strike suddenly without warning, like a catastrophic sandstorm blowing in out of the desert. But in truth, a storm had been brewing for generations, and it brought as much devastation and upheaval to Barra-Dohn as King Amhir's faithfulness had brought peace and prosperity.

A man rose to the top of the Kalonian priesthood, a man intent only on subjugating the office of king beneath the office of Amhura. He might have succeeded too, for he was as clever as he was devious. He knew that the people of Barra-Dohn attributed their success to the Cord more than they did to either the king or the priests, a fact the kings had used in their favor from the beginning, since it had been a king who had given them the Cord.

So he decided that the priests would take the Cord from the Room of Life and parade it through the streets of the city. He would present a spectacle to the masses that could replace the distant memory of a king emerging from a great chasm, grasping the Cord. No one alive had ever seen the Cord outside the Temple, and many had never even seen it there, as the rituals surrounding the Cord had become increasingly restrictive and removed from the ordinary lives of the people of the city. Now all would see the great Golden Cord and behold its glimmering beauty, carried and cared for by a small army of Kalonian priests.

It was a sad and sorry nadir. The Cord that Kalos had given Zeru-Shalim to be a symbol of his power and presence had been reduced to a pawn in a power struggle between almost equally unworthy parties. And worst of all, the man who should have been most concerned to promote the worship of Kalos and to guard most vigorously the integrity of the Cord was the architect of the plan that would be perhaps the final step in elevating the Cord above its maker.

However, some health remained in the Kalonian priesthood, and a man named Armond tried to stop the parade from happening. The Amhura, though, would not be deterred, and he had Armond struck down in the Temple. That was when the disaster came, for even as the blood of the faithful priest stained the floor of the Temple, a plague struck the city. Thousands and thousands died, including a majority of the priests themselves.

Kalos directed that the Golden Cord be divided into six fragments and distributed to the six sons of Armond. Kalos charged them to take the pieces away from Barra-Dohn. He said that the six pieces were to be kept apart and never reunited, or else the wrath of Kalos would be aroused again. This time the price to be paid would be even more disastrous.

So the six sons of Armond left their homes in Barra-Dohn. The older ones took their wives and children with them, for they knew they would never return. The descendants of the sons of Armond came to be known as Amhuru, for Armond was remembered by all those who held to the worship of Kalos as the last faithful Amhura, even though he never held that office.

You have guessed at the rest. Though we have mixed and married with many peoples over the long years of our exile, we remain true to the charge we were given. We wander still, or at least most of us do much of the time. Even so, we still remember, and always will, that Barra-Dohn was our ancient home.

Nara had been watching Tchinchura as he spoke, and when he stopped, she started. "All right, I see the connection between the Amhuru and the king Amhir, but how is any of this connected to the anniversary?"

Tchinchura had come to a stop on the broad street that went past the front of the Academy. He stood under one of the bright streetlights and pointed across at the statue of the craftsman who had discovered meridium. "You see him?"

"Yes," Nara said, looking over at the statue.

"When he cut himself, he was making the ornate tray that was going to be used by the faithless Amhura to carry the Golden Cord through the streets."

Nara looked back at Tchinchura, a slight frown creasing her brow. "That's what he was making?"

"That's what he was making."

"But," Nara said, looking back across the street at the statue, "if Barra-Dohn was turning away from Kalos, if they were about to be hit by a plague and punished, why would he choose that moment to give the city meridium?"

"That, Nara," Tchinchura said, "is a very good question."

Even in the partial light of the meridium streetlight, the Amhuru could see Nara blush. They stood together, looking at the statue floating in the middle of the empty square, still impressive even as it towered over nothing.

"I think," Tchinchura went on, "that the gift of meridium was an act of mercy."

"The Cord was about to be taken," Nara said, "so Kalos gave the people of Barra-Dohn meridium?"

"I think he gave them a second chance," Tchinchura said. "By valuing it too highly, they squandered the right to the Cord and lost it, so Kalos gave them a lesser gift. A chance to remember, even in the painful days following the plague, that Kalos had not forgotten them."

"A lesser gift? Meridium?"

"Oh, yes," Tchinchura said, turning to Nara. "You have no idea the power that the Golden Cord represented. The power of meridium is derived from the Arua field that Zerura generates. The Cord is Zerura itself."

Nara's eyes grew wide. "You said Eirmon stole something. You don't mean he stole the Golden Cord, do you?"

"Yes and no," Tchinchura said. "The Cord remains in six fragments, and not since the day that Armond's eldest son divided it into those pieces has any man brought them all together. But Eirmon has one of the original six pieces, and I'm here to get it back."

"What do you mean, 'original'? Are there pieces that aren't original?"

"Yes," Tchinchura said.

"I don't understand," Nara said, confused again.

"The six original fragments can be subdivided over and over again, and they are never exhausted, not even diminished."

"That's impossible," Nara said.

"It would seem so," Tchinchura answered, "But I have seen it done with my own eyes. An original piece of the Golden Cord can be cut almost in half, and both pieces will expand until they are the same size. The only difference between the two, if you know how to handle them, will be that the original—the piece that grows out of the larger portion of the original—can be subdivided again and again, whereas the new piece cannot. The replica, if cut, remains cut and loses its power."

"That's . . ." Nara stumbled, looking for words. "That's utterly fantastic. It's unbelievable."

"I know."

"And terrible," she added. "If Eirmon has one of these, then he can replicate it endlessly."

"Yes," Tchinchura said. "All the more reason I need to get it back."

"How . . ." Nara started, looking for the question she wanted to ask. "How did he get it in the first place?"

"I don't know how, only when," Tchinchura said.

"When?"

"About fifteen or twenty years ago, as near as any of us can tell."

"As near as any of you can tell?"

"We're nomadic, Nara. It's the nature of our charge," Tchinchura said. "And while some of us can communicate over limited distances in the way that I've shown you, we don't usually travel in pairs or stay in contact frequently. Zangira is with me, only because we've been given the task of recovering this piece of the Cord."

Nara looked at Tchinchura, searching his face. "The way you just said 'this piece,' it sounded almost like there's more than one piece that needs recovering."

Tchinchura smiled. "I hadn't decided if I would tell you that, which is why I hesitated. You're an astute observer."

"Tchinchura, how many pieces are missing?"

"Two," the Amhuru said, "just two."

"Does Eirmon have them both?"

"No," Tchinchura said, shaking his head. "I don't think so. The other piece has been missing for more than fifty years."

Nara looked stunned. "More than fifty years? Isn't that a problem?"

Tchinchura laughed. "Yes, it's a problem. But it isn't one we need to worry about tonight. We've been tending the fragments of the Golden Cord for a thousand years, Nara. Mishaps have happened before."

"Mishaps?"

"Things happen. No matter how tough you are, how clever you are, no matter how many safeguards you build into your routines and plans to make sure they don't. Things happen."

"I'm sure that's true," Nara conceded.

"Besides, I have enough to worry about recovering the piece that Eirmon has taken without worrying about the other one."

"Fair enough," Nara said, rubbing her hands along her arms as she looked across the street at the Academy and the statue beside it. "So what now?"

"Well," Tchinchura started. "I need to break in there and take a look around."

"Break into the Academy?" Nara asked.

"Yes," the Amhuru replied. "It might be there, but, of course, it might not. Eirmon could be wearing it."

"Wearing it," Nara muttered turning and looking at Tchinchura and the ring of Zerura encircling his bicep, as though for the first time. "Like you're wearing it right now. That's a fragment of the Golden Cord or one of the replicas, isn't it?"

"Yes."

"Amhuru don't just wear Zerura, they wear pieces of the Cord," Nara said so softly it was all but a whisper, "or pieces made from pieces."

"That's right," Tchinchura said. "That's where it all comes from. As far as I know, the Golden Cord is the only piece of Zerura ever mined. We get all our pieces from the six originals."

"Tchinchura, is that," Nara began slowly, as though measuring each word, "is that an original piece?"

Tchinchura smiled. "It is a great honor to wear one of the originals, so I will take it as a compliment that you would even ask."

Nara nodded and looked back at the Academy. "So if the king might be wearing his, why break in there?"

"I know Eirmon has been experimenting with Zerura," Tchinchura said. "Kaden used weapons made of meridium that had been enhanced with it against Garranmere. Zangira saw them."

"From what you've said, I'm guessing they'd be pretty powerful?"

"Yes," Tchinchura said, "and in Eirmon's hands, terrible."

"And he can make a limitless supply of them because he has an original piece."

"Yes."

Nara nodded. "If they've been doing experiments like that, they will have been doing them in there."

"How strange," Tchinchura began, but he didn't finish his thought.

"What is?" Nara asked.

"That my search would lead me here." He pointed across the street again. "What you call the Academy was once the Temple that housed the Golden Cord."

"The Academy was the Temple?"

"It was indeed," Tchinchura said.

"That seems, well, wrong," Nara said. "Eirmon's stolen a piece of the Cord and brought it here, and now he's experimenting on it in there?"

"There's a lot wrong here," Tchinchura said. "That's just part of it."

"How can I help?"

"After I break into the Academy, I won't be coming back to the palace," Tchinchura said. "If I find what I'm looking for, I'll disappear from Barra-Dohn."

"Just like that?"

"Just like that."

"But shouldn't Eirmon be punished?" Nara asked, perhaps a hint of hope in her voice.

"Yes, and he will be," Tchinchura said, "but by Kalos, not by me. My job is to recover the fragment. If I'm able to retrieve it from in there, my responsibility will be to take it safely away."

"And if it's not in there?"

"Then I will need to recover it from Eirmon."

"If he's wearing it, you mean."

"Yes, I'll have to come for him," Tchinchura said. "And coming for him will be dangerous. There will be blood."

"I see," Nara said, taking a deep breath. "What do you want from me?"

"Just two things," Tchinchura said. "First, though you'll probably be watched, make a habit of walking through the city. Come routinely to the market, not predictably, but frequently. I'll contact you there if I can."

"All right," Nara said, a little uncertainly. "And what's the other thing?"

"Be careful. I won't come for Eirmon right away. I'll wait for Zangira's help, which means Deslo will be back by then too. If fighting breaks out in the palace, get him out of there, and keep him safe."

Nara swallowed. "I'll try."

"You won't be in any danger from us, of course," Tchinchura hastened to add. "But Eirmon is already under heavy guard. If we breach the Academy, he'll know and be afraid. I don't know what he'll do to save himself, but he'd do just about anything. He knows I've befriended you. He might use that against me."

"You think he might hurt me?" Nara said. "Do you think he was trying to hurt us both the other day?"

"No," Tchinchura said. "I don't. And I hope he wouldn't hurt you. I just think you should stay clear of any fighting in the palace. Kaden might have to make a hard choice if he's there."

"Will you kill Kaden if he defends Eirmon?"

"I'll try not to."

"He wouldn't, you know," Nara said, "if he knew what you've told me."

"I can't risk telling him," Tchinchura said. "And I'm trusting you not to either. If he's caught in the cross fire, he'll have to make his choice and accept its consequences—as do we all."

"But you'll try not to hurt him?"

"I give you my word," Tchinchura said, and turning to head back to the palace, he waited for Nara to lead the way.

Later, as he squatted in his room, Tchinchura thought over his conversation with Nara. He'd done what he wished to and now felt free to move on with what was necessary. Still, he didn't like deceiving anyone, even if he'd avoided an outright lie.

Of course, he didn't know if she'd actually been deceived. She hadn't pursued the matter further when it came up, but that didn't mean his misdirection had worked. He fingered the fragment of Zerura that lay around his bicep. He'd told her so much. Perhaps he'd been silly to withhold that one piece of information from her.

He did wear an original piece of the Golden Cord, of course, and had for a long time. That was why he'd brought Zangira. When they recovered Eirmon's piece, Zangira would have to wear one. He could not wear both.

That he'd come to Barra-Dohn within Eirmon's grasp wearing another of the original pieces would only have made Nara anxious. There was risk involved, certainly, but sometimes risks had to be taken. The same skills that had earned him the right to wear this piece would help him to recover the one Eirmon had taken. And then, only one would be missing.

Maybe, when they'd returned this missing piece, they'd go get that one too.

24

THE ACADEMY

Deslo ducked under the prow of the large sandship and disappeared around the far side.

Zangira paused on top of the Arua field, trying to decide if he'd chase him around or cut down this side of the ship and try to catch him at the back. It might be a ruse. Once out of sight on the far side, Deslo might have turned away from the ship, and any time Zangira took running parallel to it might just slow him down. He decided to go around the front.

Zangira ducked under the prow himself and found Deslo standing still on his meridium soles not far away, the chase forgotten as he stared toward the ruined shell of Garranmere in the distance. It had taken the better part of a week, but the city, or what was left of it, no longer smoked and smoldered. It just lay there, empty and dead.

"You're not supposed to take it easy on me just because I'm old and slow," Zangira said, coming to a stop beside Deslo.

"Like it would even be a game if you really tried," Deslo murmured, not even turning to look at Zangira. "I think some more of the messengers have come back."

Zangira noticed the sliders in the distance and the men just then getting off of them. Kaden had told them about the warnings being sent to the other cities of Aralyn to comply immediately with Eirmon's demands, and Zangira knew about Deslo's fears that another city would defy his grandfather and in return be reduced to rubble. Earlier that morning, the messengers sent to Jerdan had returned with the news that they would do all that Eirmon demanded. Zangira knew Deslo would be anxious until the other three had also been heard from. "Do you want to go back?"

"I guess," Deslo said.

They started walking together, the long line of sandships from Barra-Dohn stretched out on a great arc behind them. Between them and the place where Kaden was now preparing to receive the newly returned messengers, lay the sands so recently soaked with the blood of Garranmere. The dark splotches were fading, but Zangira noticed Deslo's determined lack of attention to them as they passed.

When they'd reached their sandship, they found Kaden with Greyer standing upon the deck. Kaden looked from Zangira to Deslo, and without needing to hear it asked, answered their question. "They're back from Perone."

"And?" Deslo asked, almost breathless with anticipation.

"They have agreed to everything," Kaden said. Gazing at the boy, he allowed a smile to play at the corners of his mouth for a moment. Then he reached down and tousled Deslo's hair playfully. "That's two."

"That's two," Deslo echoed, sounding relieved and looking pleased.

"Of course, there was never much doubt about Perone," Kaden added. "Fehrin would have given in even if all we'd done was send him a nasty letter."

Greyer smirked at that, which wasn't at all surprising. During the time since the messengers had first been dispatched to their appointed destinations, Zangira had heard Kaden and his captain frequently denigrate Fehrin. The Amhuru thought of the man he'd watched eating at the king's banquet on his first night in Barra-Dohn and had to admit that the fellow wasn't very impressive. Of all the representatives at the table, he did seem like the one least likely to take a strong stand against Eirmon's unjust destruction of Garranmere.

But even as Greyer smirked, a frown crossed Kaden's face as he turned away from them to look out over the sand, the frown replacing the smile that had lingered there only a moment. "Still, it is strange that we've heard from Perone before Amattai."

"You knew Jona would hold out longer than Fehrin," Greyer said, not sounding worried.

"Longer is relative," Kaden answered. "My message insisted that compliance must be immediate. It warned that consequences would follow."

"Yes, it did," Greyer agreed. "But that's the point. 'Immediate' to Fehrin would have meant falling immediately on his face in order to implore the messenger to leave as soon as possible and bring word of their agreement back. 'Immediate' for Jona would probably have a more liberal interpretation."

Kaden grunted. "He'd better hope it isn't too liberal. If I hear from Saris in Dar-Holdin first, I'll be forced to act."

"Well," Greyer said, "since Dar-Holdin is more than twice as far away and Saris might have almost as liberal a take on 'immediate,' as Jona, I'd say that if you haven't heard from Amattai by then, we'll have cause to be concerned."

"But we can wait awhile, right?" Deslo asked, and Zangira could hear the boy's anxiety over any further destruction creeping back into his voice.

"Yes, we can wait a little while," Kaden said, and Zangira's gaze was pulled from the son to the father by the gentleness of his reply.

While in Barra-Dohn, Zangira had observed the distance and awkwardness between these two. That Kaden had been trying to reach out to Deslo since the start of the trip, he had also seen. Those attempts had been strained and awkward. That had changed with the assault on Garranmere. Somehow, some way, the death of this city had brought them life. To be sure, it was a fragile seed, and Zangira had no idea if it would survive the return to Barra-Dohn and the poison that lurked there in the palace. But their long dormant relationship seemed to have sprung to life out of these very ruins.

Maybe it was the shared trauma of witnessing the death of a great city. As much as Kaden tried to play the dutiful son fulfilling his father's commands, Zangira knew he hated what he had done. He probably hated himself as well. Certainly, Kaden hated Eirmon.

And that might be the answer. Perhaps Kaden had picked up on Deslo's anger over not just Garranmere's destruction but the unjust cause of it. Maybe in Deslo's freedom to express that anger, Kaden had found the connection with his son that he had long failed to see or perhaps refused to see. Whatever it was, Zangira was glad of it. So many had died as a result of this expedition, the least it could do was give Deslo back his father. Or at least, give him a chance to have his father back.

The Zerura on his bicep vibrated, imperceptible to anyone but himself. The sun was hanging low in the evening sky, and soon they would have dinner. It would be hard for Zangira to slip away to see what Tchinchura wanted to tell him. He might have to wait until later that night when he was sure Deslo was asleep.

After he got Tchinchura's message, he would send one of his own. He'd had a chance yesterday to examine one of the railguns, so he was sure now that they contained Zerura along with meridium. It wouldn't be much of a revelation, but he thought Tchinchura should know.

Of course, it might not matter much at this point. The king had already tipped his hand by ordering that first attack against

Tchinchura. There was little doubt now that he had what they were after. Most likely, Tchinchura had already decided to leave the palace and infiltrate the Academy. Maybe even tonight.

The Zerura vibrated again gently and then stopped. Zangira thought of Tchinchura, sitting in his room at Barra-Dohn, and wondered if tonight would be the night they finally recovered what had been stolen. Either way, if they made an attempt, his days of traveling with Eirmon's son and grandson would soon be numbered.

Tchinchura shut the door to his room behind him. Despite the late hour, the hall was well lit, and he moved quickly. Listening carefully at the intersection with the larger hall, he waited until he was sure none of Eirmon's soldiers were nearby, then crossed to the narrow stairs that led upward and disappeared into the darkness.

Making his way quietly through the remote portions of the palace on into the servant's quarters, he became increasingly relaxed. He would never grow careless, since that was not in his nature. Still, Eirmon's concern would be for his own safety, and the farther away from Eirmon's chambers Tchinchura went, the more unlikely it was that he'd encounter a substantial presence of the king's men. At last he reached the large attic space that contained the trapdoor up onto the roof, and soon Tchinchura was outside, crouching on top of the palace.

He ran lightly along the clay tiles, his bare feet padding softly along. The tiles were smooth, and if his balance wasn't extraordinary, they would have been slippery. The fine sand rested in a light coat upon the tiles. But Tchinchura stayed low and moved quickly until he was at last crouching at the corner of the palace that was closest to the wall that ran beside the great square in which the crowd had gathered outside the palace on the day after his arrival.

Down below in the square, a handful of talking soldiers were huddled together near the steps that led up to the main front entrance to the palace. The sound of laughter echoed softly from them across the square, and Tchinchura quickly surveyed as much of the wider area before him to see if these were the only soldiers on this side of the palace. The hour was late, and most of the city, like the palace, was asleep. Even so, Tchinchura had to be careful.

As he crouched on the corner of the roof, he rubbed his Zerura along the soles of his feet and against the palms of his hands, then put it back around his bicep. Gazing down into the square, he concentrated, summoning the wind. Soon several strong gusts whipped across the square, picking up the sand that lay every-where in fine layers on the stone and swirling it in a growing cloud around the soldiers.

For their part, they were taken aback by this turn of events, and all of them pulled their shirts up over their mouths as they raised their hands in a futile attempt to keep the sand from their eyes. As they were thus distracted, Tchinchura stepped from the corner of the roof and dropped lightly onto all fours on the Arua field several stories below him beside the wall. A quick glance confirmed that he hadn't been seen, and staying low, he ran along the wall until he'd exited the square by a narrow alley on the far side.

Tchinchura made his way along the less frequented and darker streets away from the main thoroughfares, though he'd have to avoid lights along any road in Barra-Dohn. He heard and saw few signs of life, but still he made his way carefully until he came upon the Academy, though not from the front as he had approached it with Nara.

If Eirmon knew why he was there and if the fragment of the Golden Cord was in the Academy somewhere, then Tchinchura expected that soldiers would be waiting on the other side of any of the entrances. He moved along the back of the building in the shadows until he was standing directly beneath a large window a few stories up. He might not be able to avoid trouble once inside, but he intended to enter and see as much as he could without rais-ing alarm.

He leapt from the Arua field and planted his axe head into the stone wall. Chips of stone and dust showered down on his head as he reached up his other hand and sank his knife into the wall a little farther up. His feet pushed up off the wall, and he reached up higher with his axe and sank it in again. And so he climbed, blow by blow up the wall until he was beneath the window and could open it and enter. The whole process took very little time, and only the faint echo of his blades on the stone could have signaled to anyone around that he was there. He was in through the window in no time, and if any had heard him, they'd find nothing behind the Academy if they walked around to check.

He brushed the dust from his smooth scalp and shook off his vest, looking around him. The room he'd pulled himself into was small and dark, and Tchinchura was grateful for the excellence of his night vision. He scanned the few plain pieces of furniture and saw that it was only an office of sorts. He took the Zerura from his arm in his hand and passed it over and around the desk and drawers in the room, knowing that if another original fragment was close enough and not synced with the heartbeat of the person wearing it, he should be able to pick up the vibration with his own fragment.

He detected nothing, so crossing to the door, he listened carefully before opening it quietly and peering out to see what he could see. The hall was dimly lit by meridium runners placed periodically along the hallway at the joints between the wall and ceiling, and Tchinchura was relieved that there weren't any more or any brighter. He'd need to make his way systematically from room to room, and though several hours of night were left, he knew he might need them all, especially if he found himself in a situation where he could no longer rely on stealth. So without waiting further, he padded down the hall toward the door closest to him.

Tchinchura squatted beside the large hole in the ground. Next to him was a rope attached to a heavy-duty pulley, while across the way a sturdy ladder descended down into the darkness. He could go down into the shaft either way, but he hesitated. He'd been below ground for quite a while, so he'd not seen outside and had no firm grasp on the time. The dawn might already have come, and his chance of slipping away unnoticed might be disappearing with the night.

Even so, curiosity pulled him irresistibly downward. He'd seen many interesting things in the Academy so far and understood most of them, but this hole perplexed him. He'd not found in the floors above what he was looking for nor anywhere that would be a likely place to store it, and this didn't look any more promising. Could he be sure without checking? And if the fragment wasn't down there, what was? Why was there a gaping hole yawning before him in the floor of what seemed to be the lowermost level of the many subterranean chambers of this place?

He had worked his way down from the upper stories of the Academy, which appeared upon closer inspection to be essentially administrative. The main floor consisted of several large chambers dedicated to projects of all kinds, none of which as far as Tchinchura could tell having anything to do with Zerura. Below the main floor, the search had grown more interesting, both because of the marked increase in guards and because he'd found evidence of Barra-Dohn's Zerura experiments.

Several large rooms on multiple subterranean layers held objects that had been made with Zerura and meridium mixed in varying proportions. Some of these objects Tchinchura could easily understand. He saw various weapons, including some like the railgun Zangira described. Several objects appeared to be more powerful versions of their commonplace meridium counterparts—lights, ovens, and more, including a thing that looked like the core for a large and powerful slider. In addition to these were some other things that defied the Amhuru's immediate grasp.

Next to one of these rooms, he found a locked storage unit filled with replicas of the missing fragment of the Golden Cord. They were stacked, shelf on shelf, from the floor to the ceiling. Fortunately, they were inert, and their reaction to his fragment suggested that Eirmon and his researchers had yet to figure out how to cut and activate them so they could be worn like Eirmon's original piece. This comforted Tchinchura greatly, as his greatest fear was facing a squad of men wearing replicas of Eirmon's piece and who also understood how they could be used. Without that possibility, storming the palace—an event that seemed more likely with every room explored—was much less intimidating.

Emboldened by the realization that only one piece of Zerura could be worn and wielded against him and that piece was likely with Eirmon, Tchinchura made his decision. He descended into the darkness of the shaft. Down, down, and down he went until he reached the bottom. A faint sound echoed from far away, and soon his exploration of the tunnel led him to another shaft.

He didn't hesitate this time but descended down through this one too. After making his way through the tunnel at the bottom, he found himself face-to-face with a third just like it. By the time he'd reached the bottom of the third shaft, the racing in his brain had increased, keeping pace with the louder echo of the sounds coming from somewhere down the next tunnel where he expected to find yet another shaft.

Midway down this tunnel, he paused in the darkness out of reach of the nearest, fairly dim meridium light. He was suddenly struck with absolute clarity by the truth of what he'd found. Eirmon knew. He knew the Old Story about the gift of the Golden Cord. Whoever else had forgotten, he knew. He knew, and he was digging beneath the foundations of his own Academy aware it had once been the Temple built to honor the place where Kalos had opened the earth and given Zeru-Shalim, now Barra-Dohn, the Golden Cord.

But Eirmon didn't believe in Kalos, and he seemed an unlikely candidate to give the Old Stories much credence. At the same time, Tchinchura thought, Eirmon now possessed one of the fragments of the Golden Cord. He'd felt the power as it lay still yet living against his skin. He'd seen it displayed in the objects created for him by the members of the Academy. That power might well be enough for a power-hungry man like Eirmon to reconsider many things he'd once felt certain about.

Tchinchura remained where he was, fairly sure about what he'd find up ahead—another shaft, probably leading down to another tunnel. Somewhere below him, men were likely working day and night to search for more Zerura. Eirmon probably hoped to tap a vein of it. He no doubt fell asleep at night dreaming about the power a discovery like that would give him.

Tchinchura shook his head. Eirmon would never find more, not this way.

Exhaling, he felt relief wash over him again. He'd suspected that a mystery lay somewhere down here, but now that he knew what it was, or was at least pretty sure he did, he wasn't worried. Once he reclaimed the missing fragment from Eirmon, the king or his successor could dig here as long as they liked, but Tchinchura knew that what they wanted could not be found in this manner.

He turned to go, and it was then he realized that he'd been so absorbed in his thoughts that he'd not noticed the sounds of men coming down the shaft from above. Perhaps it was the next shift come to relieve those currently at work or perhaps just men returning from a break in the world above. Whoever it was, they were almost at the bottom of the shaft. Tchinchura thought about going back the other way toward the sound and the portion of the dig he hadn't explored but quickly rejected that idea. He'd probably just get caught in a less advantageous place between two groups of men. Better to choose his own ground and face the men behind him while they were still vulnerable from the climb down and the odds against him weren't any worse.

He ran to the place where the ladder from the shaft above hung on the wall just in time to see a foot step down onto the bottom rung. He reached up and grabbed the ankle of the man that foot belonged to and pulled him off the ladder. He fell onto the floor and cried in pain. Tchinchura grabbed him by the head and slammed it back against the stone so his eyes fluttered up into his skull. He hoped the man would wake up long after he was gone, alive but with a terrible headache.

Above him, another man higher up on the ladder had heard his friend's cry and seen Tchinchura's head-slamming routine. Now he was scrambling back up as fast as he could go. Tchinchura leapt up and grabbed the highest rung he could, scrambling up after him. He closed the gap, but the man was moving quickly too. By the time he was close enough to grab hold of the man, pulling him from the ladder would almost certainly prove fatal. On the other hand, to pursue him all the way up would mean still being on the ladder himself when the man reached the tunnel above, which meant, of course, being much more vulnerable.

The man was probably a miner, not a soldier. Even if he tried to turn the tables on Tchinchura at the top of the ladder, he was alone, and the Amhuru felt confident he could outmaneuver him. Besides, the man had chosen to run down below, so Tchinchura felt sure he'd keep running. Most likely, he would try to get up above and alert the guards to Tchinchura's presence. The Amhuru felt as if he had more than enough time to make sure that didn't happen without killing the poor fellow.

Sure enough, once out of the shaft, the man went running down the tunnel toward the bottom of the next shaft. Tchinchura flew after him, closing rapidly. Perhaps sensing he wasn't going to make the next ladder before being caught, the man turned and raised the pick as though to strike out with it. Before he could swing, though, Tchinchura struck him in the gut with the haft of his axe, and the man doubled over, the wind knocked out of him. Using the flat of the axe head, Tchinchura dealt him a vicious blow on the back of the skull that knocked him to the ground where he lay unmoving.

Tchinchura made his way quickly upward. He climbed up the second shaft and then the first until he was gliding once more through the most subterranean of the many levels of the Academy. As he made his way through it, he listened, wondering if more miners were on their way down from the world above, but he encountered nothing more difficult to negotiate than he had on the way down. Three times he had to reverse directions to avoid detection, but each time he was able to find his way again. At last he stood before a door near the back of the Academy that emptied out into the same back alley he'd approached the Academy from in the first place. Looking over his shoulder one last time, he pushed the door gently open and stepped out into the night.

He tensed. Not ten feet away from him, half a dozen guards stood chatting with twenty or more miners who were just now approaching the Academy in the murky light of daybreak.

25

BENEATH THE SAND

As the shock on the soldiers' faces turned to resolve, Tchinchura released his knife, burying it in the throat of the only soldier who had raised his long, black spear with the nasty serrated blades that the Davrii carried. As the knife flew back into his hand, the Amhuru whirled to the side, closing the gap on the soldier closest to him, who had been stunned by the sudden death of his comrade and was now moving to defend himself.

Tchinchura's axe fell with all the force he could summon, and the man's collarbone snapped beneath the blow. His spear clattered on the paving stones even as his scream shattered the early morning stillness.

The scream snapped the miners from their reverie. The emergence from the Academy of this wild figure had stunned them as much as it had the soldiers. But now that two of the men they'd just been speaking with had been either killed or incapacitated in such an efficient fashion, they realized they were also in the man's way.

As the miners quickly ran from the square, the four remaining soldiers fanned out to face Tchinchura. Pulling his axe from the shoulder of the hobbled man groaning at his feet, Tchinchura whirled back to defend himself against the spear thrust coming from the soldier who'd moved quickly in to strike from behind. The Amhuru severed the spear with a quick chop of the axe and stepped in close so he could jam his knife in between the man's ribs. A short gasp was the only sound the man made as he slumped to his knees.

The other three decided not to wait and rushed toward him as he turned back. He flicked his knife at the man in the middle, but he only hit the man's arm, then he sidestepped, grabbing the spear haft of the man nearest him, redirecting the blow past his side, and pulling the man between himself and the others.

Now on the side of the small line of soldiers, Tchinchura let go of the spear and struck the man who'd just missed him in the back with his axe. It wasn't a fatal blow, but it was enough to incapacitate him, and the man fell sprawling onto the paving stones. Now only two men were left uninjured, and as they watched the man between them and Tchinchura fall, they realized that their numerical advantage had been all but eliminated, and the Amhuru still stood unwounded.

The one with Tchinchura's knife in his arm reached down as though to grab it, but the Amuru raised his hand and summoned it back. That must have been the last straw, because the wounded soldier dropped his spear and ran. The last soldier hesitated a moment, and then he followed his friend, running as fast as he could out of the square.

The four soldiers that Tchinchura had either killed or fatally wounded lay scattered around him, two of them moaning. Tchinchura took a step back and almost slipped on a patch of slick blood, but he quickly regained his balance.

As he turned to go, he heard the door of the Academy behind him start to open. He spun to see it swinging outward, and raising his foot, he kicked it hard, jamming it back against the arm of whoever was on the other side. He heard a cry of pain from inside before the door closed with a bang. With that, Tchinchura ran down the dim alley, putting as much distance between himself and the Academy as he could.

Tchinchura dodged around the corner and flattened himself against the wall. He listened, hoping to hear if he was being followed by whoever had been behind that door. Since he didn't hear anything, he imagined that whoever had been drawn to the door by the racket outside it, now saw the scene of death that lay just beyond it. No doubt he thought twice about pursuing whoever had attacked those men.

Tchinchura jogged through the smaller, back streets of Barra-Dohn, navigating them effortlessly. He had walked these streets many times during his stay in the city so he'd be able to find his way in time of need, long after he'd realized he'd need to investigate the Academy.

Having come up empty-handed in his search of the Academy, his next step would be to wait for Zangira's return. Together, they would move on Eirmon in the palace. Until then, he'd need to slip out of the city and take refuge nearby. The only person inside Barra-Dohn he knew he could trust was Nara, and she couldn't hide him. He'd have to leave, and hopefully he could get out without having to kill anyone else, though he realized that might not be possible.

He turned the next corner and ducked into a doorway. Down the street, a man was wrestling with a large cart, either trying to get it out of a narrow doorway or in, he couldn't tell. Tchinchura waited up against the door behind him, watching. The morning sun was just beginning to peek above the rooftops, and he knew the city would soon be stirring to life beyond the odd straggler like this fellow. He needed to be gone.

Just then, the door behind him opened, and a pair of strong hands gripped him by his upper arms, pulling him back into darkness.

Kaden set his hand gently on Deslo's shoulder. He could feel the boy trembling, and though it didn't stop, it seemed to settle down.

It looked like time had run out for Amattai.

"I'm sorry Deslo, but we have to go."

"Can't we wait a little longer?" Deslo implored.

"Enough time has passed to send messengers here and back from Amattai four or five times over, and yet we've heard nothing. If they were going to agree or even stall, we'd have heard something by now."

"We've heard from Dar-Holdin already," Greyer said. "It's just Amattai now."

"And they're the closest." Kaden frowned, looking north across the sand. When he spoke again, his voice was quiet and angry. "They've killed or imprisoned my men."

"We don't know that," Deslo said.

"Yes, we do, son," Kaden answered without taking his eyes off the horizon. "The embassy had clear instructions. If they haven't returned by now one way or another, it can only mean they've . . ."

"Look . . . ," Zangira said, pointing toward the horizon.

Kaden looked when he heard Zangira's voice trailing off. He saw what had drawn the Amhuru's attention. A few sliders were approaching from the other side of the Behrn.

"Maybe that's them!" Deslo said, moving forward.

Kaden could tell right away that it wasn't. It didn't look like the sliders that had borne his messengers to Amattai. There were too many, for one thing. For another even from a distance, he could see the colorful clothes this party was wearing. They didn't have the uniform look of soldiers from Barra-Dohn or anywhere else.

"Greyer," Kaden said. "Find out who this is and what they want."

"Yes, sir," Greyer said, and a few moments later a large company of men was moving to intercept the party on its way.

Not long after, Greyer returned but not with the whole party. He was escorting a man and woman, both dressed garishly. The woman stood out especially, bedecked with jewelry and a yellow-and-scarlet outfit. Neither seemed especially nervous as Greyer brought them forward. In fact, the woman especially appeared to be comfortable with being escorted by a large company of soldiers.

Kaden watched her, while Greyer introduced Kaden to her. A slight look of surprise showed faintly. That was all he could see when the woman was introduced to the son of Eirmon Omiir, king of Barra-Dohn. The man with her was less able to contain his reaction, but even he gathered himself admirably. Kaden was impressed.

"And this," Greyer continued, motioning to the woman next to him, "is Captain Elil D'Sarza, a merchant, who would like to trade with Garranmere."

"That will be difficult," Kaden said drily.

"I can see that," D'Sarza replied, glancing sidelong at the ruined walls of the city. "Obviously, I would not have made the trek from my ship if I'd known what I'd find."

"Obviously," Kaden said. He sized D'Sarza up. "You left your ship at the coast?"

"I did; it doesn't do well on land," D'Sarza said. Then, perhaps noting the cloud that passed over his face, she seemed to realize she'd been too glib and added, "Garranmere wasn't my original destination. I'm improvising, bringing some samples of my wares here, in case I could find a market among the nobility."

Kaden nodded. "An expensive cargo, then?"

D'Sarza hesitated, and Kaden wondered what passed through her head. A significant portion of the army of Barra-Dohn had surrounded her. She was far from her ship and any aid, and now being asked about the value of her cargo. Of course, any merchant who made a living dealing with the powerful faced risks, but those risks were never as visible as they were for her at the moment.

"Very expensive," D'Sarza said. "I only traffic in the finest."

"The finest what?" Kaden asked.

"You name it," D'Sarza said with a shrug. "I have brought samples with me, if you'd like to see them. Or if there's something particular you're after that you don't see, I either have it at my ship or I can get it."

Kaden laughed, noting as he did the relief in the face of D'Sarza's companion, even if no change registered directly on the face of the captain. "I'm not in the market for any of your wares just now," Kaden said, "however luxurious they might be. Perhaps if you come to Barra-Dohn sometime, we can discuss it then."

D'Sarza nodded, ever so slightly. "I'd be happy to. I'm headed to Barra-Dohn next."

Kaden's eyes narrowed. "So, you're coming from the east?"

"Yes," D'Sarza said without hesitation, though a shift in her posture showed that the captain had also registered the shift in Kaden's tone.

"You've been to Amattai?"

"Yes," D'Sarza said, measuring her words carefully, "but not on this trip."

Kaden studied her for a moment. "Why not? Amattai has a larger population, would be a more likely market, and is easier for you to access."

"We had planned to go to Amattai," D'Sarza said, after considering the question for a moment. "That's the improvising. We'd planned to go there, not here."

"So why didn't you?"

D'Sarza fixed Kaden with a level gaze. "A large fleet was in the harbor, flying colors I didn't recognize. I thought it best to move on."

"You didn't even dock?"

"No."

Kaden nodded. "When you say fleet . . ."

"I mean fleet," D'Sarza said. "There were a lot of ships under uniform colors."

"What colors?"

"A golden fist on a green background," D'Sarza said.

Kaden turned to Greyer. "Have you heard of that insignia?"

Greyer shook his head.

"Zangira?" Kaden said, looking back at the Amhuru for the first time.

"No," Zangira said, shaking his head too. "I don't recall ever seeing that one."

Kaden frowned. None of this made sense. He'd never heard of that insignia, and Amattai didn't have a fleet anything like what D'Sarza described. "I don't like it. No word, a strange fleet. How long ago did you see this?"

"Nine, maybe ten days," D'Sarza said.

Kaden turned to Greyer. "We need to go now."

"I agree," Greyer nodded. "But are we going back to Barra-Dohn or to Amattai?"

"That's the question," Kaden said. "They know we'd be coming by land. That fleet isn't defensive."

"They also know we won't have left Barra-Dohn defenseless," Greyer said. "Besides, Barra-Dohn's harbor has great natural defenses. It would be a gutsy call to attack by water, not that attacking by land would be any wiser."

"I think," Zangira said, inserting himself into their conversation for the first time, "we all need to concede that we have no idea what this strange fleet represents. Even if it was seen nine or ten days ago, it's not a reaction either to our coming or even to Eirmon's ultimatum. Amattai couldn't have assembled it without considerable effort, time, and planning, if indeed they assembled it."

"What do you mean, *if*?" Kaden asked, turning more fully to the Amhuru. He felt a sudden rush of gratitude that he had a man of Zangira's experience and wisdom with him, as wild thoughts ran rampant through his mind.

"I mean, it was seen there, but we don't know how it got there."

"So what do we do?" Kaden looked back and forth between Greyer and Zangira. He felt a total loss. A fleet might be evidence that Eirmon had been right. Perhaps the Five Cities had been planning a rebellion.

"If I may make a suggestion?" Zangira said.

"You came to advise," Kaden said, "so advise."

"If Captain D'Sarza will cooperate, perhaps she might agree to take Deslo and me back to Barra-Dohn—for the right price, of course," Zangira added, turning to the captain and smiling. Kaden could see that Zangira understood the language of a merchant captain well. "We can take warning to your father, just in case a warning is needed, while you go to Amattai and investigate both this fleet and their silence."

"And if you run into a hostile fleet on the way?" Kaden asked.

"Captain D'Sarza strikes me as someone who knows her business," the Amhuru said. Then he spoke directly to the merchant. "You can keep us away from any potential trouble, yes?"

"*The Sorry Rogue* is hard to catch," Captain D'Sarza said proudly, "and I have a valuable cargo. I generally try to avoid being boarded."

Kaden studied her for a moment. "I would want to send a contingency of my men along as an escort for my son, perhaps twenty. You would be willing to take them, Captain?"

"For the right price," she said, echoing Zangira. "This sounds like a potentially risky job . . . with precious cargo." Her eyes flitted from Kaden to Deslo just long enough for her to smile at the boy before looking back to his father.

"When you've delivered them safely, go see my father at the palace. He'll take care of you," Kaden said, not sure if he was still impressed with the captain's nerve or merely aggravated by her presumption. He turned to Deslo and Zangira. "Gather your things. As soon as Greyer has gathered your escort and I've considered what message I want you to tell Eirmon, you need to be on your way."

Just a short time later, all was ready for Zangira and Deslo to depart with the captain and their escort.

Kaden asked Zangira for a word. "I want to thank you for everything," Kaden said, taking the Amhuru's hand firmly. The other's penetrating, golden eyes watched him carefully. "For taking such good care of Deslo, for advising me well, for understanding."

Zangira nodded, acknowledging the gratitude. "You are welcome. I have tried to serve both you and Deslo well."

"You have," Kaden said. "Now I ask you one more thing: keep him safe. I don't like this news from Amattai."

"He'll be safe with me," Zangira said, smiling.

"Good," Kaden said, returning the smile. "Hopefully, I'll see you again in Barra-Dohn before too long."

"Hopefully," Zangira said, but he did not then turn to go, even though Kaden said nothing further. "May I say something, Prince Kaden?"

"Of course, Zangira," Kaden said, "and please, just call me Kaden."

"Your father casts a long shadow, and I can see that you fear lest it will swallow you."

Kaden tensed, turning ever so slightly to make sure no one was close enough to hear. Only Greyer was near, and he wasn't close enough to hear the Amhuru's softly spoken words.

"All I wanted to say," the Amhuru hurried on, seeing Kaden's discomfort, "is that I think you're on the right road to be free of him. The more you are the husband, the father, and one day, the king that you ought to be, that you can be, that you were meant to be, the more his shadow will melt away like mist before the midday sun. Farewell," Zangira added, and he turned to walk away.

"Farewell," Kaden replied, but he wasn't sure he said it loud enough for anyone but himself to hear.

As Devaar stood behind him watching, the Jin Dara concentrated. He could almost feel the ripples of sand in the distance as the creatures heard his summons and responded, turning from their course. As they drew nearer, they also became visible, or at least, the large furrows of sand their progress created revealed their coming.

At first, there were only a few, as those that had been closest when he called them arrived. They would draw near and surface, their long bodies covered with those cruel hooks briefly visible before they'd dive again, spraying sand all over. Soon the desert all around them was in a state of constant upheaval as dozens and dozens were now circling them, some fairly deep beneath the surface.

"They've grown so big," Devaar said, the wonder clear in his voice. "I think we're ready."

"Almost," the Jin Dara said.

The ground he was sitting on and that Devaar was standing on remained steady and unshaken, but the ring of writhing sand, rising and falling around them, grew larger and larger. Clouds like smoke drifted in all directions, and even the sound of the ordinarily silent sand echoed on the wind as it crashed in whooshing waves.

He reached out, calling the others. He was the Jin Dara, and gigantic hookworms were not the only dark things he would bring with him when he finally returned to his ancestral home. He'd never been there, of course, but Barra-Dohn was the city that had cast his family out, even if it had been called by another name at the time.

Like the churning sandstorm around him, the ancient hatred for that city rose within. Years had passed, and generations came and went, but the hatred wouldn't die. Indeed, it lived and grew, and Barra-Dohn would reap its full measure.

26

ALLIES

The hands that gripped Tchinchura were strong. He was held fast, arms pinned against his side. The man holding him seemed content to keep him still, and Tchinchura stood ready to move as soon as he relaxed his grip or shifted his hold.

The room he'd been pulled into was dimly lit and musty, though Tchinchura detected a strong scent of sage oil coming from somewhere behind him. A man in a dark robe and bare feet walked silently past and closed the door to the street. He turned, calmly considering the Amhuru.

He stood, hands clasped before him. "Let him go, Owenn."

The man behind Tchinchura released him and then walked around to stand by the other. He was huge, towering over both Tchinchura and the man who'd closed the outside door. He wore a black robe like the other, but his hair was short, neat, and blond, while the smaller man had long dark hair that hung down to his shoulders.

"You're Devoted?" Tchinchura asked as the two men stood quietly opposite him.

"We are," said the shorter man. "I'm Marlo, and this is Owenn, and we've been waiting for you."

"Waiting for me?" Tchinchura asked.

"Why don't you come through?" Marlo said, gesturing toward the interior of the house. "We can offer you food and drink, as well as shelter."

"Shelter?"

"Yes, we've prepared a room for you," Marlo said. "You may stay as long as you need to."

Tchinchura looked behind him for the first time at the door leading into a more brightly lit interior room where a rough wooden table sat, and then back at Marlo and Owenn. His puzzlement had turned to shock. "I don't understand."

Marlo walked past him to the open doorway. "Come, eat. I'll explain."

Tchinchura followed Marlo into the next room. The table was bare, but Marlo brought out a platter with a loaf of warm bread, and despite the stronger smell of sage oil here, the scent of the bread rose and filled Tchinchura's nostrils, stirring the hunger he had held at bay through the night. Marlo broke off a hunk and handed it to Tchinchura, before breaking off another for Owenn. Tchinchura ate hungrily while Marlo also poured water from a pitcher for each of them.

When the bread was gone, Marlo cleared the platter and returned with another bearing quail, and Tchinchura helped himself to the cold meat. As though on cue, a lean black dog padded into the room and waited expectantly, and soon not only Marlo but all of them were passing it quail bones that it crunched noisily on the floor. Tchinchura sat back, his stomach full and his fingers greasy. He held a cup of water as he watched Marlo.

"You look tired," Marlo said. "Would you like to sleep first or talk?"

"Talk," Tchinchura said. "I'm grateful for your hospitality, but I don't understand it. Why were you waiting for me?"

"Deras told us to expect you."

"Who's Deras?"

"Deras was our Guardian of Truth," Marlo said.

Tchinchura nodded. He'd heard that term before. "He led your sect, but something happened to him?"

"Not just our sect, but he also was Guardian for all of Aralyn," Marlo said. "And yes, something happened to him. He came ahead of us to Barra-Dohn to deliver a message and prepare the way."

The image of the elderly Kalosene standing in the great square outside the palace of Barra-Dohn flashed before Tchinchura as understanding finally dawned on him. He saw the man, bold and unafraid, and heard his voice ringing like a bell, delivering the message that would cost him his life.

Forty days, oh, king, is all the time you have left. Forty days. Even now, your doom comes, and before the sunset of the fortieth day, Barra-Dohn will be destroyed, and her empire shall fall. For elevating a created thing above the Creator, for forgetting where you came from and what matters most, for pride and for arrogance, the price must be paid.

"Deras is dead," Tchinchura said. "I'm sorry."

"We know," Marlo said. "He told us when he left that he would not return."

"And he told you to wait for me?"

"Yes."

"He told you when and where?"

"Yes."

Tchinchura sat quietly, drinking his water, taking it in. Deras had known all along that he himself would die and that Tchinchura would be in Barra-Dohn. "What else did he tell you?"

"He told us you would need a place to stay, you and the other Amhuru. He told us we should help you, and you would help us."

Marlo looked at Owenn, who still had not said a word, but now he broke his silence. "Deras said you would know what was going on beneath the Academy of Barra-Dohn."

"I do know," Tchinchura said. "I just found out, actually. That's where I was coming from when you grabbed me."

"We're sorry about that," Marlo said. "We couldn't be sure of the exact time when you would come, so we'd been waiting awhile and didn't want to miss our chance to speak with you."

"It's all right," Tchinchura said, waving away their concern. "You're just fortunate I didn't break Owenn's hold and kill you both before I knew you were friends."

"It was a chance we had to take," Marlo said. "Besides, Owenn's grip is very strong."

"It's not bad," Tchinchura agreed, and both he and Owenn smiled.

"Deras said you would tell us what was going on beneath the Academy," Owenn repeated, returning them to the subject at hand.

"He didn't tell you?"

"He didn't know," Marlo said. "All he knew was that Kalos told him it was an abomination."

"Eirmon is mining for Zerura," Tchinchura said. He paused, considering what else to say, but there was really no deliberating to be done. His lot was already thrown in with these men; they might as well know the truth. "He already has some, because he has a fragment of the Golden Cord. Still, it would seem he wants more."

It was Marlo's turn to look surprised. "He has a fragment of the Golden Cord?"

"For now," Tchinchura said. "I'm here to take it back."

Marlo nodded, then leaned forward over the table. "The king is really mining beneath the foundations of the Temple?"

"He is," Tchinchura said. "I've not been all the way to the bottom, but the shafts are deep and staggered to minimize the structural instability, I suppose."

Marlo sneered. "The fools. Isn't it enough that they've turned the Temple of Kalos into an altar to their silent god?"

"That's fine with me," Owenn said. "They've made our job easier."

"What's your job?" Tchinchura asked.

"Deras says Eirmon has been experimenting with some new and devastating weapons," Marlo said. "Did you see evidence of that?"

"I did," Tchinchura said.

"Among them," Owenn continued, "are some explosives. They're supposed to be potent."

Tchinchura thought of the stacks and stacks of the round meridium balls he'd seen below the Academy that matched Zangira's description of the projectiles used to demolish the walls of Garranmere. His eyes widened as he looked from one man to the other. "You're going to destroy the Academy."

"We are," Marlo said. "The Room of Life and the Temple of Kalos will be defiled no longer."

For several days, Tchinchura had nothing to do but wait. Having a place to stay inside the walls of Barra-Dohn was a fortuitous turn of events, but having to stay inside the house and out of sight was the unfortunate by-product. He wasn't restless exactly, but having traveled so far and looked so long, he felt the waiting keenly.

He'd heard from Zangira and knew he was moving north from Garranmere with Deslo and a small contingency of soldiers to travel home by ship. The good news, of course, was that Kaden and the army of Barra-Dohn under his command was not returning with him. It was true that plenty of soldiers were still in Barra-Dohn to make their task at the palace challenging, but Tchinchura had hoped Kaden would not be pulled into the matter.

The mysterious fleet that the captain of the merchant vessel had spotted was a curiosity, but Tchinchura felt sure that even if Amattai did have a hostile intent toward Barra-Dohn, their plans to retake the Cord would not be threatened. It was unlikely an army of any size would reach Barra-Dohn before the smaller, faster-moving party Zangira was with, and even if they did, Tchinchura wasn't worried. The distraction created by such an attack might divert the king from his precautions against them or provide cover for their escape. Now, though, all he could do was wait.

Marlo and Owenn were waiting too. The Devoted lived in small, fairly isolated communities outside the big cities of Aralyn, and word had been dispatched to those close enough to Barra-Dohn to gather here. Over the next week and a half, perhaps twenty more Kalosenes would come in answer to the call. They were working on a definite timeline, for the night appointed for the attack on the Academy had already been determined and announced.

The plan was to destroy the Academy the night before the fortieth day after Deras had delivered his warning to Eirmon. Neither Marlo nor Owenn knew any more about what would happen to Barra-Dohn on that day, but both were confident that Deras's warning foreshadowed more than their plans for the Academy. Something terrible was coming to Barra-Dohn, and the destruction of the ancient temple would serve as harbinger for the greater calamity to come.

Tchinchura had told them about the destruction of Garranmere and the move currently under way against Amattai, as well as about the mysterious fleet that had been spotted there. And, while both men agreed with Tchinchura that the timing of these events was curious, they couldn't be sure if either were directly linked to the fate of Barra-Dohn. Perhaps the move on Amattai was simply a decoy, the moving of Kalos's providential hand, so that when doom fell on the city, the main contingency of its army would be far away. Or perhaps the fleet spotted there was the doom Deras had foretold. For now, they could only speculate and prepare.

A light knock on Tchinchura's door drew him from his thoughts, and Marlo called from the hall outside. "Owenn's back. He found her this time."

Tchinchura rose and followed Marlo out to the front room where Nara stood with Owenn. "Tchinchura!" she called and ran to him.

"It's all right," Tchinchura whispered as she held on tightly. "I'm all right."

"I'm so glad," she said, stepping back and wiping tears from her cheeks with both hands. "Eirmon's been in an absolute fury since you disappeared. I hoped that was a good sign."

"Perhaps not for those who have to put up with him now that I'm gone," he said with a twinkle in his eye, "but good for me."

Nara smiled, and he turned to Owenn. "Thanks for finding her."

Owenn nodded, and both he and Marlo excused themselves so Tchinchura could be alone with Nara. He took her to the table and brought water when she refused his offer of food. "I hope Owenn didn't startle you too much."

"Well, he did," Nara said, laughing. "I was walking aimlessly through the market, like I have been since you disappeared from the palace, and then there he was, looming above me. He about scared me to death."

"I'm sorry," Tchinchura said, and he meant it, even though he couldn't help but laugh at the picture she created. "It seemed safer than coming for you myself."

"No, it's all right. I understand why you did it," she said, smiling again. "I'm just so glad to see you. I don't think I understood until you weren't there to talk to just how much I'd come to enjoy having a real friend again."

"Well, it is in the spirit of friendship that I wanted to see you."

"What is it?"

"I have news," Tchinchura began.

"About Deslo?" Nara asked eagerly. She reached across the table and took his hand in her own. "You've spoken to Zangira recently?"

"I have," Tchinchura said. "They're on their way home."

Nara's eyes fluttered closed. She sat still, holding his hand tightly, and the tears she'd repressed earlier rolled down her cheeks. This time she made no effort to stop them, and when her eyes opened, she squeezed his hand still harder. "Thank you."

"They're coming back but not with the army."

"What do you mean?" Nara asked, surprised.

"Deslo and Zangira and a small band of soldiers are on their way north from Garranmere to take an ocean-going ship home while the rest of the force under Kaden heads to Amattai."

"Oh," Nara said, letting go of his hand and sitting back. "I didn't know they took a ship like that with them."

"They didn't," Tchinchura said. "Zangira says they'll be sailing on a merchant ship with some captain who ventured down to Garranmere."

"Oh," Nara said again. "I see."

"I wanted you to know, but you must still be careful. You can't spend all your days now at the quay or give anything away at the palace. If messengers come from Kaden to the king, you must act surprised should he pass on the news."

"I know, Tchinchura," Nara said. "Besides, no one pays attention to me."

"I wouldn't be too sure about that," Tchinchura said.

"I'll be careful," she said.

"Good," Tchinchura said. "And there's another thing. My work here won't be finished before Deslo and Zangira return."

"You said you'd wait for him to return if what you were looking for wasn't in the Academy," Nara said. "So, it wasn't there."

"No," Tchinchura said. "Eirmon must have it."

"I'm sorry," Nara said.

"We'll do what we have to," Tchinchura said. "Nara, the Academy isn't a safe place for you to visit."

"The Academy?" Nara said. "Why would I go there?"

"I'm not sure why," Tchinchura said, "but don't."

"All right," she said, peering at him curiously from across the table. "You know you can trust me, Tchinchura."

"I do trust you," he said. "That's why I'm telling you this. Stay away from the Academy. And if something happens there, I want you to take Deslo and get out of the palace."

"If something happens at the Academy, get out of the palace?" Nara asked. "Why? Is that when you're coming?"

"You remember the Kalosene who told Eirmon that Barra-Dohn would fall in forty days?"

"Of course," Nara said. "How could I forget?"

"Well, it's going to happen," Tchinchura said, "and I have reason to believe that Barra-Dohn's fall will begin at the site of the ancient temple—the Academy."

"You're serious," Nara said, studying him.

"I am."

"If the city is going to fall," Nara said, "where should we go? Where can I take Deslo and be safe? And what about Kaden?"

"I don't know, Nara," Tchinchura said. "Just be prepared to go. We still have to reclaim the missing fragment from Eirmon, and the confusion and turmoil that is coming to Barra-Dohn might be our best chance."

"Take us with you," Nara said, and she leaned over the table, reaching across to take Tchinchura's hand again. "I mean it. I've sometimes thought since I knew why you were here that I'd like to escape too, to disappear with Deslo when you disappear. I've held back, not wanting to take him from his inheritance. But if Barra-Dohn is about to collapse, then there's nothing for Deslo here but danger."

It was Tchinchura's turn to study her. "And Kaden? Do you think he'll want to come too?"

"I . . . I . . ." Nara faltered. "I don't know what Kaden wants. I have to think of Deslo and what's best for him."

"Nara . . . ," Tchinchura started.

"If Kaden's really gone to Amattai," Nara said more firmly, "then it is up to me to keep Deslo safe, and the best chance of that is for me to take him and go with you. Perhaps we can come back for Kaden later."

"I don't know what promises I can make," Tchinchura said softly. "If we recover the fragment, my obligation is to the Golden

Cord, to get it safely away. But if we can help you and Deslo in the process, we will. We'll help Kaden too, if he wants it."

"And if you have to kill Eirmon to get the fragment back?" Nara asked. "What then?"

"Then Kaden will have to make a choice, won't he?"

For a moment they sat in silence, and then Nara nodded. "Yes, I guess he will."

"So steer clear of the Academy, and if you hear of trouble, get out of the palace."

"I will."

"It's possible the trouble will come to Barra-Dohn from the sea," Tchinchura said, "but if it doesn't, try to make your way to the harbor. Almost certainly, Zangira and I will try to get out of Barra-Dohn that way if we can."

"All right," Nara said, looking relieved that she had something concrete to hold on to, no matter how tentative or uncertain. "I'll try to get Deslo to the harbor."

"And we'll do what we can," Tchinchura said. "But remember—"

"Your duty is to the Golden Cord," Nara finished. "I understand."

They sat a moment longer, and just as Tchinchura was about to rise and summon Owenn to escort Nara back to the market-place, she said, "I had an idea, something that might help you get the fragment back."

"Something that might help?" Tchinchura said.

"Well, someone, really," Nara said. "Gamalian. I think he could help you."

"Nara," Tchinchura said, gently shaking his head. "He's Eirmon's counselor. "

"Wait," Nara said. "Listen before you dismiss it, all right?"

"All right," Tchinchura said. "Tell me."

"He is Eirmon's counselor, but if he knew what I know, that the king was responsible for the death of an Amhuru, he'd be horrified. He'd do the right thing."

"Do you think he could ever see betraying his master as the right thing?"

"Absolutely," Nara said. "I've heard him teach my son for years. He may not believe in Kalos as you do, but he knows there are higher laws than the laws of the state. He's spoken with contempt about the despots of the past."

"It's easier to despise a dead king than to disobey a live one."

"True, but I think you should trust him like you trusted me. Soldiers have been crawling all over the palace since you left like you said they would. Maybe he can help you figure out how to get in, or maybe he can help you once you're there."

Tchinchura thought about it. If they were to help the Devoted with their plot against the Academy, then they wouldn't have a lot of time to get the fragment of the Golden Cord before whatever calamity that was coming on the fortieth day. Having someone placed inside the palace close to the king might prove helpful.

"If I meet with him," Tchinchura said at last, "and I don't feel I can trust him, I won't be able to let him go. I won't be able to risk the possibility he might warn the king."

"How will you know?"

"The same way I knew with you."

"How did you know with me?" Nara asked.

Tchinchura smiled. "I knew."

Nara reached up and brushed back a few hairs that had fallen over her eyes. "So, what are you saying?"

"You know what I'm saying," Tchinchura said. "I'm asking you how sure you are that he'll see this like you do."

"I'm pretty sure," Nara said.

"Pretty sure?" Tchinchura said. "His life might be at stake."

"All right, I'm sure," she said. "Of all the people in the palace, the only person I completely trust is Gamalian. He tries to be a good influence on Eirmon, but it's just that there isn't much anyone can do in that regard."

Tchinchura nodded. "Well, I'll meet with him. I just wanted you to understand what was at stake before I do."

"I understand," Nara said, looking a little pale at the thought. "What should I do? How do you want to arrange it?"

"See if you can get him to walk with you in the marketplace tomorrow afternoon, but don't tell him why."

"Then what will I tell him?"

"Whatever you like, but he can't know he's coming to see me. I can't risk betrayal before I've had a chance to talk to him personally."

"All right, so just get him to the market?"

"Just get him there," Tchinchura said. "We'll take care of the rest."

27

TIME TO GO

Eirmon clenched and unclenched his fists and ground his teeth. He could almost feel the veins in his temples bulging. He took a deep breath. And another.

"Captain," Eirmon began slowly, deliberately. "With the better part of our army gone, I understand the strain on those who remain. Nevertheless, I want you to maintain the increased guard at the palace, as well as the patrols in and around the city. I want the Amhuru found."

"Yes, Your Majesty," the captain said. Eirmon could see the man was aware that he'd said all that a wise man might about his objections to the king's wishes. He would now acquiesce to whatever Eirmon said, regardless of how he felt about it, and Eirmon was fine with that.

"He's a big man," Eirmon continued. "And very distinctive looking, so he'll almost certainly be cloaked and hooded if he's out and about. If you need to begin stopping and searching any and all people you find who are covered up, then do so."

"Yes, Your Majesty."

"And if you need to extend your searches to the coastal towns within a day's walk of Barra-Dohn in case he's sought refuge in any of them, then do so."

"Yes, Your Majesty."

"And if you have any suspicion of his whereabouts, whatsoever, then do what you need to do to see if there's anything to it."

"Yes, Your Majesty."

"You think I'm angry now, Captain," Eirmon said, stepping closer to the man, "but you have no idea how angry I'll be if he isn't found."

This time the captain didn't reply. He stood, keeping his face as stoic as he could, but Eirmon knew he was worried and should be. Eirmon's men knew he could be generous with his rewards and exacting with his punishments.

"I think you understand me," Eirmon said. "You may go."

The captain was too disciplined to show any elation or relief at being dismissed, but Eirmon thought he stepped a little more lively on the way out than he had on the way in. The captain would impress upon the men under his command the anger of their sovereign and thus the urgency of their mission, and in turn those men would impress upon the men under them the same. All that could be done to find Tchinchura would be done.

He knew that it was unreasonable to expect his men to simply produce the man, especially since a solitary individual could hide in a million places if he had stayed in or around Barra-Dohn. It wasn't even certain he had stayed. Oh, Eirmon was quite sure the Amhuru wasn't finished with him or Barra-Dohn, not since the man had been found coming out of the Academy after attacking a pair of his miners inside of it. He must know Eirmon's little secret now. That the Amhuru would take steps to recover the fragment of the Golden Cord was certain.

What was uncertain was whether he would seek help from more Amhuru. Zangira was off with Kaden, surrounded by Eirmon's men, and Eirmon had already given the order for him to be arrested the moment he set foot back in the city. Even if Zangira was somehow reunited with Tchinchura, they were still only two men. Two Amhuru could be difficult, to be sure, but Eirmon was worried that perhaps Tchinchura had left Barra-Dohn, planning to return with more. And so, while he didn't like the thought of Tchinchura hiding somewhere under his nose, plotting to recover what he had taken, he found himself hoping Tchinchura was somewhere close by—and alone.

Eirmon closed his eyes and felt the Zerura against his skin. He realized it was probably unwise to keep wearing it now, but it had become so hard to take off. Even when he only took it off long enough to make the replicas the Academy used, he missed feeling it against his leg. The world felt duller without it, less colorful, less vibrant, less . . . alive.

His eyes popped open when the knock at his door interrupted him. "Who is it?"

"Just me."

Rika. What did she want?

"Come in," Eirmon called. He watched her slip stealthily into the room. Everything she did was stealthy, he thought, not for the first time since the episode at the Academy. He didn't yet have hard evidence against Rika and Barreck, and they'd been careful not to be seen together outside the Academy and only met infrequently inside of it. Still, Eirmon's suspicions remained, and he felt as certain as ever that he was right.

She walked toward him slowly, her eyes locked on his with that practiced look of allurement she often wore when they were together. Reaching him, she slid an arm around his waist and stood up on her toes to kiss him. He allowed it and felt perhaps the smallest pang of regret that these were the lips of a liar that would soon be silenced.

"What is it, Rika? I have things to do."

She let go and stepped back, feigning an injured look. "Maybe I've just missed you."

"Maybe," Eirmon said, "but I doubt it. What is it?"

"You asked me some time ago to be aware of the growing friendship between the king's daughter-in-law and the Amhuru."

"Yes," Eirmon said brusquely, wondering where Rika was going with this.

"Well, something curious happened yesterday in the market."

"Go on," Eirmon said. He already knew his soldiers had seen Nara in the market, but nothing curious had been reported. Certainly, at least, nothing involving the missing Amhuru.

"Well, I was on my way to the Academy when I saw her approaching the market, and remembering what you'd said and knowing you were looking for Tchinchura, I thought I'd see where she went."

"You followed Nara?" Eirmon asked.

"I did," Rika replied.

Eirmon could imagine what would follow from this beginning. He felt the irony of Rika's attempt to deflect his suspicions from her by raising them about Nara, but he tried to keep it from showing. She must think him gullible indeed if she expected him to suspect his son's wife, the most guileless woman he'd ever met, of harboring the Amhuru or being part of any conspiracy to keep him hidden. Eirmon had been concerned that Nara might somehow inadvertently give away the secret that was now clearly out of the bag, but he had long since turned his attention elsewhere. Rika had no shame.

"So what curious thing did you find?" Eirmon asked.

"Only this," Rika said. "She seemed to be wandering almost aimlessly through the market, and for a moment I lost her in the crowd. But then I found her again, and this time she was walking with clear purpose, following a rather large fellow in a cloak."

"You think she was with Tchinchura?" Eirmon asked, his suspicious regard for Rika slipping almost against his better judgment. He couldn't deny feeling traces of hope that the object of his search had been found in this most unlikely of ways.

"Well, no," Rika said, sounding a little flustered. "It wasn't Tchinchura. This man was bigger and fair-skinned with short blond hair, but she followed him around a corner, and by the time I made my way to the same corner, they were nowhere to be seen."

Eirmon pursed his lips as he strained to subdue his anger. "You think you saw her following a big man, and then they disappeared."

"I did see her following a big man," Rika said, doggedly.

"You saw her behind him, but you don't know that she was following him."

"Your Majesty, I think I know—"

"You're a researcher and a scientist. What exactly do you think you know about things like this?" Eirmon asked, watching her closely.

Rika blushed, even if only slightly. "Well, he could have been leading her to the Amhuru. It certainly couldn't hurt to search the houses in the area."

"You're sure they disappeared into a house nearby?"

"Like I said, when I reached the corner, they were nowhere to be seen."

"How soon after they turned the corner did you get there?"

"Only a few moments."

"A few moments," Eirmon said, sighing.

"The market was crowded."

"Of course, it was," Eirmon said, turning away from her. "Which, of course, means they could have turned another corner before you got there, which of course means they could have been heading anywhere in the city, providing they were even traveling together in the first place."

"She was following him," Rika said, determined.

Eirmon turned around and faced her again. "As you know full well, Rika, my daughter-in-law is very lonely. She has precious little in her life aside from her son, who's been gone from the city for some time. If she's been keeping company with a man from the city, it is likely for more obvious and less nefarious reasons than treachery and betrayal. Even that, though, seems unlikely, as she's a very honorable girl."

"I don't know how likely or unlikely anything is, Your Majesty, but as you'd noticed their connection before yourself and pointed it out to me, I naturally thought you'd be interested in my news."

"If it were news, I would be interested," Eirmon said. "All you've brought me, however, is idle conjecture, which would be laughable if I were in a better mood. You may go."

"But, Eirmon," Rika began.

"I said," Eirmon glared at her, "you may go."

Rika left without delay, leaving Eirmon to fume privately. He'd intended to wait until after Kaden's return and the resolution of the matter with the Amhuru to dispose of her, but he was beginning to wonder if that was wise. He had too many important matters to attend to without her transparent ploys to save her own neck.

"Nara," he said out loud, scoffing to himself at the idea of his daughter-in-law somehow being a party to the Amhuru's schemes. The idea was as laughable as the idea that those three researchers he'd had executed were the real conspiracy behind the missing Zerura.

Zangira watched Deslo dip his hand over the edge of the skiff that was ferrying them out to *The Sorry Rogue*. They'd waited ashore with the soldiers Kaden had sent with them while the larger boats took out the sliders and cargo samples Captain D'Sarza had carried with her down to Garranmere. Now, though, the ship was loaded, and it was time for them to board.

He'd spent enough time with the boy to read his moods pretty well. After the long, anxious wait at Garranmere for word of the other cities' responses to his grandfather's ultimatum, Deslo was anticipating his first sea voyage. Although he had been out in the Barra-Dohn harbor on Eirmon's barge many times, but never outside the harbor, this was just what the boy needed for a diversion. Zangira could see his eagerness as they climbed the dangling rope ladder and stepped onto the deck.

They were met there by none other than D'Sarza herself, who seemed, Zangira felt, fully aware of the value of making a good impression on Eirmon's grandson, as well as the possible price of making a bad one. "Welcome aboard, Deslo, Zangira. *The Sorry Rogue* is at your disposal."

After a brief but courteous exchange of pleasantries, they were shown to a comfortable cabin, which Zangira suspected belonged to the captain's first mate, Geffen, the older man that had been brought with D'Sarza before Kaden. He didn't exactly complain about it, but he seemed a bit muttery every time Zangira crossed his path for the rest of the day.

A few hours after getting under way, Zangira stood with Deslo along the portside rail, watching the sea spray splash up against the side of the ship. Sadly for Deslo, it wasn't coming quite high enough for him to feel it. "What do you think, Deslo?"

"About what?"

"The feel of the ship," Zangira said. "You said you wanted to see how it compared to a sandship."

Deslo shrugged. "I don't know. There's more up and down, I guess."

"You're right," Zangira nodded. "There is more up and down. Does the motion bother you?"

"No," Deslo said, looking up at Zangira. "Does it bother you?"

"Sometimes, when the waves are high, and the seas are rough. It isn't bothering me now, though."

Deslo looked back out over the rail. "I really like it. I knew I would too. When I'm older, I want to sail all over the world. I even want to cross the Madri."

"Well," Zangira said, appreciating the adventurous spirit bubbling out of the boy and not wanting to squash it, "that's an ambitious goal. I hope you get your chance."

Deslo looked up at him. "Have you crossed the Madri, Zangira?"

"Me?" Zangira said, a little surprised by the question, though he realized it would be natural for a boy like Deslo to ask. "No, I've never crossed the Madri. Amhuru don't normally do that."

Deslo looked puzzled for a moment. "Crossing the Madri isn't normal for anyone, is it?"

"Well," Zangira said, seeing he'd need to be clearer. "I guess not. Some people do make the crossing from time to time as part of their trade. What I meant was that the Amhuru don't cross at all, ever."

"Not ever?"

"No."

"Why not?"

"It's complicated," Zangira said, wondering how much of the Amhuru's story he should tell if the boy persisted.

"So there aren't any Amhuru in the northlands?"

"There are," Zangira said, "but the Amhuru in the northlands stay above the Madri, like we stay below it."

"Oh," Deslo said. He seemed satisfied by this and turned back to face out to sea, adding as he did, "I'm still going to cross it one day."

Zangira smiled. "Maybe you will." For a long while, they stood, enjoying their view of the bright sunlight dancing on the waves, the shores of Aralyn visible in the distance.

Zangira knew his time with Deslo was drawing to a close. It was unfortunate that he'd have to disappear without saying goodbye, but what had to be done, had to be done. Still, he was hopeful that he and Tchinchura could finish before Kaden returned. With any luck, the seeds planted between the boy and his father on this trip, though sown in the midst of a difficult time, would grow and bear fruit. Certainly, Zangira hoped they would. The boy might dream of distant and grand adventures, like crossing the Madri, but Zangira knew that what he needed most was far closer to home.

Rika waited in Barreck's office. She couldn't keep her hands from shaking. Eirmon had unnerved her by the way he looked at her and talked to her. He'd been angry and rude to her before, but this was different. Barreck had been right.

Eirmon knew.

"You shouldn't have come here," Barreck said quietly as he slipped inside the room and checked the hall before closing the door. "We agreed not to meet alone like this."

"We have to go," Rika said, "as soon as we can."

Barreck looked at her. "What happened?"

"What do you mean, what happened?" Rika snapped. "Eirmon happened. You were right. He knows."

"Rika," Barreck said, crossing to her and taking her hands in his. "You've been saying we were safe, and now you say he knows. Something happened."

"Nothing I can explain," she said. "I just went to him with information I thought he'd want, information he would normally have been interested in, but he wasn't. Not at all. That's when I knew. He was so consumed with examining me, of suspecting me, he couldn't see that what I was telling him might actually be useful. He knows."

"So why hasn't he done anything about it?" Barreck asked.

"I don't know, and I don't want to find out. How soon can you be ready to leave?"

"I'm ready now," Barreck said. "The only catch will be getting the Zerura on board the ship. That could take a few days if we want to be discreet about it."

"Then start tonight," Rika said. "Talk to the captain. Get as much help as you can to get it done."

"More help means splitting the profit more ways."

"I don't care. I want to be gone as soon as we can."

Barreck watched her silently for a long moment and said, "You must really want to go."

Rika glared at him. "That's what I've been trying to tell you."

Barreck ignored the glare, but he also took any hint of teasing out of his tone and demeanor. "A change in plan might make the captain nervous, especially if he thinks Eirmon's going to be chasing after us."

"I don't care what the captain thinks," Rika said. "He knows what's at stake, for him and for us. He wants to be wealthy too."

"Hey, you're shaking," Barreck said gently. "Don't worry. We're almost there."

Rika laid her head against his chest. "He scared me today, Barreck, and I don't scare easily."

"It's all right, Rika. I'll make the arrangements, and then we'll go. All right?"

Rika nodded and let Barreck hold her tightly. A few more days in Barra-Dohn meant a few more days at the palace. She didn't know if she could bear it, but she didn't think she had a choice.

28

LOOK HOMEWARD

The look on Rika's face was priceless. Even as calm as she tended to be, Eirmon had known his little surprise would faze her. He'd looked forward to it, and he wasn't disappointed.

Almost two full days had passed since she'd come to him with the foolishness about Nara and the Amhuru, and already Rika had been seen by the men he'd assigned to keep tabs on her when she went to see that young researcher, Barreck—twice. For his part, the man had spent a considerable amount of time the previous evening at the quay. Eirmon felt sure that whatever they might be up to, aside from stealing Zerura from him, they were most likely focused now on getting away from the city and from him.

He had no intention of letting that happen, so he'd had the two soldiers who'd obviously aided and abetted their plot brought to him. Before allowing either of them to speak and before saying a word himself, he'd pointed at one of them. Two Davrii moved

swiftly in, stabbing the man repeatedly. Other soldiers held the
uninjured man as he struggled, but no words were spoken, and
soon there was little to do but watch the dying man writhe in his
own blood on the floor.

. Eirmon had spoken then. He offered the remaining man one
chance to tell the truth about what had happened at the Academy
on the day in question, and the soldier was more than happy to
oblige him. Eirmon didn't know if he actually believed that by
turning Rika and Barreck in that he'd live, but turn them in he
did, explaining in great detail how Rika had recruited them, what
she'd promised, and more. If Eirmon hadn't given the order for
him to join his friend, he'd probably still be talking.

All that had been left to do to prepare for Rika's arrival, other
than securing Barreck, which of course Eirmon had already seen
to, was to arrange the bodies of the deceased to greet her in an
appropriately shocking manner. In the end, lacking any truly
creative ideas, he'd simply ordered his men to drive their spears
through the backs of the dead, so that the blades wedged in
through their rib cages. This enabled the men to hold up the bodies well enough so that at first glance, you might think they were
standing under their own power.

It was this gruesome scene which Rika was even now taking in
as she stood, speechless, just steps from the door through which
she'd been ushered a moment before. She stood, looking horrified, then covered her mouth with her hand and convulsed like
she might vomit. It was a sign of Eirmon's distrust of her that he
found himself wondering if her horror was over the gory sight or
its obvious implication that she had been discovered.

Eirmon motioned to the soldiers holding up the dead men,
and they let go of the spears and let the bodies slump to the
ground. As they did so, Rika looked over her shoulder, but two
of the Davrii had slid in quietly behind her and closed the door.
There was no escape for her there. At the same time, a small
door on the side of the room opened, and Barreck, his hands tied
behind his back, was led in and brought to a place where he stood

between his guards, equidistant between Rika and the dead soldiers on the floor. Both faced Eirmon.

"I hope you don't mind," Eirmon said, walking forward and looking back and forth between them, "but I started without you. We're making good time though. Your guilt has been established by some damaging testimony from the deceased."

Eirmon stopped long enough to motion vaguely in the direction of the two dead guards, who had come to rest in an odd position on their knees, leaning against one another, spears protruding from their backs. The king continued. "All I need to know now is where I should look to recover what you have stolen. I'm not feeling terribly inclined to be merciful, but quick, complete cooperation may affect your sentencing."

The king watched his prisoners, but neither spoke. Rika had regained some of her composure, but she hadn't moved an inch from where she'd stopped on the way in, and her eyes remained focused on the dead men on the floor. Since his initial entrance into the room, she'd not looked at Barreck nor had she looked at Eirmon.

Barreck, for his part, also stood quietly. Eirmon could see fear in his body language, but he also saw defiance. Unlike Rika, he did not shy away from meeting Eirmon's gaze. The king, though, stared until Barreck eventually looked away. Eirmon crossed his arms and waited, but neither spoke.

"Very well," he said at last. "I'm sure I'll find it eventually. I just thought I'd save myself some trouble. Well, not me personally, of course. I have more important things to do. I can't be expected to run an empire and personally recover stolen goods from every common thief in Barra-Dohn."

Eirmon paused to enjoy his taunt, though if he thought either Rika or Barreck would be embarrassed by it, they didn't show it. "Well, my dear," he said, taking a step toward Rika, "all good things must come to an end."

"Wait," Rika said, looking at Eirmon for the first time since entering the room. "You're making a terrible mistake."

"I am?" Eirmon said. He'd expected Rika to try something desperate, and for a moment, he'd thought she might disappoint him.

"Everything I've done, I've done for you," Rika added, as though she was worried Eirmon might stop her. Clearly, she had no idea how much he'd been looking forward to just this moment.

"You stole Zerura from the Academy and orchestrated the deaths of three innocent men all for me? I'm so flattered."

"I did what I needed to do to get and maintain Barreck's trust."

That had Barreck's attention. He looked at her in shock.

"When he came to me with his ideas about stealing the Zerura and selling it to the enemies of Barra-Dohn—"

"When I came to you?" Barreck sounded furious.

Eirmon felt gleeful. Rika hadn't waited long to stab her coconspirator in the back.

Eirmon almost felt bad for him.

"I knew it wouldn't be enough to turn him over to you," Rika hurried on, as though she'd never even been interrupted. "I needed to go along with it until I could identify for you whoever bought the Zerura from him so you'd know who your enemies were—all of them."

"Weren't the three researchers you accused my enemies? You said they were."

"Barreck knew you were aware that Zerura was missing. He insisted on the ruse."

"I insisted?" Barreck shouted. He struggled against his restraints, but the guards held him back. "It was your idea!"

Rika stepped closer to the king, but soldiers moved closer to make sure she intended no harm to Eirmon. She dropped to her knees. "Barreck told me just yesterday that he had found a buyer for the Zerura. I had hoped to discover who it was and bring the whole matter before you, perhaps even today—"

"Lies, every word you say is a lie—"

"As it is, Your Majesty," Rika continued, "I cannot tell you who that buyer is. Still, I submit myself to your judgment and mercy, only I implore you not to execute Barreck until you have extracted that name from him. Then Your Majesty will know how deep the conspiracy against you really runs."

She stopped, her head bowed as though in submission to an unjust but inevitable fate.

Barreck stood staring, his mouth open in stunned disbelief.

Eirmon had to admit it—she was good. Cold but good. She knew Eirmon couldn't disprove her claim that Barreck had approached her and that she'd gone along out of loyalty. She knew his great fear was a conspiracy among the powerful in the Five Cities against his throne. She knew and had used both admirably in her appeal. She couldn't possibly believe it would work, but she had only one play left and had made it pretty well.

Eirmon looked down at her, and he shook his head. He looked over from her at Barreck.

The look of stunned disbelief was gone, replaced now by a mixture of hurt and betrayal. "I realize things haven't worked out like you planned," Eirmon said to him, speaking softly but loud enough to be heard throughout the utterly silent room. "But take heart. Now that you've seen what she's really like, you know the future you'd envisioned could never have been. Sooner or later, she'd have tired of you. I'm guessing sooner."

Eirmon motioned to the guards. "Take them to the dungeon, and lock them up side by side. Until I've thought of a suitably public way in which to execute their sentence, I'd like to give them a little more time together. I'm just that generous."

The king smiled, and the guards moved in on Rika and Barreck. Neither looked happy, and both were led quietly away.

Kaden gazed at Amattai in the distance. The walls were nowhere near as formidable as the walls of Garranmere, though the gates were renowned for being ornate. Today, however, what attracted his attention was not the style of the gates but the fact that they were standing open wide.

It would certainly seem that an open gate was a good thing, given what they'd come to do, but it was amazing how a little thing like this could throw off all his plans. He'd intended to relay a verbal ultimatum by means of a messenger sent close to the city and then to follow that message by pounding the city when the ultimatum was refused. It was a simple strategy, but the open gate had given him pause from the moment they arrived.

He suspected a trap. Amattai was by now aware of the power of his weapons. The demand for their surrender had counted on it. Perhaps they had left the gate open as an invitation for him to enter so that his soldiers might be engaged at close quarters and the city could avoid the deadly barrage that Garranmere had endured. It was a risky play, but he could see its merits to Amattai and disadvantages for himself, and so he hung back.

The situation had been further complicated when word came back from his scouts that the Amattai harbor was essentially empty. They'd gotten close enough to see that with the exception of some vessels in drydock that might not have even been seaworthy, there were not only no ships there flying the strange insignia mentioned by Captain D'Sarza, but there were no ships at all.

His first thought was that the merchant captain had lied to him, and he felt a pang of worry for Deslo. That feeling was strangely reassuring and painful all at the same time. The thought of his son being used in some way against Barra-Dohn or worse, being hurt, struck him like a blow to his gut. He wasn't really sure just exactly where or when he'd decided to embrace his role as a father, but he apparently had, and he would make anyone who hurt Deslo pay.

Fortunately, he quickly moved on from this suspicion of D'Sarza, based not on facts but on his own ability to judge people. He didn't think D'Sarza had been lying, and neither had Zangira, and he trusted the Amhuru's judgment as much as his own. Besides, it wasn't just that these particular ships weren't there, but no ships were there. He had no idea what that might mean.

It was time to find out. He'd been watching the city for over an hour, and none of the facts had changed. Even with the open gates, no one had been seen stirring within the city. They didn't seem disposed to come out, and he wasn't going in, at least not yet.

He'd felt bad unleashing the full strength of Barra-Dohn against Garranmere. They had no choice and no chance. That wasn't true of Amattai, and he didn't feel the same compunction here. He had to protect his men.

Kaden turned to Greyer. "Give the order."

Greyer relayed his command, and soon the railguns unleashed a ferocious attack on the walls beside the gate. The projectiles blew the walls to bits, and stone and dust sprayed high in the bright morning sun. Greyer motioned to the crews manning the railguns, and the attack ceased.

The full force of it had been directed against a small section of wall on either side of the gate. Kaden hoped that if soldiers were concealed there, waiting to spring their trap, he might demolish them and force the rest either to surrender or come out. The dust settled over the newly created rubble heaps by the gates, but still no signs of life from within the city were visible.

Kaden watched and waited, but the complete lack of response from the city was eerie. No one stirred or cried out; there was neither attack nor surrender, only silence. Kaden called for meridium soles, and when they were brought to him, he began to run toward the city.

"Kaden! Kaden!" he heard Greyer calling from behind him. "After him! Fall in, everyone, after him!"

He didn't look back. He didn't need to. He knew that every soldier within the sound of Greyer's voice was following him. By the time he was midway to the city, some had overtaken him and formed a vanguard to escort him.

If he was going in, they were going in with him.

He reached the gate and slowed, peering both to the right and the left. He saw no one, alive or dead. With only a barely perceptible pause, he passed through the gate.

Motioning to the nearest buildings that remained standing
and intact, soldiers spread out and explored the structures. They
found nothing. Farther and farther they penetrated into the city,
but always the findings were the same. All buildings were empty.
All shops and stalls abandoned. They found no one anywhere.

"What's going on, Kaden?" Greyer asked as they stood once
more at the gate, a little while later, waiting for a complete sweep
of the city to be completed.

"I don't know," Kaden said. "But I don't like it."

"Perhaps they had second thoughts about defying you and
decided to flee."

"Perhaps," Kaden frowned, "but as we discovered at Garranmere, evacuating a city is no small venture. This wasn't done on
a whim."

Kaden paced back and forth at the entrance to the city, rubbing the back of his neck and wiping the sweat on his shirt. He
didn't like surprises, especially when he didn't understand them.
"The fleet is gone. The city is empty."

He stopped pacing, lifted his head, and looked not at the city
but homeward, back across the desert in the general direction of
Barra-Dohn. Perhaps the army of Amattai had fled, along with
the people, but it was also possible that they had moved toward
trouble, not away from it.

"Greyer," Kaden said quietly.

"Yes?"

"Gather everyone, as quick as you can. We're headed home."

Greyer followed his gaze. "They wouldn't dare."

"Why wouldn't they?"

"Surely, they know we wouldn't leave Barra-Dohn defenseless," Greyer said, gesturing dismissively, as though nothing could
be more obvious.

"I'm sure they do know," Kaden said. "Nevertheless, here we
are, and we're a significant portion of Barra-Dohn's army. If I was
desperate enough, I might try."

"I'll gather the men," Greyer said, and he moved quickly into the city.

Kaden now stood with his back to Amattai. Where were they? The mysterious fleet? Had the unprovoked attack on Garranmere been the catalyst that set in motion some already existing plan to move on Barra-Dohn? If so, how much of a head start did they have, and could he get back before they struck against the city?

Then it occurred to Kaden that if they really hurried, he could probably be home by the fortieth day since the Kalosene's prophecy. And if there was time for him to get there by then, then there was . . .

Kaden shrugged off that thought. It was mere superstition and coincidence. Whatever else his father was wrong about, he wasn't wrong about this.

Barra-Dohn was too strong, and its fall inconceivable.

Part 3

THE DARKER ROAD

29

THE THIRD PIECE

Though they were walking fast, it was all Nara could do to keep from running. Deslo was home, safe and sound, and she was on her way to the quay to see him. The men with her were on their way to the quay for a different reason.

As excited as she was to see Deslo, she was also scared. As soon as word had come to the palace of the arrival of the merchant ship bearing Deslo and Zangira, Eirmon had lost no time in organizing an escort of fifty men selected from among the Davrii to bring them to the palace. Nara knew they were being sent to deal with Zangira, and that this was why the king had urged her to remain with him and wait for them to bring Deslo back. But she had insisted on going, and in the end, the king had relented, having nothing aside from the truth that he would not tell to offer as a reason for her to stay.

And so Nara was scared that Deslo could be hurt, even though she knew neither Zangira nor the Davrii would deliberately hurt him, scared for Zangira, and even scared for Tchinchura. If Eirmon's strike against Zangira succeeded, then Tchinchura would have to move on Eirmon alone. Even with the Kalosene plot against the Academy, that would be difficult. If it failed, then Eirmon's crimes might go unpunished.

The soldier she was following turned onto the commercial wharf that stretched out into the harbor. Several ships lay anchored along it, and the wharf was alive with the hustle and bustle of dockhands loading and unloading cargo.

The large party of soldiers moving swiftly up the center of the wharf drew attention. People moved aside, and most stopped once out of their way to watch the curious procession.

Nara scanned the ships ahead, and her heart skipped a beat when she spotted *The Sorry Rogue*. She started to jog. She couldn't help it. A cart with wooden wheels bearing bolts and bolts of cloth rumbled down the wharf in front of her, and she darted around it and forward toward the ship. A strong scent of mint flooded her one moment and then was gone the next. She could see the gangway now. She ran.

Her feet echoed on the wood as she raced up onto the ship. Fortunately, no one was loading or unloading anything, and her path to the top was unabated. She paused there, searching the deck. She heard heavy feet start up the gangway behind her, and then she saw him. He was standing with a woman in colorful clothes by the rail on the far side of the ship. "Deslo!" she cried as she started across the deck.

He turned, and when he saw her, his face lit up. He ran to her and threw his arms around her. She pulled him close and squeezed him tightly.

For a moment, she held him, unaware of anything else in the world. But only for a moment. Soon she was all too aware of the soldiers swarming over the deck of the ship. The woman Deslo had been standing with started to protest but was immediately surrounded and silenced at spearpoint.

"Mom?" Deslo said, now also aware of what was going on around them. "What's happening?"

"Come with me, Deslo," Nara said, taking his hand firmly and leading him quickly toward the top of the gangway.

Deslo didn't resist, but he followed slowly, distracted by the turmoil around him. The sailors had stopped doing anything, and most of the soldiers from the palace were searching the ship, while a few of them were huddled together, talking to the ones that had traveled back from Garranmere.

"Mom, what's going on?" Deslo asked again more insistently as they started down the gangway.

Nara didn't pause to answer until they were back on the wharf and walking away from the ship. She'd thought that perhaps if she'd found Zangira with Deslo she could have warned him with a look or a signal or something, but she knew that she could do nothing now. Getting Deslo away from there was all she could do.

"They're looking for Zangira," she said at last, after Deslo had asked a third time about the soldiers.

"Why?" Deslo said, worry creasing his brow as he turned to look back at the ship as they made their way away from it.

"I will tell you," Nara promised, "but I can't right now."

She had known that in order to prepare Deslo for what Tchinchura had told her was coming, she'd have to bring him into her confidence, at least, as far as she could. She felt pretty confident that he'd agree with her in condemning Eirmon's actions, even though he was Deslo's grandfather. But she thought the matter delicate enough that she didn't want to get anywhere near it now. Her attention and effort were directed entirely toward getting her son as far away from *The Sorry Rogue* as possible.

"Deslo," she said as they approached the quay. "I didn't see Zangira on deck when I looked for you. Was he still on board?"

"I think so," Deslo said. "After he sent the messenger to the palace, he waited with me and Captain D'Sarza. I suggested we go with the messenger, but he thought we should wait. He thought you might like to see the ship and meet the captain."

"Was that the captain you were standing with when I arrived?"

"Yes."

"But Zangira wasn't there," Nara said. "Had he been gone long?"

Deslo thought about that for a while. "I don't know. I don't think he was gone very long. He said he wanted to go back to our cabin, but I don't remember why. I just know I was talking with Captain D'Sarza, and then you were there."

Nara felt a momentary surge of hope. Maybe bloodshed would be avoided today. Maybe Zangira had gotten away.

Zangira crouched behind the stack of crates, watching the two men at the doorway to the warehouse. They pointed down the quay, laughed, and then disappeared back inside. He glanced around, making sure no one else was around, then darted quickly across to the side of the building and away from the waterfront.

Near the back, standing in the warehouse's shadow, was a hulking man with short blond hair.

When Zangira approached him, the man simply extended his hand, which held a long brown robe. Zangira nodded his thanks, and with no more ceremony or conversation than that, he pulled the robe and hood over his head and followed the Devoted through the city.

Once safely inside the house and reunited with Tchinchura, Zangira dried off, changed clothes, and joined the others. More than a dozen Devoted had gathered here already, and more were on their way. Tchinchura had suggested as much when he'd instructed Zangira on where to go once they arrived in the harbor of Barra-Dohn, and the presence of so many Kalosenes comforted him. After being for so long with an army where the only person he knew he could trust was a ten-year-old boy, it was a relief to be once more among friends.

The Devoted offered food and water, but Zangira took only the drink. He'd had plenty to eat that morning on *The Sorry Rogue* and was eager to hear from Tchinchura more fully about his plans. Perhaps sensing this, the Devoted made themselves scarce, and the two Amhuru soon found themselves at the table alone.

"The circle of our conspiracy has grown," Tchinchura said. "Nara brought Gamalian, the king's advisor, to me three days ago. He's with us."

"Oh?" Zangira said.

"Yes," Tchinchura said. "He seemed reluctant to accept that Eirmon could have killed an Amhuru himself or even just had one of us killed, but he still acknowledged that the king's possession of a fragment of the Golden Cord was a serious indictment of his character. He actually offered a formal apology on behalf of Barra-Dohn for Eirmon."

"Did he now?" Zangira said.

"He did indeed."

"So he believes Eirmon has the fragment and has used it?"

"Oh, he doesn't believe it. He knows the king has it."

Zangira's eyebrows rose.

"Yes," Tchinchura continued. "He's seen it with his own eyes."

"He already knew about this?"

"No, not exactly," Zangira said. "I'd no sooner explained my belief that Eirmon wore the fragment on his person when he talked about seeing a curious golden ring around the king's calf years ago when his cloak snagged and tore on a table. He didn't know what he was seeing at the time, of course, but he knows now."

"Around his calf," Tchinchura said. "That's it."

"That's it," Tchinchura agreed.

"Will he help us get it back?"

"Yes," Tchinchura said. "We haven't finalized anything yet. I wanted to wait for you, but there are a few possibilities. They all depend on how things go when we help the Devoted with their plan to destroy the Academy."

"So you do intend to help," Zangira said.

Tchinchura nodded. "I know it isn't why we came, but I can't ignore that they found me, as their Guardian said they would."

"The Devoted that Eirmon executed?"

"Yes," Tchinchura said. "He told them when and where to find me, and he said I'd help with their scheme for the Academy. So I plan to."

"If you are convinced," Zangira said, "that's good enough for me."

"Depending on how all that goes," Tchinchura said, "we will move on the king after. It will be hard and bloody, but when it is finally over, if Kalos wills it, we can return what was stolen."

The Jin Dara stood with Devaar looking north toward the sea. The coastline was just close enough that they could see a hint of the evening sun sparkling on the water. The world around them was relatively quiet, for even though they were an impressive force, all told, the day was still relatively hot. Few men had shown an inclination to do more than rest since he'd called a halt to their slow progress across the sand.

Jona, his bushy red beard blowing in the warm wind, approached. The Jin Dara turned to him and smiled. "Lord Jona," he said, "I trust you've had a good day."

"Yes, well, fairly good, I'd say," Jona replied.

The Jin Dara maintained his smile, amused at the man's hopelessly awkward ability to deal with basic social niceties. He was intense and all about business, which was fine most of the time, but if subtlety or delicacy were ever required, he couldn't imagine how Jona would handle such a thing. He waited, sure that Jona would come to his point in short order, which he did.

"We're a large force," Jona began, "and this blasted heat is pretty unrelenting. But I think we should be pressing on a bit longer before stopping each day. I know we're only a few days away, but if the report of our scouts is accurate, young Omiir could still overtake us."

"I certainly hope so," the Jin Dara replied, looking from Jona to Devaar and laughing. "Otherwise, all this dragging of our heels has been for nothing."

Jona's eyes kept growing wider, and his mouth dropped open until a moment later he stood, watching them laugh, mouth agape. "But we'll lose our advantage! We'll reach Barra-Dohn and find it as well defended as it might have been at any time!"

"Ah, yes, very true," the Jin Dara replied, losing the smile and the laugh, and turning his penetrating gaze back to Jona. "I suppose I owe you an apology. I haven't been entirely forthright with you."

Jona went through a rapid progression of mood swings, all of them visible on his face. A brief surge of anger swept across it, and he turned quite red, but as the Jin Dara's own eyes lost their mirth and he met the man's eyes gaze for gaze, Jona paled, and fear replaced the anger.

The Jin Dara didn't look away or soften his look. He intended Jona no harm and meant to keep the rest of the bargain. But the man might as well know right now that this was not a partnership, a fact he felt should have already been clear.

"I mean to destroy Barra-Dohn, to crush it utterly," the Jin Dara said. "Not just the physical structure but the entire city. Everything. If I moved on the city before the king's son and his men returned, I'd just have to fight them later. I might as well do it right the first time."

"But I told you about their new weapons," Jona sputtered. "The reports . . . ?"

"You did," the Jin Dara said. "And I told you not to worry about that."

They stood, eyes locked in a silent struggle. After a moment, Jona swallowed and nodded.

"I apologize about the deception," the Jin Dara said, reaching over and placing a firm hand on Jona's shoulder. "I told you what I thought you needed to hear to get you to come along, and despite your obvious disappointment at this moment, I think you'll be gratified by the results. When Barra-Dohn lies in rubble, this will all be forgotten. We'll return with you to Amattai, collect our ships, which your people will no longer need to hide on since the threat against them will have been neutralized, and be on our way."

"And we will be grateful," Jona said. "Hopefully young Omiir didn't do too much damage to the city before realizing what had happened."

"Hopefully not," the Jin Dara said. "But whatever he did can be repaired. Stone can be replaced. The city will live because the people live. Barra-Dohn won't be so lucky."

Perhaps it was the idea of Barra-Dohn's annihilation that consoled him, but Jona relaxed visibly, and the Jin Dara released him. The big man shifted where he stood, turning his intense gaze from the north to the west toward Barra-Dohn. "I still hope we can get there by the fortieth day."

"Yes," the Jin Dara said, "we were just talking about that. It would be a nice touch."

Jona's jaw clenched and bulged in his cheek, and when he spoke, it sounded as if he were talking through gritted teeth. "Oh, you have no idea. I just want to see Eirmon's face when he realizes that the crazy Kalosene's prophecy has come true."

"If the prophecy comes true," Devaar interjected, turning to the others, "wouldn't that suggest the Kalosene wasn't crazy?"

"Devaar," the Jin Dara said, "our friend here doesn't know you well enough to realize you aren't serious." He leaned toward Jona and whispered loudly. "He's not serious. He thinks the Kalosenes are as crazy as we do."

"Generally, yes," Devaar said. "But you have to admit. It's a pretty big coincidence."

"I don't know what it was or what the man thought or why he thought it," the Jin Dara said, "but if the idiot Kalosene had been a real prophet, why didn't he foresee his own death and keep his mouth shut?"

The others didn't answer, and after a moment, Jona took his leave and headed back toward the sandships.

Devaar hung behind longer, but after a while, he too left to go back.

The Jin Dara, though, remained, looking northward once more to the sea. He could not see them, not from here, anyway. But when he closed his eyes and felt for them, he could almost imagine their majestic forms gliding along, some above and some below the water, parallel to the coast. More were coming in answer to his summons each day, and though these were not as large as the ones he'd manipulated back at Amattai, they'd certainly help.

He understood Jona's fear. Eirmon's weapons would frighten someone who didn't know what a piece of the Golden Cord could do. But he was not afraid. He was the Jin Dara, and he wielded more power than the king of Barra-Dohn could imagine.

30

BITTERSWEET RETURN

At first, Deslo thought being back at the palace was great. He'd enjoyed the sandships, being with Zangira, and most of all, being noticed by his father. Still, he'd missed the comforts of home, and more than that, he'd been distressed about what his grandfather had sent the army of Barra-Dohn to do.

His dreams had been haunted since Garranmere by images of mangled men in the sand, of the city on fire, by the sounds of crying and screaming in the dark, and most of all by the little girl he'd seen, crushed by a block from a building that should have sheltered, not killed her. He'd told Zangira about some of his dreams, but not all of them. Not the ones about her. They were too hard to talk about.

So he'd looked forward to being home. To sleeping in his own bed. To having his mother there if the nightmares continued. To being surrounded by tranquility and routine, far from the awful things that had transpired at Garranmere, and perhaps by now, also at Amattai.

But as much as he'd looked forward to being back at the palace, he found his heart sinking as he realized his mother was taking him straight to the king. He felt silly for thinking she'd do anything else, for not realizing that this meeting had been inevitable, but that didn't make it any easier. He had tried to reconcile himself to his grandfather's terrible command to destroy Garranmere, but it still made him angry. Now he had to face him. What's more, as inevitable as the meeting itself was the fact that his grandfather would want him to talk about what he'd witnessed, and while he might be angry about it, he didn't want to show that to the king. He generally didn't like to disagree with Eirmon or disappoint him. Nobody did.

Deslo's thoughts turned to his father. He'd felt angry with him too for doing what the king had told him to do. Kaden hadn't ordered the destruction of Garranmere, but he'd overseen that destruction, and Deslo felt let down by them both.

Then it dawned on Deslo: Kaden was afraid of Eirmon, just as much as he was.

It seemed obvious now. He'd known they frequently disagreed and argued, but he'd never really understood that his father could be afraid of the king like he was. But he was. Everybody was. He wasn't sure why that should comfort him, but it did. And just in time too because the room Nara was entering contained the king, and he wasn't alone.

Deslo almost stopped walking when he saw how many soldiers were there, but his mother didn't stop, so he didn't either. He followed her into the room, looking timidly around at all the men lining the walls and bunched at the end of the room where his grandfather stood with Gamalian. He'd sailed across Aralyn to war with his father and the army of Barra-Dohn, but he didn't think he'd felt so completely surrounded by so many soldiers in all that time as he did now.

The king saw them enter, and smiling, came walking toward them, arms wide open. Deslo soon found himself being hugged, and instinctively he hugged back. Even so, he felt relief when his grandfather let go and stood up straight again.

"Welcome home, Deslo," the king said in a booming voice. He sounded lighthearted and welcoming, but Deslo saw the look in his eyes and wasn't fooled. He knew when he was being carefully examined. "I didn't expect you to arrive by sea and without your father. Is he well? What happened?"

"He's fine," Deslo said, and though he felt he should say more, he wasn't sure where to go from there. Should he report about Garranmere first, or explain about Amattai's silence, or go right to how he ended up with Captain D'Sarza? Gamalian, understanding his silent confusion, intervened.

"Why don't you start at the beginning, Deslo," he said, walking over and placing a welcoming hand on Deslo's shoulder. "How did things go at Garranmere?"

"Good, I guess," Deslo said. Inwardly, he flinched as soon as the words *I guess* were out of his mouth. If he was to keep his disapproval of Eirmon's commands to himself, he'd have to do a better job. He hastened to add, "The city is empty and in ruins."

The king smiled at that and asked, "Did Kaden lose many men?"

"No," Deslo said.

"Good." Eirmon nodded, looking serious for a moment. "The best wars, Deslo, are the ones you fight on your own terms. Fighting at the time of your choosing, on the field of your choosing is the best way to minimize losses."

Your own losses, Deslo thought, as he struggled to push the anger down. The king didn't care about the losses to Garranmere or even if the war had been necessary in the first place. He'd often spoken to Deslo about the responsibility of the throne and the one who sat on it to all of Aralyn, but Deslo understood now that these were only words. The king only cared about Barra-Dohn. Maybe not even that. Maybe he only cared about himself.

"So," Gamalian said, prompting Deslo to continue, "where's Kaden? And the army? Why didn't you return with them?"

"They left Garranmere for Amattai."

"Amattai?" Eirmon said, scowling. "I should have known Jona would be fool enough to test me."

"Why didn't you go with him?" Gamalian asked.

"A merchant captain came to Garranmere, and Father wanted to send word home about Amattai, so Zangira suggested we come back too."

"And where is Zangira now?" his grandfather said, peering down at him.

Deslo shook his head, almost as a defense against the possibility of the king's displeasure. "I don't know. He disappeared."

"Disappeared," Eirmon growled, anger flashing in his eyes as he looked up and motioned to one of the soldiers nearby. The man headed immediately for the door, and the king turned back to Deslo. "I want to hear all about your trip, Deslo. But now I need to talk to some of the soldiers who came back with you. We'll talk later."

Deslo nodded. He was glad to be dismissed.

"We'll talk later too," Gamalian added. "I know your mother wants you to herself now."

It was then that it occurred to Deslo that Rika was the missing piece from this scene. He couldn't believe she'd have missed his return if she'd been in the palace or near it when the messenger came.

"Where's Rika?" he blurted out.

"I think that's one of the things you'll need to talk to your grandfather about later," his mother said before anyone else could answer him.

His grandfather's whole countenance changed at the mention of her name like the dark clouds of a sandstorm swirling without warning across a blue sky.

His mother's hands guided him swiftly away from Eirmon and Gamalian then, and he risked only one look back over his shoulder. It didn't tell him anything, though, for the king was already speaking quietly with another soldier, while Gamalian, who was watching him leave, waved to him with a forced smile.

The doors had barely closed behind his daughter-in-law and grandson before the soldier the king sent to bring the others in returned. They entered and confirmed the boy's story, adding that Kaden had thought that by the time *The Sorry Rogue* reached Barra-Dohn, he should have dealt with Amattai and be on his own way home.

"Good," Eirmon said to Gamalian while the soldiers who'd given the report were led out. They stood, waiting for D'Sarza to be brought in. "I expected it would all be over by now."

The doors opened again, and a pair of soldiers escorted D'Sarza in. While it was a rare privilege for a merchant to receive an audience with the king, she didn't look pleased to be there.

"You are Captain D'Sarza?" Eirmon said, thinking she looked a little young to be the captain of her own merchant vessel.

"I am," she said.

"I am Eirmon Omiir, King of Barra-Dohn and all Aralyn," Eirmon said, "but you probably know that."

"Thank you for your welcome, Your Majesty," Captain D'Sarza said, giving a slight bow. Very slight, and when she rose, she added, "Still, I'm not clear about why my ship was boarded and searched in what appeared to me a less than friendly manner."

Eirmon smiled tolerantly. Whatever her age, she had the courage and the heart that all really successful merchant captains had. "I had reason to believe you were carrying an enemy of Barra-Dohn on your ship. Precautions were necessary."

D'Sarza frowned. "Enemy of Barra-Dohn? I had your soldiers and your grandson."

"And the Amhuru, Zangira?"

"What about him?" D'Sarza said, returning Eirmon's stare, levelly, hands on her hips.

"He wasn't on board when my men searched," Eirmon said.

"No, he wasn't," D'Sarza said. "He must have slipped away shortly before they came. I don't know where he went."

"Did you help him?"

"Help him?" D'Sarza said. "I gave him passage from Garran-mere. Is that helping him?"

"I'd watch your tone," Eirmon said.

D'Sarza took a deep breath, then started again more civilly. "I'm sorry, Your Majesty, but I'm a little confused. Your son told me to bring your grandson and the Amhuru here, and that for this I'd be rewarded. My only reward so far has been an unfriendly welcome and vague accusations that I don't understand."

"My son did not know certain things about the situation here in Barra-Dohn."

"Then how would I?" D'Sarza asked, her inflection inching back toward indignation.

"The voyage, I'm sure, provided many opportunities to speak with the Amhuru. He might have confided things in you that he wouldn't have confided in my son." Eirmon said, hardening his tone. He respected bravery, but the woman needed to remember who she was talking to.

D'Sarza caught the shift. When she spoke again, she sounded once more like a supplicant before a superior and not like an indignant and shrewish wife scolding her husband. "I spoke with the Amhuru on a number of occasions," D'Sarza said, "but he never said anything that would indicate there was trouble between the two of you. What's more, I had no idea, up until the moment your men told me he was not on the ship that he had left. I was on deck the whole time, and I don't think he could have left by the gangway without my notice. He must have slipped overboard."

Eirmon watched her silently for a moment, then nodded thoughtfully. "Captain," he said, "I am grateful that you have brought Deslo safely home. You will be compensated. I regret that your reception wasn't warmer and will provide letters of introduction to some of Barra-Dohn's leading citizens by way of apology. Perhaps, if time permits, I may even view some of your finer wares here at the palace before you leave the city."

"I would be honored," D'Sarza said.

Eirmon motioned to the soldiers that had brought her in. "These men will take you to my chief steward. He'll settle with you for my grandson's passage."

"Thank you, Your Majesty." D'Sarza bowed and then followed the soldiers who led her from the room.

Even when she was gone, Eirmon stared after her, lost in his own thoughts. Where had Zangira gone? Had he simply guessed that Eirmon would try to take him immediately upon his return? Could he somehow have already known that Tchinchura had left the palace and that the silent war between them was now out in the open?

He noticed that Gamalian had come forward and was waiting for the king to acknowledge him. He looked at his advisor and said, "What is it, Gamalian?"

"I haven't asked about all the extra security in the palace, Eirmon," Gamalian said quietly as though desiring to keep a secret from all the soldiers in the room, "and I haven't pursued the matter of Tchinchura's disappearance since my first question to you about it went unanswered. I can't help but wonder if it isn't time you confided in me about what's going on. Maybe I can help."

Eirmon listened to Gamalian and sighed. He'd held back from letting Gamalian in on the nature of the conflict between the Amhuru and himself, feeling sure that Gamalian would disapprove of what he'd done. Eirmon had hoped to deal with the problem of the Amhuru as quietly as possible. Now there seemed no way the matter would be resolved quietly unless they just left, which he didn't think they'd do. And if they did, they'd just come back—in greater numbers. They knew his secret, and they weren't going to leave him alone.

"I'm sorry, Gamalian," the king said at last. "There are things I should have told you, and I will but not now."

"I am, as always, at your service," Gamalian said.

"I know that," Eirmon said, "and I appreciate your counsel. We'll talk soon."

Gamalian bowed slightly and withdrew.

With his departure, Eirmon's thoughts returned to the Amhuru. No one knew where Zangira was, but Eirmon could only guess that by now he'd rejoined Tchinchura. He had meant what he said earlier to Deslo about fighting your enemies on your own terms. He'd had his chance to control the manner in which the Amhuru were engaged, and he'd let it slip away, a little too confident in his control of the situation. Now, he knew he could no longer force the issue. They would come at him, when and where they would. He'd just have to be ready.

Gamalian turned the corner and paused against the wall, looking around to see if anyone had followed him from the palace. Few people walked along the streets, and the only soldiers he could see were coming from the opposite direction and couldn't have been sent to track him. He didn't think Eirmon had anyone watching him as a matter of course, at least not yet, but he needed to be sure. Even though he was only going to meet the Kalosene, Marlo, he knew Marlo could in turn be tracked back to the Amhuru, and he didn't want to give them away.

Eirmon had betrayed not only Barra-Dohn but also all the values of nobility and common decency that Gamalian had labored to teach him, not to mention his son and grandson. Whatever measure of revenge the Amhuru exacted would be deserved, and Gamalian would happily see Kaden seated on the throne in Eirmon's place.

A change in Barra-Dohn was long overdue.

31

A LARGER PURPOSE

K aden unwound the scarf that covered his mouth but left his goggles on. The worst of the sandstorm had passed, but the winds were still fairly strong. Ever since he'd been a boy, he'd hated the feel of sand in his eyes.

He looked to the skies, encouraged by the signs that with the passing of the storm, the thick, solid bank of clouds were passing too. If he were going to press on through the night in one last desperate push to reach Barra-Dohn before the force from Amattai, then to do it he'd need the light of the stars and moon, which was thankfully almost completely full.

Greyer, who'd removed his goggles already, approached him on the foredeck, where Kaden had been monitoring the storm. Kaden knew Greyer had been busy debriefing the scouts that had returned shortly before the storm hit, so he took a deep breath as he waited for the news, whatever it was.

"I know it doesn't make a lot of sense," Greyer said, shrugging with his hands raised as though to underscore his own lack of comprehension about what he was saying, "but they all say that we're almost even with them now and moving faster. We should get there first."

Kaden shook his head. It was good news, of course, as he'd been pressing hard in the very hope that he'd be able to bypass the force from Amattai and reach Barra-Dohn first to aid in its defense. Even so, he was mystified, and as a general rule, he mistrusted inexplicable good fortune.

"Walk through this with me," Kaden said.

"All right."

"I'm Jona, or whoever is leading their army," Kaden said.

"It has to be Jona," Greyer said, the confidence of this assertion a marked contrast with the uncertainty he'd displayed a moment before. "Who else would be so bold?"

"Well, whoever it is, I'm Jona," Kaden said.

"All right," Greyer said. "You're Jona."

"I'm Jona," Kaden continued, "and I hear that an army from Barra-Dohn has just demolished Garranmere. Leveled it with some mysterious new weaponry. I'm told to surrender, or I'll be demolished too. Right?"

"Right."

"So I've been given an ultimatum," Kaden said, "and apparently, I deliberate my options for a while. They seem to be three in number: submit, defend my city, or attack Barra-Dohn."

"Maybe it doesn't matter, but how do we know they deliberated?" Greyer asked.

"Because even though I eventually decide to attack, I don't leave right away. I wait a while."

"Waiting doesn't necessarily signal deliberation," Greyer said. "They might have known from the moment they heard the ultimatum that they weren't going to give in or wait for us to come to them. But getting ready to launch the attack could easily have required the time that passed."

"True," Kaden agreed. "Whether I deliberated or not, I've obviously been considering aggression against Barra-Dohn already. Or else how do I get an army ready at all, even in the time it did take to depart?"

"You don't," Greyer replied. "Just making the crossing with that many men would be almost logistically impossible to arrange on short notice, not to mention conducting a siege against the strongest city in Aralyn on the other side."

"Not to mention evacuating my own city, because I don't want them defenseless when an angry army from Barra-Dohn comes calling to fulfill their threat."

"That's right. Organizing both those things would take quite a while."

"I can't even imagine," Kaden said, rubbing his cheek thoughtfully and shaking his head. "So I needed the days of preparation that I took before launching my attack. They were essential. Some planning for the assault I could do while en route, but some things I just had to do before leaving."

"You do, but you get everything together as quickly as you can, and then you head out."

"And why do I do this as quickly as I can?" Kaden asked.

"Because you have to launch before the army from Barra-Dohn comes. If they arrive before you leave, you're trapped inside the city. You'll miss your chance."

"Yes, I'll be trapped, but that's not the only reason I move as quickly as I can."

"True, you launch quickly because you know that if you get to Barra-Dohn first, you have, in addition to the tactical advantage of surprise, the advantage of knowing a significant portion of Barra-Dohn's army is gone."

"Exactly," Kaden said, pointing emphatically at Greyer. "If I've been harboring hopes of attacking Barra-Dohn, then news of the surprise attack against Garranmere and the ultimatum, despite any initial concern, is actually good news. In fact, it's better than I could ever have hoped for."

"Your enemy is out of position and vulnerable."

"Out of position and vulnerable," Kaden repeated, "but only if I get there first. So why do I dawdle on the crossing?"

"I wouldn't say they've dawdled," Greyer said. "I mean, we've pushed pretty hard to catch them, and we're only just going to do it."

"I don't care," Kaden said, becoming animated. "I'm launching a desperate attack against a superior foe. And both of my tactical advantages will be lost if I don't get there before their army, and I have a head start of a couple of days. I move heaven and earth to get there first. There's no way I don't. I leave any ships, men, or materiel behind, within reason, if they're slowing me down. I don't get caught, and I don't get passed. Period."

"No," Greyer agreed, almost reluctantly. "You don't."

"So how?" Kaden said. "How did we do this? How are we going to pass them and get there first?"

"I don't know," Greyer conceded. "Maybe there's more to the rumors than we thought."

"Rumors?" Kaden scoffed. "You mean the bizarre tales of strange creatures and monsters marching with the enemy?"

"I know," Greyer said. "The scouts have been vague and inconsistent, unable to describe anything that makes sense, but maybe they've really seen glimpses of something, you know, non-human. Maybe that explains the slower pace."

Kaden gazed out over the sand. The storm was gone now, the sky clearing up. He took his goggles off. He found it difficult to give rumors like these credence, but they did seem persistent. What's more, it might explain not only Jona's slower pace but also his evident confidence.

Kaden had approached Garranmere with confidence, knowing the power of the weapons he carried with him from Barra-Dohn. Was Jona approaching Barra-Dohn with a similar confidence? Did he have a secret weapon that meant he didn't care if Kaden passed him and got there first?

Eirmon had been clear in giving Kaden his instructions. If at all possible, he wanted the submission of the rest of the Five

Cities to be completed by the fortieth day. Morning would bring that day, and it would also bring him home. But what else would the morning bring?

Suddenly, the image of Nara in her silk robe, her long hair flowing down over both shoulders as she stood in her doorway framed in light, popped into his head. He thought that perhaps he was already too late to salvage a relationship with her. His time with Deslo had encouraged him that it wasn't too late to be a real father but to aspire beyond that to a whole and healthy family seemed naïve.

He'd like a chance to find out. Whether he reached the city first or not, he'd throw everything he had at the enemy and do whatever it took to save Barra-Dohn.

Tchinchura squatted on the floor, looking at the evening light falling through the window on the far side of the room. Centuries of nomadic wandering had bred restlessness into the Amhuru. At the best of times, he itched to be moving, and the time he'd spent cooped up in this house had seemed to drag on interminably. Tonight, though, when the city went to sleep, he'd go forth with the Devoted and be free again—free to face whatever the night and the new day might bring.

He looked around him at the many Kalosenes stretched out on the thin mats scattered around the house. More than twenty of them had gathered now, and most of them were sleeping, or at least lying still, resting while they could. Even if things went well, it would be a long night.

The front door opened and closed, and a moment later, Marlo came silently through from the front room. Tchinchura watched him stepping carefully over the forms of the sleeping men covering the floor on his way to the small kitchen. After a moment, Tchinchura rose and went to join him.

He found Marlo sitting at the small wooden table against the kitchen wall. The table was just barely big enough for two, and

Tchinchura crossed the room to sit down on the other side. "It's almost time," he said softly.

"Yes," Marlo said, "it is."

"This kind of work is not common for the Devoted," Tchinchura said, trying to read Marlo's face. He had found the Devoted to be almost as good at hiding their emotions as he was. "It will be dangerous work."

"It will," Marlo acknowledged. "But it's not the danger that worries me."

"No?"

Marlo shook his head. "The Devoted don't kill. The loss of life is to be avoided at all costs. And this, this task . . ."

"I know," Tchinchura said. "Despite our plans to do this in the middle of night, men will die."

"Yes and those lives are precious, theirs as well as ours."

"I wish it weren't so," Tchinchura said, "but there will be casualties. We can't let anyone who is in the Temple leave when we get there. They will die, as will some that we bring, perhaps many. Perhaps even all."

"Perhaps," Marlo said, "but I don't think so. Deras hinted we had more work to do than this."

"He did?" Tchinchura said.

"Yes, and I think it might have to do with you."

"With me?" Tchinchura said, continuing to examine the expressionless man across from him. "You haven't mentioned this before."

"No, I haven't," Marlo said. "Deras told us exactly how to find you, and why, and what we were to do. This is different. It's a sense, a feeling I had sometimes when he talked. Like this would be the beginning of something bigger. Something important."

"For me or for you?"

"For all of us, maybe," Marlo said. "If Barra-Dohn is to fall tomorrow, then something none of us can understand or foresee is about to happen. It makes me wonder how many other things that we think of as certain tonight will be shaken tomorrow."

Tchinchura reached for the pitcher of water on the table, poured a cupful, and took a long slow drink. He knew Marlo wasn't offering his suspicions as prophecy, that Deras hadn't promised the Amhuru would survive what was to come, but he was encouraged all the same. If there had been hints of a larger work and longer journey that Marlo was to take with them, then Tchinchura was glad. Like all Amhuru, he would die to protect the Golden Cord, or in this case, to reclaim it. Still, he wanted to live.

"About the only thing we can say for sure about tomorrow is that we both believe we can neither predict nor control it," Tchinchura said, setting his cup down. "So, I can't make any promises, but if you feel there's something to this feeling of yours about a larger destiny, then you're welcome to come with us when we go."

Marlo seemed to consider this as he also took a drink of water. He set his cup down and leaned over the table. "I appreciate that," he said, a fierce intensity suddenly visible in his look. "Could I bring Owenn as well? He's felt it too, this sense of destiny about our work with you."

"If you make it through what lies ahead, you should do what you think is right and bring who you think you should bring," Tchinchura said. "If we're able to secure what we've come for, we plan to make our way to the quay. Zangira thinks the merchant captain that brought him back to Barra-Dohn could be persuaded to take us away for the right price, of course, especially if chaos breaks out all over the city."

"And if the catastrophe prophesied for Barra-Dohn comes to the harbor as well?" Marlo asked.

"Then we must each of us save ourselves as we may," Tchinchura said, smiling, "and trust that if Kalos has a larger purpose for us, that it will indeed come to pass, whatever happens."

They sat together in silence. The light coming through the small kitchen window disappeared, and the room grew dark. Eventually, Marlo stood. "I should wake the others."

"Yes," Tchinchura agreed. "We must gather the materials and prepare ourselves."

"We must," Marlo said, "and when we've done all we can do to prepare, we will pray for strength to do what Kalos requires."

32

ENOUGH

Gamalian took the lamp from the steward who had pre-
vailed upon him to come down into the old dungeon in
the first place. The door swung open, and he followed
the man into the dark, musty circular staircase that led down and
down and still farther down.

The glow of the lamp grew paler the farther down they went,
and Gamalian looked at the brackets on the walls that had once
held torches and wondered if they shouldn't have brought one
down. The picture in his mind of men holding burning torches
seemed strange and primitive, but sometimes old ways were better
than new ways.

Gamalian almost smiled to himself at the irony of that
thought. Despite his reputation as a lover of antiquity, it was a
reputation not fully deserved. He loved stories of antiquity, to be
sure, not necessarily antiquity itself. Old ways might sometimes
be better than new ways, but he believed that history taught as

often by displaying the mistakes and folly of mankind as it did in any other way. Astute students of the world could learn as much about virtue and wisdom by examining what happened when those things were absent as they could by remembering the times when they were faithfully modeled.

The dungeons to which they were descending might in fact be examples of days long forgotten that ought to be remembered but not for anything virtuous or enlightening. For Gamalian, they were relics of a dark time in Barra-Dohn's history. With the discovery of meridium—so recently celebrated as the source of the city's power and prosperity—came darker things too, like greed and betrayal.

Not that greed or betrayal hadn't been there before, but the more powerful the throne became, the more desperate people became to seize it, within the royal family as well as without. Many of these had languished in these very dungeons, as well as some who'd actually held the throne. More than one king in the long history of Barra-Dohn, having lost his crown above, lost his head below.

That all seemed a long time ago. With little or no need for private cells to hold rival claimants to the throne or deposed sovereigns and with separate facilities in the city for holding anyone accused of criminal offenses against the general welfare, this whole area of the palace had been nearly forgotten. Gamalian even wondered how long it had taken Myron to locate the keys for the cells themselves, despite the chief steward's well-established competence. Certainly, Gamalian could not remember the dungeons being used for anything like their original purpose in all the years he'd served as an advisor in the royal household.

They neared the bottom of the stairs, and the sound of the steward's fumbling with the door there snapped Gamalian's attention from musings about the distant past to the situation at hand. Rika and the other researcher from the Academy had both been down here since the day Eirmon had accused them of theft and betrayal. Over the past few days, Rika had been working on the steward who tended their cells to plead with Gamalian to come and see her, pleas that he had ignored until now.

On the one hand, it was odd that she'd decided to focus her attentions on him. He was well aware that despite his own attempts to respect Eirmon's decision to appoint her as a tutor for Deslo by refusing to ever undermine her authority with the boy, she'd not returned the favor. He knew from any number of conversations with Deslo that she openly challenged things he'd taught the boy on numerous occasions, and if neither Eirmon nor Deslo were around, she was barely able to bring herself to be civil with him.

On the other hand, she didn't have many options. The natural haughtiness of the brilliant and ambitious woman who'd risen quickly within the ranks of the Academy researchers had been amplified when she'd become the king's mistress. Gamalian wondered if perhaps she had actually believed that she might become queen, though he was quite sure Eirmon would never legitimize any of the long succession of women he'd dallied with since the queen's death.

For that, he'd almost pitied her, though she did make it hard. All the same, she didn't have any other friends in the palace, which was probably why she'd focused on him. She knew he was kindhearted by nature, and as he had finally acquiesced to her insistent pleas for him to visit, he supposed she'd been correct to do it, in a strange sort of way.

Still, she didn't know what he knew about the Amhuru's plans for tonight and tomorrow. His coming to her had been an easier concession to make with those plans in mind. Though he couldn't trust her with what he knew, of course, it would be easier to resist whatever strategem she'd contrived to employ with him, knowing that being locked in the dungeon might actually be the safest place for her to be in the near future.

The dungeons were dimly lit by older meridium lights, and while there were half a dozen cells—three on either side—Gamalian noted that Rika and the researcher, Barreck, had been put right next to each other. No doubt Eirmon had insisted on it. He'd have enjoyed the thought of leaving Rika and the man she'd betrayed so callously in her hope of saving her own skin to spend all day, every day, just a few feet apart. They didn't seem to be enjoying it.

He was sitting against the back wall on the opposite corner from her, knees drawn up under his chin, eyes closed. She was standing at the front of her cell, watching them come through the door and down the row of cells to her. The steward left Gamalian there, received a warm smile from Rika that made him blush, and retreated to just outside the door where he said he'd wait to take Gamalian back up when he was finished.

"Oh, thank you for coming, Gamalian," Rika said, not wasting any time once the door slid closed and the steward was gone. "I know how busy you are."

"What do you want, Rika?" Gamalian asked, perhaps a little colder than he'd intended.

If his tone surprised or hurt her, she didn't show it. She simply answered the question. "Just to live, Gamalian."

"That's out of my hands. You know that."

"Eirmon listens to you," she said, "as much as he listens to anyone."

"Which isn't much," Gamalian replied. "You know that too, now. A lesson learned at a high cost."

"I guess I do," Rika said, losing the affected tone of a damsel in distress. When she spoke again, she was clear and firm and seemed as genuine as she could be. "Maybe you can help me another way."

"How's that?"

"You can get me out of the palace," she said quietly.

A slight movement from the neighboring cell showed Gamalian that Barreck was very much awake.

"I can't . . . ," Gamalian started.

"You can," Rika insisted, cutting him off. "The steward who led you down here says he can show you where the keys are kept.

He says they aren't locked up at night. He won't do it himself because he knows he'd be suspected. He wants to establish an alibi. Just tell him which night you want to do it, and it can be done."

"Even if it would be as easy as you suggest, Rika," Gamalian said, shaking his head, "why would I?"

"Because you're not a bloodthirsty tyrant, like Eirmon," she said coolly. "I know you don't like me, that I haven't endeared myself to you, but that's not a good reason to sit back and let me die. Just let me out. I'll leave Barra-Dohn forever. You'll never see me again."

"Rika, you know Eirmon fears for his life with the Amhuru on the loose. You know the palace is crawling with soldiers," Gamalian said, shaking his head. "I can't do this. It won't work."

He turned as though to go, and her hand shot out through the bars of the cell and grabbed his sleeve. "I can make you rich, Gamalian," she said, "very rich."

Gamalian jerked his arm away. He pursed his lips and his whole body tensed. When he spoke, he didn't try to keep the disdain from his voice. "Appealing to greed? You insult me. Better to have appealed to honor."

"Honor?" Barreck scoffed from his dark corner. "You think she understands honor? She thinks everyone can be bought."

"Be quiet," she hissed, turning toward him with a vengeance, her fists clenched by her side.

Gamalian started again for the door. "I can't help you."

"Wait, Gamalian!" she called.

The door opened and closed. He was gone.

Tchinchura stooped beside the dead man at his feet and wiped the blood from his axe on the man's tunic. He tried to ignore the stunned, staring eyes, and the fact that the "man," on closer inspection, looked barely older than a boy.

The Amhuru were hard men who lived hard lives. Squeamishness didn't enter into his reaction. If this was the will of

Kalos, they would do what was required. In forbearance, Kalos had waited for generations while His worship was abandoned, His house desecrated, and His name forgotten. No longer. There comes a day when even divine mercy says, "Enough."

Still, Tchinchura thought as he straightened up and Zangira appeared at his side, he wished sometimes that everything were simpler. If it came to it, he'd have no trouble burying his axe in Eirmon. This was harder.

"I think that's everyone," Zangira said.

"Good," Tchinchura said. "Did we lose any more?"

"No, still just the three."

"It could have been worse."

"It could have been."

"I'll go down with the Devoted," Tchinchura said, watching the Kalosenes who'd been with Zangira as they moved to the stairs. "To keep an eye on everything. Just in case."

"And I'll wait up here," Zangira said, "just in case. The doors seem pretty secure, and it shouldn't take long, but if we've missed anything or anyone, I'll be here."

"I'll be as quick as I can," Tchinchura said, and gripping his axe firmly in hand, jogged down the stairs toward the dig.

There, the remaining Kalosenes would already be moving with care the scores of round, explosive projectiles that Eirmon had enhanced with Zerura down into the tunnels beneath the Academy. Zangira, who had watched the soldiers of Barra-Dohn use the things against Garranmere, had confirmed both their power and the relative safety of handling them. Marlo thought they'd been designed to be triggered on impact and likely a fairly substantial impact, which made the thought of dropping one less alarming. But the Devoted intended to move and place them carefully, nonetheless.

Tchinchura had already been down to the bottom of the dig once that night. While Zangira remained with a handful of the Kalosenes above to bar the doors and make sure no warning escaped the Academy, Tchinchura and those with him cleared and secured the lower levels so the Devoted could start moving the stockpiles of explosives down into the dig. Resistance had been stiff at first, for the Academy was better guarded this time, no doubt a direct result of Tchinchura's initial infiltration, but only three of the Devoted had fallen in the fighting.

Now those who remained were stationed strategically throughout the dig to ferry baskets of explosives down below. They would work their way out from the bottom up. The twin problems of how to ignite the explosion that would hopefully destroy the Academy and how to do it without committing suicide, appeared to have one common solution—if it worked. No one wanted to think about what they would do if it didn't.

Tchinchura was surprised to find them as far along as they were, already finished with the bottom two levels of horizontal tunnels and in the midst of moving their operation to the one above. When the Amhuru expressed his surprise to Marlo, who had just climbed up out of the deep vertical shaft to join them, sweat glistening on his face, the Devoted said, "It's not like the plan is complicated."

Tcinchura smiled. "No, I guess not."

"It may not work," Marlo said, "but it isn't complicated."

"We'll know soon enough," Tchinchura said. "When the first one is dropped, it'll detonate and trigger the ones in the tunnel at the bottom of the shaft or it won't."

"And if it does," Marlo said, picking up the thread, "and the stack we've left at the edge of the next shaft tumbles over and drops more of them into the next shaft, then the process should repeat itself."

"And on and on, until hopefully all the tunnels and shafts and the whole dig collapses in on itself, bringing the Academy down with it."

"It will be a sad end to the majestic structure that was once the center of the worship of Kalos," Marlo said.

"Yes," Tchinchura agreed, "a sad end for the Temple that housed the Room of Life and the Golden Cord."

Marlo nodded and sighed. "Though I guess, it hasn't been a temple for a long time."

"Oh, it's still a temple, all right," Tchinchura said. "It's just not Kalos that's worshiped here."

"You're right, of course," Marlo said. "We all worship something, but not all the things we worship deserve our devotion."

"They certainly don't," Tchinchura said.

The last of the Devoted came up over the edge of the shaft, and the ones already gathered there began to carefully lay a foundation of about half a dozen or more of the round projectiles next to the hole, but they hesitated before moving on to put the next layer on top.

Marlo motioned to Tchinchura to follow him. "Come, I'm sure they'd feel more comfortable doing this if we went back up."

Tchinchura shrugged. "I'm in no greater danger here than they are. If one of these things falls before they're ready, we're all in trouble."

"True, but if they die taking down the Temple, they'll die knowing they've done what they came for," Marlo said. "They know you have more to do."

"Yes," Tchinchura said, starting back toward the last vertical shaft with Marlo, "I do."

They climbed back out, and Tchinchura squatted by the top of the shaft, peering down through the darkness at the dimly lit opening far below. Soon, the rest of the Devoted, having laid out a trail of sporadically placed projectiles all the way down the tunnel, placed the ones they had left except for a few at the bottom of the shaft. Then, having done what they could do down below, they climbed out and joined them.

All the Devoted stood together by the edge of the shaft with the Amhuru, staring silently downward. Amongst them, they had three of the Zerura-enhanced meridium explosives.

Tchinchura supposed they'd brought more than one, just in case the first one didn't detonate, though he couldn't imagine why a second or third one would if the first one wouldn't.

"Well," Marlo said at last, "we might as well see if this is going to work, because if it isn't, we'll have to figure something else out in a hurry. Daylight's probably not that far away."

Owenn turned to Marlo. "Let me do it."

Marlo smiled but shook his head. "I have to do this. The rest of you need to go upstairs. Get Zangira, and unbar the door. I'll give you a few minutes, and then I'm going to drop this thing and run."

No one budged. Finally, Marlo shrugged and turned to Tchinchura. "They won't listen to me, but they'll follow you. Take them up. If this works, you'll all know I'm on my way long before you see me."

Tchinchura reached out and shook Marlo's hand. "We'll see you upstairs shortly."

He started away, and the Devoted finally stirred into motion. He led them to the base of the stairs that led up to the next level of the Academy, and when he looked back, he saw Marlo standing beside the shaft, watching them leave, holding one of the projectiles while the other two lay at his feet.

33

FALLING DOWN

Eirmon sat up with a start. His arm was tangled awkwardly in his sheet. He thrashed around for a moment before he was free of it. Something had startled him, breaking through his deep sleep and into his dreams. A movement, or maybe a sound . . .

BOOM! BOOM! BOOM! BOOM! BOOM!

He was out of bed now and moving toward his balcony. The sound had seemed both loud and distant at the same time, a strange and alarming combination. He pushed open the door and stepped outside. It was still dark, but his senses and intuition told him it was early morning.

The city lights glowed in the square below and in as much of the city as he could see. Visually, the world beyond the palace looked like it should, and yet such loud and disruptive sounds suggested that something, somewhere, was very wrong.

Boom! Boom! Boom! Boom! Boom! Boom! Boom! Boom! Boom!

Eirmon gripped the stone rail, peering into the dark in the direction he thought the sounds had come from. These hadn't been as loud. They'd sounded like muffled echoes of the ones he'd heard earlier. Were there two different places within earshot where huge explosions were happening? Could Barra-Dohn be under attack of some sort? He resisted the thought. He didn't see smoke or other evidence of an attack. For a moment, he felt a flash of fear, fear that someone might be using weapons like those he'd used against Garranmere against him.

But of course, how could that be? There were no other weapons like those he'd used against Garranmere. There were lesser weapons, of course, but nothing else that potent. Who else could have mixed Zerura and meridium together to create them?

He thought of the missing Amhuru. It hadn't occurred to him before that the Amhuru might be more than keepers and protectors of the fragments of the Golden Cord, but they could be. Over the long centuries of their possession, perhaps they too had explored the possibilities. Maybe they'd discovered things Eirmon as yet could only dream of. Maybe they'd brought these discoveries with them to Barra-Dohn, and perhaps today they were being unleashed.

A distant rumbling might have been more sounds like those he'd heard before, but if so, they were even farther away, more muffled and less distinct. A third location, perhaps, or maybe even a fourth, if the sounds that had first roused him from his sleep had been from someplace else as well.

A loud pounding at his door echoed within his room, and he turned to see his door swing open as members of the Davrii flowed in from the hallway. One of the soldiers saw Eirmon on the balcony and turned, calling something through the still open doorway. From the hall, one of the captains who shared the responsibility of keeping the palace secure, a man named Brennin, walked confidently into the room and over to the entrance to the balcony.

"Your Majesty," he said, bowing as he stopped in the doorway.

"Captain?" Eirmon replied.

"With the explosions in the city," the captain said matter-of-factly, as though explosions in the city were an everyday affair, "we thought we should have a detail with you until we knew more."

"In the city?"

"We believe so. The first ones sounded close enough."

"Any idea where?" Eirmon asked.

The captain shook his head. "We've sent runners to have a look, but the rest of the men have taken defensive positions below. We just wanted to make sure you were secure."

"Thank you, Captain."

Eirmon turned to look back over the city. It seemed an oddly incongruous thought to have at that moment, but he suddenly felt relieved that he hadn't brought the new girl to his chamber last night. He'd considered it for a while but then decided to stick to the original plan, which had been to wait until tonight. She was to be a reward for the passing of the fortieth day in the Kalosene's absurd prophecy. Disturbed in their sleep by strange booming sounds and then barged in upon by the Davrii wasn't how he'd envisioned their first night together.

Suddenly, another loud sound rumbled across the city to their ears, but this one was different than the earlier ones. It was deep and strong, like a mountain groaning, like rocks being ripped in half. Not small rocks you could hold in your hand, either, but ones that if they fell upon you would grind you into dust.

The rumbling, groaning, ripping sound grew louder and louder, and the Davrii inside were drawn from their positions out onto the balcony too. Soon they were all standing along the stone rail, peering through the gloom of early morning, hoping to see some evidence of what was going on.

"Is that smoke?" one of the men said, and Eirmon peered but couldn't be sure of anything.

"I can't tell," someone else chimed in, and they all continued to stand and stare, transfixed.

After a few moments, the sound settled down a bit, though it didn't disappear, and a slight breeze picked up. It was warm and blew toward them from the direction that the sound had come, and it carried with it fine layers of dust. The men raised their hands to shield their eyes and turned their heads to the side for further protection.

Eirmon turned to Brennin. "Captain, round up an escort. I want to go see what has happened."

"Your Majesty, you'll be safer here . . ." Brennin began to protest, but Eirmon didn't let him get any further.

"Captain, you have no idea what just happened, and thus can't possibly pretend to know where I will or will not be safe."

Eirmon turned to head back inside, first motioning to the captain and his men to precede him. As they filed back inside, Eirmon glanced back over his shoulder for one last look at the city, but the breeze and dust were still strong, and he couldn't look that way for long. He stepped inside.

"Should I leave some of my men with you?" Captain Brennin asked when Eirmon had pulled the door shut behind him.

"In the hall, outside my door," Eirmon said. "I'll change and then join you downstairs."

Brennin bowed and walked to the door, which he held open as his men filed out. When the rest were out, Captain Brennin bowed to Eirmon and closed the door.

Instead of getting dressed though, Eirmon walked over to the windows. They were now coated with a film of the gray dust that the wind had carried here from who knew where. Eirmon raised his hand and felt the glass, as though hoping to touch the dust on the other side and uncover its secret. Whatever it was and wherever it came from, it wasn't sand.

It was the fortieth day. According to the prophecy of the Kalosene, before the sun that was shortly to rise would set that night, Barra-Dohn would fall.

It was certainly alarming that loud explosions, at least some of them apparently coming from within the city, had awakened him from his sleep on this day. And yet, whatever had happened and wherever it had come from, Eirmon still couldn't conceive how it might signal the end of his empire.

Perhaps the Kalosene had associates in some plot against himself and Barra-Dohn. Perhaps he and the Amhuru had arrived on the same day for a reason. Perhaps they'd been in on this together, whatever this was, from the beginning.

But that didn't make sense. The Amhuru had seemed as surprised as anyone by the appearance of the Kalosene, and they had both stood by and watched the man be executed.

Eirmon shook his head, looking for answers he didn't have. He'd known at some level inside that the appearance of two Amhuru together had something to do with the fragment of the Golden Cord he now wore around his right calf. And while the struggle between the Amhuru and himself had been essentially unstated, he'd thought he had the measure of things.

It didn't feel that way at all now. Something was going on, and it felt to him like some vast and terribly important object was moving just outside his field of vision. He could sense it, but he couldn't see it. It felt as if even the slightest turn of the head would bring it into view, but he couldn't turn and therefore couldn't see.

Eirmon pulled himself physically away from the window, but the sense that something was lurking out of sight didn't go away. It might be the Amhuru come into the open at last to reclaim what he had taken. It might be some plot hatched by whoever had sent the Kalosene. It might be any number of things, but whatever it was, now that it was actually upon him, he felt something akin to relief. He planned and prepared, maneuvered and orchestrated, but when push came to shove, Eirmon was chiefly a man of action. Whatever this was, he wouldn't wait for it here in the palace like a cornered and frightened animal.

He would go see what had happened with his own eyes, come what may.

After a brief argument about the king's usual mode of transport through the city being too dangerous, which Captain Brennin lost, Eirmon's platform was brought. He stepped onto it and settled into his seat. The sun was not yet visible above the rooftops, but Eirmon let the canopy spread across his ornate chair be, even though he had no need of shade. The platform moved out, a large company of perhaps a few hundred Davrii running before, alongside, and behind. They glided smoothly across the square and out into the main thoroughfare that led through the city in the direction of the explosions.

It was very early, but the city was alive with activity. Hardly a building didn't have someone standing out front, hanging out of a window, or otherwise looking around in various states of surprise, concern, and alarm, wondering what had just happened. A sizable number were also walking cautiously along the same street that the king was traveling on, as though curious to see what had happened but afraid to know. Invariably, when these pedestrians became aware of Eirmon and his men behind them, they would move to the side and watch silently as their sovereign passed.

Eirmon might just have imagined it, but he felt that the faces of many of these onlookers were relieved when they saw him, and he took that as evidence that he'd made the right decision. There was great uncertainty down this road and possibly great danger, but for many, the fact that Eirmon was out and among them gave reassurance that whatever had happened, all would be well.

The road grew more congested, and though the crowds continued to move aside for Eirmon, their progress was slowed. The Davrii were clustered close together all round the platform, watching the crowds intently. Their weapons were in their hands, and wherever they looked, people grew still and quiet under their watchful eyes.

Eirmon couldn't help but scan the crowds too, looking for any sign of golden eyes or golden plumes of hair falling from the back of smooth, bald heads. Fear and hope mingled within as he saw no such signs. He pushed down both the hope that perhaps the Amhuru had simply left Barra-Dohn, as well as the fear that whatever lay ahead was part of a move on their part that he hadn't foreseen and would be helpless to counter.

Even if it was, he'd had to come. If he wasn't safe moving about his own city today, surrounded by hundreds of his own men, then there was no reason to think he'd ever be safe there again. Taking this short journey from the palace to wherever he was going was an essential step into his own future. The Amhuru now knew his secret, and he had no idea what response would come from them.

The vague sense that this moment must surely come someday had been replaced by the awful reality that he'd never had a clear plan about what to do when it did. Now that it was here, he felt all he could do was face whatever came his way and hope that the power his theft had given him was enough to see him through.

Eirmon looked up from the immediate crowd around the platform to survey the street ahead, and amazement seized him as he rose almost involuntarily from his chair. The street ran on for as far as his eyes could see with a steady stream of people upon it, but a sizable gap in the line of buildings on his right caught his attention immediately. A cloud of dust swirled in the air there, and it took him a moment to process what he was seeing. When he had, he sank back into his chair.

The Academy was gone.

As the platform navigated the remaining distance to the place where the Academy had formerly been, Eirmon sat in stunned silence. The building had obviously collapsed into the dig beneath it, despite all the precautions his engineers had taken to ensure it's structural stability. Had he not heard the explosions with his own ears, he might have thought that finally the dig had gone too deep and the foundation been weakened too much, but it seemed clear now what had happened. The explosives stored within the lower levels—explosives he had commissioned be made and stored there—had blown up and taken down the Academy. But how? How had this happened?

Drawing near enough now to have a better view, Eirmon realized that how this had happened was something he might never
know. Chunks of what had once been the Academy were scattered
in the street and the open square beside it, but where the building itself had been was only a great crater. Rubble protruded here
and there, but in most places, there was only empty space. How
far down into the dig parts of the Academy had tumbled, Eirmon
couldn't tell, and he couldn't imagine how they'd ever know.
Cranes large enough to extract all the crumbled remains from
the deep, deep shafts below couldn't possibly exist. If there were
secrets buried below, they would likely stay there.

Despite the solid mass of people in the street, the square
beside the crater was largely empty. He called back to Captain
Brennin, who was standing with the pilot by the meridium rudder, and they guided the platform into the square as he directed.
They stopped a short distance off the road with a clear view of the
crater but not close to the edge.

For a long time, he stared at the crater in silence, trying to take
in the Academy's sudden and almost incomprehensible collapse.
After a while, though, he turned his attention to the enormous
statue he'd commissioned for the anniversary celebration. It was
drifting on the Arua field, rotating slowly a short distance from
the crater. As it turned, Eirmon noticed that one of the arms—the
one that wasn't held aloft, holding the knife—had been blown
off, presumably by a piece of the Academy that now lay scattered
around at odd intervals.

Just as his shock at this was turning to irritation and even
anger, something flashed through Eirmon's peripheral vision and
fell to the ground in the open square. A loud *BOOM!* echoed in
the still morning air, almost deafeningly loud, leaving Eirmon's
ears ringing. Another *BOOM!* was followed by yet another, and
as Eirmon covered his ears and cowered in his seat, he saw a flash
right below the statue and braced for the echoing *BOOM!* that
followed.

He stared once again full of disbelief at what he was seeing. The enormous platform tilted downward on the side near the crater so that the statue of the craftsman tipped increasingly over. It moved quickly at first, then slowed, then seemed to stop at a severe angle. For a moment it hovered, striking an odd equilibrium that it couldn't possibly maintain, hovering there as though trying to decide whether to go all the way over or pop back upright into its normal position.

Then it moved again, tilting farther over, now fully committed to its own fall. Down it crashed, adding yet another earsplitting sound to the rest. The head and raised arm sheered off and slid over the edge of the crater into a gaping hole, while the torso, feet, and platform broke into a couple of pieces on the ground beside it. As the piece of statue with the head and arm snapped and fell, Eirmon caught a brief glimpse of the stylized red blood on the knife as it flashed in the morning sun, and then it was gone.

For the briefest of moments, there was silence, and then another *BOOM!* from even closer rocked the king's platform. Both Eirmon and his chair were knocked over, sending him sprawling first onto and then off the side of his platform as it slid closer in the direction of the crater.

34

THE SPRINGING OF THE TRAP

Kaden sped along beside the long row of sandships, which were disgorging their cargo rapidly in the early morning light. He didn't like the uneven and almost haphazard way they had come to rest in a line outside the walls of Barra-Dohn, but there was no time. So long as the defenses being prepared from them took on a more purposeful and organized shape, he would bear with the untidy arrangement of ships themselves.

Runners raced back and forth on the Arua field as the captains under Kaden's command tried to execute his orders as quickly as possible and position the railguns both efficiently and effectively. How much time they had before the other fleet arrived, Kaden had no idea. That it wouldn't be long, he did not doubt.

He slowed his slider, bringing it to a stop in front of his command ship, which he'd placed in front of the main city gate. He'd sent a messenger to the palace with news of his arrival and the situation as he understood it as soon as he'd had a chance to dispense his orders for the city's defense, but he wouldn't order the gate closed until he knew the enemy was approaching. Of course, if the defense he was preparing couldn't stop the army that was coming with all the power at his disposal, he wasn't sure how much help the gate would be.

Leaving the slider, he walked up the gangway onto the ship, taking the field glasses that Greyer held out. He surveyed the units assembling the long line of railguns as their first defense, as well as the thousands of soldiers moving into position behind them. The quick, competent arrangement of the powerful railguns and their ammunition, as well as the orderly ranks of infantry taking up position behind them filled him with confidence and pride, helping him to forget the less orderly row of ships behind them. He didn't approve of how Eirmon wielded the power of Barra-Dohn, but he loved the city and would defend it against anyone who thought they could threaten or destroy it.

"What's the mood of the men?" Kaden asked as he lowered the glasses and turned to Greyer.

"Good," Greyer said. "They're home, they're well trained, and they have weapons that just ripped the walls of Garranmere to pieces. What chance do sandships and soldiers have against them?"

"Can it be that easy?"

"It was at Garranmere."

"I know," Kaden said, sighing, lifting his glasses to survey the horizon for any sign of his enemy.

"Listen to me, Kaden," Greyer said, and Kaden turned to him again. "I know you think there has to be some catch, some weapon or strategy that explains why they'd take this chance, but we've had a lot of time to think of what that might be, and we can't."

"That doesn't mean we're not missing something."

"No, it doesn't," Greyer agreed. "But power like the power we displayed at Garranmere makes people desperate, and desperate people do desperate things."

Kaden thought about this for a moment and then nodded reluctantly. "I hope you're right."

"Me too," Greyer said and smiled.

Kaden lifted the glasses again and surveyed the defense prep-arations. As he did so, a flash of light caught his eye. He waited for it to happen again, and when it did, he handed the glasses to Greyer and pointed. Greyer looked for a moment, then nodded, handing the glasses back as he pulled a mirror from his pocket. Raising it, Greyer signaled the unit that had signaled them.

Kaden watched the exchange of messages, waiting. When Greyer finally lowered his mirror, Kaden asked. "Is it time?"

"It is."

"Well," Kaden said, looking over his shoulder at Barra-Dohn behind them. "Send a runner. It's time to close the gate."

Eirmon felt himself falling, and then he felt himself being caught. Many hands reached up and took hold of him, buoying him up so that for a moment, he hung almost suspended above the heads of his soldiers. They'd seen him slide over the edge of the platform and dropped their weapons so they could secure him.

There seemed to be momentary confusion among them about what to do now. Eirmon felt himself being slowly lowered, but then he caught sight of Captain Brennin scrambling over to the edge of the platform and motioning to the men to lift Eirmon back up, and he surged upward as they responded to these same motions.

Reaching up, Eirmon took Brennin's hand and crawled back onto his platform. Despite the confusion and chaos of what was going on all around him, he found himself hoping that his efforts to regain his place on the platform didn't appear too undignified to the people of Barra-Dohn who might be watching. That the Amhuru must be somewhere nearby, orchestrating all this, filled him with rage. Whatever they might do to him, he wouldn't let them laugh over him as though he were an infirm old man. He got to his feet as quickly as he could and stood tall, gazing around for any sign of his enemies.

Unfortunately, the dust from the collapse of the Academy that had settled had been stirred up by the recent explosions, and now a thicker cloud swirled around them at or near ground level, mirroring the dissipated thinner cloud that still hung higher in the air above. Consequently, Eirmon could see little of what was going on around him, though from the sounds coming from the road, it wasn't hard to figure out that the crowd that had been assembling there was dispersing.

"I don't like this," Captain Brennin said. "I can't see anything, and we're too exposed."

"What do you . . ."

Eirmon never finished his question. With the low visibility, they hadn't even had the visual clue of an object flashing across their peripheral vision to warn them, and another *BOOM!* nearby stirred up more dust and blew chunks of loose rock their way. Captain Brennin forced Eirmon down on his knees and crouched over him to shelter him from the blast and any debris stirred up by it. Another *BOOM!* rocked the platform so it tilted, and they slid a little sideways toward the crater again.

"I have to get you out of here," Captain Brennin called over the din to Eirmon.

"How?" Eirmon called back. "The pilot can't possibly see where he's going in all this dust. Besides, the street's even more confined than this square. It might be worse."

"I have an idea," Captain Brennin called back, though softer, for the echo of the most recent explosion was subsiding. "Will you trust me and do as I say?"

Eirmon looked up at the captain's earnest face and nodded. "Get me out of here, Captain, and I will be much obliged."

That was all the encouragement Brennin needed, and being a man of action more than words, he said no more. Staying low and guiding Eirmon back to the edge he'd only recently tumbled over, he helped the king down onto the ground below. He spent a brief moment in earnest and quiet conversation with a few of his men, who when he was finished with them, scrambled up onto the platform. Then gathering the rest of the king's guard around him, he explained his plan.

A few moments later, Eirmon, wrapped in the grey cloak that marked a soldier of his guard, made his way through the swirling dust across the open square on foot. They were moving parallel to the crater, away from the main road down which they had come a few moments earlier. He flinched with every noise, waiting for the *BOOM!* that would announce their ruse uncovered and blow him into as many pieces as the Academy.

And yet, with every step they took, that *BOOM!* didn't come, and he began to hope that they'd reach the smaller backstreets that Brennin hoped would conceal their return to the palace. If the Amhuru were occupied here, springing their trap and unloading their arsenal of explosives in their attempt to blow up Eirmon as they'd blown up the Academy, then the palace would once more be his place of refuge.

Looking over his shoulder, Eirmon could only dimly make out the platform moving through the thick cloud of dust in the other direction, still surrounded by the larger share of his personal guard. With any luck, the Amhuru would reposition themselves on the rooftops of the nearby buildings to assault the platform when it made its way into the street and thereby miss Eirmon's escape altogether.

They reached the entrance to the small backstreet toward which they'd been heading and turned into it, moving rapidly away from the open square. The farther they went, the less the dust swirled, and while Eirmon missed the cover it provided, he drank in the cleaner air, inhaling deeply.

For several moments, they kept on, their only aim to put as much distance between themselves and the gaping hole that now yawned in the very center of Barra-Dohn. Just then, another *Boom!*—this one echoing from a distance, broke the relative silence and brought hope that their plan had indeed succeeded.

"It worked," Eirmon said, not really speaking to anyone in particular but smiling as he looked around at the men who'd escorted him out of the confusion and chaos behind.

"It worked," Captain Brennin replied, his relief evident now that the imminent threat of harm was past.

The smile on Eirmon's face slipped away and grim determination replaced it as he stepped up close to Captain Brennin. "As soon as we are safely back in the palace, I want you to take every man you can find and go back. See that they don't get away."

"I can't leave you unguarded," Brennin said, shaking his head slightly at the prospect.

"Then leave a skeleton guard behind," Eirmon replied, "but take the rest. An opportunity like this might not present itself again. We have to act. The sooner they're dead, the sooner I'll be safe."

"Well," Brennin said, "let's get you back to the palace."

They started jogging down the street again. Eirmon, now with a little distance from what had happened and what he'd found, believed that the demolished Academy represented a trap set for the express purpose of luring him out of the palace. An elaborate trap, to be sure, but a trap nonetheless.

He would turn the tables. The trap meant to catch him would instead become a trap for his enemies. He'd had no success finding the Amhuru, but he had them now. Captain Brennin had ordered his men left behind to abandon Eirmon's platform once they'd negotiated it into the main road and to disperse and surround the nearby buildings. With any luck, the Amhuru would be cornered, and if cornered, then hopefully also killed.

That was why he was determined to send back with the captain every able-bodied soldier he could reasonably spare. He'd not secured the fragment of the Golden Cord by being timid, and he wouldn't keep it unless he was bold now.

It also occurred to him as he jogged toward the palace that the destruction of the Academy might also provide another opportunity. Once he had Tchinchura and Zangira in hands, he would let it be known that they had been behind the destruction of the Academy. If he were careful enough, he might be able to sow among the people animosity for the Amhuru as a whole. That way, if more came to recover what he had taken, they might find the will and collective power of Barra-Dohn directed against them. He'd no longer have to plot in secret. He could simply call on the people to remember what these Amhuru had done.

And if no further attempt came in his lifetime, he would eventually pass on the importance of being prepared against such a day to Kaden when he gave him the fragment itself. As he said many times to his son, when you are king, there can never be rest and complacency. At all times, you either grow stronger or you grow weaker.

As they drew nearer to the palace—he could see it towering over the smaller buildings in his immediate view—his mind drifted to the new girl. He still hoped to enjoy her for the first time tonight. The thought made him smile. Losing the Academy had been unexpected, but if the Amhuru were taken care of, if his power were made more secure both now and for the future, and if she still came to him as expected, then he would gladly mark the passage of this "fortieth day" and the failure of the Kalosene's prophecy.

Tchinchura dropped down on the other side of the wall, and pulling up his hood, crouched down, waiting for Zangira to join him. The small garden was empty, as he'd suspected it would be at this early hour.

Once Zangira was there crouching beside him, they stole silently across the small courtyard to the door and rapped firmly but quietly. It opened immediately, and they slipped inside. Gamalian nodded to them as they entered, then closed the door. He led them a short distance down the hall to a small sitting room and locked the door behind them.

"Did it work?" Gamalian asked, and when Tchinchura cocked his head slightly to the side as though asking him to clarify the question, he added, "The Academy, is it destroyed?"

Tchinchura nodded. "It has fallen, as will Eirmon."

"And the city he loves," Zangira added.

"Then you'd best be about your business here," Gamalian said, "so we can be well away before that happens."

"Is he back yet?" Tchinchura asked.

"I haven't seen him," Gamalian replied, "but I think so. Things haven't been exactly quiet here since the explosions began, but there was a particular frenzy a few moments ago. Suddenly, soldiers were jogging throughout the palace, all summoned to receive instructions of some kind I take it. In fact, I was half afraid you would arrive during the midst of it all, and I wouldn't be able to get you in."

"They've left now?" Zangira asked.

"It appears so," Gamalian said. "There was a storm of activity for a few moments, but then it was over, and things are positively quiet now. There had been so many guards moving through the palace for so long, it almost feels deserted."

"You were right," Zangira said, turning to Tchinchura. "He's sent them back out after us."

"He couldn't know we'd have help from the Kalosenes," Tchinchura replied, "and he certainly couldn't resist the temptation to finally get us. He thinks he'll avenge Barra-Dohn for the loss of the Academy and secure himself at the same time."

"The longer the soldiers are gone, though," Gamalian said, "the more he'll wonder if he's done the right thing by sending them away. The more aware of his vulnerability he'll be."

"True," Tchinchura said, "so we will shortly be about our business, as you put it. But first, tell me of Nara and the boy. Are they gone?"

"Yes," Gamalian said. "I found them during the first flurry of activity when the explosions began this morning. In all the commotion, I took her aside and passed on your message."

"They've gone to the quay?"

"Yes," Gamalian said, "I saw them to the door myself."

Tchinchura nodded and reached out a hand to Gamalian, which the other took willingly. "We owe you thanks," the Amhuru said.

"You owe me nothing," Gamalian replied. "I am grateful to have had this chance to help repay the debt my city owes you. I'm just sorry I couldn't do more."

"You've done enough," Zangira said.

"Have you decided yet?" Tchinchura added. "Will you come with us?"

"Perhaps," Gamalian said. "Though I was hoping there'd be some sign by now of what form this calamity will take that is to befall Barra-Dohn today. I might be able to do some good here in its aftermath."

"You may not know before you have to choose," Tchinchura said. "If things go well, we may be shortly on our way."

"I know," Gamalian answered. "Hopefully, when the time comes, I'll know my own mind."

Tchinchura nodded and turned to Zangira. "We've waited a long time for this."

"And come so far."

"Let's take it back."

35

A DIFFERENT KIND OF POWER

Kaden held the field glasses, watching the line of enemy sandships that didn't move. For the better part of an hour, they'd been stopped in the distance, not so far away that his railguns couldn't do serious damage, but far enough that he might exhaust more ammunition doing it than he'd like to.

He'd not fired on them, and they'd shown no openly aggressive signs yet either. No messengers had been sent by slider, no soldiers emerging to gather for a charge, no movement or signs of any kind. Kaden felt that as the invader and aggressor, the first move was theirs. He didn't feel especially threatened and therefore thought there was no real need to do anything precipitously. Perhaps, just perhaps, the enemy was having second thoughts about what they'd come to do. Maybe this would be settled more or less peaceably.

Of course, the possibility of second thoughts and misgivings wasn't the only explanation for why the enemy might not be moving. Could the ships before him be a decoy of some sort? Might there be more that Kaden was unaware of, trying some flanking maneuver? Surely, the messengers he'd sent inside the city had spoken with his father by now, and the king was aware of the need to provide for the defense of the city on all sides.

And of course, there were the less quantifiable but nonetheless no less important psychological aspects of waging war. He knew the power of an enemy showing itself outside your walls, even when those confronted with the appearance felt secure. Hadn't he come to Garranmere, knowing they'd be confident in their own strength, but also knowing that when an enemy appeared on your doorstep, no matter how strong you thought you were, hidden insecurities were bound to surface?

There was no way to be sure if the earlier confidence of his own men was being shaken by the silent showdown between the two armies as they waited, staring at one another across the sands. Perhaps he should have a few of the railguns open up on the enemy ships at the center of their line. Not a full-scale launch, of course. He'd save the bulk of his explosives for use later should the fleet move closer. Then closer together and closer to him, the enemy sandships would be easy prey.

He could, though, launch just enough to be sure of destroying a few ships. Perhaps a visible demonstration of the power his enemy had only heard of and never witnessed might induce the misgivings he hoped they were already feeling, as well as stem the tide of any dissipating confidence among his own men. If so, then a minimal expenditure of effort might produce maximum results. He called for Greyer.

"Perhaps a demonstration is in order," Kaden said when Greyer appeared.

"What did you have in mind?"

"Have a dozen or so of the closest railguns target the same three sandships at the center of their line—any three near the center will do, but make sure it's the same three." Kaden turned

from the horizon and looked his subordinate in the eyes. "Let's
see if we can force their hand one way or another."

Greyer smiled. "Yes sir. Gladly."

The Jin Dara, whose golden-flecked eyes didn't need field glasses
to survey the line of enemy ships in the distance or the long line
of soldiers waiting patiently in their orderly ranks in front of them,
turned to Devaar who stood yawning beside him. "There's movement at last."

"What is it?"

"A slider," the Jin Dara said, "Moving up and down their front
line, stopping off at a handful or so of those round platforms."

"They're preparing to open fire?"

"It looks like some of them are."

"Good," Devaar said. "I was getting bored."

The Jin Dara smiled. "Well, I'd say things are about to get
interesting."

He concentrated, reaching out for the hookworms, summoning them to come. After he had demonstrated the ineffectiveness
of his enemy's weapons, he would begin to display the power of
his own.

Having delivered his message, Kaden waited for the demonstration of his power to take place. It would take a moment for the
different crews to coordinate their attack so that their combined
power would be equally directed and distributed among the three
sandships singled out to receive it. He watched, anticipating the
damage his weapons would do. If they had blown the great stone
walls of Garranmere to bits, what would they do to sandships?

A sudden gust of wind was his first clue that anything unusual
was going on with the weather. That first clue was soon followed
by a second and far more disturbing one. Swirling clouds of sand

began to appear all up and down the line he had established with his men and railguns. It was like nothing he'd ever seen before. Not one great swirling sandstorm but fifty or a hundred small and localized ones.

He frowned as he examined them with his field glasses. His eyes weren't deceiving him. Spinning vortexes of sand had appeared up and down his own line, dispersed at almost even intervals. Looking farther afield, he saw none in the great open stretch of sand between his own line and his enemy, nor did he see any around or among the sandships in the distance.

He lowered his field glasses. Surely, it was impossible that his enemy had conjured the swirling winds. What kind of power could do that? Who could harness the wind and direct it where to blow?

And yet how could it be a coincidence? For an hour the two armies had waited in the hot, still morning, hardly any breeze to speak of. And then, just moments after he gave the order to demonstrate the power of their railguns, these strange mini-storms had appeared. Somehow, someway, his enemy was controlling them.

But to what end? To obscure his visibility? They might indeed do that, but they couldn't do much more. The railguns launched both the spherical explosives and the long meridium bolts with tremendous force. It would take more than swirling winds to stop them from hitting their targets.

Greyer approached, and Kaden saw in his captain's face the same wonder and confusion he was himself feeling. Greyer opened his mouth, but before he could say anything, Kaden spoke. "Give the command."

"But Kaden, the whirlwinds . . ."

"I see them," Kaden said, "and I can't explain them, but they can't stop the railguns. Give the command."

Greyer signaled to the crews below, and Kaden watched as they drew ammunition for the supply ships and moved toward the railguns. At the same time, though, the whirlwinds began to move. They swept in closer, until they were no longer in front of the circular platforms that held the railguns, but they were upon them. Then Kaden saw the power of the whirlwinds and the problem they created.

The force of the swirling winds was too much for the soldiers assigned to swivel the round platforms and aim the railguns to counter. The platforms began to spin round and round uncontrollably. Some soldiers hung on desperately for a while and were spun around and around with the platforms before being flung off into the sand, while others were thrown down immediately. In every case, though, the platforms were soon spinning out of control, and Kaden understood his peril immediately. If he couldn't aim the railguns, he couldn't use them. The spinning whirlwinds, if they continued, had neutralized his greatest weapons.

Hardly had this thought dawned upon him, when fresh movement in the distance raised new fears. The enemy ships had not moved, but there was movement in the sands. Great mounds and burrows were appearing and shifting, rapidly. He tried to focus on what was happening beyond the wildly spinning railguns, but it was difficult. The rippling motion was familiar, but for a moment he couldn't place it. When at last he recognized it, he gasped.

"Hookworms," he said, turning his stunned gaze upon Greyer. He pointed and handed the field glasses over. "Look!"

Greyer raised the field glasses, held them for a few minutes as he gazed in the direction Kaden had indicated, and then lowered them with a trembling hand. "I think you're right."

"They must be massive," Kaden said, whispering.

"And so many," Greyer said, "all moving in concert."

Kaden started to ask what to do but stopped, knowing there was neither time to ask nor any point. Greyer wouldn't know any more than he would. Their defense was spinning out of control, while a completely unforeseen weapon was being unleashed. His men would have to respond and defend themselves as best they could against this new development.

The small huddle of guards outside the king's spacious private chambers were leaning casually against the wall beside the door when Tchinchura and Zangira appeared at the other end of the long hallway. By the time they'd looked up, Zangira's axe had struck one of them in the chest, and even as he slid slowly down the wall onto the floor, the axe was already flying back into Zangira's hand.

Another fell as Tchinchura's axe likewise struck home. The remaining soldiers, though, moved quickly into action. Tchinchura saw immediately that these were better-trained men than those he'd encountered on the dock or at the Temple. The two who led the way down the corridor soon had their weapons out, long, cruel-looking curved knives that could be easily wielded in the confined space of the hallway.

Behind these two, the others fell in closely, but not before one had drawn and thown a long narrow-bladed knife, which Zangira only barely dodged by dropping instantly to the floor and allowing it to fly overhead and strike the wall behind them. As smoothly as he'd dropped down, Zangira was back on his feet, his own knife flashing out of his hand and down the hall.

The soldier out in front on Zangira's side of the hallway, dodged sideways adroitly, but the man who'd fallen in behind him, effectively using him as a shield as they moved, wasn't so fortunate. The knife hit his stomach, burying itself to the handle. Zangira summoned it back, and it returned to his hand as bloody as his axe. The man didn't drop, though. If anything, he charged faster, rushing past the soldier who'd been in front of him, eager to close the gap with the Amhuru while strength remained.

As he drew nearer, Zangira suddenly leapt sideways, avoiding the arcing swipe the soldier made with his curved knife, planted his right foot high up on the wall and pushed up and off hard. His left foot, which he'd held back, kicked out strongly, striking the man squarely in the face and sending him flying backward. As he dropped, Zangira soared past him, swinging his axe to counter the knife stroke coming from the soldier behind him. The Amhuru's momentum carried him forward so both of them tumbled to the floor together.

Not waiting to see how that engagement played out, Tchinchura moved sideways to get a better angle on the two soldiers who'd been coming straight at him. Throwing his axe at the one in the back, he raised his knife to deflect the attack of the one in the front. His axe hit home, but he was unable to retrieve it, as for a few moments, he matched stroke for stroke, simply blocking the vicious attack coming his way. He didn't have to wait long for his opening, though, as his opponent overextended himself in his eagerness, and Tchinchura ducked under his arm and drove his knife home.

The fight was over. He looked up to see Zangira removing his knife from the body of one of the soldiers on the floor. They didn't stop to wipe off the blood, though, for they knew that as quickly as it had transpired, the fight in the hallway was certain to have attracted attention inside the room.

They approached the door. Tchinchura tried the handle, which revealed that the door was unlocked. Turning it, he pushed the door open as they stood clear on either side of the frame while it swung open. It was a good thing they did, because not one but two knives flew through the opening into the hall. The Amhuru didn't hesitate after the blades soared past but ducked rapidly inside the room.

The knives had come from the only two soldiers in the room, who were both moving forward and drawing their longer blades to place themselves between danger and their king as the Amhuru entered. Beyond them, standing behind a large chair in the expansive sitting room, Eirmon stared, wide-eyed with fear.

"Stop!" Tchinchura called in a commanding voice, and the two men froze where they stood.

Zangira closed the door behind them.

"What are you waiting for?" Eirmon called out hysterically, gesturing angrily from the soldiers to the Amhuru. "Kill them!"

The men hesitated, then continued forward as their king commanded.

Tchinchura felt the fragment of the Golden Cord around his bicep pulse as Zangira reached out through his replica to seize hold of the Arua field, which was always like trying to grab hold of the wind, especially this far above the ground where it felt so much less substantial than it did at ground level.

Even so, Zangira was skilled in his manipulation of the field, and soon the soldiers had dropped their weapons and fallen to the ground. Falling to their knees, they clasped their stomachs and were violently ill all over the floor. Even rippling the Arua field very slightly could radically affect the fine balance between it and any living thing close enough to be disturbed by it, and Zangira did not ripple it gently. It was a testimony to Zangira's adeptness that both Eirmon and the Amhuru, on opposite sides of the ripple Zangira created, did not also fall writhing to the floor.

Tchinchura saw Eirmon glance down at his leg. He wasn't being made ill, but he'd felt what Zangira was doing, just as surely as Tchinchura had. He was wearing the stolen fragment.

"It's time to restore what you have stolen," Tchinchura said quietly.

Eirmon looked up and stared across the room at him, but he made no verbal reply. Tchinchura could feel him fumbling with the power of the Cord. He was trying to reach out, probably hoping to wield the same control over it that Zangira had just demonstrated, but lacking the Amhuru's mastery, was failing to do anything that might threaten them, who knew the power and ability of the Cord so intimately. That he could reach out through the Zerura he wore for the Arua field at all was likely a new revelation to Eirmon, who'd never had the ability demonstrated for him before. Given but a little time to experiment with it, however, he would become considerably more dangerous.

There was no reason to prolong this. Tchinchura stepped closer as the two soldiers continued to languish on the floor in extreme discomfort. "You can't stop us from taking it back. Whether we leave you behind, alive or dead, is up to you."

"Even if I give it up, you won't let me live," Eirmon scoffed.

"We won't leave you unpunished. Your crime certainly deserves it," Tchinchura answered, "but we will let you live. We'd hate for you to miss your empire's collapse, after all, which we believe the Devoted said would happen today."

Eirmon opened his mouth as though to reply, but it suddenly dropped open farther, and he said nothing at all.

Tchinchura didn't need to wonder why, for he knew immediately, as did Zangira, who looked at Tchinchura with eyes wide with wonder.

Someone immensely strong and capable was using Zerura to violently manipulate the Arua field and more somewhere in the city, or if not inside it, close enough to it that they could sense it as though it was happening right there in the room. The power and mastery that Tchinchura could sense was like the power only an Amhuru who'd been raised with Zerura might have, and yet no Amhuru would wield that power in such a way. His mind raced, fitting the pieces of the puzzle together. There could be only one explanation for what he was sensing, as incredible as that conclusion was.

"Tchinchura," Zangira said, letting go of his lighter and more tenuous hold on the Arua field.

"I know," Tchinchura said. "The other fragment is here."

36

POWER UNSEEN

Chaos and confusion surrounded him. Everywhere he looked, his orderly defenses were in disarray. Whether they moved back and forth on the sand itself or above it on the Arua field, his soldiers could focus on little else beyond the seething, roiling sand beneath their feet. And Kaden couldn't blame them, for even from his safer vantage point on the deck of his sandship, his eyes were drawn irresistibly to the burrows and troughs being cut and recut across the sands by the giant hookworms surging in and out of his line of sight.

The hookworms moved up and down, seemingly at random. Most of the time they were submerged, but then one would surface and show itself before diving back down. Sometimes the surfaced hookworm would open its mouth and take hold of a man and either gulp him down or more likely simply grab ahold and pull him screaming down into the sand as it disappeared again.

More often, though, the surfaced hookworm didn't bother to open its mouth. Rather, it would simply push through a crowd of men and let it's razor-sharp hooks do their work as they ripped open anyone unlucky enough to get pulled sideways against the hardened side of the creature as it passed. And then, after leaving a swath of destruction behind, the worm would dive back down below.

Kaden wasn't sure which was more disconcerting, the hookworms aboveground or below. Aboveground, the hookworms were deadly and fearful, but they also provided targets, even if the scrambling men had not yet figured out how to take advantage of it. Some attempts had been made at launching meridium spears into great gaping mouths when the opportunity arose, but few had struck home and even when they had, the hookworm in question, spear and all, had simply disappeared a moment later.

Still, though frightful, a giant hookworm aboveground was visible, a thing that could be seen. A thing that could be seen was, at least theoretically, a thing that could be killed. Belowground the hookworms were phantoms. The sands surged and sprayed, and suddenly a great trough would open up and swallow men whole, or suddenly a great mound would rise up and displace both men and sand into the air. A man could throw a spear against the hardened exterior of a surfaced hookworm and feel that he had struck a blow, even if for all intents and purposes he had done nothing. When the hookworms stayed down below, a man could do nothing but wait to be bitten, bowled over, or buried.

Kaden felt despair wash over him. He didn't understand how anyone could command either hookworms or whirlwinds, but someone was. He understood even less how he was to fight against that kind of power.

He looked at the long row of railguns on their round platforms, still spinning wildly. The first time he'd journeyed to the quarry, some distance from Barra-Dohn where the railguns had been tested and where he'd seen their capabilities displayed, he'd been in awe of their power and maneuverability. He'd thought they rendered the armies of Barra-Dohn invincible. How wrong he had been.

As he gazed at them, he saw a soldier from one of the units that had been trained to operate them, struggling against the whirling wind that controlled the railgun closest to him. In his outstretched hands was a round meridum ball with the special explosive Zerura core. Kaden was too far away to be heard over the din of the howling winds, but he shouted all the same for the man to stop. The man did not hear, and he did not stop.

Reaching the spinning railgun, the soldier held out the explosive, pushing as hard against the strong winds as he could. For a long, suspended moment, he inched closer to the rails. Then his movement, which had been like the slow-motion steps of a bad dream, suddenly changed as everything happened at once. The meridium ball was caught by the pull of the rails and propelled forward, while the man, who couldn't let go in time was picked up by the whirling wind and flung to the side. The platform continued to whirl, and as a result of the almost half-spin the platform was able to make while the meridium ball was held and accelerated by the rails, the explosive was shot at an angle back toward the city and ripped through one of the sandships farther down the line before hitting the wall of Barra-Dohn with a *Boom!*

He stood and stared, as pieces of stone from the wall fell in chunks into the sand at the base of the wall. Plumes of fine masonry dust mixed with the coarser sands being tossed around by the whirling winds close by. As stunning as it was to see Barra-Dohn struck by the very weapon that was supposed to defend it, what soon grabbed Kaden's attention was down at the base of the wall.

Kaden noticed for the first time that some of the burrows being created by the hookworms as they tore along belowground headed toward and then disappeared at the foot of the wall. He didn't know how far down below the surface of the sand the wall went, but it occurred to him that if they dove down far enough, there was no reason to suppose the walls could keep the hookworms from passing beneath Barra-Dohn. He didn't know how much mischief they could create inside the city, as the buildings all rested on solid foundations and most of the roads were paved, but then again, he wasn't sure how much of a deterrent a few feet of paving stones would be for one of these things if it decided to surface inside the city.

"Kaden!"

He turned, finding Greyer nearby, wearing goggles for protection against the increasingly sand-saturated wind. He held out a pair for Kaden. At first, Kaden shook his head, but Greyer simply took his free hand and pointed insistently out over the area that Kaden had thought would be a battlefield, but which at the moment was the calmest part of the landscape. To look up and over it would be to expose his eyes to the full blast of the sand, so Kaden took the goggles and put them on.

Once protected, Kaden looked where Greyer was pointing, and if he wasn't already overwhelmed by what they faced, he was now. Enormous rhino-scorpions were walking toward them in a great line, not single file like rhino-scorp herds normally did, but spread out like a military line advancing together slowly. Hanging above them in the relatively calm wind of the sands beyond the railguns were their scythe-like tails, curved, barbed, and wickedly dangling. And strangest and most fearful of all were the riders standing on the backs of the largest of them. They wore green and held long reins secured somehow to the flat heads below them, and they were spaced out at fairly even intervals along the front of the line.

Beyond the rhino-scorpions at something of a distance and almost lost in the spectacle before them were lines and lines of men. The army he had expected to face was now coming, but in the last hour, he'd lost all hope that he could repel them.

"You see them, right?" Greyer asked.

"I see them," Kaden answered.

"I'm not dreaming then. This is really happening—the winds, the hookworms, and now these . . ."

Kaden turned to Greyer, and slipping off his goggles, handed them back. "Greyer, I have to go to the king."

Even with the goggles on, Kaden could see Greyer react. He'd never seen Greyer reluctant to do anything that he asked, but he could see fear in his eyes now. Stark, unadulterated fear. He grabbed Greyer by the shoulders, hard, and he got right up in his face. "Greyer, the king has to know what's going on. I will return if I'm able, and I'll bring or send what help I can."

Greyer seemed reassured, and he not only nodded, but he also mustered a relatively calm and firm, "Yes, sir."

Kaden let go of him and made his way to the top of the gangway where for a long moment he stood, looking down at the tumultuous sands below. He didn't want to go down there, but he had to get inside the city. He had to speak to the king. He'd let Greyer think he was going only to inform him of their plight and seek aid, but he knew his message for Eirmon would be darker and more specific than that.

Against power like this, the defense of Barra-Dohn was untenable.

The Amhuru stood, staring at each other, while his soldiers lay hunched on the floor. Eirmon stood, for the moment ignored, on the opposite side of the room. They'd come to demand the fragment of the Golden Cord from him, offering to spare his life if he gave it up voluntarily. Though cryptically, they'd assured him he would still be "punished," whatever that meant.

And then the pulsing, throbbing surge of power he'd felt against his right calf, mediated through the Zerura he wore there, had spoken of something remarkable happening. He'd felt Zangira use the Zerura on his arm a moment earlier to disable his two men, had felt him seize control of the Arua field and warp it somehow in the center of the room, but this had been categorically different—larger, stronger, and more violent. He felt it still, and the Zerura on his calf still pulsed and throbbed with it.

After that, the Amhuru had turned to each other and exchanged words he'd heard but wasn't sure he'd understood. Tchinchura had said something about another fragment. In context, all Eirmon could think of was that the Amhuru meant another missing fragment of the Golden Cord, but surely this was impossible.

Eirmon had learned, as he sought information about the Amhuru and the six fragments of the Golden Cord that they protected, that only three were kept on this side of the Madri. In fact, some of the stories that supported this idea suggested that the Amhuru had themselves created the Madri to keep the three pieces above it and the three below it from ever being brought together, but Eirmon saw in this claim the telltale signs of myth growing up alongside fact. That the Madri existed, a swath of danger and disturbance that encircled the world, dividing north from south, he knew to be true. That the Amhuru had created this dividing line instead of merely using it, seemed altogther unlikely.

All the same, Eirmon did believe there were only three original fragments of the Golden Cord below the Madri, which made his own acquisition of one so remarkable and, at least until the Amhuru had come to reclaim it, fortuitous. Consequently, he greeted with skepticism this statement from Tchinchura that seemed to suggest that the disturbance he was currently feeling coming from somewhere outside the palace had been created by another missing fragment. That two of the three southern fragments were missing seemed impossible, that two of three could be missing and somehow both be at Barra-Dohn, really had to be.

He had to have misunderstood the Amhuru's reference. And yet, whatever was going on outside, whatever had interrupted their showdown inside, definitely involved Zerura. There could be no doubt of that.

Tchinchura suddenly turned from Zangira and fixed Eirmon with his eerie, golden stare once more. "It would seem that at last we have an explanation for the Devoted's riddle."

"You're the one speaking in riddles," Eirmon said. "The Kalosene spoke nonsense."

Tchinchura shook his head. "I had my own questions about his prophecy, I admit, but now I know he spoke rightly. As do you, for you must feel it as surely as I do."

"I don't know anything of the sort," Eirmon said sharply.

"Yes, you do," Tchinchura said. "The Devoted prophesied Barra-Dohn's downfall for today, and what you're feeling right now is as sure a sign that Barra-Dohn's downfall has come as our entrance here into your chamber is a sign that your personal downfall has come."

Eirmon wasn't sure how to respond to this. There was no bragging or gloating in Tchinchura's voice, only cold certainty that whatever they were feeling was utterly compelling, though to what end exactly, Eirmon didn't know. He connected the only dots that were clear to him and responded along those lines. "You're saying that whoever is doing this, this whatever it is that we're feeling, is the threat to Barra-Dohn the Kalosene spoke of?"

"I am," Tchinchura replied. "Take it from one who knows, whoever is doing this has an original fragment like you do, but he knows how to wield it and understands its true potential far more than you do."

"You say he has an original fragment," Eirmon said.

"He does."

"And of course, I have one, which is why you're here," Eirmon said, knowing it was pointless not to admit it.

"Of course."

"And do either of you have one?" Eirmon asked, looking intently at the two of them.

"We do."

"Then you expect me to believe that all three of the southern fragments are here, in Barra-Dohn and that only one of them is in the hands of the Amhuru?"

"It is fantastical," Zangira admitted, "but it is true."

"How do I know this isn't a trick?" Eirmon asked. "Maybe what I'm feeling is something another Amhuru is doing somewhere outside just to induce me to give up my piece."

"It isn't your piece," Zangira said, almost growling, "and we don't need tricks to take it from you."

Zangira raised his bloody axe as though to prove his simple claim.

Tchinchura motioned to him, and he stopped. He remained still but kept the axe raised. Even in the midst of the utterly bizarre conversation he was having, Eirmon couldn't help but stare at the blood dripping steadily from the blade onto the floor.

"Listen," Tchinchura said, "you are not the first to have coveted a fragment of the Golden Cord for yourself, nor are you the first to have taken one. A few times before you, a piece has been taken. In every case, the fragment has been recovered, though it can take a while, for reasons that should be obvious but that I don't have time to explain. A piece was already missing when you took yours. It's been missing longer than yours has, and multiple teams like ours have tried to trace it, to this point unsuccessfully."

"And now," Zangira said when Tchinchura stopped, for it was to the other Amhuru that he spoke, really, not to the king, "here it is. Both missing pieces, brought together, within our reach."

Tchinchura nodded, taking a step forward, toward Eirmon. "Eirmon, at some level, even if you've never admitted it to yourself, you know you could never have hoped to keep it. Even if your plans had worked and you'd somehow killed us, more would have come, and they'd keep coming until the fragment was reclaimed. I know you well enough by now to know that you took it to ensure the security of your empire and your line, but if you passed the fragment down to Kaden and then to Deslo, you would only endanger them. But now, you have a chance to help us and help them at the same time."

"How's that?" Eirmon asked, surprised at the quiet, seemingly defeated tone in his own voice.

"Give us the fragment you took," Tchinchura said. "The two of us, both wielding original pieces, may just be strong enough to stop whoever has come with the third from completely destroying your family and your city, though if the Devoted is right, it may be too late to save your empire."

"That's your offer?" Eirmon said, trying to inject more strength into his words, but though he was successful in sounding more strident, he wasn't sure he'd been successful in projecting more strength. "You'll use the fragment I have to take back the other one you're missing, and in return, you'll leave me a crumpled empire and a humbled city?"

"Not you," Tchinchura said, pointing at him. "Don't misunderstand us. Your son. You will give us the fragment, and you will give him the throne."

"What a deal," Eirmon said, sarcastically.

"Don't deceive yourself," Tchinchura said in a voice that would brook no nonsense. "Your reign is over. Whoever is out there has come to destroy you, as the Devoted said he would. You can give us the fragment you carry, and we can try to defend the city against him and preserve the throne and as much of its influence and power as we can, or we can take the fragment from your dead body and decide for ourselves the best way to proceed in recovering the third piece. You choose."

Eirmon sighed. His dreams for Barra-Dohn had crumbled, and if he didn't want the actual city to crumble too, he knew what he had to do. He reached down and removed the fragment.

As Eirmon removed the fragment he had stolen, Tchinchura removed the fragment of the Golden Cord that he wore around his bicep and handed it to Zangira. In turn, Zangira handed him the replica that he had been wearing, which he put on his own bicep. It had always been the plan to hand over the original that he wore when they recovered the piece they were tracking, since of course, no Amhuru would wear two original fragments at the same time. That was forbidden. That they'd not expected the recovery to happen in circumstances quite like this went without saying.

Eirmon handed Tchinchura the fragment he'd been wearing around his right calf. Tchinchura took it in hand and felt a shiver, perhaps of wonder, perhaps of gratitude, run down his spine. They'd come a long way over many years to track this down, and now they had it. What's more, if things went well in the next few hours, they might have both the missing pieces, though what they'd do with the third if they successfully recovered it was a puzzle. Still, it was a puzzle for later. Perhaps this was what the elderly Devoted, Deras, had meant when he told Marlo and Owenn that they had more to do with the Amhuru. Perhaps one of them was to take the third fragment back with him to his people.

Tchinchura held the recovered fragment in his hand, felt it gyrating there, and felt also the longing to put it on and bond with it. At the same time, he knew each piece of the Golden Cord, though they shared many basic elements, were nevertheless a little different. Perhaps it would be best for what they had to do now to simply hold it and reach out through the replica of the piece he was more familiar with that rested on his bicep. If it worked, he could draw on the power of the original, while controlling it through the replica. There'd be plenty of time later to get used to the feel of the new piece.

He turned to Eirmon. "It would help to see what's going on. You'll need to come with us. Your soldiers have been told to kill us on sight."

Eirmon nodded. "Lead on."

They made their way through the palace out into the courtyard. Twice along the way they paused briefly while Eirmon explained what was going on as best he could to some of the Davrii, who both times fell in behind them. When they encountered more soldiers outside, there was less explaining to do. Word of the battle outside the walls had reached them already, along with strange tales of unnatural things going on in the midst of it.

Tchinchura pointed to the wall in the distance that stood between them and the place where this battle was taking place. "Can you get us up there?"

"Yes," Eirmon said. "There are stairs at the corner, not far from here."

"Good," he said. "I don't want to reach out blind. The more we know first, the more effective we can be."

They jogged together as a group through the streets, running roughly parallel to the northern wall that ran beside the palace grounds. The corner where the northern and eastern walls met was the corner the king had indicated. Beyond the eastern wall lay the answer to a fifty-year-old mystery.

At the top of the stairs, the group hesitated as Tchinchura peered out through the door, looking over the land outside the wall. The line of sandships up against the wall didn't come quite this far north, but they stretched south along the eastern wall as far as Tchinchura's excellent eyes could see.

It didn't take long for both Amhuru to take the measure of the battle. They could see the whirlwinds that were incapacitating the railguns, the great hookworms gliding in and out of the Barra-Dohn battle lines, and the fearful rhino-scorpions, creating havoc with the Barra-Dohn foot soldiers wherever they were to be found, their deadly tails lashing out violently at any soldier within striking distance. The battle lines of the enemy, by contrast, were orderly, intact, and simply waiting at a short distance to be called in when the enemy commander deemed it necessary.

Tchinchura led Zangira out onto the wall, glad that the parapet was high. Whoever was out there with a fragment of the Golden Cord probably had eyesight as good as their own, and while seeing the Amhuru on the wall wouldn't be necessary for him to have a fair idea where they were, it was still better that they remain unseen. For his part, Tchinchura didn't know where exactly their enemy was, but he was not on the enemy sandships. He was among the men on the field. The epicenter of the strength manipulating the Arua field was there.

Eirmon took the small group of soldiers that had accompanied them up onto the wall and distributed them, half on the far side of the Amhuru, half on the near side. He had picked up on their attempts at concealment, for the soldiers crouched down, out of view, not facing the battlefield but surveying the wall itself in both directions. After placing his men, Eirmon came up beside the Amhuru.

"I don't know what you have to do here, or how long it will take, but they'll guard you against attack for as long as they can."

Tchinchura nodded. "I'm not exactly sure how long it will take either, but we appreciate your help."

"It's madness down there," Eirmon said. "And my son is probably in the middle of it. Stop it if you can."

With that, the king moved back toward the group of soldiers stationed at the corner to watch from a distance. Tchinchura looked at Zangira, who nodded, and they clasped hands.

At first, they didn't reach for the Arua field, they simply felt for it, trying to see how it was being warped to create the whirlwinds and control the beasts below. After they had done that, Tchinchura struck out. It wasn't that the fragments themselves represented any certain quantity of power, but they provided a certain amount of comfort and control when trying to establish a connection with the Arua field, or in this case, to wrest control of it away from someone else.

Zerura flowed through the veins of the earth like blood flowed through the veins of the body, generating the Arua that regulated the life cycles of all living things. That was where the power lay— "out there" in the unseen world of the living matter belowground and in the field that emanated from it. The fragments of the Golden Cord simply opened doors and provided access to that unseen power.

He reached for and attacked the whirlwinds first, completely cutting off their enemy's control of them. Suddenly, up and down the battle line below, the whirling tempests died, and the sands whipped up by the storms settled back down to the ground. The spinning platforms slowed to a halt, and as the soldiers who'd given up manning them noticed the sudden change, they returned to their posts as soon as they were able.

Tchinchura turned his attention to the hookworms and rhino-scorpions. Controlling living creatures was always more delicate than controlling forces of nature, like winds and storms. Natural forces didn't have minds of their own, and to simply interrupt the control that their opponent had established didn't really indicate what the hookworms and rhino-scorpions would do once freed from that control. Tchinchura wanted not only to break the hold on them but also to redirect their destructive power against the now vulnerable army in green, watching the battle comfortably from a distance.

As he worked on this, he felt resistance to his attempt to take control. His nemesis, wherever he stood, was of course aware by now that someone was interfering with his work and was trying to hold on to the hookworms and rhino-scorpions. For a moment, they wrestled for that control, and Tchinchura felt the power of his adversary—his ability, his control, his will, but in the end two things doomed him. The first was Tchinchura's superior situation. The access granted by one fragment was no match for two. The second was the fact that Kaden's men down below were beginning to open fire with the railguns, and a distraction like that would interrupt anyone's concentration.

The hookworms turned and dived, heading back away from the wall, and the rhino-scorpions, thrown into a frenzy by their sudden release, turned first on their riders and then, seemingly, on each other. For the moment, whoever their adversary was had let go of his attempt to resist Tchinchura. But Tchinchura knew that was only for the moment. Whoever it was would regroup, so he held onto Zangira and steeled himself for the backlash.

37

THE SERPENT'S LAST STING

F ury. That was the only word to describe what the Jin Dara felt as his control over the whirlwinds disappeared and as he watched the massive, churning clouds of sand suddenly dissipate over the enemy lines. Someone who knew what they were doing had struck out from close by and seized control of the Arua field, pulling it like a prized possession from his grasp.

He clenched his jaw as the rage surged through him, even as he struggled inwardly for control. He knew a second strike was coming. Whoever had interfered would not be satisfied with stopping the whirlwinds, but he'd want to stop the hookworms and rhinoscorpions too. He hadn't anticipated that Barra-Dohn might harbor someone with either the ability or the material necessary to thwart his work with the Arua field, but somehow, it did, and the outcome of this battle was no longer a foregone conclusion.

The second attack came, and it was as precise, as forceful, and ultimately as successful as the first. He struggled, resisting as much as he could, but in the end, he felt his control of the hook-worms and rhino-scorpions slipping away. Even when he'd known it was coming, his resistance to the attack had been futile.

He let go. He needed to regroup and assess the situation. He could feel the fragment around his neck pulsing and throbbing with the power of the field as it was being twisted now to very different ends than his own by someone who couldn't be very far away. He didn't think it was anyone on one of the enemy sand-ships or among the soldiers on the ground. It felt, in fact, like it had come from somewhere off to his right, near the far northern end of the wall before him.

Without the concentration required to maintain control of the Arua field, his mind was free to examine the puzzle before him. He possessed one of the six original fragments of the Golden Cord. It had been in his family for fifty years. He'd been raised with it and experimented with its power all of his life. He was on intimate terms with it. And yet, he'd just been bested in his attempt to direct for his own purposes the Arua field through it, as though he'd been a mere novice in its world of secrets.

At the very least, this meant he was dealing with someone else who had an original fragment. As improbable as it seemed that two might be in Barra-Dohn at the same time, he couldn't account for what had happened any other way. What's more, the person wielding it was experienced in its use, as experienced as he was or even more. That meant someone raised with it, which meant an Amhuru.

That an Amhuru might be here wasn't that hard to believe. That he was one of the few who carried an original fragment was just plain unlucky. Still, the Jin Dara didn't understand how a con-test that should have matched roughly equal strength and mastery had gone so decidedly against him. Perhaps it was just his pride, but he didn't reckon that any single Amhuru, despite his lineage, should really be that much better and more able than he was in working his will through a fragment of the Golden Cord. He had long explored the potential of his fragment and experimented with its power and potential in ways that any Amhuru would have found abhorrent.

A small island, far away, bore the marks of those experiments, as did the unlucky few who still lived there.

So what was he missing? How had this happened? How had his grasp on not just the winds but on creatures he had been both directing and enlarging for months been suddenly taken from him?

He didn't have much time to consider the issue. His enemies were beginning to regain control of their railguns and use them to good effect. He could see them spraying meridium bolts in the direction of the lumbering rhino-scorpions who were now lashing out in all directions at anything near them, even each other. As yet, the attacks from the railguns were sporadic and directed at the creatures and not his men, but he knew that this would change. Soon the orderly command of a well-disciplined army would return and they would direct more systematic attacks his way.

"Devaar!" he called to his second in command. The man appeared, looking uncertainly at him.

"What's going on?" Devaar asked.

"There's a problem," the Jin Dara said. "Perhaps temporary, perhaps not. So there's a change of plan. Order all but a few of our units forward. We need to close the gap on the railguns before they start ripping us apart."

"But without the whirlwinds—"

"Do as I say," the Jin Dara yelled, his own frustration showing in a rare outward display of anger. "The objective of the attack is to seize control of the railguns in the center, then use them to neutralize the others."

"Yes, sir," Devaar said simply.

"Once we control all of them, or at least all of them that are still working, we'll turn them on the city as originally planned."

"Yes, sir," Devaar said again.

"Well, what are you waiting for?"

Devaar hurried off, and before long, the Jin Dara watched the units arrayed along the front of his current line begin to advance at a quick pace as he waited with the reserves. They'd have to negotiate the remaining rhino-scorpions, of course, as well as the resistance that was sure to come from the railguns as more and more crews, separated from their posts and demoralized by the hookworms some time ago, returned to them. Still, the Jin Dara had brought his men in fairly close, only hanging back far enough so as not to confuse the creatures under his control.

If all had gone as planned, he would have held them back until the enemy was completely routed and had abandoned all sem-blance of a defense. Then he would have ordered them forward to seize the railguns. As it was, a victory here looked like it would be more costly than he had anticipated, but he didn't doubt that a victory was still within reach. He'd come too far and carried his ancestors' hatred too close to his heart for too long to be turned back now.

Besides, if he could be surprised and bested by his unseen enemy, then perhaps he could turn the tables and regain control himself. He looked up at the wall, scanning it for the first time. It made sense, of course, that whoever had countered him was up there. If whoever it was had been out here with the army when the Jin Dara had first struck, why wait until now? No, he had been inside the city when the attack began.

If the tables were turned and it had been he, the Jin Dara thought as he kept scanning the wall, if he'd been inside the city and felt someone manipulating the Arua field like that, he'd have sought a vantage point where he could see what was going on. The difficulty of being high up aboveground when working with Arua would have been more than made up for by the fact that he could see what was going on.

The Jin Dara lingered behind his attacking men, but he watched the wall and not the battle unfolding before him. He would try, when he had gathered himself, to seize control again. If that failed, he would wait for the gate or the wall to be breached, then he would enter the city and find his opponent personally. Either way, easy or hard, he would not be denied, even if it cost him his life.

Eirmon found it difficult to watch and know that his city hung in the balance, and he was helpless to do anything about it. Now that he no longer wore the fragment around his calf, he felt a void, a longing, an aching to have the Zerura against his skin again. It felt like life had lost its color, that his eyes had dimmed, and his senses as a whole had faded.

He also realized now that he wasn't wearing the Cord how much easier it had been to think he could somehow hold onto it and avoid the fate Tchinchura had made sound so inevitable. He hadn't just felt more alive with the Zerura, but he'd also felt more confident and more powerful. Over the years he'd worn it, he'd lost his ability to measure his own vulnerability, perhaps even his own mortality.

He wouldn't make that mistake again. Whatever happened now, for better or for worse, he knew he couldn't live forever. His empire couldn't stand forever. He couldn't escape justice for his wrongs forever. Surprisingly, that thought didn't discourage him. If anything, it emboldened him. He'd been defeated, and he probably would be again, but that didn't mean he was out of options. Sand adders were always at their deadliest when wounded. As his father had always said, "Beware the serpent's last sting."

As he watched the two Amhuru, silent and focused on the battlefield below, and as he watched the tide of that battle shift, a daring thought occurred to him. The whirlwinds were gone, and the hookworms had retreated from beneath the feet of the army of Barra-Dohn. The railguns were slowly returning to action, and the enemy army had just begun to move in. Even they could see that the tide had shifted, and they were moving now in the hope of striking a finishing blow before his railguns tore them apart. Just a few moments more, maybe, especially if things went his way down below, and the way might be clear for Eirmon to seize this opportunity . . .

But did he dare? It would be a bold move, and if it failed, his life would be forfeit. But what of that? The Amhuru had said he would live but lose his throne. He'd always envisioned handing Kaden a powerful empire, but he'd never anticipated being around to watch him rule it. Now that he considered the idea, he didn't much like it, especially if the power of Barra-Dohn was going to be greatly diminished as both the prophecy of the Kalosene and the assurances of the Amhuru suggested it was. Death didn't sound so bad compared with that future, so the risk of it was hardly the deterrent it would have been even just a few hours earlier when he had feared for his life in the confusion surrounding the Academy.

He deliberated a little more, internally, as he watched the railguns open fire on the advancing ranks of the enemy. He deliberated as he watched the foremost ranks of his enemy fall, but he knew that he'd already decided. He might fail, and he might die, but he would never not be king. He took aside the highest ranking officer from among the Davrii on the stairs beside him and whispered in his ear.

The man seemed thunderstruck by Eirmon's words, but the king simply fixed him with an intense stare, and before long the man's excellent training to obey without question kicked in and wiped the wonder from his eyes. Instead, he turned and began to spread the word to the soldiers with them.

Eirmon turned back to survey the scene, both on the wall and down below. The tide of battle continued to shift, though perhaps it was still too early to say the army of Barra-Dohn had seized the upper hand. They would though, Eirmon believed, now that the armies were engaged in a more conventional battle. Even if the control of the Amhuru over the Arua field faltered, there seemed little that hookworms or rhino-scorpions could do now that the soldiers from both sides had drawn so close together.

He looked past the Amhuru at the soldiers posted on the wall beyond them. For a moment he considered walking behind the Amhuru to inform them of his plan. As focused as they were, the Amhuru might not even notice him, and if they did, they probably wouldn't suspect what he was up to. He held back, though. The risk seemed to outweigh the reward. They'd figure out what was going on quickly enough without being told. He'd rather their reaction be a bit slower to what he intended than run any risk of giving the Amhuru forewarning. Facing one angered Amhuru with the other dead or incapacitated would be risky, but two Amhuru on alert would be suicidal.

He could do nothing now but go. He started out from the door to the stairs where he'd been standing, walking briskly straight toward Tchinchura. The Amhuru didn't turn from the battle below or seem to notice his approach, at least not until Eirmon drove his knife into the Amhuru's back. He heard a cry of pain, a gasp, and Tchinchura let go of Zangira's hand and sank to his knees.

From there, things happened quickly. The soldiers who'd been with him by the stairs were already moving past him to engage Zangira, who had turned from the battlefield and was drawing both his axe and knife. He fought off their attack furiously. The Davrii on the far side, as Eirmon had hoped, had only needed to be summoned once before they likewise converged upon the Amhuru.

All this Eirmon saw unfolding in a flash, and he didn't hesitate to reach down and seize the fragment of the Golden Cord that Tchinchura held in his left hand. Not a fragment, Eirmon thought, his fragment. Once bent over Tchinchura, he hesitated. The knife he'd stabbed Tchinchura with was still protruding from the Amhuru's back, and part of him wanted to take it, pull it out, and make sure the job was finished. A bigger part of him, though, cried out for the Zerura to be immediately wrapped around his calf. He wanted to feel it once more against his skin.

He took a few steps back from the fallen Amhuru. The feeling of the Zerura going around his leg was like the feeling he sometimes got when the sun, having been blocked by banks of clouds for days and days on end, finally emerged. Brilliant. Radiant in all its splendor. At least, it was kind of like that, only a thousand times as powerful. It was almost intoxicating. The world returned to normal, and Eirmon knew his cause was not yet lost.

Even so, Zangira fought on. So far, he was successfully holding his enemy at bay. In fact, several of the soldiers who had converged on him had either fallen or withdrawn from the fight with serious wounds. Zangira, with his golden eyes flashing in the midday sun, had slid down along the parapet so that he was now fighting more or less over the still crumpled body of Tchinchura.

Eirmon watched this fight progress, a little conflicted. He'd hoped Zangira would fall quickly so he could seize both pieces of the Golden Cord. He knew he didn't understand their potential as well as the Amhuru did, but he figured what he did know would only be that much better with two fragments. And if things went well for his army down below before the day was out, he might have all three of the southern fragments. An hour ago, that thought would have seemed like madness, but now it seemed indispensable to his hopes for the future.

But as he watched the battle with Zangira, he could see that the end of that fight was certainly in doubt. His men held the numerical advantage, but the Amhuru fought like a man possessed. Everywhere Eirmon looked, his Zerura-lined blades flashed in the sun, and the confined space of the wall didn't give the king's soldiers much of a chance to fully enjoy their superior numbers.

He knew that if he slipped down the stairs now, he could get away and go to the battlefield where he would be on hand to maintain the effort against his new enemy. If Zangira fell, he could claim the fragment for himself later, and if he didn't, then he'd at least have a chance of taking the piece that was somewhere down below to combine with his own. He'd need it if Zangira somehow survived and came for him.

And then, unexpectedly, the decision was made for him.

Kaden was not at all prepared for what he saw as he emerged onto the city wall. A furious engagement between the Davrii and Zangira was under way. It looked like Tchinchura was down, and Zangira fought alone. It also looked like Eirmon had ordered the attack. Certainly, he was doing nothing to stop it.

He'd found Gamalian in the palace when he arrived, looking for his father. Gamalian had not seen them leave, but he'd heard of the king's departure with the Amhuru from the palace not long before. Wild stories were already circulating about what was going on outside the walls, and rumor said that the king and Amhuru had gone to intervene in the battle. Outside the palace they'd found soldiers who'd seen the original party heading toward the stairs that led up onto the wall. Kaden had brought both the soldiers and Gamalian with him.

"Father!" Kaden shouted, anger erupting at the outrage of what he was seeing. "What's the meaning of this?"

Eirmon walked to Kaden and slapped him. Hard. As Kaden recoiled, Eirmon hissed, "Don't ever shout at me."

Kaden recovered and stood his ground, meeting Eirmon glare for glare. "We were told the Amhuru were helping you, that you'd come here together to help our army," Kaden said.

"They were helping me," Eirmon said, "but the tide of battle has changed. We don't need them anymore."

Kaden glanced back down the wall at Tchinchura on his knees and Zangira, covered with blood, still fighting over him. He looked back at his father, but only for a moment before stepping past him to move down the wall. Passing Eirmon, he murmured with disgust. "What have you done?"

He wanted to hurt Eirmon, but helping Zangira seemed the more pressing need. Zangira was not an outsider. He was his friend.

"Come," Kaden called back to the men who had followed him out onto the wall. "We need to break this up."

Eirmon watched the soldiers Kaden had brought move in to try to break up the fight between the other Davrii and Zangira, but he had no intention of waiting to see how the scene on the wall played out.

Kaden had always been weak. His mother had doted on him, and though Eirmon had tried to toughen him, obviously he'd failed. His choice to act was confirmed. If his gamble succeeded, he would once more rule Barra-Dohn. If he failed, it would all collapse. Fine. Kaden wasn't fit to rule, anyway. He was sorry for Deslo, but perhaps he could still salvage victory, and after he dealt with Kaden for his betrayal here, he could groom Deslo for the throne.

Eirmon turned and started rapidly down the stairs. His only chance now to stay alive and keep his dreams alive too was to somehow get out onto the battlefield and secure the third fragment.

38

REAPING THE WHIRLWIND

The Jin Dara reached up to feel the fragment of the Golden Cord around his neck. The throbbing, pulsing sensation that had marked his enemy's interference was gone. All he could sense now was the normal, rhythmic feel of Zerura against his skin.

He took a deep breath as he waited, looking back to the top of the wall. For what seemed a long time he stood there, waiting. Nothing happened. The Zerura against his skin remained "normal." He frowned. The battle was far from over, so why had his enemy let go? Was he being dared to reach out and seize the Arua again? Was it a trap of some kind?

If it was a trap, he couldn't think of what the stakes might be. His enemy had seized conrol and made it possible for Barra-Dohn to mount a real defense. What possible objective could there be in letting go now before the outcome of the battle had been decided? Did his enemy anticipate that a renewed attempt by the Jin Dara to summon and control the whirlwinds and living weapons he had created for this day was coming? Was his antagonist simply encouraging him to do it now, to get it over with, so he might despair and quit the field?

Well, the Jin Dara thought, if that's what he wants, that's what he'll get. He struck out suddenly, violently, seizing hold of the Arua field. He took hold of it, calling forth, not the many whirlwinds from before, but one great whirlwind. It appeared in the sky above the center of the enemy line, and slowly, gradually, descended. Men and railguns were alike tossed about by the wind like grains of sand. Even massive sandships slid sideways taking their moorings with them.

For a moment, he held the whirlwind out like a challenge, but no response from the city came. No interference, no intervention, no counter. The Jin Dara released the whirlwind and began immediately to bring back the smaller, more focused storms from before. Soon they had reappeared up and down the line, once more rendering the railguns impossible to control.

Now for the hookworms and what was left of the rhinoscorpions. It would, of course, be impossible for the creatures to be directed against only the soldiers from Barra-Dohn. They couldn't possibly move into an active engagement and only kill the soldiers from one of the two armies. Still, the prospect of their killing, indiscriminately, large numbers of both armies didn't bother him terribly much.

For one thing, Devaar was a bright and capable commander. Now that the whirlwinds had reappeared, he'd figure out that the problem the Jin Dara had spoken of earlier had been overcome. And with the return of the hookworms, he'd do what he could to disengage and let the creatures do their work.

For another thing, most of the men who'd followed Devaar forward were soldiers of Amattai. Lord Jona might be distraught by their sacrifice, but the Jin Dara didn't especially care. He'd come for one reason and one reason only—to utterly destroy Barra-Dohn, the city once known as Zeru-Shalim. He'd come prepared to sacrifice his own men as well as himself, so sacrificing soldiers from a city that meant nothing to him? That was easy. As easy as hate itself.

The soldiers that Eirmon had set upon Zangira had taken a step back, disengaging as Kaden directed, but Zangira still had both his knife and axe raised, and he looked ready to use them on anyone who dared move a step closer.

"Zangira!" Kaden called from where he stood a few feet behind the nearest withdrawn soldier. "It's me. It's Kaden. I've commanded these men to stop. No one will hurt you or Tchinchura. Eirmon is gone."

Zangira turned his head and fixed Kaden with his golden eyes. He was a mess. In addition to the blood dripping from his weapons and staining his clothes, Kaden could see he'd been cut in several places. His arms were cut and bleeding, a slash ran horizontally across his right thigh, and a knife or spear had punctured him on his left side.

No one spoke or moved, and after a moment, the Amhuru began slowly to lower his weapons. Kaden stepped forward, and the soldiers who'd already parted a little bit so he could address the Amhuru, parted farther so he could slip through. Without speaking, both Zangira and Kaden stooped over Tchinchura to examine his wound.

It was deep and wide and blood was seeping out of it at an alarming rate. Tchinchura groaned as he lay there. He was conscious, but his eyes were closed, and he seemed only vaguely aware of what was going on around him.

"We need to get him down from here," Zangira said, speaking at last. "Perhaps there are bandages in the palace?"

"Of course," Kaden said, automatically. "I'm sure that even if Gamalian doesn't know where to find some, Myron can get us whatever we need."

Zangira took off his vest, ripped a strip out of the back where there was less blood on it and applied pressure to the wound with it. "I'll have to carry him down."

Before he could hoist Tchinchura up onto his shoulder, though, Kaden reached out and put a hand on his arm. "Zangira, can't you, I mean, isn't there something you can do for him?"

Zangira looked at Kaden. "I'll take him back to the palace, cleanse the wound, and do all I can do there."

"I mean something more," Kaden said, glancing at the Zerura wrapped around his left bicep. "Look, I don't pretend to understand how someone could call down whirlwinds or control an army of hookworms, let alone how you could stop them. But, the fact is they did, and you did. Can't you, you know, use some of that power to heal him?"

"I appreciate your concern for Tchinchura," Zangira said, "but you need to understand that the Amhuru have safeguarded the fragments of the Golden Cord for a thousand years. There are things that wearing Zerura does automatically to us and for us, and these things are accepted as part of the job. There are things Zerura can be made to do, and they are permitted as a reward for the price we pay to do what we must. And, there are things Zerura can do that are forbidden, for they are seen as overreaching the purpose for which the Cord was given in the first place.

"The line between these categories can be blurry, and who can say where reasonable action to preserve the gift of life ends and presuming upon the prerogative of Kalos begins? All I can tell you, my friend, is that I will do for Tchinchura all that I can in good conscience do. The rest is not up to me."

Suddenly, Zangira's eyes grew wide, and his head whipped around so that he stared up and over the parapet. The sky had begun to darken. Kaden stood too and watched as a mammoth whirlwind began to form not far away near the gate to the city. The great, swirling cloud began to slowly descend, and even as far

away as they were, they felt the sand being picked up and blown
every which way, whipping their faces.

Kaden leaned forward to stare down over the parapet. He saw
the bottom of this whirlwind touch the ground, saw men and platforms in the distance tossed about. Even his own sandship broke
lose from its moorings and was pushed sideways into the gate,
which it struck with a mighty crack.

He turned to Zangira. "If I take Tchinchura down, will you
stay and do what you were doing before? Will you stop this?"

Zangira, still crouched over Tchinchura and holding the now
soaked strip of cloth against the other Amhuru's wound, was no
longer looking at the sky, and he did not look now. He shook his
head. "This is no longer my fight."

Kaden stooped back down and seized Zangira by the arm.
"My men are down there. Don't punish them for what my father
did. I'm asking as a friend."

"I'm not punishing them," Zangira replied, "but I'm telling
you as a friend that I can't help them. The die is cast. The other
fragment of the Golden Cord has left with your father, and even
if we could somehow recover it now, the one who could best wield
it to defend your city lies here wounded."

"But you're here," Kaden pleaded. "You can do something."

"Maybe," Zangira said, "but without Tchinchura and without
the other fragment, I am pretty evenly matched with whoever is
out there. I might be able to slow him down, but I don't know if
I can stop him."

"You have to try!"

"Listen," Zangira said, as vehement as Kaden himself had
been. "I didn't come here to save Barra-Dohn. I came here to
recover what your father stole. And we had it, Kaden. We had it!
And despite what your father had done to get it, we were using it
to protect the city, your city. But Eirmon couldn't let it go. I can,
and I will. That means leaving Barra-Dohn to the fate your father
has chosen."

"But why?" Kaden persisted. "It's not too late. If you help me win this battle, then you can still do what you've come to do."

Zangira shook his head, and when he spoke, he spoke quietly, so quietly that Kaden had to strain to hear him. "Your father thinks he can win this battle, but he doesn't understand. He doesn't know what whoever is out there can do. He'll lose the battle, and most likely, lose the fragment too. Our mission has failed."

"You don't know that. We can go after him. Maybe we can reach him first."

"Maybe we could," Zangira said, "but if we failed, and if whoever has the third piece gets the fragment your father has before we do, I won't be able to stop him. I'm not afraid to die, Kaden, but if I fall, then we could also lose the fragment I now bear, and none of the Amhuru will know what we discovered here. I can't take that risk. They have to know."

"Well, I have to go back," Kaden said, when it was clear that Zangira wasn't going to change his mind.

It was Zangira's turn to reach out and seize Kaden by the arm. "Not only do you not have to go back, you shouldn't."

"Greyer—and my men—I have responsibilities."

"They will neither be saved nor lost by your return," Zangira said. "The issue is beyond you. However, your wife and son are somewhere out on the quay, waiting for us. You might be able to save them. Are they not also your responsibility?"

"On the quay?" Kaden asked, looking confused. "What do you mean?"

Zangira shook his head, let go of Kaden's arm and lifted Tchinchura, putting him over his shoulder. "There's no time to explain all that has transpired while you were away. I've delayed too long already. Barra-Dohn is falling. You need to decide where your priorities lie."

"I need to know what you're talking about!"

Zangira continued toward the stairs, but as Kaden jogged beside him, he tried to explain. "Believing the prophecy that

Barra-Dohn would fall, we offered Ellenara and Deslo a chance to come with us when we left."

"And she accepted? She thinks she can just leave and take Deslo?"

They hesitated at the entrance to the stairwell, and Zangira stood there, holding onto Tchinchura, looking at Kaden. "Until just now, your whereabouts were unknown. She had to protect Deslo, didn't she?"

"Well, yes," Kaden sputtered, but before he could speak further, Zangira hurried on.

"Kaden," he said. "Eirmon has ensured the fall of the city. You may never be a king, but you can still be a husband and a father. That's up to you."

Kaden could think of nothing to say. In his peripheral vision, he could see the mammoth storm that had blown up below begin to dissipate. He turned, seeing the smaller whirlwinds that had plagued his defenses earlier return. Zangira was right. He could go back down there, but he couldn't do a thing to stop what was happening.

Suddenly, an image of Nara and Deslo, alone and afraid in the confusion that must inevitably ensue when the city was overrun, flashed before his eyes.

"All right," Kaden said. "I'll come."

The gate was up ahead. Eirmon was eager to pass through and see if the army of Barra-Dohn had continued to fend off the enemy attack. He was at least encouraged that he'd felt no throbbing or pulsing from the fragment wrapped around his calf, which meant that even without the Amhuru on the wall, whoever had summoned the whirlwinds and hookworms before had not done so again.

It had been bold, perhaps even foolish to stab Tchinchura before his army had been able to do more damage with the rail-guns, but that was why it had been necessary. If either of the Amhuru had even suspected that Eirmon might betray them, surely they wouldn't have expected it might happen before they had secured the victory he so desired. Had Eirmon waited until the battle was decided and it was safe to strike, it might have been too late. So, he'd struck when he had, knowing he was risking more than himself. He was risking Barra-Dohn.

And yet, that risk seemed to be paying off. A few minutes had passed since the Amhuru's hold on the Arua field had disappeared, and still no counterstroke occurred. Perhaps the railguns had already routed the enemy. Perhaps he'd pass through the gate, out onto the battlefield, only to find little more than mopping up to be done.

The Davrii at the gate opened it enough for him and the men with him to pass through. That the fighting was not yet over, he could tell right away. More than that, though, he couldn't see, mostly because the line of sandships was moored between him and the thick of the fighting. He saw that the ship right in front of him was Kaden's command ship, and he made for the gangway. Captain Greyer, or whoever Kaden had left in charge, would be directing the battle from there.

He had not yet reached the bottom of the gangway when the fragment of the Golden Cord alerted him to the counterstroke that he had feared. It was the same, strong, violent seizing of the Arua field that he had felt from the palace, but it was more intense now. Eirmon didn't know if this was because he was closer to the source, or if the one doing it was simply seeking to take a firmer hold. Either way, Eirmon almost stumbled to a halt as the sky above his head began to darken.

He'd felt Zangira's work with the Arua field earlier, when he made the soldiers guarding him sick, and he'd felt some of what his opponent was doing now, before. Eirmon believed he could do it too, so he tried to reach out through the Zerura on his leg and take control of the Arua field away from his enemy. He concentrated, and he tried, but his efforts were wholly ineffectual. Either it was harder than it had seemed, or his enemy had such a firm hold of it that he couldn't even come close to getting his own grip.

The dark sky had become a roaring maelstrom of wind. Eirmon was suddenly afraid. He abandoned all efforts to resist what was happening above and around him. It struck him suddenly, like a physical blow that what was taking place here was something he was powerless to stop.

His mind raced. He'd burned his bridges with the Amhuru. Even if Tchinchura still lived, they would not help. He could not go back.

Ahead of him, the swirling winds picked up one of his precious railguns and blew it away across the sands like a feather blown before a strong summer breeze. Whatever lay behind him, ahead of him was death.

He turned, thinking that if he moved quickly, he might arrive at the gate before the storm became too strong to navigate. He was wrong. The next moment, he felt himself being picked up and blown to the side. He crashed into the side of the neighboring sandship and blacked out as he fell to the sand.

39

SETTLING AN ANCIENT SCORE

Inside the palace, Gamalian found Myron almost immediately, or rather, Myron found Gamalian. No sooner had Gamalian announced his intentions to go in search of the chief steward, when the chief steward appeared. Gamalian gave a brief account of the situation, and soon a small army of stewards was at Zangira's disposal, bringing him whatever he needed to wash and dress Tchinchura's wound. While that work proceeded, and while Kaden went to quickly gather a few things to take with them, Gamalian hung back, wrestling with his own conscience.

From the moment it had been clear on the wall that the time to abandon Barra-Dohn was here, he'd been deliberating about what to do with the two prisoners locked in the dungeon beneath the palace, if anything. Personally, he didn't care a great deal about what happened to Rika, but he did feel sorry for the other one, who'd had the great misfortune to get mixed up with her.

Gamalian knew it wasn't his responsibility to do anything about them, but he also knew that Barra-Dohn was likely to be overrun. Whatever chance the ordinary citizens stood of escaping or even just surviving that calamity, as minuscule as it might be, the two locked in cells didn't have even that much of a chance. He sighed, and drawing Myron aside, secured the help of a steward who was sent to bring him the keys to the relevant doors.

Meanwhile, Kaden returned, and as Tchinchura's wound had been cleansed and closed and bandaged as well as could be hoped for, Kaden helped Zangira put Tchinchura back on his shoulder for the trip out to the quay. The steward had not yet returned with the keys, so Gamalian offered to stay behind. "There's something I need to take care of," he said. "Go ahead of me, and I'll catch up."

"If it won't take long," Kaden said, "we'll just wait."

"There's no need," Gamalian said, smiling reassuringly. "I won't be long, and even though I'm old, you'll be slowed down by having to carry Tchinchura. Please, go. You not only need to find the captain and the ship, but you need to find Nara and Deslo. I'll be fine."

They hesitated still but soon acquiesced and left for the quay. No sooner had they gone than the steward returned with the keys.

Gamalian moved quickly through the palace. He was drawing near the door that opened on the stairs that went down to the dungeon when he paused, his attention drawn to a small, tangled heap of belts with sheathes and knives lying nearby at the base of a wall. Which of the soldiers had put them there and for what reason he couldn't guess, but it struck him that now might be the time to carry a weapon. He walked over, picked a couple of them up, and went to the door.

There was no guard at either the top or the bottom of the stairs. Perhaps multiple locked doors had rendered that job redundant or perhaps word of the events in the city and outside it had pulled attention away from the prisoners. At any rate, Gamalian found both Rika and Barreck alone in the dank and dimly lit dungeon, much as he had found them last time.

No sooner did Rika see him enter, when she was on her feet, moving to the front of her cell. There was no pretense of being calm or cool as there had been last time. Gamalian could see in her eyes the desperation to get out.

"Gamalian, you have the keys," she said simply, looking at what he held in his hand. Then she saw what was in his other hand. "And knives. What's going on?"

"There's something going on out there," Gamalian said, nodding back toward the stairs with his head. "Which is why I'm here."

"What's going on?" Barreck said, also rising and moving forward in his cell.

"Barra-Dohn is under attack," Gamalian said simply. "It looks like the Kalosene's prophecy is about to come true."

"You can't mean you think the attack will succeed?" Rika said. "Who could possibly defeat Barra-Dohn?"

"I don't have time to explain," Gamalian said, beginning to fumble with the key ring. "I'm going to let the two of you out, but then you're on your own. I have to go help Kaden find Nara and Deslo at the quay."

"Thank you," Rika exclaimed, but when Gamalian stepped toward Barreck's cell, she reacted immediately. "You have to let me out first!"

Both men looked at her, but it was Gamalian who asked. "Why?"

"If you let him out and give him one of those knives, he'll kill me. He might wait until you're gone, but he will."

Gamalian looked back at Barreck, who stared blankly back. Gamalian didn't see murder in his eyes, but he didn't see denial either, even though he said, "I want nothing to do with her."

"Don't listen to him," Rika said. "You haven't been down here. You haven't heard the things he says when no one else is around."

Gamalian took a step back, assessing the situation, while the two of them exchanged verbal attacks. "All right, you first," he said, moving toward Rika's cell, "but you'll have to go as soon as I let you go. I can't linger just to give you a head start."

"Thank you, Gamalian. Thank you so much," she said, and she stepped back from the door so Gamalian could experiment with the keys. After a few tries, he found the one that worked on her cell, and soon she was free.

"Here you go," Gamalian said, handing her one of the belts. "Good luck."

"Thanks," Rika said, strapping the belt quickly around her waist.

Gamalian turned to go back over to Barreck's cell, when the sound of light footsteps and the sudden, sharp feel of a burning, intense pain in his back told him he shouldn't have trusted Rika. She stabbed him again. Then a third time. He dropped the keys as he fell to the floor.

There was a jingling sound as Rika kicked the keys away from Barreck's cell. Barreck was yelling something at Rika, but Gamalian was struggling to push himself up off the floor. He couldn't focus.

"I'm sorry, Barreck," he heard Rika say when the other's shouting stopped, "but I'll feel a lot safer out there if I know you're down here."

The footsteps disappeared down the hall, toward the stairs, and Gamalian, unable to push himself up off the floor, collapsed.

There was madness at the harbor. The quay was crawling with people. By now, the destruction of the Academy that morning was old news. The battle going on outside the city walls wasn't. The two things combined had driven anyone in Barra-Dohn who had a ship, had access to a ship, or had any hope whatsoever of getting near a ship, to the quay.

With the crowds, and all the bumping and jostling going on, Kaden led the way for Zangira, who followed close behind with Tchinchura still draped over his shoulder. On their way, Zangira had told Kaden that ultimately they were looking for Captain D'Sarza and *The Sorry Rogue*, so Kaden was looking both for Nara and Deslo and for any sign of the ship or its crew. He'd never actually seen the ship, but he remembered both the captain and her first mate from Garranmere.

"Zangira!"

The voice that called to them had come from behind. It was a man's voice, but when they turned, they didn't see Gamalian. It was two Kalosenes, pushing their way through the crowd to join them.

"What happened to Tchinchura?" they asked as they drew closer.

"I can tell you later," Zangira said, "that is, if you're still coming with us?"

"We'd like to," one of them answered, "if it's still all right."

"Of course," Zangira said, "especially if Owenn will carry Tchinchura for a while. I'm exhausted."

In response, the bigger of the two men reached down without saying a word and lifted Tchinchura up off Zangira's shoulder with ease and placed him gently over his own. Zangira flexed and massaged the arm that had been holding Tchinchura securely in place, wincing at the pain.

"Did you get it?" the other asked in a quiet voice, looking around as though someone might hear him.

Zangira shook his head, and the two Kalosenes exchanged meaningful glances. "I'm sorry."

"And you?" Zangira said. "I'm glad to see you avoided capture. What about the rest?"

They looked at each other again and shrugged. "The last I knew," the Kalosene said, "all of us who survived the night survived the morning too. It looked for a while like we might be pinned down on the rooftops, but as word spread inside the city about the battle outside the walls, the patience of the soldiers waiting for us in the streets seems to have been severely tested."

"Whether they were summoned to the defense of the city or just went of their own accord," the one called Owenn added, "they disappeared."

"Or maybe they were freaked out by the enormous hookworm that smashed up through the street, sending paving stones flying every which way before it disappeared again, leaving behind a substantial hole in the ground," the other added.

Kaden hadn't followed a lot of what he heard, but when the Kalosene said that, he gaped, and even Zangira's eyes grew wide.

"It might have been that," Owenn agreed, "though I thought that happened later."

"Whatever it was, we got down and made our way here," the other added, wrapping up their account of the morning since creating the diversion in the square.

"What was it like?" Kaden said, speaking to the Kalosenes for the first time. "The mood of the city?"

"Panicked," the Kalosene said, observing Zangira's companion carefully. "And why not? They woke to the collapse of one of their greatest buildings, and the day only got worse from there."

Kaden looked confused, glancing from the Kalosenes to Zangira. "What building?"

It was the Kalosenes' turn to look confused. "You don't know?"

Zangira stepped in. "There are lots of things about today that will need some explaining, and we can discuss all of them when we're under way. Let's find Captain D'Sarza and our other companions, and let's get going."

Eirmon's eyes flickered open. His head hurt, and it took a few moments for his eyes to adjust to the light. He was lying on wooden flooring. Decking, to be exact, as it didn't take much looking around for him to figure out he was on a sandship. He could see no one else, save for a man with reddish hair, watching him intently.

The man noticed Eirmon's eyes open, and he rose from where he'd been sitting and walked over to him. Stooping down, he handed him a cup of water. Eirmon wasn't sure who this man was, or even if the water was safe to drink, but he was powerfully thirsty. He drained the cup in a single gulp.

When he handed the cup back to the man, he noticed for the first time that his hair wasn't completely red. Flecks of gold were in it. And in his bright blue eyes too.

Instinctively, he recoiled, pushing himself back across the decking, away from the man. He didn't know for sure that the golden eyes and hair that marked the Amhuru was the result of wearing Zerura against their skin from the time they were children, but it was a logical guess. He'd possessed his fragment for more than a decade, but neither his hair nor his eyes were marked at all with these golden signs. This man's were.

If he was seeing correctly and thinking clearly, he was looking at the mystery man. The bearer of the third fragment.

It was then that Eirmon realized there was no Zerura on his calf. He lurched as he reached down and grabbed his leg. His hand searched up and down from his ankle to his knee, but to no avail. It was gone.

All this, the man with the red hair just watched as he stood above him, looking down. He didn't say anything, though, and after a moment, Eirmon broke the silence. "Who are you?"

"We'll come back to that," the man said. "One of your soldiers identified you as the king of Barra-Dohn. And given what I found you wearing around your calf, what you were obviously just searching for, I'm inclined to think he was right."

It hadn't been framed as a question, but Eirmon suspected the man was waiting either for confirmation or a denial. He might be captured, and very likely facing death, but he didn't feel like giving this man what he wanted. Stubbornly, he kept his mouth shut.

"Well, you don't deny it, anyway," the man said after a moment. "You may be descended from the ancient kings of Zeru-Shalim, if the royal lineage has proceeded unbroken all these years. But between you and me," he said, stooping down and whispering, "it seems rather unlikely."

"Nevertheless," he said, standing again and resuming his previous tone of voice, "it does seem a rather extraordinary coincidence that you and I should be here, and up until just a short time ago, both of us had fragments of the Golden Cord in our possession. Rather ironic, don't you think?"

"Is it?" Eirmon asked, having no idea what the man was talking about.

"Oh, my, yes," the man said. "But to understand just how ironic, I'll have to tell you a story. A little sad, really, that you'll have to learn such an important chapter of your own history from me, but there it is. That too, can wait a few moments. First, tell me who interfered with my whirlwinds and hookworms earlier. It certainly wasn't you."

Again, Eirmon retreated to silence.

If it angered or irritated his questioner, he didn't show it. Instead, he simply kept talking. "Was it an Amhuru? It was wasn't it? That makes the most sense. If it was, why'd he stop interfering? And how did you get the fragment? I can't figure that one out."

When Eirmon didn't offer any answers, the man kept going.

"Of course, I did have one idea, and a very intriguing idea at that. It occurred to me, as improbable as this would be if actually true, that maybe, just maybe, the Amhuru who tried to stop me was really here to take that fragment away from you."

Eirmon could keep his mouth shut, but he couldn't keep his face from giving away some of what he felt.

"I'm right, aren't I?" the man asked. "Yes, I can see it. Fascinating. I wondered about that, because of course, the Amhuru have tried to recover my fragment too. We've encountered a few teams here and there along the way since we seized it.

"And that's why I thought, when I found you, that maybe a team of Amhuru was here trying to recover the piece you have. It would explain a few things, like how my hold on the Arua field was taken away so thoroughly and so quickly."

The man was talking to Eirmon. No one else was there, but he was pacing back and forth, almost taking no note of the king now.

It was like he was talking only to himself. "But, if two Amhuru were with you, and if—and this is the truly fantastic part—if one of them had an original fragment too, then I can understand what happened."

He stopped pacing and stood still. "Imagine that. Imagine the odds. All the years I've searched for this place. All the work and the planning, and I arrive here while not one, but two original fragments of the Golden Cord just happen to be in the city."

He stared back down at Eirmon, and the king, who'd been shielding his eyes against the sun as he looked up at the man, simply laid his head back down and looked away.

"It could have been disastrous, of course," the man continued. "Two fragments in one place. It very nearly was disastrous. So while I don't know what happened to make them stop interfering with me and protecting the city—though I suspect I have you to thank for that somehow—I'm certainly glad that they did stop. I would have been most distraught after coming so far to be turned back now."

For a while, the man was quiet. He stood not far from Eirmon, looking deep in thought.

It was Eirmon's turn to speak, so he asked, "How did I get out here?"

"Pardon?" the man asked, looking down at Eirmon as though he hadn't heard him correctly.

"How'd I get all the way out onto one of your sandships? Was I really unconscious that long?"

"You're not on one of my sandships," the man said.

"What?"

"Look," the man said, pointing beyond Eirmon. "Just turn around."

Eirmon lifted himself as far up off the deck as he dared. His head throbbed as he raised it up, and he groaned with the pain. Turning, though, he saw that the man was right. The walls of Barra-Dohn lay behind him.

Eirmon sank back down. If this man was sitting unconcerned and alone with him on the deck of one of Barra-Dohn's own sandships, it couldn't be a good sign about the outcome of the battle.

"Your army has been routed and your city has fallen," the man said, as though he'd read Eirmon's mind.

Eirmon's head was still throbbing, and he suspected that the bright light from the early afternoon sun hanging high overhead wasn't helping. He closed his eyes. "What are you going to do with me?"

"Kill you, of course," the man said, matter-of-factly. "Though Lord Jona won't be pleased about that."

"Lord Jona hates me," Eirmon said. "Why wouldn't he be pleased?"

"Ah, too true," the man replied. "He hates you very much. Perhaps I was unclear. He won't object to you being killed. He will be angry that I've done the killing. He was hoping to do it himself, I believe."

Eirmon looked up at the man again. "Lord Jona is here? This is Amattai's army?"

"Some of it is Amattai's army. We formed an alliance of convenience. Two men, one goal, and all that. Well, you understand the concept of an alliance."

Eirmon was no longer an afterthought to the man. The talking was no longer half to himself. He was completely focused.

"I know why Lord Jona hates me," Eirmon said. "Why do you hate me?"

"Ah," the man said, and he sat down cross-legged on the deck not far from Eirmon. "That is the question."

Again, Eirmon suspected that the man wanted him to ask what the answer was, but his earlier stubbornness returned. He was going to find out, whether he asked or not. He didn't feel like playing games. Sure enough, after a moment the man simply launched into his story.

"A long time ago, before Barra-Dohn was even called Barra-Dohn, there was a priest. He was a very important and powerful priest. He served in a great temple in this city, which was called Zeru-Shalim at the time."

Zeru-Shalim. Eirmon had heard the name of course, probably as a boy when Gamalian taught him the history of Barra-Dohn. It was an obscure fact about the distant past, though, and he wondered what relevance any event from those ancient times might have to this man's life or his hatred of Eirmon and Barra-Dohn.

"Anyway, that influential priest was beloved by the people. The king was jealous, because influence is power, and kings never like it when someone else has any of that. I'm sure you understand. Anyway, a plague struck the city, killing many, many people, including the priest. Not content simply to enjoy the death of his enemy, the king, wanting someone to blame, suggested the plague was actually the fault of the dead priest!"

The man was growing agitated. After this exclamation, he paused, as though half expecting that Eirmon would confirm that any such thing was absurd. Eirmon didn't speak, and the man continued.

"Well, as if smearing the name and reputation of his dead enemy wasn't enough, the king exiled the priest's widow and children from the city. In the midst of their grief, he cast them out into the world, poor and alone, with no one to protect or care for them. And this, more than anything else, is what I cannot forgive."

Eirmon looked over at the man, and he could see that his bright blue eyes were burning as he sat, staring across the deck at him. "Wait," Eirmon said, "You're . . ."

"Yes," the man said. "I'm a descendant of the priest."

Silence. For the first time, Eirmon could hear sounds from beyond the ship's deck upon which he lay. Men were moving about beyond the sandship, though none of the sounds he could hear were of battle. He was here with this man, and no help was coming.

"So you see why my claim to your blood is superior to Jona's," the man said. "He's hated you his whole life, but I and my family have hated you and this place for a thousand years."

"But wait," Eirmon started, "like you said, I'm almost certainly not descended from that king, whoever it was. In fact, I know I'm not. My family has only held the throne for five generations."

"I believe you," the man said, "but nevertheless, you are the king of the city once known as Zeru-Shalim, and killing you and razing your city has been our goal for a very, very long time."

"You said it was ironic that we both had a piece of the Golden Cord," Eirmon said, reaching for straws. He could sense the man was drawing to a close, and he suspected that unless he could think of something soon, that meant his death was near. "Why? Because I was the one you'd come to kill?"

"Don't you know?" the man said. "The Golden Cord was what my ancestor, the priest, served and protected. The king's claim that the plague was caused by him was based on some crazy accusation about my ancestor's misuse of the Cord.

"And now here I am, and here you are too. Both with a fragment of the Golden Cord. My piece was the basis of my power and the reason I defeated you. That would have been sweet, all by itself, but what makes it sweeter is that you had one too. In fact, if I was right before, and the more I think about it the more I think I was, you even had access to two. And still I beat you.

"Perhaps this is vindication. Perhaps the Golden Cord, after all these years, is itself testifying against this city, in which so great an injustice was done and against its cruel and unjust kings. What do you think?"

The man rose and stood over him, staring down. Eirmon knew the end was near. His head was pounding, and his body was weak. He wanted to resist, to fight, to flee—to do something, but he just couldn't muster the energy or the courage to try. He was defeated, and he knew it. "You said you'd tell me your name."

"I did," the man said. "But I lied. You don't deserve to know my name."

Eirmon was out of ideas.

"Well," the man said. "The time for talk has passed."

He pulled a wicked-looking knife with a curved blade about a foot and a half long from wherever he'd had it tucked away behind him. The man stood there, looming over Eirmon ominously. What was delaying the deathblow, Eirmon had no idea. He felt a slight twinge of hope, but he tried not to indulge it.

Eirmon inhaled. He wanted only to meet his end without whimpering or begging for mercy. For a moment, he thought he might fail and break down. And then, just when he thought he didn't have the strength to hold on, acceptance swept over him.

He was going to die, and that was all right. He hadn't bowed the knee to the Amhuru. He'd fought to the end.

"Before I kill you," the man said calmly, softly, "I want you to know with certainty what I'm going to do to your city. I said I was going to raze it, and I mean that. I'm going to burn and destroy everything, and I'm going to kill every living thing I find. Everything. I'll wreak so much havoc on the Arua here, that no plant will grow for years, no animal that walks the ground will survive, and even the birds of prey that now circle in the skies above will flee from the feast I shall leave them. I will leave behind no traces of your city or your people or you. Nothing. Zeru-Shalim, now Barra-Dohn, is gone. The sun sets on her tonight to rise no more."

Eirmon thought with horror of Deslo, and he opened his mouth to scream. He was still screaming when the curved blade separated his head from his shoulders.

40

THE FLIGHT OF *THE SORRY ROGUE*

The quay was packed with people, and the crowd was getting rough. They hadn't found Nara and Deslo. They hadn't found Captain D'Sarza or *The Sorry Rogue*. And if Gamalian had followed them from the palace, he hadn't found them either.

Kaden was growing worried. He was starting to think they should make their way back to the palace. Perhaps they could secure a few, very fast sliders, and maybe they could outrun their enemy on those. To turn back now would mean to abandon Nara and Deslo, and from the moment Zangira had told him they were somewhere here, on the quay, he'd known that whatever happened, he couldn't do that.

And then he saw D'Sarza, dressed as colorfully today as she had been when they'd first met outside Garranmere. She must have seen them coming, because she and her first mate were already making their way through the crowd toward them. They

met in the midst of the crowd, and ignoring the disgruntled protests of those having to make their way around them, they spoke
briefly together.

Captain D'Sarza had been ready to give up on waiting for
them, when her first mate, Geffen, had seen a large man in black
carrying one of the Amhuru. Coming over to investigate, they'd
seen Zangira and then recognized Kaden. They'd not known he
was back home, but they asked no questions and accepted his
presence as though it had always been part of the plan.

They agreed that they should make their way to *The Sorry
Rogue* for Tchinchura's sake to get him out of this crowd, and that
Kaden would come back to look for Nara and Deslo. D'Sarza was
none too pleased about the prospect of delaying their departure any
longer from the chaos in the city and on the quay, but in the end
she agreed. "An hour, and no longer," she had said, several times.

Kaden, in reply, had promised that by himself, with no
wounded Amhuru to encumber him, he would scour the entire
quay and be back in less time than that. If his family and Gamalian were out there, he would find them. Hopefully, they would
find each other in the meantime and make his job easier.

Perhaps it was the fact that they were headed somewhere specific, not aimlessly wandering, that the journey to the dock where
the ship was moored didn't seem to take very long or be too difficult. They soon had Tchinchura aboard and in a bed, and all
were encouraged when the elder Amhuru's eyes fluttered open for
a moment, and he managed a weak smile at the news that they
would be ready to sail from Barra-Dohn soon.

Kaden didn't wait for anything else before heading back
across the deck to disembark. Zangira offered to come too, but
Kaden could see that the toll of the day had drained him. None
of his wounds were life threatening, like Tchinchura's, but he had
many and had exerted himself both on the wall and since. He
needed rest, and Kaden needed to be quick.

A growing number of D'Sarza's crew were at the bottom of the
gangway, turning away would-be passengers, who were desperate

to get aboard a ship, any ship. Kaden slipped past them onto the dock and made his way against the grain, back in the direction of the quay. He moved through whatever crack of daylight appeared in the mass of people before him, searching all the faces he could see in every direction.

He pushed through the crowd to the front of a warehouse and found a large stone propping open one of the warehouse's great doors when loading and unloading goods for nearby ships. He stepped up onto the stone so that he was head and shoulders above the crowd and pivoted slowly in a complete circle, and he scanned the crowd in every direction. He saw no sign of any of them. He stepped back down.

The quay was long and ran both back toward the palace and a fair distance in the other direction. On the one hand, he didn't think Nara would wait on the far end, since she had known that the Amhuru would be coming from the palace. On the other hand, they had already traversed the quay between this dock and the palace and seen no sign of her. He might not have time to thoroughly investigate in both directions, so he wanted to pick right.

He gazed first one way, then the other. As he was staring, thinking more about the choice he had to make than Nara or Deslo, the crowd seemed to part, and he saw them. The tiny slice of daylight through which he'd glimpsed them disappeared again, and all he knew was that he'd seen Nara, clutching Deslo's hand, trying to negotiate the great tumult of people.

Kaden moved immediately, pushing roughly past whoever got in his way. He knew Nara had to be scared and worried, maybe even terrified. The thought that he might not be able to get through to them and lead them safely back to *The Sorry Rogue* terrified him. He pushed harder, trying to move faster. As much as he strained to see them, he didn't catch another glimpse. He pushed through the crowd on an angle he'd hoped would intercept them, but he began to despair. Had they moved faster than he had? Had they turned back somewhere along the way, and had he missed it? Had he somehow lost them again?

"Nara! Deslo!" he shouted, but he was now acutely aware of just how loud the crowd around him was. Children cried in their parents' arms, sailors on nearby ships barked out commands as their vessels prepared to sail, and the general din of the masses was magnified by the small space. "Nara! Deslo!"

He pushed on, not willing to turn back. He'd seen them going this way, and he would go this way until he found them or until he'd reached the end of the quay, then he'd turn back and push through the crowd again. If *The Sorry Rogue* left without him, then he would search on and seek another way out of the city.

He was no longer the prince of Barra-Dohn. His life no longer revolved around a throne he'd never really wanted in the first place. He was losing his home and identity, but he was suddenly adamant that whatever else he lost, he would not lose them. He would not lose the chance to care for them, to be a husband and a father, even if he'd never seriously attended to those tasks before.

"Nara! Deslo!" he shouted again, so loud it hurt his voice. He was growing desperate. A handful of men, who seemed frustratingly tall, were coming the opposite direction, and they cut off what little he could see of the crowd up ahead. As they were going past, he prepared to shout again. He opened his mouth to bellow out Nara and Deslo's names once more, when he suddenly stopped.

They were standing there, side by side, staring right at him, just a couple feet away. They'd heard him and turned around but had not been able to see him because of the same handful of men.

Kaden rushed to them, and though he saw the hesitant confusion in Nara's face, threw his arms around her anyway. She just stood there at first, letting him hug her. He knew this must be perplexing to her, knew he hadn't touched her in years, knew he might not even have a right to touch her now, but he didn't care. He was just glad he'd found her and that she was safe.

He let go, and embarrassed by the stunned look of bewilderment on her face, turned to Deslo. He felt almost as awkward with him as with Nara, but he leaned over and put his hand on the boy's shoulder. "I'm so glad I've found you," he said. "Are you ready to get out of here?"

This last question was directed to them both, and they nodded in ready agreement. Nara, though, added a little tentatively, "We were supposed to meet the Amhuru here."

"I know," Kaden said. "They're on the ship already. I came to find you."

"Oh," Nara said, looking at him as though reappraising the situation.

Kaden knew he could explain later, so he urged them to follow. "Have you seen Gamalian?" he asked, as they started slowly along the quay.

"No," Nara said, shaking her head. "Not since we left the palace this morning."

Kaden sighed. "Well, let me get you two safely to the ship, and then we'll figure out if there's time for me to come back."

He took Nara's hand and turned to go. She didn't move though but clasped his hand and pulled him. He turned back to her. When he faced her this time, she threw her arms around him and clung on tightly. All the while, Deslo stood beside her, watching curiously. She didn't hang on long, and when she let go, he could see tears in her eyes. He felt awkward and a little embarrassed but smiled almost reflexively, then turned to lead them back.

At the entrance to the dock where *The Sorry Rogue* was moored, Kaden thought he heard a voice calling shrilly above the din. "Kaden! Deslo! Kaden!"

He turned, scanning the crowd. He wasn't absolutely sure he'd heard anything, but if he had, it hadn't been a man's voice. He didn't see anyone he recognized, so he turned onto the dock and began to pick his way toward the ship, which thankfully, he could see was still there, waiting.

"Kaden!" This time he knew he'd heard it. He turned again, as did Nara and Deslo, and all three looked to see who had called. A moment later, they saw Rika pushing through the crowd.

Her hair was unkempt, her face smudged, and her clothes dirty. She wasn't at all the neat, fastidious Rika that Kaden had last seen on the day he'd left for Garranmere. He watched her approach, not sure what to say or do. Nothing had been said by any of the others about expecting Rika, and he himself was an addition to the plan, so he didn't know what authority he did or didn't have to extend an offer to her, if escape from the city was her object.

It was Nara, though, who addressed her as she approached, "I thought you stood accused of treason and were locked in the palace dungeon?"

Kaden was surprised, not just by the question, but by the tone in his wife's voice. She'd always been pleasant with everyone, but she sounded much colder and more unwelcoming than he'd ever thought she could sound.

Rika flashed her a quick, angry glare before assuming a much softer demeanor. "I was accused," she said, "but with the danger to the city, Gamalian let me go."

"Gamalian?" Kaden said. "Is he with you?"

"No," she said, and it looked to Kaden like she was fighting back tears. "He came to us, to Barreck and me, and said he was coming here to meet up with the rest of you. He even offered us a chance to leave with you, but when he let us out, Barreck went crazy. He tried to kill me."

"Tried to kill you?" Kaden said.

"Yes," Rika said, sniffling. "He blamed me for the charges your father brought against us, and when Gamalian let us out, he saw his chance to get even. But then Gamalian intervened, and Barreck killed him instead of me."

"Gamalian's dead?"

"Yes," Rika said.

"If Barreck killed Gamalian, how'd you escape?" Nara asked, her voice still cold and distrustful.

"When I saw him kill Gamalian, I ran," Rika said as she wiped the tears from her eyes. "I knew the palace better than he did, I guess, and I lost him. Gamalian saved my life."

There was silence for a moment, and then Deslo began to cry. As Nara bent over to comfort him, Rika looked up at Kaden. "Please, you have to take me with you."

Kaden looked at her. He had no idea what had happened while he was gone, how his father's mistress had fallen so far from favor as to wind up in a cell, or why this other man had wanted her dead. Still, if Gamalian had died to save her, then surely letting her take his place in their party couldn't be too far from what he would have wanted.

"All right," Kaden said. "Come on, we're almost there."

Nara glanced up at him, not angrily, but Kaden could tell she didn't like it. There was no time now to sort things out, though. They could do that later. For now, they just needed to be gone.

Zangira sat against the rail, feeling the breeze against his face. It felt good to be under way, but he knew he would feel better when they had successfully navigated the congested harbor and slipped out to sea.

The Arua field still felt odd, as though it was being manipulated, even though he could tell something had changed. Of course, the Arua always felt odd when he was on the water, but this was different. He didn't think whoever had come to attack Barra-Dohn was still using his fragment of the Golden Cord to summon whirlwinds or command hookworms, but he was doing something.

It was hard for Zangira to think of what he was leaving behind. They'd found, not just the fragment they'd been tracking but both missing pieces of the Golden Cord. Not only had they found them, but both had been within reach. Except for Eirmon's betrayal, all three might even now be in their possession.

Still, he had to look forward. All was not lost. Tchinchura was alive. What's more, if he could escape from Barra-Dohn and keep the fragment safely that he now wore, he could take word of what they'd found to other Amhuru, and they could decide from there what steps should be taken to recover what was lost. At least, they'd know where to start looking. Before he looked too far ahead, though, they needed to get away, and for some reason, Zangira wasn't ready to accept that simply putting out to sea guaranteed anything.

The sound of sailors crying out on other nearby ships was the first clue that something was going on ahead, and before he could rise and walk to the bow, sailors from *The Sorry Rogue* had likewise taken up the cry. Soon everyone who could navigate the deck of the ship was crowded around, looking ahead at the incredible sight.

Coming straight at them and the other ships trying to flee Barra-Dohn, right from the mouth of the harbor, were countless wind-rays soaring above the water. As they watched, some of them began to dive, while others that were evidently already below water began to surface. Ship after ship on the horizon found itself in the grips of a thrashing wind-ray, it's twin tails intent on puncturing that ship's hull and taking it down.

Kaden pulled Zangira aside. "Is it him? Is he doing this like he did with the hookworms? Can you stop him?"

Zangira didn't wait for the flood of Kaden's questions to stop before he reached out through the fragment of the Golden Cord around his bicep. He could feel the Arua field, mediated here through the deep waters, being manipulated. He could sense, vaguely, how the wind-rays were being directed, but he knew that even if he could interfere, he didn't know how to counter the other's commands. He didn't know how to send them back out of the harbor, how to keep them from crushing the ships they'd already taken hold of. The man directing the wind-rays had obviously already manipulated them physically, fundamentally changing them. He could not undo in mere seconds or minutes what had been done to them over a much longer period of time.

Nevertheless, Zangira tried to interfere, to oppose the operations of his mysterious nemesis. He wrestled quietly and with determination, to pull the Arua field from his enemy's grip. He tried and was somewhat successful. He could feel his enemy drawing back. It was a victory of sorts but a hollow one. No doubt the main goal had been to get the wind-rays here, and they were here. He couldn't do anything about that, not in the time before him. They would either run the gauntlet and make it through the mouth of the harbor unscathed, or they wouldn't.

No sooner had that thought passed through his mind when the ship below shuddered beneath their feet. He could feel it. Everyone could feel it. A wind-ray had attached itself underneath the hull. The tips of its great wings wrapped themselves over the rails on the sides of the ship, and some of D'Sarza's sailors moved to strike at them, even though they must have known that they wouldn't be able to do nearly enough damage that way to drive off a wind-ray before it could crush *The Sorry Rogue* to pieces and take it down.

Zangira unhooked his axe and handed it to Kaden, who looked wonderingly at him. Zangira drew his knife and climbed up on the ship's rail. For a moment he hesitated, his baggy pants billowing as the stiff breeze tossed his golden ponytail about. Then, without another word, he leapt into the roiling water below.

Kaden watched Zangira leap overboard and felt a strange mixture of fear and hope. He'd seen a wind-ray destroy that ship on the day of the anniversary, seen it shatter into hundreds of pieces and planks, floating hither and yon on the turbulent water. He knew the power the creatures possessed and knew that it had taken many men spearing the thing that day to do any damage and drive it off. He didn't know how Zangira, armed only with a single knife, could save them, but he thought if anyone could, it was Zangira.

One of the great tails of the wind-ray wheeled back so that the hard, pointed end flung water the entire length of the ship. The wind-ray had been coming from the direction they'd been heading, so the tails were near the bow, and everyone on the deck had backed right back down the length of the ship to the stern to be as far away as possible. The tail jabbed forward, and Kaden saw Deslo trembling at the sound of the wooden hull being ripped open by the blow.

He pulled Deslo close, and Nara too.

Deslo's tears, which had so recently flowed over the loss of his beloved tutor, Gamalian, flowed again. This time, though, Kaden knew they flowed for himself. He felt it too. It wasn't right. It wasn't fair. They'd come so far and overcome so much. They were together. They were fleeing for their lives, but they were together. They couldn't die like this. Not here, not now. Not like this.

Nara stooped down and wrapped her arms around Deslo, trying to comfort him. She didn't speak, didn't tell him it would be all right, she just held him. He looked up at Kaden, standing guard over him and holding the Amhuru's axe so tightly that his knuckles were blanched white. Kaden turned away, not toward the bow, but toward the place on the side of the ship where Zangira had gone overboard.

And then, something remarkable happened. The wingtips of the wind-ray uncurled themselves from the place where they'd wrapped over the rail and gripped it tightly. The two tails rose up and splashed back into the water. They could feel the wind-ray letting go. A moment later *The Sorry Rogue* felt free and unencumbered.

A voice calling out drew them all to the stern, and soon the crew had dropped a rope to Zangira and hauled him back on board. There the weary Amhuru sat on the deck, gasping for breath as he leaned against the rail; the entire crew and every last passenger on the ship stared at him in awe.

At least, they stared for a moment, before Captain D'Sarza started barking out orders. "Stations! We're not safe yet, mongrels. Every man to his station, and let's get out of this accursed place!"

The crew scrambled to get the ship back under way at full speed, and it didn't take long to regain their lost momentum.

That only left Kaden and his family, Rika and the two Kalosenes, huddled around Zangira. One of the Kalosenes, the big one, handed Zangira water, and he gulped it down eagerly. When the Amhuru had caught his breath, Deslo knelt beside him and said, "What do you see?"

Kaden didn't quite understand the significance of the question, but Zangira looked at Deslo and laughed. The hand that wasn't clasping his knife playfully tousled Deslo's hair. "Very good, Deslo," he said quietly. "I see my friend."

Nara stooped down on the other side of him and kissed his forehead. "Thank you," she whispered.

"Yes," Kaden echoed her. "You saved us. I don't know how, but you saved us."

"How did you do it?" Deslo asked, still kneeling beside him. He pointed at the knife in Zangira's other hand. "Is it that? Is it magic?"

"No, Deslo," Zangira said. "It isn't magic."

"Then how?"

"Well," Zangira said, "it's simple, really, once you think about it."

"Simple?" Kaden asked, incredulous. "Single-handedly delivering us from a gigantic wind-ray that had already fastened itself to our ship with only a knife?"

"I didn't say it was easy, but the question was how, and that's relatively simple. Tell me Deslo," Zangira said, looking the boy in the eye, "where would you attack a wind-ray?"

"I don't know," Deslo said, shrugging, as though overwhelmed by the question.

"Come on," Zangira said gently. "Think. When I first arrived at Barra-Dohn, you'd just killed a large hookworm. How'd you kill it?"

"Speared it."

"Speared it where?"

"Through it's open mouth."

"Why?"

"Because that's where it's vulnerable."

"Exactly," Zangira said, nodding. "So where would you stab a wind-ray if it was latched onto your ship and you wanted to make it let go?"

Deslo frowned, thinking. "Does my knife cut through the wind-ray's skin?"

"Yes," Zangira said, "but the body of the wind-ray could absorb hundreds of your stab wounds and still have the strength to crush your ship, so you don't have time to inflict sufficient wounds to the body and make it let go."

Deslo thought a little longer, a little harder, and then he had an idea. "In the eyes?"

"Yes," Zangira said, clapping wearily and smiling, "only, to stab both eyes would be a critical mistake."

"Why?"

"Well, if you swim under the wind-ray and find its head, and then you stab both eyes, what would happen to it?"

"It would be blind."

"That's right," Zangira said. "It would be blind, in great pain, afraid, and very, very angry. It wouldn't know where you were or where to go to get away from you. Having lost its sight, it would only have its touch, and what it felt would be your ship, already in its grasp, and it would wreak a terrible vengeance. It would cling to your ship until it had crushed it to splinters, even if it was the last thing the wind-ray did.

"That's why you'd only stab one eye. One eye does everything you want to do, only it leaves the wind-ray a reason to let go. You show it fear and pain and darkness, as it feels the stab, but it can still see, even if poorly. It still has something to lose. Aware that you are still there, that while it holds the ship it can't defend itself against you, it will let go. It will let go and swim away, removing to a safe distance to reassess the situation, to preserve the eye that can still see. And then? Then your ship will be safe."

"Remarkable," Kaden whispered when Zangira was finished.

Zangira smiled. "Not remarkable. Simple."

Kaden thought of Zangira, stabbing the eye of the wind-ray and then waiting for it to just let go and leave. The epic undersea battle had been mental, not physical. The Amhuru had swum under the creature's head, found his eye, and stabbed. The rest had taken care of itself. Leaning forward, he clasped Zangira's arm. "Friend, we are in your debt."

Zangira shook his head. "No, you saved me on the wall. We're even."

"I'm not so sure you needed saving," Kaden said.

Zangira let his eyes flutter closed as he smiled.

Not long after, *The Sorry Rogue* passed out of the harbor of Barra-Dohn, entering the open sea.

41

THE WANDERING

The Jin Dara sat on the edge of the crater he had discovered near the center of Barra-Dohn, his legs dangling. He didn't need to turn around to see the buildings burning behind him, or the streets littered with the bodies of the dead to know they were there. Ahead, beyond the crater, more buildings burned and more bodies lay dead.

Finding the building that had been the ancient temple of Zeru-Shalim—the building where the Golden Cord had been stored and where his ancestor had served—in this condition, had been a surprise. At some level, he'd always known it might not still be here, but he'd gathered from more than one citizen of the city before he killed them that this dramatic destruction had taken place only that morning.

It robbed his victory of a little of its sweetness. Only a little bit, but he felt robbed, nonetheless. He should like to have seen it, to have seen its rooms and walked its corridors. Maybe in the

473

building that had once been the home of the Golden Cord he would have found wisdom for the decisions that now faced him.

He had thought his entire life that if he could just do what he had done this very day—destroy Zeru-Shalim and avenge his family's ancient grievance—that then his life would be complete. He had no need to think or plan for after, for there was no after worth thinking about. Only this and nothing more.

He looked down at the fragment of the Golden Cord that he had recovered from the last king of Barra-Dohn. It danced rhythmically in the air above his outstretched hand.

He'd never imagined what he'd find here, never imagined that a second piece would essentially fall into his lap. His family had sought the piece he wore around his neck for generations. It had been purchased at a great price as his grandfather and several of his uncles had died in its taking. His father had raised him with it, learning about it and instructing him in its use just to prepare him for this task. He'd lived for nothing more than to use it to wreak this terrible vengeance. But now what? What did fate have in store for him now?

He didn't imagine that outside the Amhuru themselves anyone would know more about the Golden Cord than he did. He knew, of course, that the six pieces had been divided among the six sons of his ancestor's rival, another priest and the father of his ancient enemies, the Amhuru. He knew about the curse that was supposed to be upon the fragments, that their reunion was forbidden on pain of death. Although they'd been entrusted with all six fragments, no Amhuru would even think of putting two original fragments on.

Now he had two. But could he wear two? Did he dare? Wouldn't wisdom suggest giving one to Devaar or perhaps another of his men? Working together, they could be powerful.

Of course, if he could wear both, then he wouldn't have to share any of that power. If the curse was just a legend, a story to frighten the greedy and ambitious, then he could do anything. He could even get more pieces, perhaps. After all, as incredible as it now seemed, a third piece had been in this very place just a few hours earlier.

He looked at the fragment again, and he knew. He didn't care if it killed him. He'd already achieved his life's work. If he died, he would die happy. If he lived, well, then he would be more powerful than anything or anyone in the world.

He swung his legs around and lay down on the warm stone. He set the fragment of the Golden Cord down on his chest. There it twisted and squirmed for a moment in no discernible pattern. Then it shifted downward, and soon it was rolling and wriggling across his stomach. It kept rolling until it had crossed over his right hip. Down and down it went, over his thigh, up and over his knee until it reached his right calf. There it stopped rolling. The Jin Dara sat up.

He picked up the fragment and held it tightly while he rolled up his pants leg. Then, without hesitating, lest he lose his nerve, he laid the fragment against the bare skin of his calf.

The fragment wrapped itself around his leg, and he closed his eyes, waiting for death.

Death did not come. Instead, he only felt the wondrous feeling of the fragment syncing its own internal rhythm in some inexplicable way with his heartbeat. He felt both the fragment around his neck and the fragment around his calf beating faintly with his pulse. He felt them and through them felt the Arua field.

He opened his eyes and looked around him, half expecting to see it, the Arua field. It felt so real, so close, so tangible. Still, it was just as invisible as before. Even so, he could tell that his powers of perception had improved still further. He saw individual ashes fluttering over buildings in the distance, visible against the fading twilight. He heard flames crackling, the wind stirring, a man groaning for water several streets away as he lay dying.

The Jin Dara stood. At his feet lay the wreckage of the past, and all around him lay the accomplishment of the present.

Wrapped around his neck and his calf were promises of the future. Without even needing to think about it, he was now committed to a new goal, a greater goal, a higher vision even than destroying the city once known as Zeru-Shalim. He would take for himself all the fragments of the Golden Cord. Not just the three below the Madri, of which he now had two, but all of them. All six.

He had come a long way to get here, and the way had been dark at times. Now, a darker road lay before him.

The sun setting over the water was a deep and brilliant orange. Tchinchura, supported by Zangira, leaned against the rail of *The Sorry Rogue* and looked back in the direction of Barra-Dohn, although the city and the smoke rising from it were no longer in view.

"The captain would like to know where we want to go," Zangira said.

"We'll worry about that tomorrow," Tchinchura said, glancing behind him at the other passengers.

Kaden sat talking quietly with Nara, as he had been for the last hour, while Rika played with Deslo a good distance away.

Marlo and Owenn had offered their help to the crew and were below decks patching the hole the wind-ray had made.

"For now, putting as much distance between us and Barra-Dohn is the right direction," Tchinchura said.

"The Devoted was right," Zangira said. "Before sunset on the fortieth day, the city fell."

"Yes," Tchinchura echoed, "so far, all he has spoken about Barra-Dohn has come true."

"But there was more."

"There was. He also said the city would lie empty and in ruins for seventy years while a small and harried remnant wandered in exile."

"Yes," Zangira said, "for elevating a created thing above the Creator, for forgetting where she came from and what matters most, for pride and for arrogance, the price must be paid."

"The price must be paid," Tchinchura echoed, whispering. "The wandering has begun."

THE END

THE END

THE DARKER ROAD GLOSSARY

Amattai (AM-uh-tie) – Coastal city, one of the Five Cities.

Amhir (AM-here) – Faithful king of Zeru-Shalim, to whom the Golden Cord was first given.

Aralyn (ERR-uh-lin) – The continent on which Barra-Dohn lies, and over which Barra-Dohn rules.

Armond (AR-mond) – High Priest of Kalos who sacrificed his life to keep Kartain from using the Golden Cord to increase his power and the power of the Kalonian priesthood.

Arua (UH-RUE-uh) – The invisible field generated by Zerura that governs the biological cycles of all living things, and to which materials made with meridium react.

Barra-Dohn (BEAR-uh-DOAN) – The city of might and power, where meridium was discovered, center of power in Aralyn, ruled over currently by the House of Omiir.

Calsura (CAL-sur-uh) – Son of Armond, High Priest of Kalos. He leads his five brothers forward from Zeru-Shalim with the six fragments of the Golden Cord and the charge to keep them forever separate.

Captain Elil D'Sarza (uh-LEEL duh-SAR-za) – Merchant and Captain of *The Sorry Rogue*.

Captain Greyer (GRY-er) – Officer in the army of Barra-Dohn, friend to Kaden.

Davrii (Duh-VREE) – Private guard for Eirmon Omiir.

Deslo Omiir (DES-low O-MEER) – Son of Kaden and grandson of Eirmon, he senses the estrangement between his mother and father, and more to the point, between his father and himself.

Devaar (De-VAR) – The Jin Dara's right-hand man.

Eirmon Omiir (AIR-mun O-MEER) – King of Barra-Dohn, eager to tighten his control over Aralyn and extend it, as well as advance the financial empire of Barra-Dohn that is based on the trade of meridium and meridium technologies.

Ellenara Omiir (EL-len-NAR-uh O-MEER) – Known more commonly as Nara, the wife of Kaden. Has struggled since marrying into House of Omiir, particularly as she has ended up something of a lightning rod for the tension between Eirmon and Kaden.

The Five Cities – The league of cities over which Barra-Dohn presides, and made up of Amattai, Dar-Holden, Garranmere, Jerdan and Perone. Once, there six cities in the league, but Barra-Dohn crushed Rezin for its rebellion, leaving it in ruins and empty, and making it an example for the rest of the Five Cities.

Garranmere (gair-en-MEER) – Inland city of Aralyn, one of the Five Cities, surrounded by massive stone walls.

Geffen (GEF-en) – First mate on *The Sorry Rogue*.

Jin Dara (JIN DARR-uh) – Literally means "dark things," and is the name adopted by the mysterious man who has an ancient grievance against Zeru-Shalim and is coming to Barra-Dohn to pay it back.

Gamalian (Guh-MAY-lee-un) – Royal tutor to House of Omiir and sometime advisor to Eirmon.

The Golden Cord – A piece of Zerura once kept in the Temple of Zeru-Shalim and divided into six fragments after a plague struck the city about a thousand years before our story opens. The six original fragments have remarkable powers and have been kept apart from one another and managed during all that time by the Amhuru, a nomadic tribe of sorts largely descended from Armond, the last faithful priest and true Amhura of Zeru-Shalim.

Kaden Omiir (KAY-den O-MEER) – Son of Eirmon Omiir, king of Barra-Dohn, and heir to the throne.

Kalos (CAL-oss) – Spoken of in the Old Stories as the God who made all things. He is forgotten by all but the few, such as the Kalosenes, the Amhuru and a few others.

Kalosenes (KAL-O-seens) – Also called "the Devoted," they are seen as mystics and outsiders by most. They see themselves as the remnant of true servants of Kalos in a world that no longer worships Him.

Kartain (KAR-tane) – Amhura whose killing of Armond profanes the Temple of Kalos and causes the plague that kills many in Zeru-Shalim.

Madri (MOD-dree) – An equatorial band that runs around the world, dividing the Southlands from the Northlands. To pass through the Madri makes one very ill, and it is rumored that the effect is many times more severe for anyone bearing Zerura, like an Amhuru.

Meridium (Meh-RID-EE-um) – Discovered a thousand years ago in Barra-Dohn, it is the metallic alloy that when mixed with biological materials from plants or animals can create remarkable light, heat, and force reactions that play off the Arua field. It is both the source and currency of power in Barra-Dohn, Aralyn, and the world at large.

Mordain (More-DANE) – King of Zeru-Shalim who exiles the family of the dead Amhura, Kartain.

The Old Stories – These tales of the world when it was young have been passed down for many centuries, though they are believed by most to be only myths, valuable – if at all – for the lessons they teach. Some, like the Kalosenes and Amhuru, see them as more than that, as truth not myth.

Rhino-Scorpions – Desert animals peculiar to Aralyn that move in herds and usually avoid human habitations.

Room of Life – A special room in the Temple of Kalos where the Kalonian Priesthood kept the Golden Cord.

Rika (REE-ka) – Member of the distinguished Academy of Barra-Dohn and also a tutor for Deslo Omiir, grandson of King Eirmon.

Tchinchura (Chin-CHER-uh) – The older Amhuru, leading the two-man team sent to recover a missing fragment of the Golden Cord.

Zangira (Zan-GEAR-uh) – The younger Amhuru who journeys to Barra-Dohn with Tchinchura, seeking a missing fragment of the Golden Cord.

Zeru-Shalim (Zey-RU-SHA-leem) – The city of life and peace, now known as Barra-Dohn, city of might and power.

Zerura (Zeh-RUR-uh) – Sometimes called "living matter." According to the Old Stories, Kalos, the creator of all things, placed veins of Zerura beneath the ground to govern the ecology of all living things, to place limits and boundaries on their growth cycles. The Golden Cord is the only piece of Zerura that has ever been seen aboveground.

ABOUT THE AUTHOR

L. B. Graham writes fantasy/sci-fi and contemporary adult fiction. In 2005, his novel *Beyond the Summerland* was a finalist for a Christy, a national fiction award. Check out his website www. lbgraham.com for more information on his previously published works and his forthcoming titles. He lives and teaches high school in St. Louis, Missouri.

OTHER BOOKS/SERIES
BY L. B. GRAHAM

The Binding of the Blade (a 5 book fantasy series)
Beyond the Summerland
Bringer of Storms
Shadow in the Deep
Father of Dragons
All My Holy Mountain

Avalon Falls—a crime novel

The Raft, The River, and The Robot—a futuristic/sci-fi novel
with a *Huck Finn* twist